P. W. (Patrick Weston) Joyce

The origin and history of Irish names of places.

(First [-second] series)

I0592353

P. W. (Patrick Weston) Joyce

The origin and history of Irish names of places.
(First [-second] series)

ISBN/EAN: 9783741154188

Manufactured in Europe, USA, Canada, Australia, Japa

Cover: Foto ©Andreas Hilbeck / pixelio.de

Manufactured and distributed by brebook publishing software
(www.brebook.com)

P. W. (Patrick Weston) Joyce

The origin and history of Irish names of places.

THE

ORIGIN AND HISTORY

OF

IRISH NAMES OF PLACES.

(First Series.)

BY

P. W. JOYCE, LL.D., T.C.D., M R.I.A.,

ONE OF THE PROFESSORS IN THE TRAINING DEPARTMENT OF THE COM-
MISSIONERS OF NATIONAL EDUCATION, IRELAND.

Cnıallam cımõeall na Poõla.

FOURTH EDITION.

DUBLIN:

M'GLASHAN & GILL, 50, UPPER SACKVILLE-STREET.

LONDON: WHITTAKER AND CO.; SIMPKIN, MARSHALL AND CO.

EDINBURGH : JOHN MENZIES.

PREFACE.

RIaLLam cImcheaLL Na
poOhLa—Let us wander round
Ireland : So wrote the topogra-
pher John O'Dugan, five hundred years
ago, when beginning his poetical description of Ireland, and so I address
my readers, to-day. The journey will
be at least a novel one ; and to those who are inte-
rested in the topography of our country, in the origin
of local names, or in the philosophy of language, it
may be attended with some instruction and amusement. ·

The materials for this book were collected, and
the book itself was written, in the intervals of serious
and absorbing duties. The work of collection, arrangement, and composition, was to me a never-
failing source of pleasure ; it was often interrupted
and resumed at long intervals ; and if ever it in-

volved labour, it was really and truly a labour of love.

I might have illustrated various portions of the book by reference to the local etymologies of other countries; and this was indeed my original intention; but I soon abandoned it, for I found that the materials I had in hands, relating exclusively to my own country, were more than enough for the space at my disposal.

Quotations from other languages I have, all through, translated into English; and I have given in brackets the pronunciation of the principal Irish words, as nearly as could be represented by English letters.

The local nomenclature of most countries of Europe is made up of the languages of various races; that of Great Britain, for instance, is a mixture of Keltic, Latin, Anglo-Saxon, Danish, and Norman French words, indicating successive invasions, and interesting and valuable for that very reason, as a means of historical research; but often perplexingly interwoven and difficult to unravel. In our island, there was scarcely any admixture of races, till the introduction of an important English element, chiefly within the last three hundred years—for, as I have shown (p. 104), the Danish irruptions produced no appreciable effect; and accordingly, our place-names are purely Keltic, with the exception of about a

thirteenth part, which are English, and mostly of recent introduction. This great name system, begun
thousands of years ago by the first wave of population that reached our island, was continued unceas-
ingly from age to age, till it embraced the minutest
features of the country in its intricate net-work ; and
such as it sprang forth from the minds of our ancestors, it exists almost unchanged to this day.

This is the first book ever written on the subject.
In this respect I am somewhat in the position of a
settler in a new country, who has all the advantages
of priority of claim,but who purchases them too dearly
perhaps, by the labour and difficulty of tracking his
way through the wilderness, and clearing his settlement from primeval forest and tangled underwood.

On the journey I have travelled, false lights glim-
mered every step of the way, some of which I have
pointed out for the direction of future explorers.
But I have had the advantage of two safe guides,
Dr. John O'Donovan, and the Rev. William Reeves,
D.D.; for these two great scholars have been specially distinguished, among the honored labourers
in the field of Irish literature, by their success in
elucidating the topography of Ireland.

To the Rev. Dr. Reeves I am deeply indebted for
his advice and assistance, generously volunteered to
me from the very beginning. He examined my
proposed plan of the book in the first instance, and

afterwards, during its progress through the press, read the proof sheets—all with an amount of attention and care, which could only be appreciated by an actual inspection of the well annotated pages, abounding with remarks, criticisms, and corrections. How invaluable this was to me, the reader will understand when he remembers, that Dr. Reeves is the highest living authority on the subject of Irish topography.

My friend, Mr. William M. Hennessy, was ever ready to place at my disposal his great knowledge of the Irish language, and of Irish topography. And Mr. O'Longan, of the Royal Irish Academy, kindly lent me some important manuscripts, from his private collection, of which I have made use in several parts of the book.

I have to record my thanks to Captain Berdoe A. Wilkinson, R.E., of the Ordnance Survey, for his kindness in procuring permission for me to read the Manuscripts deposited in his Office, Phœnix Park. And I should be guilty of great injustice if I failed to acknowledge the uniform courtesy I experienced from Mr. Mooney, Chief Clerk in the same office, and the readiness with which both he and Mr. O'Lawlor facilitated my researches.

I have also to thank the Council of the Royal Irish Academy for granting me permission—long before I had the honor of being elected a member of that learned body—to make use of their library, and to consult their precious collection of Manuscripts.

Dublin, *July*, 1869.

The following is a list of the principal historical and topographical works on Ireland published within the last twenty years or so, which I have quoted through the book, and from which I have derived a large part of my materials:—

The Annals of the Four Masters, translated and edited by John O'Donovan, LL. D., M. R. I. A.; published by Hodges and Smith, Dublin; the noblest historical work on Ireland ever issued by any Irish publisher—a book which every man should possess, who wishes to obtain a thorough knowledge of the history, topography, and antiquities of Ireland.

The Book of Rights; published by the Celtic Society; translated and edited by John O'Donovan. Abounding in information on the ancient tribes and territories of Ireland.

The Battle of Moylena: Celt. Soc. Translated and edited by Eugene O'Curry, M. R. I. A.

The Battle of Moyrath; Irish Arch. Soc. Translated and edited by John O'Donovan.

The Tribes and Customs of the district of Hy-Many: Irish Arch. Soc. Translated and edited by John O'Donovan.

The Tribes and Customs of the district of Hy-Fiachrach :
Irish Arch. Soc. Translated and edited by John
O'Donovan (quoted as "Hy-Fiachrach" through this
book).

A Description of H-Iar Connaught. By Roderick O'Flaherty:
Irish Arch. Soc. Edited by James Hardiman, M. R. I. A.

The Irish version of the Historia Britonum of Nennius :
Irish Arch. Soc. Translated and edited by James Henthorn Todd, D. D., M. R. I. A.

Archbishop Colton's Visitation of the Diocese of Derry,
1397 : Irish. Arch. Soc. Edited by the Rev. William
Reeves, D. D., M. R. I. A.

Cambrensis Eversus : By Dr. John Lynch, 1662 ; Celt.
Soc. Translated and edited by the Rev. Matthew
Kelly.

The Life of St. Columba : By Adamnan : Irish Arch. and
Celt. Soc. Edited by the Rev. William Reeves, D. D.,
M. B., V. P. R. I. A. This book and the next contain a
vast amount of local and historical information, drawn
from every conceivable source.

Ecclesiastical Antiquities of Down, Connor, and Dromore.
Edited by the Rev. William Reeves, D. D., M. B.,
M. R. I. A. (Quoted as the "Taxation of 1306," and
"Reeves' Eccl. Ant.").

The Topographical Poems of O'Dugan and O'Heeren :
Irish Arch. and Celt. Soc. Translated and edited by
John O'Donovan.

The Calendar of the O'Clerys, or the Martyrology of
Donegal : Irish Arch. and Celt. Soc. Translated by John
O'Donovan. Edited by James Heathorn Todd, D. D.,

M. R. I. A., F. S. A.; and the Rev. William Reeves, D. D., M. R. I. A. (quoted as " O'C. Cal.").

The Wars of the Gaedhil with the Gaill. Published under the direction of the Master of the Rolls. Translated and edited by James Henthorn Todd, D.D., &c. (Quoted as " Wars of GG.").

The Chronicon Scotorum. Published under the direction of the Master of the Rolls. Translated and edited by William M. Hennessy, M. R. I. A.

Cormac's Glossary; translated by John O'Donovan; edited with notes by Whitley Stokes, LL.D.

Lectures on the Manuscript Materials of Ancient Irish History; delivered at the Catholic University, by Eugene O'Curry, M. R. I. A. Published by James Duffy, Dublin and London.

The Ecclesiastical Architecture of Ireland; comprising an Essay on the Origin and Uses of the Round Towers of Ireland. By George Petrie, R. H. A., V. P. R. I. A.

Among these, I must not omit to mention that most invaluable work to the student of Irish Topography and History, "The General Alphabetical Index to the Town-lands and Towns, the Parishes and Baronies of Ireland:" Census, 1861: which was ever in my hands during the progress of the book, and without the help of which, I scarcely know how I should have been able to write it.

I have also consulted, and turned to good account, the various publications of the Ossianic Society, which are full of information on the legends, traditions, and fairy mythology, of Ireland.

On the most ancient forms of the various Irish root-words

and on the corresponding or cognate words in other
languages, I have derived my information chiefly from
Professor Pictet's admirable work, "Les Origines Indo-
Européennes, ou les Aryas Primitifs:" Zeuss' masterly
work, Grammatica Celtica, in which the author quotes
in every case from manuscripts of the eighth, or the
beginning of the ninth century: Ebel's Celtic Studies;
translated by William K. Sullivan, Ph.D., M. R. I. A.:
Irish Glosses; a Mediæval Tract on Latin Declension;
By Whitley Stokes, A. B.; and an Edition, with notes,
of Three Ancient Irish Glossaries; By the same accom-
plished philologist.

ADDENDUM.

Lectures on the Manners and Customs of the Ancient
Irish. By Eugene O'Curry, M. R. I. A. Edited, with
Introduction, Appendices, &c., by W. K. Sullivan,
Ph. D. Published in 1873.

PREFACE TO THE SECOND EDITION.

S the first edition of this book went off very quickly—it was sold in six months—I have thought it right to issue a second edition with as little delay as possible.

I have considerably enlarged the book, partly by the expansion of some of the articles, which want of space obliged me to curtail in the first edition, and partly by the insertion of additional names.

For the favourable reception of the work by the Press, in England and Scotland as well as in Ireland, I here offer my thankful acknowledgments. It has been noticed in a great number of newspapers and magazines; and while most of the reviews are elaborate and critical, not one is unfavourable. Several of the writers take exception to some of my statements, but in the whole of their criticisms I cannot find one unfriendly or unkind remark.

I have examined with great care the objections of those who question the correctness of some of my conclusions. Many of them are palpably wrong; while others, carrying more weight, and requiring more investigation than I can now afford time for, are held over for further consideration. Although I adopted every available precaution to ensure correctness, yet where such a vast number of names and places were concerned, complete freedom from error was a thing scarcely to be hoped for; accordingly a few undoubted mistakes have been detected and pointed out, some publicly by the reviewers, and some privately by my literary friends. These I have corrected in the present edition.

Soon after the appearance of the book, I received communications from correspondents in various parts of Ireland, containing information, more or less valuable, on the topography of their respective localities. Among these I may mention specially Mr. John Fleming, of Rathgormuck in the county Waterford, who has brought his knowledge of Irish to bear in elucidating the topography of the Cummeragh mountains, and who has communicated to me without stint, the results of his investigations. Mr. O'Looney of the Catholic University also furnished me with a large quantity of valuable topographical notes taken

from the Irish Lives of several of our early saints.
To these, and to all others who gave me their aid, I
return my best thanks. At the same time I take
this opportunity of soliciting further information
from those who are able to give it, and who are
anxious to assist in the advancement of Irish literature.

The head-pieces have been copied by permission—
with some modifications in the arrangement—from
the marginal illuminations in "The Cromlech of
Howth," a work in which are faithfully reproduced
the beautiful ornamental designs of the Book of
Kells, and other very ancient Irish manuscripts.
I have to thank the Council of the Irish Archæo-
logical Society for the use of four of their ornamental letters, which were likewise copied from the Book
of Kells.

Dublin, *April*, 1870.

CONTENTS.

PART I.

THE IRISH LOCAL NAME SYSTEM.

PART II.

NAMES OF HISTORICAL AND LEGENDARY ORIGIN.

PART III.

NAMES COMMEMORATING ARTIFICIAL STRUC-
TURES.

PART IV.

NAMES DESCRIPTIVE OF PHYSICAL FEATURES.

IRISH NAMES OF PLACES.

PART I.

THE IRISH LOCAL NAME SYSTEM.

CHAPTER I.

HOW THE MEANINGS HAVE BEEN ASCERTAINED.

HE interpretation of a name involves two processes: the discovery of the ancient orthography, and the determination of the meaning of this original form. So far as Irish local names are concerned, the first is generally the most troublesome, while the second, with some exceptions, presents no great difficulty to an Irish scholar.

There are cases, however, in which, although we have very old forms of the names, we are still unable to determine the meaning with any degree of certainty. In some of these, it is certain that we are not in possession of the most ancient orthography, and that the old forms handed down to us are nothing more than corruptions of others still older ; but in most cases of this kind, our ignorance is very probably due to the fact that the root-words of which the names are composed became obsolete before our most ancient manuscripts were written. Names of this class challenge the investigation, not so much of the Irish scholar, as of the general philologist.

With respect to the names occurring in this book, the Irish form and the signification are, generally speaking, sufficiently well known to warrant a certain conclusion ; and accordingly, as the reader may observe, I have interpreted them in almost all cases without any appearance of hesitation or uncertainty. There are indeed names in every part of the country, about whose meanings we are still in the dark ; but these I have generally avoided, for I believe it to be not only useless but pernicious, to indulge in conjecture where certainty, or something approaching it, is not attainable. I have given my authority whenever I considered it necessary or important ; but as it would be impossible to do so in all cases without encumbering the book with references, and in order to remove any doubt as to the correctness of the interpretations, I shall give here a short sketch of the various methods by which the meanings have been ascertained.

I. A vast number of our local names are perfectly intelligible, as they stand in their present anglicised orthography, to any person who has studied the phonetic laws by which they have been reduced from ancient to modern forms. There can be no doubt that the Irish name of Carricknadarriff, in the parish of Annahilt, county of Down, is *Carraig-na-dtarbh,* the rock of the bulls; that Boherboy, the name of a village in Cork, and of several places in other counties, means yellow road (*Bothar-buidhe*); or that Knockaunbauu in Galway and Mayo, signifies white little hill.

But this process requires check and caution; the modern forms, however obvious in appearance, are often treacherous; and whoever relies on them with unwatchful confidence will sooner or later be led into error. Carrick-on-Suir is what it appears to be, for the Four Masters and other authorities write it *Carraig-na-Siuire*, the rock of the Suir; and it appears to have got its name from a large rock in the bed of the river. But if any one should interpret Carrick-on-Shannon in the same way, he would find himself mistaken. The old English name of the town was Carrickdrumrusk, as it appears on the Down Survey map; but the first part should be Carra, not Carrick, to which it has been corrupted; for the place got its name not from a rock, but from an ancient *carra* or weir across the Shannon; and accordingly the Four Masters write it *Caradh-droma-ruisc*, the weir of Drumroosk. Drumroosk itself is the name of several townlands in the north-western counties, and signifies the ridge of the *roosk* or marsh.

II. In numerous other cases, when the original forms are so far disguised by their English dress, as to be in any degree doubtful, they may be discovered by causing the names to be pronounced in Irish by the natives of the respective localities. When pronounced in this manner, they become in general perfectly intelligible to an Irish scholar—as much so as the names Queenstown and Newcastle are to the reader. Lisnanees is the name of a place near Letterkenny, and whoever would undertake to interpret

it as it stands would probably find himself puzzled ;
but it becomes plain enough when you hear the
natives pronounce it with a *g* at the end, which has
been lately dropped :—*Lios-na-naosg* [Lisnanueosg],
the fort of the snipes.

There is a small double lake, or rather two little
lakes close together, three miles from Glengarriff in
Cork, on the left of the road to Castletown Bere-
haven.   They are called on the maps Lough Avaul—
a name I could never understand, till I heard the
local pronunciation, which at once removed the difficulty; the people pronounce it *Lough-auc-icoul*, which
any one with a little knowledge of Irish will recognise
as *Loch-dha-bhall*, the lake of the two spots, a name
that describes it with perfect correctness.

Take as another example Ballylongford near the
Shannon in Kerry: as it stands it is deceptive, the
first part of the name being apparently Bally, a town,
which in reality it is not.   I have a hundred times
heard it pronounced by the natives, who always call
it in Irish *Beal-atha-longphuirt* [Bellalongfort], the
ford-mouth of the fortress.   The name was originally
applied to the ford over the little river, long before
the erection of the bridge ; and it was so called, no
doubt, because it led to the *longphort* or fortress of
Carrigafoyle, two miles distant.

Of this mode of arriving at the original forms of
names I have made ample use ; I have had great
numbers of places named in Irish, either in the very
localities, or by natives whom I have met from time
to time in Dublin ; and in this respect I have got
much valuable information from the national school-
masters who come twice a year from every part of
Ireland to the Central Training Establishment in
Dublin.   But in this method, also, the investigator

must be very cautious; names are often corrupted in Irish as well as in English, and the pronunciation of the people should be tested, whenever possible, by higher authority.

The more intelligent of the Irish-speaking peasantry may often assist the inquirer in determining the meaning also; but here he must proceed with the utmost circumspection, and make careful use of his own experience and judgment. It is very dangerous to depend on the etymologies of the people, who are full of imagination, and will often quite distort a word to meet some fanciful derivation; or they will account for a name by some silly story obviously of recent invention, and so far as the origin of the name is concerned, not worth a moment's consideration.

The well-known castle of Carrigogunnell near the Shannon in Limerick, is universally understood by the inhabitants to mean the candle rock, as if it were *Carraig-na-gcoinneall;* and they tell a wild legend, to account for the name, about a certain old witch, who in times long ago lived on it, and every night lighted an enchanted candle, which could be seen far over the plain of Limerick, and which immediately struck dead any person who caught even its faintest glimmer. She was at last vanquished and destroyed by St. Patrick, but she and her candle are immortalised in many modern tourist books, and, among others, in Mrs. Hall's "Ireland," where the reader will find a well-told version of the story. But the Four Masters mention the place repeatedly, and always call it *Carraig-O-gCoinnell,* with which the pronunciation of the peasantry exactly agrees; this admits of no exercise of the imagination, and banishes the old witch and her candle more ruthlessly than even

St. Patrick himself, for it means simply the rock of the O'Connells, who were no doubt the original owners.

The meaning of a name, otherwise doubtful, will often be explained by a knowledge of the locality. Quilcagh mountain in the north-west of Cavan, at the base of which the Shannon rises, is called in Irish by the inhabitants, *Cailceach* [Calkagh], which literally signifies chalky (Ir. *caile*, chalk; Lat. *calx*) ; and the first view of the hill will show the correctness of the name ; for it presents a remarkably white face, due to the presence of quartz pebbles, which are even brought down in the beds of streams, and are used for garden walks, &c.

Carrantuohill in Kerry, the highest mountain in Ireland, is alway called throughout Munster, Carraunthoohill, and the peasantry will tell you that it means an inverted reaping-hook, a name which is apparently so absurd for a mountain, that many reject the interpretation as mere silliness. Yet whoever looks at the peak from about the middle of the Hag's Valley, will see at once that the people are quite right; it descends on the Killarney side by a curved edge, which the spectator catches in profile, all jagged and serrated with great masses of rock projecting like teeth, without a single interruption, almost the whole way down. The word *tuathail* [thoohill] means literally left-handed ; but it is applied to anything reversed from its proper direction or position ; and the great peak is most correctly described by the name *Carrán-tuathail*, for the edge is toothed like the edge of a *carrán*, or reaping-hook ; but it is a reaping-hook reversed, for the teeth are on a convex instead of a concave edge.

III. The late Dr. O'Donovan, while engaged in

the Ordnance Survey, travelled over a great part of Ireland, collecting information on the traditions, topography, and antiquities of the country. The results of these investigations he embodied in a series of letters, which are now deposited in the Royal Irish Academy, bound up in volumes, and they form the most valuable body of information on Irish topography in existence.

His usual plan was to seek out the oldest and most intelligent of the Irish-speaking peasantry in each locality, many of whom are named in his letters; and besides numberless other inquiries, he caused them to pronounce the townland and other names, and used their assistance in interpreting them. His interpretations are contained in what are called the Field name Books, a series of several thousand small parchment-covered volumes, now lying tied up in bundles in the Ordnance Office, Phœnix Park. The names of all the townlands, towns, and parishes, and of every important physical feature in Ireland, are contained in these books, restored to their original Irish forms, and translated into English, as far as O'Donovan's own knowledge, and the information he received, enabled him to determine.

There are, however, numerous localities in every one of the thirty-two counties that he was unable to visit personally, and in these cases, instead of himself hearing the names pronounced, he was obliged to content himself with the various modes of spelling them prevalent in the neighbourhood, or with the pronunciation taken down by others from the mouths of the people, as nearly as they were able to represent it by English letters. He had a wonderful instinct in arriving at the meanings of names, but the information he received from deputies often left him in great doubt, which he not unfrequently expresses; and his interpretations, in such cases, are to be received with caution, based as they often are, on corrupt spelling, or on this doubtful information.

So far as time permitted, I have consulted O'Donovan's letters, and the Field name Books, and I have made full use of the information derived from these sources. I have had frequently to use my own judgment in correcting what other and older authorities proved to be erroneous; but I do not wish, by this remark, to underrate the value and extent of the information I have received from O'Donovan's manuscript writings.

I will give a few illustrations of names recovered in this way. There is a townland in Cavan called Castleterra, which gives name to á parish; the proper pronunciation, as O'Donovan found by conversation with the people, is *Cussatirry*, representing the Irish *Cos-a'-tsiorraigh*, the foot of the colt, which has been so strangely corrupted; they accounted for the name by a legend, and they showed him a stone in the townland on which was the impression of a colt's foot.

In the parish of Kilmore, in the same county, the townland of Derrywinny was called, by an intelligent old man, *Doire-bhainne*, and interpreted, both by him and O'Donovan, the oak grove of the milk; so called, very probably, from a grove where cows used to be milked. Farnamurry near Nenagh in Tipperary, was pronounced *Farranymurry*, showing that the name is much shortened, and really signifies O'Murray's land; and Ballyhoos in Clonfert, Galway, was stripped of its deceptive garb by being called *Lilechuais*, the old tree of the *coos* or cave.

IV. We have a vast quantity of topographical and other literature, written from a very early period

down to the 17th century,·in the Irish language, by
native writers. Much of this has been lately published and translated, but far the greater part remains
still unpublished.

Generally speaking, the writers of these manuscripts were singularly careful to transmit the correct
ancient forms of such names of places as they had
occasion to mention; and accordingly it may be
stated as a rule, subject to occasional exceptions, that
the same names are always found spelled in the same
way by all our ancient writers, or with trifling differences depending on the period in which they were
transcribed, and not affecting the etymology.

At those early times, the names which are now
for the most part unmeaning sounds to the people
using them, were quite intelligible, especially to
skilled Irish scholars; and this accounts for the almost
universal correctness with which they have been
transmitted to us.

This is one of the most valuable of all sources of
information to a student of Irish local names, and it
is, of course, of higher authority than those I have
already enumerated: with the ancient forms restored,
it usually requires only a competent knowledge of
the Irish language to understand and interpret them.
I have consulted all the published volumes, and also
several of the unpublished manuscripts in Trinity
College and the Royal Irish Academy. Great numbers of the names occurring in the texts have been
translated in foot notes by the editors of the various
published manuscripts, and I have generally availed
myself of their authority. A list of the principal
works already published will be found in the Preface.

Many of the local names occurring in these manuscripts are extinct, but the greater number exist at

the present day, though disguised in an English dress, and often very much altered. In every such case it becomes a question to identify the ancient with the modern name—to show that the latter is only a different form of the former, and that they both apply to the same place. A great deal has been done in this. direction by Dr. O'Donovan, Dr. Reeves, and other editors of the published manuscripts, and I have generally adopted their identifications.

This method of investigation will be understood from the following examples:—At the year 586, it is stated by the Four Masters that Bran Dubh, King of Leinster, gained a battle over the Hy Neill "at the hill over *Cluain-Conaire;*" and they also record at the year 837, that a great royal meeting took place there, between Niall Caille, king of Ireland, and Felimy (son of Criffan), king of Munster. In a gloss to the Calendar of Aengus the Culdee, at the 16th of September, *Cluain-Conaire* is stated to be "in the north of *Hy Faelain;*" and this clearly identifies it with the modern townland of Cloncurry, which gives name to a parish in Kildare, between Kilcock and Innfield, since we know that *Hy Faelain* was a territory occupying the north of that county. As a further corroboration of this, the old translator of the Annals of Ulster, in rendering the record of the meeting in 837, makes the name Cloncurry.

Once we have arrived at the form *Cluain-Conaire*, the meaning is sufficiently obvious; it signifies Conary's lawn or meadow; but who this Conary was, we have no means of knowing (See O'Donovan's Four Masters, Vol. I., p. 457).

Ballymagowan is the name of some townlands in Donegal and Tyrone, and signifies MacGowan's town.

But Ballymagowan near Derry is a very different name, as will appear by reference to some old authorities. In Sampson's map it is called Ballygowan, and in the Act 4 Anne, "Ballygan, alias Ballygowan:" while in an Inquisition taken at Derry in 1605, it is designated by the English name Canons' land. From all this it is obviously the place mentioned in the following record in the Four Masters at 1537:—"The son of O'Doherty was slain in a nocturnal assault by Rury, son of Felim O'Doherty, at *Baile-na-gcananach* [Ballynagananagh], in the Tormon of Derry." This old Irish name signifies the town of the canons, a meaning preserved in the Inq. of 1605; while the intermediate forms between the ancient and the modern very corrupt name are given in Sampson and in the Act of Anne.

In Adamnan's Life of St Columba (Lib. ii. Cap. 43) it is related, that on one occasion, while the saint was in Ireland, he undertook a journey, in which "he had for his charioteer Columbanus, son of Echuid, a holy man, and founder of a monastery, called in the Scotic tongue *Snamh-Luthir.*" In the Life of St. Fechin, published by Colgan (Act. SS. p. 136 b.), we are informed that "the place which is called *Snamh-Luthir* is in the region of *Cairbre-Gabhra;*" and O'Donovan has shown that Carbery-Goura was a territory situated in the north east of Longford; but the present identification renders it evident that it extended northwards into Cavan.

In an Inquisition taken at Cavan in 1609, the following places are mentioned as situated in the barony of Loughtee:—"Triuitie Island scituate near the Toagher, * * * Clanlaskin, Derry, Bleyncupp, and Dromore, *Snawlugher* and Killevallio" (Ulster Inq. App. vii.); Snawlugher being evidently the ancient *Snamh-Luthir.* We find these names existing at the present day in the parish of Kilmore, in this barony, near the town of Cavan, in the modern forms of Togher, Clonloskan, Derries, Blencup, Drummore, Killyvally, Trinity Island; and there is another modern townland called Slanore, which, though more altered than the others, is certainly the same as Snawlugher. If this required further proof we have it in the fact, that in Petty's map Slanore is called Snalore, which gives the intermediate step.

Snamh-Luthir is very well represented in pronunciation by Snawlugher of the Inquisition. This was shortened by Petty to Snaloro without much sacrifice of sound; and this, by a metathesis common in Irish names, was altered to Slanore. Luthir is a man's name of frequent occurrence in our old MSS., and *Snamh-Luthir* signifies the swimming-ford of *Luthir.* This ingenious identification is due to Dr. Reeves. (See Reeves's Adamnan, p. 173).

V. Some of the early ecclesiastical and historical writers, who used the Latin language, very often when they had occasion to mention places, gave instead of the native name, the Latin equivalent, or they gave the Irish name accompanied by a Latin translation. Instances of this kind are to be found in the pages of Adamnan, Bede, Giraldus Cambrensis, Colgan, O'Sullivan Beare, and others. Of all the sources of information accessible to me, this, as far as it extends, is the most authentic and satisfactory; and accordingly I have collected and recorded every example of sufficient importance that I could find.

These men, besides being, many of them, profoundly skilled in the Irish language, and speaking it as their mother tongue, lived at a time when the local names of the country were well understood; their interpretations are in almost all cases beyond dispute, and serve as a guide to students of the present day, not only in the very names they have translated, but in many others of similar structure, or formed from the same roots. How far this is the case will appear from the following examples.

St. Columba erected a monastery at Durrow, in the King's County, about the year 509, and it continued afterwards during his whole life one of his favourite places. The old Irish form of the name is *Dairmag* or *Dearmagh*, as we find it in Adamnan:—"A monastery, which in Scotic is called *Dairmag;*" and for its interpretation we have also his authority; for when he mentions it in Lib. i. Cap. 29, he uses the Latin equivalent, calling it "Roboreti campus," the plain of the oaks. Bede also gives both the Irish name and the translation in the following passage:—"Before he (Columba) passed over into Britain, he had built a noble monastery in Ireland, which, from the great number of oaks, is in the Scotic language called *Dearmagh*, the field of the oaks" (Lib. iii. Cap. 4). *Dair*, an oak; *magh*, a plain.

It is hardly necessary to remark that the name was in use ages before the time of St. Columba, who adopted it as he found it; and it has been softened down to the present name by the aspiration of the consonants, *Dearmhagh* being pronounced *Darvah*, which gradually sunk to Durrow.

Durrow, on the borders of the Queen's County and Kilkenny, has the same original form and meaning, for we find it so called in O'Clery's Calendar at the 20th of October, where St. *Maeldubh* is mentioned as "from *Dermagh* in *Hy Duach*, in the north of

Ossory," which passage also shows that Durrow, though now included in the Queen's County, formerly belonged to the territory of Idough, in Kilkenny.

There are several townlands in other parts of Ireland called Durrow, Durra, and Durha; and although we have no written evidence of their ancient forms, yet, aided by the pronunciations of the peasantry, and guided by the analogy of Durrow, we cannot hesitate to pronounce that they are all modern forms of *Dearmhagh*.

We find the same term forming part of the name of Dunderrow, a village and parish in Cork, whose ancient name is preserved in the following entry from the Book of Leinster, a MS. of the 12th century, recording an event that occurred early in the ninth :—
" By them (i. e. the Danes) were demolished *Dun-dermaigi* and *Inis-Eoganain*" (Owenan's or Little Owen's island or river-holm, now Inishannon on the river Bandon : " Wars of GG.," p. 223). Dunderrow signifies the fortress of the oak-plain, and the large dun from which it was called is still in existence in the townland of Dunderrow, half a mile south of the village.

Drumhome in Donegal takes its name from an ancient church originally dedicated to St. Adamnan (see O'Clery's Calendar at 23d Sept.). O'Clery and the Four Masters call it *Druim-tuama*, which seems to imply that they took it to mean the ridge of the tumulus. Adamnan himself, however, mentions it in his Life of St. Columba (Lib. iii. Cap. 23) by the equivalent Latin name *Dorsum Tommæ ;* and Colgan (A. SS. p. 9, n. 6) notices this, adding the words, " for the Irish *druim* signifies the same as the Latin *dorsum.*" From which it appears evident that both

Adamnan and Colgan regarded Tommæ as a personal name ; for if it meant tumulus, the former would, no doubt, have translated it as he did the first part, and the latter would be pretty sure to have a remark on it. The name, therefore, signifies the ridge or long hill of Tomma, a pagan woman's name ; and this is the sense in which Lynch, the author of Cambrensis Eversus, understands it (Camb. Evers. II. 686).

About four miles from Bantry, on the road to Inchigeela, are the ruins of Carrigannss castle, once a stronghold of the O'Sullivans. O'Sullivan Beare mentions it in his History of the Irish Catholics, and calls it *Torrentirupes*, which is an exact translation of the Irish name *Carraig-an-easa*, the rock of the cataract ; and it takes its name from a beautiful cascade, where the Ouvane falls over a ledge of rocks, near the castle.

There is another place of the same name in the parish of Ardagh, near Youghal, and another still in the parish of Lackan, Mayo ; while, in Armagh and in Tyrone, it takes the form of Carrickaness— all deriving their name from a rock in the bed of a stream, forming an *eas* or waterfall.

VI. When the Irish original of a name is not known, it may often be discovered from an old form of the anglicised name. These early English forms are found in old documents of various kinds in the English or Latin language—inquisitions, maps, charters, rolls, leases, &c., as well as in the pages of the early Anglo-Irish historical writers. The names found in these documents have been embalmed in their pages, and preserved from that continual process of corruption to which modern names have been subjected ; such as they sprang from their Irish source they have remained, while many of the corresponding modern names have been altered in various ways.

They were obviously, in many instances, taken down from the native pronunciation ; and very often they transmit the original sound sufficiently near to suggest at once to an Irish scholar, practised in these matters, the proper Irish form. Drs. O'Donovan and Reeves have made much use of this method, and I have succeeded, by means of it, in recovering the Irish forms of many names.

Ballybough, the name of a village near Dublin, is obscure as it stands ; but in an Inquisition of James I., it is called Ballybought, which at once suggests the true Irish name *Baile-bocht*, poor town ; and Ballybought, the correct anglicised form, is the name of some townlands in Antrim, Kildare, Cork, and Wexford.

Cappancur near Geashill, King's County, is mentioned in an Inquisition of James I., and spelled Keapancurragh, which very fairly represents the pronunciation of the Irish *Ceapach-an-churraigh*, the tillage-plot of the *curragh* or marsh.

There is a townland in the parish of Aghaboe, Queen's County, the name of which all modern authorities concur in calling Kilminfoyle. It is certain, however, that the *n* in the middle syllable has been substituted for *l*, for it is spelled in the Down Survey map Killmullfoyle : this makes it perfectly clear, for it is a very good attempt to write the Irish *Cill-Maol-phoil*, Mulfoyle's Church, Mulfoyle being a man's name of common occurrence, signifying St. Paul's servant.

It would be impossible to guess at the meaning of Ballyboughlin, the name of a place near Clara, King's County, as it now stands ; but here also the Down

Survey opens the way to the original name, by spelling it Bealaboclone, from which it is obvious that the Irish name is *Beal-atha-bochluana*, the ford of the cow-meadow, the last part, *bochluain*, cow-meadow, being a very usual local designation.

CHAPTER II.

SYSTEMATIC CHANGES.

There are many interesting peculiarities in the process of altering Irish topographical names from ancient to modern English forms; and the changes and corruptions they have undergone are, in numerous instances, the result of phonetic laws that have been in operation from the earliest times, and among different races of people. Irish names, moreover, afford the only existing record of the changes that Irish words undergo in the mouths of English-speaking people; and, for these reasons, the subject appears to me to possess some importance, both in an antiquarian and philological point of view.

I. *Irish Pronunciation preserved.*—In anglicising Irish names, the leading general rule is, that the present forms are derived from the ancient Irish, as they were spoken, not as they were written. Those who first committed them to writing aimed at preserving the original pronunciation, by representing it as nearly as they were able in English letters. Generally speaking, this principle explains the alterations that were made in the spelling of names in the process of reducing them from ancient to modern forms; and, as in the Irish language there is much

elision and softening of consonants; as, consequently,
the same sounds usually take a greater number of
letters to represent them in Irish than in English;
and since, in addition to this, many of the delicate
sounds of the Irish words were wholly omitted, as
impossible to be represented in English; for all these
reasons the modern English forms of the names are
almost always shorter than the ancient Irish.

Allowing for the difficulty of representing Irish
words by English letters, it will be found that, on
the whole, the ancient pronunciation is fairly preserved. For example, Drummuck, the name of
several places in Ulster, preserves almost exactly the
sound of the Irish *Druim-muc*, the ridge of the pigs;
and the same may be said of Dungarvan, in Waterford and Kilkenny, the Irish form of which is *Dun-
Garbhain* (Four Mast.), meaning Garvan's fortress.
Not quite so well preserved, but still tolerably so, is
the sound of *Baile-a'-ridire* [Ballyariddery], the town
of the knight, which is now called Balrothery, near
Dublin. In some exceptional cases the attempts to
represent the sound were very unsuccessful, of which
Ballyagran, the name of a village in Limerick, may
be cited as an example; it ought to have been anglicised Bellahagran, the original form being *Bel-atha-
grean*, the ford-mouth of the gravel. Cases of this
kind are more common in Ulster and Leinster than
in the other provinces.

Whenever it so happens that the original combination of letters is pronounced nearly the same in
Irish and English, the names are commonly modernized without much alteration either of spelling or
pronunciation; as for instance, *dun*, a fort, is usually
anglicised *dun* or *doon*; *bo*, a cow, *bo*; *druim*, a long
hill, *drum*; *leitir*, a wet hill side, *letter*, &c. In most

cases, however, the same letters do not represent the same sounds in the two languages; and, accordingly, while the pronunciation was preserved, the original orthography was in almost all cases much altered, and as I have said generally shortened. The contraction in the spelling is sometimes very striking, of which Lorum in Carlow, affords a good illustration, the Irish name being *Leamhdhruim* [Lavrum], the *drum* or ridge of the elms.

II. *Aspiration.*—The most common causes of change in the reduction of Irish names, are aspiration and eclipsis; and of the effects of these two grammatical accidents, it will be necessary to give some explanation.

O'Donovan defines aspiration—" The changing of the radical sounds of the consonants, from being stops of the breath to a sibilance, or from a stronger to a weaker sibilance :" so that the aspiration of a consonant results in a change of sound. There are nine of the consonants which, in certain situations, may be aspirated : *b, c, d, f, g, m, p, s*, and *t*. The aspiration is denoted either by placing a point over the letter (*ċ*), or an *h* after it (*ch*); by this contrivance letters that are aspirated are still retained in writing, though their sounds are wholly altered. But as in anglicising names, these aspirated sounds were expressed in English by the very letters that represented them, there was, of course, a change of letters.

B and *m* aspirated (*bh, mh*), are both sounded like *v* or *w*, and, consequently, where we find *bh* or *mh* in an Irish name, we generally have *v* or *w* in the English form : examples, Ardvally in Sligo and Donegal, from the Irish *Ard-bhaile*, high town ; Ballinvana in Limerick, *Baile-an-bhana*, the town of the green

3 *

field; Ballinwully in Roscommon, *Baile-an-mhullaigh*, the town of the summit.

Very often they are represented by *f* in English, as wo see in Cloondaff in Mayo, from *Cluain-damh*, ox-meadow; Boherduff, the name of several townlands in various counties, *Bóthar-dubh*, black road. And not unfrequently they are altogether suppressed, especially in the cud of words, or between two vowels, as in Knockdoo in Wicklow, tho same as Knockduff in other places, *Cnoc-dubh*, black hill; Knockrour or Knockrower in tho southern counties, which has been made Knockramer, in Armagh, all from *Cnoc-reamhar;* fat or thick hill.

For *c* aspirated see next Chapter.

D and *g* aspirated (*dh*, *gh*), have a faint guttural sound not existing in English; it is something like tho sound of *y* (in yore), which occasionally represents it in modern names, as in Annayalla in Monaghan, *Eanaigh-gheala*, tho white marshes, so called, probably, from whitish grass or white bog flowers. But these letters, which even in Irish are, in some situations not sounded, aro generally altogether unrepresented in English names, as in Lisnalee, a common local name in different parts of tho country, which represents tho Irish *Lios-na-laegh*, tho fort of tho calves, a name having its origin in the custom of penning calves at night within tho enclosure of tho *lis;* Reanabrone near Limerick city, *Réidh-na-brón*, tho marshy flat of the mill-stone or quern; Ballintoy in Antrim, *Baile-an-tuaidh*, tho town of the north.

F aspirated (*fh*) totally loses its sound in Irish, and of course is omitted in English, as in Bauraneag in Limerick, *Barr-an-fhiaigh*, tho hill top of tho deer; Knockanurro in Wicklow, *Cnoc-an-fhraeigh*, tho hill of tho heath.

P aspirated (*ph*), is represented by *f*, as in Ballinfoyle, the name of a place in Wicklow, and of another near Galway, *Baile-an-phoill*, the town of the
hole ; Shanlongford in Derry, *Sean-longphort*, the
old *longfort* or fortification.

S and *t* aspirated (*sh*, *th*), both sound the same as
English *h*, as in Drumhillagh, a townland name of
frequent occurrence in some of the Ulster counties,
Druim-shaileach, the ridge of the sallows, which also
often takes the form Drumsillagh, where the original
s sound is retained ; Drumhuskert in Mayo, *Druim-
thuainceart*, northern *drum* or ridge.

III. *Eclipsis.*—O'Donovan defines eclipsis, "The
suppression of the sounds of certain radical consonants
by prefixing others of the same organ." When one
letter is eclipsed by another, both are retained in
writing, but the sound of the eclipsing letter only is
heard, that of the eclipsed letter, which is the letter
proper to the word, being suppressed. For instance,
when *d* is eclipsed by *n* it is written *n-d*, but the
n alone is pronounced. In representing names by
English letters, however, the sound only was transmitted, and, consequently, the eclipsed letter was
wholly omitted in writing, which, as in case of aspiration, resulted in a change of letter.

" All initial consonants that admit of eclipsis are
eclipsed in all nouns in the genitive case plural, when
the article is expressed, and sometimes even in the
absence of the article " (O'Donovan's Grammar). *S*
is eclipsed also, under similar circumstances, in the
genitive singular. Although there are several other
conditions under which consonants are eclipsed, this,
with very few exceptions, is the only case that
occurs in local names.

The consonants that are eclipsed are *b, c, d, f, g, p, s, t,;* and each has a special eclipsing letter of its own.

B is eclipsed by *m.* Lugnamuddagh near Boyle, Roscommon, represents the Irish *Lug-na-mbodach,* the hollow of the *bodaghs* or churls; Knocknamoe near Abbeyleix, Queen's County, *Cnoc-na-mbo,* the hill of the cows; Mullaghnamoyagh in Derry, *Mullach-na-mboitheach,* the hill of the byres, or cow-houses.

C is eclipsed by *g.* Knocknagulliagh, Antrim, is reduced from the Irish *Cnoc-na-geoilleach,* the hill of the cocks or grouse; Cloonagashel near Ballinrobe, ought to have been anglicised Coolnagashel, for the Four Masters write the name *Cuil-na-gcaiseal,* the angle of the cashels or stone forts.

D and *g* are both eclipsed by *n.* Killynamph in the parish of Aghalurcher, Fermanagh, *Coill-na-ndamh,* the wood of the oxen; Mullananallog in Monaghan, *Mullach-na-ndealg,* the summit of the thorns or thorn bushes. The eclipsis of *g* very seldom causes a change, for in this case the *n* and *g* coalesce in sound in the Irish, and the *g* is commonly retained and the *n* rejected in the English forms; as, for instance, *Cnoc-na-ngabhar* [Knock-nung-our], the hill of the goats, is anglicised Knocknagoro in Sligo and Down, and Knocknagower in Kerry.

F is eclipsed by *bh,* which is represented by *v* in English. Carrignavar, one of the seats of the M'Carthys in Cork, is in Irish *Carraig-na-bhfear,* the rock of the men; Altnaveagh in Tyrone and Armagh, *Alt-na-bhfiach,* the cliff of the ravens; Lisnaviddoge near Templemore, Tipperary, *Lios-na-bhfeadóg,* the *lis* or fort of the plovers.

P is eclipsed by *b.* Gortnaboul in Kerry and

Clare, *Gort-na-bpoll*, the field of the holes: Corna-baste in Cavan, *Cor-na-bpiast*, the round hill of the worms or enchanted serpents.

S is eclipsed by *t*, but this occurs only in the genitive singular, with the article, and sometimes without it. Ballintaggart, the name of several places in various counties from Down to Kerry, represents the Irish *Baile-an-tsagairt*, the town of the priest, the same name as Ballysaggart, which retains the *s*, as the article is not used; Knockatancashlane near Caherconlish, Limerick, *Cnoc-a'-tscan-chaisleáin*, the hill of the old castle; Kiltenanlea in Clare, *Cill-tSennin-leith*, the church of Senan the hoary; Kiltenan in Limerick, *Cill-tSenain*, Senan's church.

T is eclipsed by *d*. Ballynadolly in Antrim *Baile-na-dtulach*, the town of the little hills; Gortna-dullagh near Kenmare, *Gort-na-dtulach*, the field of the hills; Lisnadurk in Fermanagh, *Lios-na-dtorc*, the fort of the boars.

IV. *Effects of the Article.*—The next series of changes I shall notice are those produced under the influence of the article. Names were occasionally formed by prefixing the Irish definite article *an*, to nouns, as in case of Anveyerg in the parish of Agh-namullan, Monaghan, which represents the Irish *An-bheith-dhearg*, the red birch tree. When the article was in this manner placed before a word beginning with a vowel, it was frequently contracted to *n* alone, and this *n* was often incorporated with its noun, losing ultimately its force as an article, and forming permanently a part of the word. The attraction of the article is common in other languages also, as for instance in French, which has the words *lhierre, lendemain, luette, Lisle, Lami*, and many others, formed by the incorporation of the article *l*.

A considerable number of Irish names have incorporated the article in this manner; among others, the following: Naul, the name of a village near Balbriggan. The Irish name is *an aill*, i. e. the rock or cliff, which was originally applied to the perpendicular rock on which the castle stands—rising over the little river Delvin near the village. The word was shortened to *n'aill*, and it has descended to us in the present form Naul, which very nearly represents the pronunciation.

The parish of Neddans in Tipperary, is called in Irish *na feaddáin*, the brooks or streamlets, and it took its name from a townland which is now often called *Fearann-na-bhfeadáin*, the land of the streamlets. Ninch in Meath, the *inch* or island. Naan island in Lough Erne, the *ain* or ring, so called from its shape; Nart in Monaghan, *an fheart*, the grave.

Nuenna river in the parish of Freshford, Kilkenny —*an uaithne* [an oohina], the green river. The river Nore is properly written *an Fheoir*, i. e. the Feoir; Boate calls it "The Nure or Oure," showing that in his time (1645) the article had not been permanently incorporated. Nobber in Meath; the *obair* or work, a name applied, according to tradition, to the English fortress erected there. Mageoghegan, in his translation of the "Annals of Clonmacnoise," calls it "the Obber."

It is curious that in several of these places, a traditional remembrance of the use of the article still exists, for the people often employ the English article with the names. Thus Naul is still always called "The Naul," by the inhabitants: in this both the Irish and English articles are used together; but in "The Oil" (the *aill* or rock), a townland in the parish of Edermine, Wexford, and in "The Obber," the Irish article is omitted, and the English used in its place.

While in so many names the article has been incorporated, the reverse process sometimes took place; that is, in the case of certain words which properly began with *n*, this letter was detached in consequence of being mistaken for the article. The name *Uachongbhail* [Oohougwal], is an example of this. The word *Congbhail* means a habitation, but it was very often applied to an ecclesiastical establishment, and it has been perpetuated in the names of Conwal, a parish in Donegal; Conwal in the parish of Rossinver, Leitrim; Cunnagavale* in the parish of Tuogh, Limerick; and other places. With *nua* (new) prefixed, it became *Nuachongbhail*, which also exists in several parts of Ireland, in the forms of Noughaval and Nohoval. This word is often found without the initial *n*, it being supposed that the proper word was *Uachongbhail* and *n* merely the article. In this mutilated state it exists in the modern names of several places, viz.: Oughaval in the parish of Kilmacteige,

* This place is called *Cunnaghabhail* in Irish by the people, and it is worthy of notice, as it points directly to what appears to be the true origin of *Congbhail*, viz., *congabhail*. I am aware that in O'Clery's Glossary, *Congbhail* is derived from *combhaile (con + baile)*. But in a passage in the "Book of Armagh," as quoted by Dr. W. Stokes in his Irish Glosses, I find the word *congabaim* used in the sense of *habito;* and O'Donovan states that *congeb* = he holds (Sup. to O'R. Dict.). The infinitive or verbal noun formation is *congabail* or *congabhail*, which, according to this use, means *habitatio;* and as Colgan translates *Congbhail* by the same word *habitatio*, there can be, I think, no doubt that *congbhail* is merely a contracted form of *congabhail*. *Congabhail* literally means *conceptio*, i. e. comprehending or including; and as applied to a habitation, would mean the whole of the premises included in the establishment.

Sligo; the parish of Oughaval in Mayo; and Oughaval in the parish of Stradbally, Queen's County;
which last is called by its correct name *Nuachonghhail*,
in O'Clery's Calendar at the 15th May. This is also
the original name of Faughanvale in Derry, which
is written *Uachonghhail* by the Four Masters. This
old name was corrupted to Faughanvale by people
who, I suppose, were thinking of the river Faughan;
which, however, is three miles off, and had nothing
whatever to do with the original name of the place.

The word *Uachonghhail* has a respectable antiquity
in its favour, for "The Book of Uachonghhail" is
mentioned in several old authorities, among others
the Book of Ballymote, and the Yellow Book of Lo-
can; the name occurs also in the Four Masters at
1197. Yet there can be no doubt that *Nuachongbhail* is the original word, for we have the express
authority of Colgan that *nua* not *ua* is the prefix, as
he translates *Nuachonghhail* by *nova habitatio;* indeed *ua* as a prefix could, in this case, have scarcely
any meaning, for it never signifies anything but "a
descendant."

The separation of the *n* may be witnessed in operation at the present day in Kerry, where the parish of
Nohoval is locally called in Irish sometimes *Uachobhail* and sometimes *an Uachobhail*, the *n* being actually detached and turned into the article (See
O'Donovan's Letter on this parish). That the letter
n may have been lost in this manner, appears also to
be the opinion of Dr. Graves, for in a paper read
before the R. I. Academy in December, 1852, he
remarks that the loss of the initial *n* in the words
oidhche (night) and *uimhir* (a number) "may perhaps
be accounted for, by supposing that it was confounded
with the *n* of the article."

The words *cascu* (or *casgan*), an eel, and *cas* (or *easóg*), a weasel, have, in like manner, lost the initial *n*, for the old forms, as given in Cormac's Glossary, are *naiscu* and *ness*.   Dr. Whitley Stokes, also, in his recent edition of this Glossary, directs attention to the Breton *Ormandi* for Normandy, and to the English *adder* as compared with the Irish *nathir* (a snake) and Lat. *natrix;* but in these two last examples, it is probable that the article has nothing to do with the loss of the *n*.

As a further confirmation of this opinion regarding the loss of *n* in *Uachongbhail*, I may state that the letter *l* is sometimes lost in French and Italian words from the very same cause; as in Fr. *once* (Eng. ounce, an animal), from Lat. *lynx;* it was formerly written *lonce*, and in the It. *lonza*, the *l* is still retained.   Fr. *azur* (Eng. azure), from *lazulus*. So also It. *usignuolo*, the nightingale, from *luscinia;* and It. *orbacca*, a berry, from *lauri-bacca*.

Another change that has been, perhaps, chiefly produced by the influence of the article, is the omission or insertion of the letter *f*.   The article causes the initial consonants of feminine nouns (and in certain cases those of masculine nouns also) to be aspirated.   Now aspirated *f* is wholly silent; and being omitted in pronunciation, it was, in the same circumstances, often omitted in writing.   The Irish name of the river Nore affords an instance of this.   Keating and O'Heeren write it *Feoir*, which is sounded *Eoir* when the article is prefixed (*an Fheoir*).   Accordingly, it is written without the *f* quite as often as with it: the Four Masters mention it three times, and each time they call it *Eoir*.   The total silence of this letter in aspiration appears to be, to some extent at least, the cause of its uncertain character.   In the

case of many words, the writers of Irish seem either
to have inserted or omitted it indifferently, or to
have been uncertain whether it should be inserted
or not ; and so we often find it omitted, even in very
old authorities, from words where it was really
radical, and prefixed to other words to which it did
not belong. The insertion of *f* is very common in
the south of Ireland (See O'Donovan's Grammar,
p. 30, and O'Brien's Irish Dictionary, p. 446).

The following words will exemplify these remarks :
from *aill*, a rock or cliff, we have a great number of
names — such as Aillenaveagh in Galway, *aill-na-*
bhfiach, the ravens' cliff, &c. But it is quite as often
called *faill*, especially in the south; and this form
gives us many names, such as Foilduff in Kerry and
Tipperary, black cliff ; Foylataluro in Kilkenny, the
tailor's cliff. *Aill* I believe to be the most ancient
form of this word, for *Aill-finn* (Elphin) occurs in the
Tripartite Life of St. Patrick. So with *uar* and *fuar*,
cold ; and Fahan on Lough Swilly, is sometimes
written *Fathain*, and sometimes *Athain*, and *Othain*,
by the Four Masters.

The *f* has been omitted by aspiration in the names
Lughinny in the parish of Killahy, Kilkenny, and
in Lughannagh in the parish of Killosolan, Galway,
both of which represent the Irish *an fhliuchaine* [an
luhiny], the wet land ; and also in Ahabeg, in the parish
of Carrigparson, Limerick, *an fhaithche beag*, the little
green. In these names, the article, after having caused
the aspiration of the *f*, has itself dropped out ; but it
has held its place in Nurchossy near Clogher in Tyrone,
the Irish name of which is *an fhuar-chosach*, the cold
foot or cold bottom-land, so called probably from its
wetness. A place of this name (*Fuarchosach*) is
mentioned by the Four Masters at 1584, but it lies

in Donegal; there is a little island in Lough Corrib, two miles and a half north-east from Oughterard, with the strange name of Cussafoor, which literally signifies "cold feet;" and Derreennagusfoor is the name of a townland in the parish of Kilcummin in Galway, signifying the little oak wood of the cold feet.

The *f* has been affixed to the following words to which it does not radically belong: *fan* for *an*, stay; *fiolar* for *iolar*, an eagle; *fainne* for *ainne*, a ring, &c. It has also been inserted in Culfeightrin, the name of a parish in Antrim, which is properly *Cuil-eachtrann*, the corner or angle of the strangers. Urney in Tyrone is often called Furny, as in the record of Primate Colton's Visitation (1397), and the *f* is also prefixed in the Taxation of Down, Connor, and Dromore (1306), both showing that the corruption is not of recent origin.

I must notice yet another change produced by the article. When it is prefixed to a masculine noun commencing with a vowel, a *t* should be inserted between it and the noun, as *anam*, soul, *an tanam*, the soul.[*] In the case of a few names, this *t* has remained, and has become incorporated with the word, while the article has disappeared. For example, Turagh in the parish of Tuogh, Limerick, i. e. *an t-iubrach*, the yew land; Tummery in the parish of Dromore, Tyrone, *an t-iomaire*, the ridge; so also Tassan in Monaghan, the *assan* or little cataract; Tardree in Antrim, *an tard-fhracigh*, the height of the heather. The best known example of this is

[*] This *t* is really a part of the article; but the way in which I have stated the case will be more familiar to readers of modern Irish.

Tempo in Fermanagh, which is called in Irish *an t-Iompodh deisiol* [an timpo deshil], *iompodh* meaning turning, and *deisiol*, *dextrosum*—from left to right. The place received its name, no doubt, from the ancient custom of turning sun-ways, i. e. from left to right in worship (See *deas*, in 2nd series).

V. *Provincial Differences of Pronunciation.*—There are certain Irish words and classes of words, which by the Irish-speaking people are pronounced differently in different parts of the country; and, in accordance with the general rule to preserve as nearly as possible the original pronunciation, these provincial peculiarities, as might be anticipated, are reflected in the modern names. This principle is very general, and large numbers of names are affected by it; but I shall notice only a few of the most prominent cases.

In the southern half of Ireland, the Irish letters *a* and *o* are sounded in certain situations like *ou* in the English word *ounce*.* *Gabhar*, a goat, is pronounced *gour* in the south, and *gore* in the north; and so the name *Lios-na-ngabhar* (Four Mast.: the *lis* or fort of the goats) is anglicised Lisnagower in Tipperary, and Lisnagore in Monaghan. See also Ballynahown, a common townland name in the south (*Baile-na-habhann*, the town of the river), contrasts with Ballynahone, an equally common name in the north. *Fionn* (white or fair), is pronounced *feoun* or *fune* in Munster, as in Dawnfoun in Waterford, and Bawn-fune in Cork, the white or fair-coloured field. In most other parts of Ireland it is pronounced *fin*, as in Findrum in Donegal and Tyrone, which is written

---

* For this and the succeeding provincial peculiarities, see O'Donovan's Grammar, Part I., Chaps. I. and II.

by the Four Masters *Findruim*, white or fair ridge ;
and this form is often adopted in Munster also, as in
Finnahy in the parish of Upperchurch, Tipperary,
Fionn-fhaithche, the white plat or exercise field.

The sound of *b* aspirated (*bh = v*) is often sunk
altogether in Munster, while it is very generally retained in the other provinces, especially in Connaught.
In Derrynanool in the parish of Marshalstown, Cork
(*Doire-na-n-abhall*, the grove of the apples), the *bh* is
not heard, while it is fully sounded in Avalbane in
the parish of Clontibret, Monaghan (*Abhall-bán*,
white orchard), and in Killavil in the parish of Kil-
shalvy, Sligo (*Cill-abhaill*, the church of the apple
tree).

In certain positions *adh* is sounded like Eng. *eye*,
in the south; thus *cladh*, which generally means a
raised dyke of clay, but sometimes a sunk ditch or
fosse, is pronounced *cly* in the south, as in Clyduff
in Cork, Limerick, and King's County, black dyke.
More northerly the same word is made *cla* or *claw;*
as in Clawdowen near Clones, deep ditch ; Clawinch,
an island in Lough Ree, the island of the dyke or
mound.

Adh in the termination of words is generally
sounded like *oo* in Connaught; thus *madadh*, a dog,
is anglicised *maddoo* in Carrownamaddoo, the quarter-
land of the dogs, the name of three townlands in
Sligo—while the same name is made Carrowna-
maddy in Roscommon and Donegal.

One of the most distinctly marked provincial peculiarities, so far as names are concerned, is the pronunciation that prevails in Munster of the final *gh*,
which is sounded there like English hard *g* in *fig*.
Great numbers of local names are influenced by this

custom. Ballincollig near Cork is *Baile-an-chul-laigh*, the town of the boar; and Ballintannig in the parish of Ballinaboy, Cork, *Baile-an-t-scanaigh*, the town of the fox. The present name of the river Maigue in Limerick, is formed on the same principle, its Irish name, as written in old authorities, being *Maigh*, that is the river of the plain. Nearly all the Munster names ending in *g* hard are illustrations of this peculiar pronunciation.

It is owing to a difference in the way of pronouncing the original Irish words, that *cluain* (an insulated bog meadow) is sometimes in modern names made *cloon*, sometimes *clon*, and occasionally *clone*; that *dún* (a fortified residence) is in one place spelt *doon*, in another *dun*, and in a third *down*; that in the neighbourhood of Dublin, *bally* is shortened to *bal*; in Donegal *rath* is often made *rye* or *ray*; and that *disert* is sometimes made *ister* and *tristle*, &c., &c.

VI. *Irish Names with English Plurals.*—It is very well known that topographical names are often in the plural number, and this is found to be the case in the nomenclature of all countries. Sometimes in transferring foreign names of this kind into English, the original plurals are retained, but much oftener they are rejected, and replaced by English plurals, as in the well-known examples, Thebes and Athens.

Great numbers of Irish topographical names are in like manner plural in the originals. Very frequently these plural forms have arisen from the incorporation of two or more denominations into one. For example, the townland of Rawes in the parish of Tynan, Armagh, was originally two, which are called in the map of the escheated estates (1609) Banragh and Douragh (*Bán-rath*, and *Dubh-rath*, white rath and black rath); but they were afterwards formed into a single townland, which is now called Rawee, that is, *Raths*.

There is a considerable diversity in the manner of anglicising these plural forms. Very often the original terminations are retained; as in Milleeny in the parish of Ballyvourney, Cork, *Millinidhe*, little hillocks, from *meall*, a hillock. Oftener still, the primary plural inflection is rejected, and its place supplied by the English termination. Keeloges is the name of about twenty-six townlands scattered all over Ireland; it means "narrow stripes or plots," and the Irish name is *Caelóga*, the plural of *caelóg*. Carrigans is a common name in the North, and Carrigeens in the South; it is the anglicised form of *Carraiglnidhe*, little rocks. Daars, a townland in the parish of Bodenstown, Kildare, means "oaks," from *dairghe*, plural of *dair*, an oak. So Mullans and Mullauns, from *mulláin*, little flat hills; Derreens, from *doirlnidhe*, little *derries* or oak groves; Bawnoges, from *bánóga*, little green fields, &c.

In other names, the Irish plural form is wholly or partly retained, while the English termination is superadded; and these double plurals are very common. Killybegs, the name of a village in Donegal, and of several other places in different parts of Ireland, is called by the Four Masters, *Cealla-beaga*, little churches. The plural of *cluain* (an insulated meadow) is *cluainte*, which is anglicised Cloonty, a common townland name. With *s* added it becomes Cloonties, the name of some townlands, and of a well-known district near Strokestown, Roscommon, which is called Cloonties, because it consists of twenty-four townlands, all whose names begin with Cloon.

VII. *Transmission of Oblique Forms.*—In the transmission of words from ancient into modern European languages, there is a curious principle very extensive in its operation, which it will be necessary to notice briefly. When the genitive case singular of the ancient word differed materially from the nominative, when, for instance, it was formed by the addition of one or more consonants, the modern word was very frequently derived, not from the nominative, but from one of the oblique forms.

All English words ending in *ation* are examples of this, such as *nation :* the original Latin is *natio*, gen. *nationis* abl. *natione*, and the English has preserved the *n* of the oblique cases. Lat. *pars*, gen. *partis*, &c.; here again the English word *part* retains the *t* of the genitive.

This principle has been actively at work in the reduction of names from Irish to modern English forms. There is a class of nouns, belonging to the fifth declension in Irish, which form their genitive by adding *n* or *nn* to the nominative, as *ursa*, a door jamb, genitive *ursan*, dative *ursain ;* and this *n* is obviously cognate with the *n* of the third declension in Latin.

Irish names that are declined in this manner very often retain the *n* of the oblique cases in their modern English forms. For example, Carhoon, the name of a place in the parish of Kilbrogan, Cork, and of two others in the parishes of Beagh and Tynagh, Galway, is the genitive of Carhoo, a quarter of land :—Irish *ceathramha*, gen. *ceathramhan*. In this manner, we get the modern forms, Erin, Alban, Rathlin, from *Eire, Alba* (Scotland), *Reachra*.

Other forms of the genitive, besides those of the fifth declension, are also transmitted. Even within the domain of the Irish language, the same tendency may be observed, in the changes from ancient to modern forms; and we find this very often the case in nouns ending in *ach*, and which make the gen. in *aigh*.   *Tulach*, a hill, for instance, is *tulaigh* in the genitive; this is now very often used as a nominative, not only by speakers, but even by writers of authority, and most local names beginning with *Tully* are derived from it; such as Tullyallen on the Boyne, above Drogheda, which is most truly described by its Irish name *Tulaigh-dlainn*, beautiful hill.

The genitive of *teach*, a house, is *tighe*, dative *tigh*, and at the present day this last is the universal name for a house all over the south of Ireland.   Many modern names beginning with *Ti* and *Tee* are examples of this; for, although the correct form *teach* is usually given in the Annals, the modern names are derived, not from this, but from *tigh*, as the people speak it.

There is an old church in King's County, which has given name to a parish, and which is called in the Calendars, *Teach-Sarain*, Saran's house.   St. Saran, the original founder of the church, was of the race of the *Dealbhna*, who were descended from Olioll Olum, King of Munster (O'Clery's Cal. 20th Jan.); and his holy well, *Tobar-Sarain*, is still in existence near the church.   The people call the church in Irish, *Tigh-Sarain*, and it is from this that the present name Tisaran is derived.

VIII. *Translated Names.*—Whoever examines the Index list of townlands will perceive, that while a great preponderance of the names are obviously Irish, a very considerable number are plain English words. These English names are of three classes, viz. really

4 *

modern English names, imposed by English-speaking people, such as Kingstown, Castleblakeney, Charleville; those which are translations of older Irish names; and a third class to which I shall presently return. With the first kind—pure modern English names—I have nothing to do; I shall only remark that they are much less numerous than might be at first supposed.

A large proportion of those townland names that have an English form, are translations, and of these I shall give a few examples. The Irish name of Cloverhill in the parish of Kilmacowen, Sligo, is *Cnoc-na-seamar*, the hill of the shamrocks; Skinstown in the parish of Rathbeagh, Kilkenny, is a translation of *Baile-na-gcroiceann;* and Nutfield, in the parish of Aghavea, Fermanagh, is correctly translated from the older name Aghnagrow.

Among this class of names, there are not a few whose meanings have been incorrectly rendered; and such false translations are generally the result of confounding Irish words, which are nearly alike in sound, but different in meaning. Freshford in Kilkenny should have been called Freshfield; for its Irish name is *Achad-ur* (Book of Leinster), which, in the Life of St. Pulcherius published by Colgan, is explained, "*Achadh-ur*, i. e. green or soft field, on account of the moisture of the rivulets which flow there." The present translation was adopted because *achadh*, a field, was mistaken for *ath*, a ford. The Irish name of Strokestown in Roscommon, is not *Baile-na-mbuille*, as the present incorrect name would imply, but *Bel-atha-na-mbuille*, the ford (not the town) of the strokes or blows. In Castleventry, the name of a parish in Cork, there is a strange attempt at preserving the original signification. Its Irish name is *Caislean-na-gaeithe*, the castle of the wind, which has been made Castleventry, as if *rentry* had some connection in meaning with *ventus.*

In the parish of Red City, in Tipperary, there formerly stood, near the old church, an ancient *caher* or fort, built of red sandstone, and called from this circumstance, Caherderg, or red fort. But as the word *caher* is often used to signify a city, and as its application to the fort was forgotten, the name came to be translated Red City, which ultimately extended to the parish.

In some of the eastern counties, and especially in Meath, great numbers of names end in the word *town;* and those derived from families are almost always translated so as to preserve this termination, as Drakestown, Gernonstown, Cruicetown, &c. But several names are anglicised very strangely, and some barbarously, in order to force them into compliance with this custom. Thus the Irish name of Mooretown in the parish of Ardcath, is *Baile-an-churraigh*, the town of the *moor* or marsh; Crannaghtown in the parish of Balrathboyne, is in Irish *Baile-na-gerannach*, the town of the trees. There is a place in the parish of Martry, called Phœnixtown, but which in an Inquisition of James I. is written Phenockstown; its Irish name is *Baile-na-bhfionnog* [Ballynavinuog], the town of the scaldcrows, and by a strange caprice of error, a scaldcrow or *finnoge* is here converted into a phœnix!

Many names again, of the present class, are only half translations, one part of the word being not translated, but merely transferred. The reason of this probably was, either that the unchanged Irish part was in such common use as a topographical term, as to be in itself sufficiently understood, or

that the translators were ignorant of its English
equivalent. In the parish of Ballycarney, Wexford,
there is a townland taking its name from a ford,
called in Irish *Sgairbh-an-Bhreathnaigh* [Scarriff-an-
vranny], Walsh's *scariff*, or shallow ford, and this
with an obvious alteration, has given name to the
barony of Scarawalsh. In Cargygray, in the parish
of Annahilt, county of Down, *gray* is a translation of
riabhacha, and *cargy* is the Irish for rocks; the full
name is *Cairrge-riabhacha*, grey rocks. The Irish
name of Curraghbridge, near Adair in Limerick, is
Droichet-na-corra, the bridge of the weir, or dam, and
it is anglicised by leaving *corra* nearly unchanged,
and translating *droichet* to bridge. I shall elsewhere
treat of the term *Eochaill* (yew wood) and its modern
forms: there is a townland near Tullamore, King's
County, with this Irish name, but now somewhat
oddly called the wood of O. In some modern authorities, the place is called The Owe; so that while
chaill was correctly translated wood, it is obvious that
the first syllable, *eó*, was a puzzle, and was prudently
left untouched.

IX. *Irish Names simulating English Forms.*—The
non-Irish names of the third class, already alluded to,
are in some respects more interesting than those
belonging to either of the other two. They are
apparently English, but in reality Irish; and they
have settled down in their present forms, under
the action of a certain corrupting influence, which
often comes into operation when words are transferred (not translated) from one language into
another. It is the tendency to convert the strange
word, which is etymologically unintelligible to the
mass of those beginning to use it, into another that
they can understand, formed by a combination of

their own words, more or less like the original in sound,
but almost always totally different in sense. This
principle exists and acts extensively in the English
language, and it has been noticed by several writers
—among others by Latham, Dr. Trench, and Max
Müller, the last of whom devotes an entire lecture to
it, under the name of "Popular Etymology." These
writers explain by it the formation of numerous
English words and phrases; and in their writings
may be found many amusing examples, a few of which
I shall quote.

The word "beefeater" is corrupted from *buffetier*,
which was applied to a certain class of persons, so
called, not from eating beef, but because their office
was to wait at the *buffet*. Shotover Hill, near Oxford, a name which the people sometimes explain by
a story of Little John *shooting* an arrow *over* it, is
merely the French Château Vert. The tavern sign
of "The goat and compasses" is a corruption of the
older sign-board, "God encompasseth us;" "The cat
and the wheel" is "St. Catherine's wheel;" Braze-
nose College, Oxford, was originally called Brazon-
huis, i. e. brew-house, because it was a brewery before the foundation of the college; "La rose des
quatre saisons" becomes "The rose of the quarter
sessions;" and Bellerophon is changed to "Billy
ruffian," &c., &c.

This principle has been extensively at work in corrupting Irish names—much more so indeed than any
one who has not examined the subject can imagine;
and it will be instructive to give some characteristic
instances.

The best anglicised form of *coill*, a wood, is *kill* or
kyle; in many names, however, chiefly in the north

of Ireland, it is changed to the English word *field*.
Cranfield, the name of three townlands in Down,
Antrim, and Tyrone, is in Irish *creamhchoill* [crav-
whill], i. e. wild garlick wood. *Leamhchoill* [lav-
whill], a very usual name, meaning "elm-wood," is
generally transformed into the complete English word
Longfield, which forms the whole or part of a great
many townland names. The conversion of *choill* into
field seems a strange transformation, but every step
in the process is accounted for by principles examined
in this and next chapter, namely, the conversion of
ch into *f*, the addition of *d* after *l*, and the tendency
at present under consideration, namely, the alteration
of the Irish into an English word. There are many
townland names in the South, as well as in the North,
in which the same word *coill* is made *hill*. Who
could doubt but that Coolhill in the parish of The
Rower, Kilkenny, means the cool or cold hill; or
that Boy-hill in the parish of Aghavea, Fermanagh,
is the hill of the boys? But the first is really
culchoill [coolhill], backwood, and the second *buidhe-
choill* [bwee-hill], yellow wood. So also Scaryhill
in Antrim, rocky wood; Cullahill in Tipperary, and
Queen's County, hazel wood; and many others.

Mointeán [moan-thaun], boggy land, and *Mointin*
[moantheen], a little bog, are in the South very generally anglicised *mountain*, as in Ballynamountain,
Kilmountain, Coolmountain, &c., all townland names;
and in both North and South, *uachtar*, upper, is
frequently changed to *water*, as in Ballywater in
Wexford, upper town; Ballywatermoy in Antrim,
the town of the upper plain; Kilwatermoy in Waterford, the church of the upper plain. *Braighid*, a
gorge, is made *broad*, as in Knockbroad in Wexford,

the hill of the gorge; and the genitive case of *conadh*, firewood, appears as *honey*, as in Magherahoney in Antrim, the field of the firewood.

Many of these transformations are very ludicrous, and were probably made under the influence of a playful humour, aided by a little imagination. There is a parish in Antrim called Billy; a townland in the parish of Kinawly, Fermanagh, called Molly; and another, in the parish of Ballinlough, Limerick, with the more ambitious name of Cromwell; but all these sail under false colours, for the first is *bile* [billĕ], an ancient tree; the second *málaighe* [mauly], hill-brows, or braes; and Cromwell is nothing more than *crom-choill* [crumwhill], stooped (*crom*) or sloping wood.

There is a townland in Kerry and another in Limerick with the formidable name Knockdown, but it has a perfectly peaceful meaning, viz. brown hill. It required a little pressure to force *Tuaim-drecon* (Four Masters: Drecon's burial mound) into Tomregan, the name of a parish on the borders of Fermanagh and Cavan; *Tuaim-coill*, the burial mound of the hazel, a name occurring in several parts of Wexford and Wicklow, is very fairly represented in pronunciation by the present name Tomcoyle; Barnycarroll would be taken as a man's name by any one; for Barny (Bernard) is as common in Ireland as a Christian name, as Carroll is as a surname; but it is really the name of a townland in the parish of Kilcolman in Mayo, representing exactly the sound of *Bearn-Ui-Chearbhaill*, O'Carroll's gap; and in case of *Laithreach-Chormaic*, in Derry (Cormac's *larha* or house-site), the temptation was irresistible to call it as it is now called, Larrycormac.

There are several places in Tipperary and Limerick

called by the Scriptural name Mountsion: but Mount
is only a translation of *cnoc*, and sion, an ingenious
adaption of *sidhcán* [sheeawn], a fairy mount; the
full Irish name being *Cnoc-a'-tsidhcain* [Knocateean],
fairy-mount hill: and Islafalcon in the parish of Ard-
tramon, Wexford, is not what it appears to be, the
island of the falcon, but *Oilcán-a'-phocáin* [Ilaun-
a-fuckaun], the island or river-holm of the buck
goat.

We have a very characteristic example of this process in the name of the Phœnix Park, Dublin. This
word Phœnix (as applied to our park) is a corruption
of *fionn-uisg'* [feeniak], which means clear or limpid
water. It was originally the name of the beautiful
and perfectly transparent spring well near the Phœnix pillar, situated just outside the wall of the Vice-
regal grounds, behind the gate lodge, and which is
the head of the stream that supplies the ponds near
the Zoological Gardens. To complete the illusion,
the Earl of Chesterfield, in the year 1745, erected a
pillar near the well, with the figure of a phœnix
rising from its ashes on the top of it; and most
Dublin people now believe that the Park received
its name from this pillar. The change from *fionn-
uisg'* to phœnix is not peculiar to Dublin, for the
river Finisk, which joins the Blackwater below Cappoquin, is called Phœnix by Smith in his History
of Waterford.

X. *Retention of Irish written Forms.*—To the general rule of preserving the pronunciation, there is a
remarkable exception of frequent occurrence. In
many names the original spelling is either wholly or
partly preserved;—in other words, the modern forms
are derived from the ancient, not as they were spoken,
but as they were written. In almost all such cases,

the names are pronounced in conformity with the powers of the English letters; and accordingly whenever the old orthography is retained, the original pronunciation is generally lost.

This may be illustrated by the word *rath*, which is in Irish pronounced *raw*. There are over 400 townland names beginning with this word in the form of *ra, rah, raw*, and *ray;* these names are derived from the spoken, not the written originals; and, while the pronunciation is retained, the spelling is lost. There are more than 700 names commencing with the word in its original form, *rath*, in which the correct spelling is preserved; but the pronunciation is commonly lost, for the word is pronounced *rath* to rhyme with *lath*. It is worthy of remark, however, that the peasantry living in or near these places, to whom the names have been handed down orally, and not by writing, generally preserve the correct pronunciation; of which Rathmines, Rathgar, Rathfarnham, and Rathcoole are good examples, being pronounced by the people of the localities, Ra-mines, Ra-gar, Ra-farnham, and Ra-coole.

The principal effect of this practice of retaining the old spelling is, that consonants which are aspirated in the original names, are hardened or restored in the modern pronunciation. To illustrate these principles I have given the following short list of words that enter frequently into Irish names, each containing an aspirated letter; and after each word, the names of two places of which it forms a part. In the first of each pair, the letter is aspirated as it ought to be, but the original spelling is lost; in the second, the orthography is partly or wholly preserved, and the letter is not aspirated, but sounded as it would indicate to an English reader, and the proper pronunciation is lost :—

1. *Ath* [ăh], a ford: Agolagh in Antrim, *Ath-gobhlach*, forked ford; Athenry in Galway, a corrupt form from *Ath-na-riogh* (Four Masters), the ford of the kings. 2. *Gaoth*, wind (gwee); Mastergeeha, two townlands in Kerry, Masteragwee near Coleraine, and Mostragee in Antrim, the master of the wind, so called from the exposed situation of the places; Balgeeth, the name of some places in Meath, windy town, the same as Ballynageeha and Ballynagee in other counties. 3. *Tamhnach*, a green field [tawnagh]; Fintona in Tyrone, written by the Four Masters *Fionn-tamhnach*, fair-coloured field; Tamnyagan in the parish of Banagher, Derry, O'Hagan's field. 4. *Damh* [dauv], an ox; Davillaun near Inishbofin, Mayo, ox-island; Madame in the parish of Kinaloda, Cork, *Magh-damh*, the plain of the oxen.

A remarkable instance of this hardening process occurs in some of the Leinster counties, where the Irish word *bóthar* [bóher], a road, is converted into *batter*. This word "batter" is, or was, well understood in these counties to mean an ancient road; and it was used as a general term in this sense in the patents of James I. It signifies in Wexford, a lane or narrow road:—"Bater, a lane bearing to a high road" ("Glossary of the dialect of Forth and Bargy." By Jacob Poole: Edited by William Barnes, B. D.). "As for the word Bater, that in English purpozeth a lane bearing to an highway, I take it for a meer Irish worde that crept unawares into the English, through the daily intercourse of the English and Irish inhabitants" (Stanyhurst, quoted in same).

The word occurs in early Anglo-Irish documents in the form of *bothir*, or *bothyr*, which being pronounced according to the powers of the English letters, was easily converted into *botter* or *batter*. It

forms a part of the following names :—Batterstown,
the name of four townlands in Meath, which were
always called in Irish *Baile-an-bhóthair*, i. e. the town
of the road; and anglicised by changing *bothar* to
batter, and translating *baile* to town. Batterjohn and
Ballybatter are also in Meath. Near Drogheda
there is a townland called Greenbatter, and another
called Yellowbatter, which are called in Irish, *Boher-*
glas and *Boherboy*, having the same meanings as the
present names, viz. *green road* and *yellow road.*

We have also some examples in and around Dublin, one of which is the well known name of Stonybatter. Long before the city had extended so far,
and while Stonybatter was nothing more than a
country road, it was—as it still continues to be—the
great thoroughfare to Dublin from the districts lying
west and north west of the city; and it was known
by the name of *Bothar-na-gcloch* [Bohernaglogh],
i. e. the road of the stones, which was changed to the
modern equivalent, Stonybatter or Stonyroad. One
of the five great roads leading from Tara, which were
constructed in the second century, viz. that called
Slighe Cualann, passed through Dublin by Ratoath,
and on towards Bray; under the name of *Bealach*
Duibhlinne (the road or pass of the [river] *Duibhlinn*),[*]
it is mentioned in the following quotation from the
" Book of Rights" :—

> " It is prohibited to him (the king of Erin) to go with a host
> On Monday over the *Bealach Duibhlinne.*

The old ford of hurdles, which in those early ages
formed the only foot passage across the Liffey, and

---

[*] *Duibhlinn* was originally the name of that part of the Liffey
on which the city now stands.

which gave the name of *Ath-Cliath* to the city, crossed
the river where Whitworth bridge now stands, leading from Church-street to Bridge-street;[*] and the
road from Tara to Wicklow must necessarily have
crossed the Liffey at this point. There can be, I
think, no doubt that the present Stonybatter formed
a portion of this ancient road—a statement that is
borne out by two independent circumstances. First
—Stonybatter lies straight on the line, and would,
if continued, meet the Liffey exactly at Whitworth
bridge. Secondly, the name Stonybatter, or *Bothar-
na-gcloch*, affords even a stronger confirmation. The
most important of the ancient Irish roads were generally paved with large blocks of stone, somewhat like
the old Roman roads; a fact that is proved by the remains of those that can now be traced. It is exactly
this kind of a road that would be called by the Irish
—even at the present day—Bohernaglogh; and the
existence of this name, on the very line leading to
the ancient ford over the Liffey, leaves scarcely any
doubt that this was a part of the ancient *Slighe Cualann*. It must be regarded as a fact of great interest,
that the modern-looking name Stonybatter—changed
as it has been in the course of ages—descends to us
with a history seventeen hundred years old written
on its front.

Booterstown (near Dublin) is another member of
the same family; it is merely another form of Batterstown, i.e. Roadtown. In a roll of about the year
1435 it is written in the Anglo-Irish form, Bally-
bothyr (*Baile-an-bhothair*—town of the road), of
which the present name, Booterstown, is a kind of
half translation. In old Anglo-Irish documents fre-

---

[*] Gilbert's "History of Dublin," Vol. I., Chap. ix.

quent mention is made of a road leading from Dublin
to Bray.   In a roll of the fifteenth century it is called
Bothyr-de-Broe (road of Bray); and it is stated that
it was by this road the O'Byrnes and O'Tooles usually
came to Dublin.* It is very probable that the Booterstown road and this Bray road were one and the same,
and that both were a continuation of the ancient
Slighe Cualann.

CHAPTER III.

CORRUPTIONS.

While the majority of names have been modernized
in accordance with the principles just laid down, great
numbers, on the other hand, have been contracted
and corrupted in a variety of ways.   Some of these
corruptions took place in the Irish language; but
far the greatest number were introduced by the
English-speaking people in transferring the words
from the Irish to the English language.   These corruptions are sometimes so extremely irregular and
unexpected, that it is impossible to reduce them to
rule, or to assign them to any general or uniform
influence except mere ignorance, or the universal
tendency to contraction.   In most cases, however,
they are the result of laws or principles, by which
certain consonants have a tendency to be substituted
for others, or to be placed before or after them, some
of which are merely provincial, or attributable to
particular races of people, while the influence of
others may be traced throughout the whole of Ire-

* For this information about Booterstown and Bothyr-de-
Bree, I am indebted to Mr. Gilbert.

land. Some of these laws of corruption have been
noticed by Dr. O'Donovan and Dr. Reeves ; and I
have given expression to others : I have here brought
them all, or the most important of them, under
one view, and illustrated each by a number of
examples.

I. *Interchange of* l, r, n, m.—The interchange of
these letters is common in most languages : it would
be easy, if necessary, to give examples from every
language of Europe. For instance, the modern name
Bologna is a corruption of the ancient Bononia ;
Palermo of Panormus ; Amsterdam of Amstel-dam
(the dam of the river Amstel) ; Rousillon of Ruscino,
&c., &c.

The substitution of these letters, one for another,
is also exceedingly common in Irish names ; and since
this kind of corruption prevails in Irish as well as in
English, the names were altered in this particular
respect, quite as much in one language as in the other.
L appears to have been a favourite letter, and the
instances are particularly numerous in which it is
substituted for the letter *r*. The word *sruthair*
[sruher], a stream, forms the whole or part of many
names ; and generally—but not always—the *r* has
been changed to *l*, as in Shrule, Shruel, Struell, Sroo-
hill, all names of places in different parts of Ireland.
Biorar, watercress, is now always called in Irish
biolar, in which form it enters into several names, as,
for example, Aghaviller, a parish in Kilkenny ; the
Four Masters call it *Achadh-biorair* [Ahabirrer], the
field of the watercresses, but the present spoken Irish
name is *Achadh-bhiolar*, from which the English form
is derived ; in Toberburr near Finglas, Dublin, the
original *r* is retained (*Tobar-biorair*, watercress well).
Loughbrickland in Down was anciently *Loch-Bricrenn*

(Four Masters), the lake of *Bricriu ;* and it received
its name from an Ulster poet of the time of king
Conor Mac Nessa (1st cent.), who, on account of the
bitterness of his satires, was called *Bricriu Nemh-
thenga*—Bricriu of the poison-tongue (see O'Curry,
Lect. III., 17).

N is also sometimes, though not often, changed
to *l*, as in the case of Castleconnell near Limerick,
which is the castle of the O'Connings, not of the
O'Connells, as the present form of the name would
indicate. The O'Connings, or as they are now
called, Gunnings, were chiefs of the territory of
Aes-Greine, extending from Knockgrean to Limerick ;
and this was their principal castle.

The change of *n* to *r* is one of frequent occurrence, an example of which is the name of Kilmacrenan in Donegal, which is called in Irish authorities, *Cill-mac-nEnain*, translated by Colgan, the
church of the sons of Enan, who were contempo-
raries and relatives of St. Columba.

The Irish name of Limerick is *Luimneach* [Limi-
negh : Book of Leinster, &c.], which was originally
applied to a portion of the river Shannon ; as the
following passage from an ancient poem on the
death of St. Cuimmin of Clonfert, quoted by the
Four Masters at 561, will show :—

" The Luimneach did not bear on its bosom, of the race of
        Munster, into Leath Chuinn,
A corpse in a boat so precious as he Cummine son of Fiachna ;"

and the modern name was derived from this, by a
change of *n* to *r*, and by substituting *ck* for the
guttural in the end.

The root of the word is *lom*, bare, of which *luimne*
is a diminutive form (see for the diminutive termi-

nation *ne*, 2nd Ser., c. II.) ; and from this again
was developed, by the addition of the adjective postfix *ach*, the full name *Luimneach*, which signifies a
bare or.barren spot of land, and which was applied
to the place long before the foundation of the city.
Several conjectural and legendary derivations of the
name are cited by Mr. Maurice Lenihan in the
"Kilk. Arch. Jour.," 1864-6, p. 425, note 1 ; but I do
not think it necessary to notice them here.

In connection with the name of Limerick, it may
be remarked that *lom*, bare, is a usual component of
local names. There is a place called Lumcloon near
the village of Cloghan in King's County, which the
Four Masters call *Lomchluain*, bare *cloon* or meadow ;
or more fully *Lomchluain-I-Fhlaithile*, from the family
of O'Flahily, or as they now call themselves, Flattery.
There are other places of the same name in Carlow
and Wicklow ; and it takes the form of Lomcloon
in Sligo.   Clonlum in Armagh, and Cloonloum in
Clare, have the same meaning, the root words being
reversed.

Luimneach itself is a name of frequent occurrence,
but only in one other place is it anglicised Limerick,
namely, in the parish of Kilcavan in Wexford.   It
takes the form of Limnagh in Sligo ; of Lumnagh
near Ballyvourney in Cork ; and of Luimnagh in
Galway.   Lomanagh, the name of some places in
Kerry ; Lomaunagh (-baun and -roe, whitish and
reddish) in Galway ; and Loumanagh in Cork, are
slightly different in formation ; but they have all
the same meaning as *Luimneach*.   The word is seen
compounded in Cloonlumney in Mayo, and in Ath-
lumney in Meath, the meadow and the ford, of the
bare place.

In some of the northern counties, the Irish speaking people cannot without difficulty articulate the combinations *cn* and *gn*, and in order to facilitate the pronunciation they change the *n* to *r*. There are about forty-five townlands commencing with the word *Crock*, all in Ulster, except only a few in Connaught and Leinster; and a person unacquainted with the present peculiarity might be puzzled by this prefix, or might perhaps consider it an anglicised form of *crunch*, a rick or piled up hill. But all these *Crocks* are really *Knocks*, disguised by the change of this one letter. In the Ulster counties, the termination *na-grow* or *nagrew* is often found in townland names, as in Tullynagrow in the parish of Muckno, Monaghan; this termination has been similarly corrupted, Tully-nagrow being properly *Tulaigh-na-gcno*, the hill of the nuts.

The change of *l* to *r* is not very common, but it is found in some names. Dromcolliher in Limerick is properly *Druim-collchoille*, the ridge or hill of the hazel wood; and Ballysakeery, a parish in Mayo, is called in Mac Firbis's " Hy Fiachrach," *Baile-easa-caoile* [Ballysakeely], the town of the narrow cataract. Killery harbour in Connemara is called at the present day in Irish, *Caolshaire* [Keelhary], from which the present name is formed; but it should be *Caolshaile*, or, as it is written more fully by the Four Masters, *Caolshaile-ruadh*, i. e. the reddish narrow-sea-inlet, a most appropriate name.

The change of *m* to *n*, or *vice versâ*, is not of frequent occurrence. In Rathangan in Kildare, the first *n* should be *m*, the correct name as written by the Four Masters being *Rath-iomghain*, Imgan's rath; and the old rath is still to be seen just outside the town, in a field near the church. The barony of Glenquin in Limerick takes its name from a townland (now divided into three), near Newcastle; the proper anglicised form would be Glenquim, for the Irish name is *Gleann-a'-chuim*, the glen of the *coom* or hollow.

N is changed to *m* in Kilmainham (near Dublin), which should have been called Kilmainen; it is written Kilmanan by Boate, which shows that it has been corrupted within the last two or three hundred years. It took its name from St. Maighnenn, who was bishop and abbot there early in the seventh century, and who is commemorated in the Calendars at the 18th of December. The termination of the last name seems to have been formed in imitation of the common English topographical suffix *ham*, home. In Moyacomb, the name of a parish in Wicklow, there is a genuine change of *n* to *m*, the Irish name being *Magh-da-chon* [Moyacon : Four Masters] the plain of the two hounds. We see the same in Slieve Eelim, the name of a mountain range east of Limerick city, which is *Sliabh-Eibhlinne* [Slieve-Evlinna] in the Annals, Ebhliu's mountain ; and it was so called, according to an ancient legend in Lebor na hUidhre, from Ebhliu, the step-mother of Eochaidh, who gave name to Lough Neagh, mentioned further on.

Several of the letter changes now examined have been evidently caused, or at least facilitated, by the difficulty of articulating the same letter twice in immediate succession, and this is a principle of considerable influence in corrupting language. It is easier to say Aghaviller than the right name Aghavirrer, and so on, in several other cases.

II. *Change of* ch, gh, dh, *and* th, *to* f.—The guttural sound of *c* aspirated (*ch*), as heard in *loch*, cannot be pronounced at all by a speaker of mere English;

and as it constantly occurs in names, it is interesting
to observe the different ways in which English sub-
stitutes are provided. When it comes in the end
of words, it is often passed over altogether, being
neither represented in writing nor in pronunciation,
as in Ballymena in Antrim, which is in Irish *Baile-
meadhonach*, middle town, the same as Ballymenagh
in other places. Sometimes, both in the middle and
end of words, it is represented by *gh*, which is often
sounded by the English-speaking natives, like the
proper guttural *ch*, as in Lough, Lughany, while
those who cannot sound the guttural, pronounce it
as *k* or *h* (Lock, Luhany); but if this *gh* occur at
the end of words, it is commonly not sounded at all,
as in Fermanagh, Kilnamanagh, &c. In the middle
of words, its place is often supplied by *h* alone, as in
Crohane, the name of a parish in Tipperary, and of
several townlands, which represents *cruachán*, a little
rick or hill; and in many cases it is represented by *k*
or *ck*, as in Foorkill near Athenry, Galway, *Fuarchoill*
cold wood.

Sometimes it is changed to *wh*, of which a good
example is seen in Glenwhirry, a parish in Antrim,
taking its name from the river which runs by Kells
into the Main. It is called Glancurry in the Inquisitions, and its Irish name is *Gleann-a'-choire*, the glen
of the river Curry, or *Coire*, this last name signifying a caldron. The caldron is a deep pool formed
under a cataract; and a rocky hill near it is called
Sceir-a'-choire, the rock of the caldron, which, in the
modernized form Skerrywhirry, is the name of a
townland.

But there is a more remarkable change which this
aspirate undergoes in common with three others. In
many names, the sounds of the Irish aspirated letters

ch, gh, dh, and *th,* are converted into the sound of *f;* and this occurs so frequently as to preclude all supposition of mere accident. *Ch* is a hard guttural, as heard in the common word *lough (loch)* ; *gh* or *dh* (both which have the same sound) is the corresponding soft guttural ; *th* is sounded exactly like English *h.*

The sound of *ch* is changed to that of *f* in the following names. Knocktopher iu Kilkenny is in Irish *Cnoc-a'-tochair,* the hill of the *togher* or causeway, and it was so called from an ancient *togher* across a marsh ; Luffany, the name of two townlands in Kilkenny, *an fhliuchaine* [au luhany], the wet land ; Clifden, the name of a well-known village in Galway, is a very modern corruption of *Clochán,* which is still its Irish name, and which means a beehive-shaped stone house ; but according to some, the *Clochán* was here a row of stepping stones across the Owenglin river ; Lisnafiffy, the name of two townlands in Down, *Lios-na-faithche,* the *lis* of the *faha* or exercise-green ; Fidorfe, near Ratoath in Meath, *Fidhdorcha,* dark wood.

The change of *gh* or *dh* to *f* is not quite so common, but we find it in Muff, the name of two villages, one in Donegal, and the other iu Derry, and of eight townlands, all in the northern half of Ireland ; it is merely a form of *magh,* a plain ; and the Irish name, as now pronounced in the localities, comes very near the English form. Balief in Kilkenny is *Baile-Aodha,* Hugh's town. In some cases, instead of the hard labial *f,* it is turned into the corresponding soft labial *r,* as in Lough Melvin in Leitrim ; which is called in the Annals, *Loch-Meilghe,* from Meilghe, king of Ireland in A. M. 4678. Adrivale in the parish of

Drishane, Cork, *Eadar-ghabhal*, a place between (the prongs of) a fork, i. e. a fork formed by rivers.

The change of *th* to *f* is often met with; but it is really a change from the sound of English *h* (which is equal to Irish *th*) to that of *f*. The parish of Tiscoffin in Kilkenny took its name from an old church called *Tigh-Scoithin* [Tee-scoheen], i. e. Scoithin's house; St. Scoithin was a relative of St. Ailbe of Emly, and erected his primitive church here towards the close of the sixth century (see O'Clery's Cal. 2nd Jan., and Colgan, A. SS., p. 9) ; Cloonascoffagh in the parish of Kilmacshalgan, Sligo, *Cluain-na-scothach*, the meadow of the flowers. In accordance with the same law, a *scruthan*, or streamlet, is often called *sruffane;* and this is almost always the case in some of the western counties, as in Ballintrofaun in Sligo, *Baile-an-tsrothain*, the town of the streamlet.

The greater number of the alterations noticed under this heading are attributable to the English language; but there are several instances of words and names corrupted similarly by the speakers of Irish. For example, the word *chuaidh* (past tense of the verb *teidh*, go), is pronounced *foo* in the south; and O'Donovan, in one of his Derry letters, informs us, that *magh*, a plain, is there pronounced in Irish "something between *mugh* and *muff*," thereby facilitating or suggesting its conversion into the present name, Muff.

Any one who had studied the English language and its letter-changes, might however, anticipate that the Irish gutturals would sometimes be converted into English *f*. Words transplanted directly from Irish, as might be expected, conform in many instances to the letter-changing laws of the English

language; of which names beginning with the word
knock may be taken as an illustration.   In such English words as "knight," "knife," "knee," &c., the
k sound is now entirely omitted in pronunciation;
but in the Anglo-Saxon originals *cnight, cnif, cneow,*
both letters—the *c* hard and the *n*—were pronounced (Max Müller, "Lectures," 2nd Series, p.
186).   The Irish *cnoc* is subjected to the same law,
for while both letters are heard in Irish, the anglicised form *knock* is always pronounced *nock*.

There is a similar compliance with English custom
in the change of the Irish gutturals to *f*.   The English language, though it has now no gutturals, once
abounded in them, and in a numerous class of words
the guttural letters are still retained in writing, as in
daughter, laughter, night, straight, plough, &c.   While
in many such words the sound of the gutturals was
wholly suppressed, in others it was changed to the
sound of *f*, as in *trough, draught, cough, rough,* &c.
It is curious that the struggle between these two
sounds has not yet quite terminated; it is continued
to the present day in Scotland and the north of Ireland, where the peasantry still pronounce such words
with the full strong guttural.

It will be seen, then, that when the Irish gutturals
are corrupted to *f*, the change is made, not by accident or caprice, but in conformity with a custom already existing in the English language.

III. *Interchange of* d *and* g.—The letters *d* and *g*
when aspirated (*dh* and *gh*), are sounded exactly
alike, so that it is impossible to distinguish them in
speaking.   This circumstance causes them to be, to
some extent, confounded one with the other; in
modern Irish, *gh* is very generally substituted for the
older *dh*.   In topographical names, this aspirated *g*

is often hardened or restored (after the manner shown
at page 43); and thus many names have been corrupted both in writing and pronunciation, by the
substitution of *g* for *dh*. But as far as I have examined, I find only one example of the reverse—*a*
for *gh*.

There are four townlands called Gargrim in the
counties of Donegal, Fermanagh, Leitrim, and Tyrone, which should have been called Gardrim; for
the Irish name is *Gearrdhruim*, i. e. short ridge or
hill, and it is correctly anglicised in Gardrum, the
name of two townlands in Fermanagh and Tyrone.
In exactly the same way was formed Fargrim, the
name of two townlands, one in Fermanagh, and
the other in Leitrim; it is in Irish, *Fardhruim* or
Fordhruim (outer ridge or hill), in which form it
appears in the Four Masters at A. D. 1153: in its
correct anglicised form, Fardrum, it occurs in Fermanagh and Westmeath. Drumgonnelly in the
parish and county of Louth, should have been
called Drumdonnelly, from the Irish *Druim-Dhon-
ghaile*, the ridge or hill of the Donnellys; Sliguff
in Carlow would be more correctly anglicised Sli-
duff, the Irish name being *Slighe-dhubh*, black road;
and the townland of Rossdagamph in the parish
of Inishmacsaint, Fermanagh, is *Ros-da-dhamh*, the
promontory of the two oxen. It was a mistake the
reverse of this, that gave their present English
name to the Ox Mountains in Sligo. The Irish
name, in all our Annals, is *Sliabh-ghamh* (which
means stormy mountain); but the natives believing it to be *Sliabh-dhamh*, i. e. the mountain
of the oxen, have perpetuated the present incorrect
name.

IV.—*Interchange of* b *and* m.—These letters are

often substituted one for the other; but so far as I have observed, the change of *b* to *m* occurs oftener than the reverse. The tendency to change *b* to *m* appears to be greatly assisted by the grammatical law of eclipse (see p. 22, *supra*); in other words, as the sound of *m* is, in case of eclipse, correctly substituted for that of *b*, there is a tendency to make the same change where there is no eclipse at all to justify it, in which case the change is merely a corruption.

When the preposition *a*, signifying "in," comes before a noun beginning with *b*, the *b* is then regularly eclipsed by *m*; and this *m* has in some cases remained after the preposition has been omitted, exactly as *t* was retained in Turagh after the removal of the article (see Turagh, p. 29, *supra*). The name of Managher in the parish of Aghadowey in Derry, is a good example of this: for it is in reality the same as Banagher (a place of gables or pointed rocks: see Banagher, further on). When the preposition *a* is used, the form of expression is *a-mBeannchair*, which is pronounced in speaking, *a-managher;* and the omission of the preposition left the name as it now stands:—Managher. This form of phrase is very common in the Irish language both spoken and written: we find it, for example, in case of this very name, *Beannchair*, in the Four Masters at A.D. 1065, where it is recorded that the king of Ulidia was killed at Bangor (*Ro marbhadh an ri a mBeannchair;* the king was killed at Bangor).

It is curious that Stamboul, the modern name of Constantinople, exhibits a complete parallel to this; for it appears that this name is a contraction of the Greek phrase "es tan polin," i. e. "in the city" (Rev. Isaac Taylor's "Words and Places"), a phrase corresponding with the Irish *a-mBeannchair*, and the *s* of the Greek preposition has been retained, just as *m* has been in Managher.

B is eclipsed by *m* in some cases where it is hard to assign the eclipse to any grammatical rule ; as in case of *Cill-mBian* [Kilmean] mentioned by the Four Masters at A. D. 583 : but here perhaps *Bian* is in the genitive plural (see p. 21, supra). It is evidently something like this that takes place in the popular pronunciation of Lisbellaw, often heard in the county Fermanagh, viz. Lismellaw; which I do not believe to be a corruption, but the correct phonetic representative of *Lios-mbél-atha* (see Lisbellaw further on).

In Derry the word *bo-theach,* cow-house, which should be anglicised *boyagh,* is very commonly made *moyagh.* It was evidently under the same influence that Emlygrennan, the name of a parish near Kilmallock in Limerick, was corrupted from the proper Irish name, *Bile-Ghroidhnin* [Billagrynin], Grynan's *bile* or ancient tree; though here the change appears to have been helped by a desire to assimilate the name to that of Emly, a well known place in Tipperary, not very far off.

The change of *m* to *b*, of which there are some undoubted examples, is a mere corruption, not admitting even partially, like the reverse change, of any grammatical explanation. Ballymoney, in Antrim, is usually called Ballyboney in early Anglo-Irish records (Reeves: Eccl. Ant. p. 80, note u), but I am convinced that Ballymoney is the correct form ; and the family name O'Amergin or Mergin, is now corruptly made Bergin (O'Donovan; Battle of Moyr. p. 290, note x). The name of Bannady near Ballaghaderreen in Mayo, originally began with *m*, for the Four Masters write it Meannoda. There

is a place called Bunnafedia in the parish of Dromard
in Sligo, which is anglicised from its present Irish
name, *Bun-na-fede*, the mouth of the *fead* or streamlet (see Faddan further on). Duald Mac Firbis, in
his Hy Fiachrach, writes the name Bun-fede; but
in a poem in the Book of Lecan, written by his
ancestor more than 200 years earlier, the place is
called *Muine-na-fede* (the shrubbery of the streamlet);
and as this is no doubt the original form, there is
here a change from *m* to *b*. A change much the
same as this occurs in the name of Bunnyconnellan
in the parish of Kilgarvan in Mayo, which was corrupted from the correct name *Muine-Chonallain* (Con-
allan's shrubbery) as we find it written by Mac Firbis
in Hy Fiachrach.

V.—*Insertion of* t *between* s *and* r.—The combination *sr* is one of rare occurrence in modern European languages; there is not a single word in
English, French, German, Greek, or Latin, beginning with it, though many of their words are undoubtedly derived from roots commencing with these
two letters.

The Irish language has retained this combination,
and in the Irish dictionaries, a considerable number
of words will be found commencing with *sr*. Of
these, there are only four that enter *often* into topographical names. These are *sráid*, a street, *srath*, a
holm or inch—the lowland along a river; *srón*, literally a nose, but in a secondary sense, applied to
points of hills, promontories, &c.; and *sruth*, a
stream, with its derivatives. It was not to be expected that the English language, which within its
own domain does not admit of the union of *s* and *r*,
would receive these names in all cases without alteration. Of the modern townland names containing

the four words just named, the *sr* has been retained
in less than half; in about forty or fifty, it has been
changed to *shr*, a combination admitted in English;
and in all the rest it has been corrupted by the insertion of a *t*.

There are about 170 modern names commencing
with *str*, and many more containing these letters intermediate. In all these, with hardly an exception,
the *t* is a late insertion; for although we have words
in Irish beginning with *str*, there are no names
derived from them, except perhaps about half a dozen.
The insertion of a *t* is one of the expedients for
avoiding the combination *sr*, which is found in several
languages, and which has been in operation from the
earliest times. We find it, for instance, in the O. H.
German *stroum* (Eng. stream), and in the name of
the well-known Thracian river Strymon, both of
which are derived from a Sanscrit root, *sru*, meaning
to flow.[*]

A few names will illustrate these remarks. In
Srugreana near Caherciveen, Kerry (*Sruth-greanach*,
gravelly stream), and in Srananny in parish of
Donagh, Monaghan (*Srath-an-eanaigh* [Srahananny],
the strath or holm of the marsh), the initial *sr* has
been retained. It has been changed to *shr* in Shrough,
near Tipperary, from *sruth*, a stream; and also in
Shronedarragh, near Killarney, the nose or point of
the oak.

In the following names, a *t* has been inserted :—
Strancally, above Youghal, the well-known seat of
the Desmonds; whose castle, now in ruins, was built
on a point of rock jutting into the Blackwater, called
Sron-caillighe, the hag's nose or promontory. Ard-

* See Dr. Whitley Stokes' "Irish Glosses;" and Dr. W. K.
Sullivan's Translation of Ebel's "Celtic Studies."

straw in Tyrone, which the annalists write *Ard-sratha*
[Ard-sraha], the height of (or near) the river holm;
Stradone in Cavan, and Stradowan in Tyrone, deep
srath or holm.

This corruption—the insertion of *t*—is found more
or less all over Ireland, but it prevails more in the
northern counties than anywhere else. In Ulster,
the combination *sr* is scarcely admitted at all; for
out of about 170 townland names in all Ireland,
beginning with these two letters, there are only
twelve in this province, and these are wholly confined to Donegal, Fermanagh, and Monaghan.

VI. *Addition of* d *after* n, l, *and* r; *and of* b *after*
m.—The most extensive agency in corrupting language is contraction, i. e. the omission of letters;
first, in pronunciation, and afterwards in writing.
This is what Max Müller calls phonetic decay, and
he shows that it results from a deficiency of mus-
cular energy in pronunciation, in other words, from
laziness. There are cases, however, in which this
principle seems to be reversed, that is, in which
words are corrupted by the *addition* of anomalous
letters. In English, for instance, a *d* is often added
after *n*, and in Greek, after both *n* and *l*; as in Eng.
thunder from Ang. Sax. *thunor; cinder* from Lat.
(*cinis*) *cineris*, &c.; and in Gr. *anér*, gen. *andros*, &c.
This tendency in English is also noticed by Lhuyd
in his "Archæologia" (p. 9). Another corruption
similar to this, which is found in several languages,
is the addition of *b* after *m*; as in Eng. *slumber* from
Ang. Sax. *slumerian; Fr. nombre* from *numerus*; Lat.
comburo, from *com* (*con*), and *uro*; Gr. *gambros*
for *gamros*, &c. Max Müller shows, however, that
the insertion of these letters is due to the same

laziness in pronunciation that causes omission in other cases.[*]

These corruptions are very frequent in Irish names, viz. :—the letter *d* is often placed after *n* and *l*, and sometimes after *r*; and the letter *b* after *m*. In the following names the *d* is a mere excrescence, and has been added in recent times: Terryland near Galway, which the Four Masters write *Tir-oiléin*, the district of the island; Killashandra in Cavan is in Irish *Cill-a'-sean-ratha*, the church of the old rath, and it was so called because the original church was built within the inclosure of an ancient rath which still exists; Rathfryland in Down is from *Rath-Fraoi-leann*, Freelan's rath; Tullyland in parish of Balli-nadee, Cork, *Tulaigh-Eileain*, Helena's hill.

D is added after *l* in the word "field," when this word is an anglicised form of *coill*, a wood, as in Longfield, Cranfield, &c., which names have been examined at page 40. The same corruption is found in the ancient Welsh personal name, Gildas, and in the Irish name Mac Donald, which are more correctly written Gillas and Macdonnell.

Lastly, *d* is placed after *r* in Lifford, which is in Irish *Leithbhearr* (Four Mast.); this is a compara-tively modern corruption; for Spencer, in his "View of the State of Ireland," calls it Castle-liffer. It is to be observed that this adventitious *d* is placed after *n* much oftener than after the other two letters, *l* and *r*.

The addition of *b* to *m* occurs only seldom; we find it in Cumber or Comber, which is the name of a town in county Down, and of several townlands in different counties, both singly and in composition.

---

[*] See Max Müller's "Lectures," 2nd Series, p. 178.

It is the Irish *comar*, the confluence of two waters,
and it is correctly anglicised Cummer and Comer in
many other places.

All these changes were made in English, but in
the Irish language there was once a strong tendency
in the same direction.   In what is called middle Irish
(from the 10th to the 15th century), and often also
in old Irish, the custom was very general of using *nd*
for *nn*.   For instance, the word *cenn* (a head) is cited in
this form by Zeuss from MSS. of the eighth century;
but in middle Irish MSS. it is usually written *cend*.
In all such words, however, the proper termination is
restored in modern Irish; and so strong was this
countercurrent, that the *d* was swept away not only
from words into which it was incorrectly introduced,
but also from those to which it properly and radically belonged.   For example, the middle Irish
word *Aiffrend* (the Mass) is spelled correctly with
a *d*, for it is derived from Lat. *offerenda;* but in
modern Irish it is always spelled and pronounced
Aiffrionn.

Some of the words and names cited under this section afford a curious example of the fickleness of phonetic change, and, at the same time, of the regularity
of its action.   We find words spelled in old Irish with
nn; in middle Irish, a *d* is introduced, and the *nu*
becomes *nd;* in modern Irish the *d* is rejected, and
there is a return to the old Irish *nn;* and in modern
anglicised names, the *d* is reinstated, and *nd* seems to
remain in final possession of the field.

There is a corruption peculiar to the northern and
north-western counties, which is very similar to the
one now under consideration, namely, the sound of
aspirated *m* (*mh* = Eng. *r*) is often represented in the
present names by *mph.*   This mode of spelling is

probably an attempt to represent the half nasal, half labial-aspirate sound of *mh*, which an ear unaccustomed to Irish finds it very difficult to catch. Under the influence of this custom, *damh*, an ox, is converted into *damph*, as in Derrydamph in the parish of Knockbride, Cavan, *Doire-damh*, the oak grove of the oxen ; *creamh*, wild garlic, is made *cramph*, as in Annacramph in the parish of Grange, Armagh, *Eanach-creamha*, wild garlic marsh.[*]

VII. *The letter s prefixed to* teach *and* leacht.—The Irish word *teach* or *tigh*, a house or church, as I shall show elsewhere, enters extensively into topographical names all over Ireland, in the anglicised forms of *ta*, *tagh*, *tee*, *ti*, *ty*, &c. In some of the eastern counties this word is liable to a singular corruption, viz., the Irish *ta* or *ti* is converted into *sta* or *sti*, in a considerable number of names, of which the following are examples. Stillorgan is in Irish *Tigh-Lorcain* [Teelorkan], Lorcan's church ; and it may have received its name from a church founded by St. Lorcan or Laurence O'Toole, Archbishop of Dublin at the time of the English invasion ; Stabannon in Louth, ought to be Tabannon, Bannon's house ; Stackallan in Meath, is written *Teach-collain*, by the Four Masters, i.e. Collan's house. So also Stirue in Louth, red house; Stapolin near Baldoyle, Dublin, the house of Paulin, or little Paul ; and Stalleen near Donore above Drogheda, is called in the Charter of Mellifont, granted by king John in 1185-6, *Teachlenni*, i. e. Lenne's house.

This corruption is almost confined to the counties

---

[*] For full information on the subject of letter changes in various languages, see Max Müller's most interesting lecture on " Phonetic Change" (Lectures on the Science of Language ; Second Series).

of Dublin, Meath, and Louth; I can find only very few examples outside these counties, among which are, the parish of Stacumny in Kildare, Stakally in the parish of Powerstown, Kilkenny, and Tyrella in Down, which is called in the well-known Taxation (1306), published by Dr. Reeves, Staghreel. But its Irish name is *Tech-Riaghla* [Tahreela : O'C. Cal.], the house of St. Riaghal or Regulus, who is commemorated on 17th Sept. There are altogether in Dublin, Meath, and Louth, about twenty-three names which commenced originally with *Ta* or *Ti*, in about two-thirds of which it has become *Sta* or *Sti*.

The Irish word *leacht*, a sepulchral monument, is also, in some of the Ulster counties, corrupted by prefixing an *s;* for example, Slaghtneill and Slaghtmanus, both in Londonderry, ought to be Laghtneill and Laghtmanus, signifying respectively Niall's and Manus's monument; and we also find Slaghtfreeden, Slaghtybogy, and a few others.

It will be recollected that all the corruptions hitherto noticed were found capable of explanation, on some previously established principle of language : the reason of the alteration now under consideration, however, is not so evident. In case of the conversion of *ta* and *ti* into *sta* and *sti*, I would suggest the following as the probable explanation. The fact that this peculiarity is almost confined to Dublin, Meath, and Louth, renders it likely that it is a Danish corruption. In all the northern languages there are whole classes of words commencing with *st*, which mean habitation, place, &c. For example, Ang. Sax. *stoc*, a dwelling-place, a habitation ; *stede*, a place, a station ; Danish, *sted*, locus, sedes ; *stad*, urbs, oppidum ; *stede*, statio ; Icelandic, *stadr*, statio, urbs, oppidum ; *stofa*, curta domus ; *sto*, statio. And I

may add, that in Iceland, Norway, and other northern countries, several of these words are extensively used in the formation of names of places; of
which any one may satisfy himself by only looking
over a map of one of these countries.

It appears to me, then sufficiently natural, that
the northern settlers should convert the Irish *ta* and
ti into their own significant *sta* and *sti*. The change
was sufficiently marked in character to assimilate to
some extent the names to their own familiar local
nomenclature, while the alteration of form was so
slight, that the words still remained quite intelligible
to the Irish population. It would appear more natural to a Dane to say Stabannon (meaning Bannon's
house) than Tabannon; and an Irishman would understand quite well what he meant.

This opinion is further supported by these two
well-known facts : first, many places on the eastern
coast have Danish names, as Waterford, Leixlip,
Howth, Ireland's Eye, &c.; and secondly, the Danes
frequently changed the Irish *inis*, an island, into
their own equivalent word, *ey*, as in the last mentioned name. If it be objected that Tabannon could
not be converted on this principle into Stabannon,
because the northern method of forming such names
is to place the limiting term first, not last, as in Irish
(for instance, the Irish order is *Sta-bannon*, but the
northern *Bannon-sta*); it may be answered that in
anglicising Irish names, it is very usual to convert
each part of a compound wholly or partly into an
English word, leaving the whole at the same time in
the original Irish order; as, for instance, Batterjohn,
Castledonovan, Downpatrick, Port Stewart, &c., in
which the proper English order would be John's
batter, Donovan's Castle, &c. .

6 *

It is only fair to state, however, that Worsae does not notice this corruption, though in his "Account of the Danes and Norwegians in England, Scotland, and Ireland," he has collected every vestige he could find of the Danish rule in these countries.

Notwithstanding the variety of disturbing causes, and the great number of individual names affected by each, only a small proportion of the whole are corrupted, the great majority being, as already stated, anglicised correctly, or nearly so.   When it is considered that there are more than 60,000 townlands in Ireland, and when to the names of these are added the countless names of rivers, lakes, mountains, &c., it will be seen that even a small fraction of all will form a number large enough to give sufficient play to all the corrupting influences enumerated in this chapter.

I have now examined, in this and the preceding chapter, seventeen different sources of change in Irish names, and I have selected these, because they are the most striking and important, as well as the most extensive in their influence.   There are other letter changes of a less violent character, such as those caused by metathesis, &c., which I have not thought sufficiently important to notice.   The interchange of hard and soft mutes (or *tenues* and *mediæ*) is extremely common ; but this, too, as not causing considerable obscuration of the names, I shall dismiss with a single remark.   In the formation of anglicised names from Irish, the change from hard to soft is comparatively rare, while the reverse occurs very frequently.   Dulane near Kells is an example of the former, its ancient name, as spelled by the Four Masters, being *Tuilen* or *Tulan*, i. e. the little *tulach* or hill ; as examples of the latter, it will be

sufficient to mention the frequent change of *dubh*
(black) to *duff*, *garbh* (rough), to *gariff*, *carraig* (a
rock) to *carrick*, &c., in the two former of which the
sound of *c* is converted to that of *f*, and in the last
the sound of *g* (in *got*) is changed to that of *k*. There
are also corruptions of an exceptional and unexpected character, which I have not been able to
reduce to any principle; but I shall not dwell on
them, as the object of these chapters is not so much
the examination of individual names as the develop-
ment of general laws.

_____ ___ ____ ___

CHAPTER IV.

FALSE ETYMOLOGIES.

In no department of Irish antiquities have writers
indulged to such an extent in vague and useless conjecture as in the interpretation of local names. Our
county histories, topographical dictionaries, tourist's
handbooks, &c., abound in local etymologies; but if
we leave out of the question a few topographical
works lately published, it may be safely asserted, that
these interpretations are generally speaking false,
and a large proportion of them inexpressibly silly.
Instead of seeking out the ancient forms of the
names, in authentic Irish documents, which in many
cases a small amount of inquiry would enable
them to do, or ascertaining the pronunciation from
natives, writers of this class, ignoring both authority and analogy, either take the names as they
stand in English, or invent original forms that they
never had, and interpret them, each according to his

own fancy, or to lend plausibility to some favourite
theory.

There are laws and method in etymology, as well
as in other sciences, and I have set forth in the
three preceding chapters, the principles by which
an inquirer must be guided in the present branch
of the subject.   But when we see men pronouncing
confidently on questions of Irish etymology, who
not only have no knowledge of these principles,
but who are totally unacquainted with the Irish
language itself, we cannot wonder that their conjectures regarding the signification of Irish names
are usually nothing better than idle and worthless
guesses.

The first who to any extent made use of the etymology of Irish names, as an instrument of historical
investigation, was Vallancey.   He built whole theories regarding the social condition and religious belief
of the early inhabitants of Ireland, chiefly on false
etymologies : but his system has been long exploded,
and no one would now think of either quoting or re-
futing his fanciful conjectures.   He was succeeded
by a host of followers, who in their literary specula-
tions seem to have lost every vestige of judgment and
common sense ; and the race, though fast dying out
under the broad sunlight of modern scholarship, is
not yet quite extinct.   I shall not notice their etymological fancies through this book, for indeed they
are generally quite beneath notice, but I shall bring
together in the present chapter a few characteristic
examples.

In Ferguson's " River Names of Europe," there
are near fifty Irish names, whose meanings are discussed.   Of these, a few are undoubtedly correct ;
there are about twenty on which I am not able to

offer an opinion, as I know nothing certain of
their etymology, and the author's conjectures are
far more likely to be wrong than right, for they
are founded on the modern forms of the names. A
full half are certainly wrong, and of these one example will be sufficient.   The name Nenagh (river)
is derived from Sanso. *ni*, to move, Gael. *nigh*, to
wash ; but a little inquiry will enable any one to
see that Nenagh is not the name of the river at all,
but of the town ; and that even if it were, it could not
be derived from any root beginning with *n*, since the
original name is *Arnach*, the initial *n* being merely
the Irish article.   The real name of the river, which
is now almost forgotten, is Owen O'Coffey, the river
of the O'Coffeys, the family who anciently inhabited
the district.

In Gibson's Etymological Geography, a considerable number of Irish names are explained ; but the
author was very careful to instance those only whose
meanings are obvious, and consequently he is generally right.   Yet he calls Inishbofin off the coast of
Mayo, *Inishbosine*, and interprets it *Bosine's island !*
and he confounds Inishcourcy in Down with Enniscorthy in Wexford, besides giving an erroneous etymology for both.

The Rev. Isaac Taylor, who also deals frequently
with Irish names, in a work of great ability, "Words
and Places," is more cautious than either.   But
even he sometimes falls into the same error ; for instance, he takes Armagh as it stands, and derives it
from the preposition *ar* (on), and *magh* (a plain),
though among the whole range of Irish names there
is scarcely one whose original form (*Ard-Macha*) is
better known.

There is a parish near Downpatrick, taking its

name from an old church, now called Inch, i. e. the
island, because it was built on a small island or peninsula, on the west side of Strangford Lough. The
full name is Inishcourcy; and as it is a historical fact
that an abbey was founded there by John de Courcy
about the year 1180, it is not to be wondered at that
Harris (in his History of Down), and Archdall, fell
into the error of believing that the name was derived
from him. But an earlier monastery existed there,
called *Inis-Cumhscraigh* [Inishcooscry], Cooscragh's
island, long before John de Courcy was born ; and
this name was gradually corrupted to Inishcourcy,
both on account of the curious similarity of sound,
and of that chief's connection with the place.

All this will be rendered evident by reference to
the Annals. We find it recorded in the Four Masters that in 1001 "Sitric son of Amlaff set out on a
predatory excursion into Ulidia in his ships ; and
plundered Kilclief and *Inis-Cumhscraigh ;*" and
Tighernach, who died in 1088, records the same
event. Moreover, Hugh Maglanha, abbot of *Inish-
cumhscraigh*, was one of those who signed the Charter of Newry, a document of about the year 1160.

Dr. Reeves has conjectured, what is highly probable, that the person who gave name to this place
was Cumhscrach, one of the sons of Conor Mac Nessa,
who succeeded his father as king of Ulster in the
first century.

It has been said by a philosopher that words go-
vern men, and we have an excellent example of this
in the name of the Black Valley, near Killarney.
Many of our guide books, and tourists without
number, describe it as something wonderful in its
excessive blackness; and among them is one well-
known writer, who, if we are to judge by his de-

scription, either never saw it at all, or wrote from
memory.

It may be admitted that the direction of this valley
with regard to the sun, at the time of day when visitors generally see it, has some influence in rendering the view of it indistinct; but it certainly is not
blacker than many other valleys among the Killarney mountains; and the imagination of tourists is
led captive, and they are betrayed into these descriptions of its gloominess, because it has been called
the Black Valley, which is not its name at all.

The variety of ways in which the original is
spelled by different writers—Coomdhuv, Coomadhuv,
Coomydhuv, Cummeendhuv, &c.—might lead any-
one to suspect that there was something wrong in
the translation; whereas, if it were intended for
black valley, it would be Coomdhuv, and nothing
else. To an Irish scholar, the pronunciation of the
natives makes the matter perfectly clear; and I almost regret being obliged to give it a much less
poetical interpretation. They invariably call it
*Coom-ee-wic** (this perfectly represents the pronunciation, except only the *w*, where there is a soft guttural that does not exist in English), which will be
recognised as *Cúm-ui-Dhuibh*, O'Duff's valley. Who
this O'Duff was, I have not been able to ascertain.

Clonmacnoise is usually written in the later Annals
Cluain-mic-Nois, which has been translated, and is
very generally believed to mean, "the retreat of the
sons of the noble," a name which it was thought to

---

* The popular pronunciation is also preserved in a slightly
different form by the writer of a poem in the "Kerry Magazine,"
vol. i. p. 24:—

  "And there the rocks that lordly towered above;
  And there the shady vale of Coomewove."

have received, either because the place was much
frequented by the nobility as a retirement in their
old age, or because it was the burial-place of so
many kings and chiefs. But this guess could never
be made by any one having the least knowledge of
Irish, for in the original name the last two syllables
are in the genitive singular, not in the genitive plural. *Nós* (gen. *nóis*), indeed, means noble, but here
it is the name of a person, who is historically known,
and *Cluain-mic-Nois* means the meadow of the son
of Nos.

Though the Irish name given above is generally
used by the Four Masters, yet at 1461 they call the
place *Cluain-muc-Nois-mic-Fiadaigh*, by which it appears that this Nos's father was Fiadhach [Feeagh],
who was a chief belonging to the tribe of the *Dealbh-
na-Eathra* (now the barony of Garrycastle in King's
County), in whose territory Clonmacnoise was situated. *Cluain-muc-Nois* would signify the meadow of
Nos's pigs; but though this form is used by Colgan
in the Tripartite Life, the correct original appears
to be *Cluain-maccu-Nois*, for it is so written in the
older Annals, and in the Carlsruhe Manuscript of
Zeuss, which is the most ancient, and no doubt the
most trustworthy authority of all: this last signifies
the meadow of the *sons* of Nos.

Askeaton in Limerick is transformed to *Eas-cead-
tinne*, in a well-known modern topographical work
on Ireland: the writer explains it "the cataract of
the hundred fires," and adds, "the fires were probably some way connected with the ritual of the
Druids, the ancient Irish Guebres." The name,
however, as we find it in many Irish authorities, is
Eas-Gephtine, which simply means the cataract of
Gephtine, some old pagan chief. The cataract is

where the Deel falls over a ledge of rocks near the town.

I may remark here that great numbers of these fanciful derivations were invented to prove that the ancient Irish worshipped fire. In order to show that the round tower of Balla, in Mayo, was a fire temple, Vallancey changes the name to *Beilagh*, which he interprets "the fire of fires." But in the Life of St. Mochua, the founder, published by Colgan (at the 30th of March), we are told that before the saint founded his monastery there, in the beginning of the seventh century, the place was called *Rosdair-bhreach*, i.e. oak-grove; that he enclosed the wells of his religious establishment with a "balla" or wall (a practice common among the early Irish saints); and that "hence the town received the new name Balla, and Mochua himself became known by the cognomen Ballensis."

Aghagower, in the same county, Vallancey also explains "fire of fires," and with the same object, as a round tower exists there. He was not aware that the original name was *Achadh-fobhair*, for so it is called in the Four Masters and in the most ancient Lives of St. Patrick: it signifies "the field of the spring," and the place took its name from a celebrated well, which is now called St. Patrick's Well. Its name must have been corrupted at an early date, for Duald M'Firbis calls it *Achadh-gabhair* ("Hy Fiachrach," p. 151); but even this does not signify "fire of fires," but a very different thing—"the field of the goat."

Smith, in his History of Cork, states that the barony of Kinalmeaky means "the head of the noble root," from *cean*, head, *neal*, noble, and *mearan*, a root. The true form of the name, however, is *Cinel-*

mBece (O'Heerin), which was originally the name, not of the territory, but of the tribe that inhabited it, and which means " the descendants (*cinel*) of Bece," who was the ancestor of the O'Mahonys, and flourished in the seventh century.

In Seward's Topographical Dictionary it is stated that Baltinglass (in Wicklow) " is derived from *Beal-tinne-glas*, or *the fire of Beal's mysteries*, the fires being lighted there by the Druids in honour of the sun ;" and the writer of a Guide to Wicklow (Curry, Dublin, 1834) says that it is " *Bal-teach-na-glass*, or *the town of the grey houses ;*" and he adds, " certainly the appearance of them bears us out in this." This is all pure invention, for neither of the original forms here given is the correct one, and even if it were, it would not bear the meaning assigned, nor indeed any meaning at all. In ancient documents the name is always given *Bealach-Chonglais* [Ballaconglas : Dinn-senchus], the pass or road of Cuglas, a personage connected with the locality, about whom there is a curious and very ancient legend : in Grace's Annals it is anglicised *Balkynglas*, which is nearer the original than the modern corrupt name. There was another *Bealach-Chonglais* near Cork city, but the name is now lost, and the exact situation of the place is not known.

— -

CHAPTER V.

THE ANTIQUITY OF IRISH LOCAL NAMES.

In an essay on Irish local names it may be expected that I should give some information regarding their antiquity. In various individual cases through this book I have indicated the date, certain or probable, at which the name was imposed; or the earliest period when it was known to have been in use; but it may be of interest to state here some general conclusions, to which the evidence at our command enables us to arrive.

When we wish to investigate the composition and meaning of a name, we are not warranted in going back farther than the oldest actually existing manuscripts in which it is found written, and upon the form given in these we must found our conclusions. But when our object is to determine the antiquity of the name, or, in other words, the period when it was first imposed, we have usually a wider scope and fuller evidence to guide us.

For, first, if the oldest existing manuscript in which the name occurs is known as a fact to have been copied from another still older, not now in existence, this throws back the age of the name to at least the date of the transcription of the latter. But, secondly, the period when a name happens to be first committed to writing is no measure of its real antiquity; for it may have been in use hundreds of years before being embalmed in the pages of any written document. While we are able to assert with certainty that the name is at least as old as the time of the writer who first mentioned it, the validity of any further deductions regarding its absolute age depends on the authenticity of our history, and on the correctness of our chronology.

I will illustrate these remarks by an example:— The city of Armagh is mentioned in numerous Irish documents, many of them of great antiquity, such as the Book of Leinster, &c., and always in the form *Ard-Macha*, except when the Latin equivalent is used. The oldest of these is the Book of Armagh, which is known to have been transcribed about the year 807 ; in this we find the name translated by *Altitudo Machæ*, which determines the meaning, namely, Macha's height.

But in this same Book of Armagh, as well as in many other ancient authorities, the place is mentioned in connection with St. Patrick, who is recorded to have founded the cathedral about the year 457, the site having been granted to him by Daire, the chief of the surrounding district; and as the history of St. Patrick, and of this foundation, is accepted on all hands as authentic, we have undoubted evidence that the name existed in the fifth century, though we possess no document of that age in which it is written. And even without further testimony we are able to say that it is older, for it was in use before St. Patrick's arrival, who only accepted the name as he found it.

But here again history, though of a less reliable character, comes to our aid. There is an ancient tract called Dinnseuchus, which professes to give the origin of the names of the most celebrated localities in Ireland, and among others that of Armagh. It is a fact admitting of no doubt that the place received its name from some remarkable woman named Macha, and the ancient writer in the Dinnsenchus mentions three, from one of whom the name was derived, but does not decide which. The first was Macha, the wife of Nevvy, who led hither a colony about 600 years after the deluge; the second, Macha of the golden hair, who founded the palace of Emania, 300 years before the Christian era; and the third, Macha, wife of Crunn, who lived in the reign of Conor Mac Nessa in the first century. The second Macha is recorded to have been buried there; and as she was by far the most celebrated of the three, she it was, most probably, after whom the place was called. We may conclude, therefore, with every appearance of certainty, that the name has an antiquity of more than two thousand years.

Following this method of investigation, we are able to determine, with considerable precision, the age of hundreds of local names still in use; and as a further illustration, I shall enter into some detail concerning a few of the most ancient authorities that have come down to us.

The oldest writer by whom Irish places are named in detail is the Greek geographer, Ptolemy, who wrote his treatise in the beginning of the second century. It is well known that Ptolemy's work is only a corrected copy of another written by Marinus of Tyre, who lived a short time before him, and the latter is believed to have drawn his materials from an ancient Tyrian atlas. The names preserved by Ptolemy are, therefore, so far as they are authentic, as old at least as the first century, and with great probability much older.

Unfortunately very few of his Irish names have reached our time.[*] In the portion of his work relating to Ireland he mentions over fifty, and of these only about nine can be identified with names existing within the period reached by our history. These are *Senos*, now the Shannon; *Birgos*, the Barrow; *Bououinda*, the Boyne; *Rhikina*, Reohra or Rathlin; *Logia*, the Lagan; *Nagnatai*, Connaught; *Isamnion Akron*, Rinn Seimhne (now Island Magee), i. e. the point of *Seimhne*, an ancient territory; *Eblana*,

---

[*] The following observations refer to Mercator's Edition, 1605.

Dublin; and another to which I shall return presently.

The river that he calls *Oboka* appears, by its position on the map, to be the same as the Wicklow river now so well known as the Ovoca; but this last name has been borrowed from Ptolemy himself, and has been applied to the river in very recent times. Its proper name, as we find it in the Annals, is Avonmore, which is still the name of one of the two principal branches that form the "Meeting of the Waters."

He places a town called *Dounon* near the *Oboka*. It is now impossible to determine the place that is meant by this; but the record is valuable, as the name is obviously the Keltic *dun*, with the Greek inflexion *on* postfixed, which shows that this word was in use as a local appellative at that early age.

There is one very interesting example of the complete preservation of a name unchanged, from the time of the Phœnician navigators to the present day. Just outside *Eblana* there appears a small island, which is called *Edri Deserta* on the map, and *Edrou Heremos* in the Greek text, i. e. the desert of *Edros;* which last name, after removing the Greek inflexion, and making allowance for the usual contraction, regains the original form *Edar.* This is exactly the Irish name of Howth, used in all our ancient authorities, either as it stands, or with the addition of Ben (*Ben-Edair*, the peak of Edar); still well known throughout the whole country by speakers of Irish; and perpetuated to future time in the names of several villa residences built within the last few years on the hill.

Some writers have erroneously identified *Edrou Heremos* with Ireland's Eye, probably because the former is represented as an island. The perfect co-incidence of the name is alone sufficient to prove that *Ben-Edar* is the place meant; but I may add, that to the ancient navigators who collected the information handed down to us by Ptolemy, Ireland's Eye would be barely noticeable as they sailed along our coasts, whereas the bold headland of *Ben-Edar* formed a prominent landmark, certain to be remembered and recorded; and connected as it was with the mainland by a low, narrow isthmus, it is no wonder they mistook it for an island. Besides, as we know from our most ancient authorities, Howth was a celebrated locality from the earliest times reached by history or tradition; whereas Ireland's Eye was a place of no note till the seventh century, when it was selected, like many other islands round the coast, as a place of religious retirement by Christian missionaries.

According to some Irish authorities, the place received the name of *Ben-Edair* from a Tuatha De Danann chieftain, Edar, the son of Edgaeth, who was buried there; while others say that it was from Edar the wife of Gann, one of the five Firbolg brothers who divided Ireland between them. The name Howth is Danish. It is written in ancient letters *Hofda*, *Houete*, and *Howeth*, all different forms of the northern word *hoved*, a head (Worsae).

The Irish names originally collected for this ancient atlas were learned from the natives by sailors speaking a totally different language; the latter delivered them in turn, from memory, to the compiler, who was of course obliged to represent them by Phœnician letters; and they were ultimately transferred by Ptolemy into the Greek language. It appears perfectly obvious, therefore, that the names, as we find them on Ptolemy's map, must in general

7

be very much distorted from the proper forms, as used
at the time by the inhabitants.

Enormous changes of form have taken place in
our own time in many Irish names that have been
transferred merely from Irish to English, under circumstances far more favourable to correctness. If
some old compiler, in drawing a map of Ireland,
had removed the ancient *Ceann Léime* (the head of
the leap) twenty or thirty miles from its proper position (as Ptolemy does in case of several places), and
called it by its present name Slyne Head, and if
all intermediate information were lost, it is highly
probable that it would never be recognised.

When we reflect on all this, and remember besides
that several of the names are no doubt fantastic
translations, and that with great probability many
of them never existed at all, except in the imagination of the voyagers, we shall cease to be surprised
that, out of more than fifty, we are able to identify
only about nine of Ptolemy's names.

The next writer after Ptolemy who has mentioned
many Irish localities, and whose works remain to us,
is a native, namely, Adamnan, who wrote his Life of
St. Columba in the seventh century, but the names
he records were all in use before the time of Columba
in the sixth century. In this work about forty Irish
places are mentioned, and here we have Ptolemy's
case reversed. The number of names totally lost, or
not yet recognised, does not amount to half-a-dozen.
All the rest have been identified in Reeves's edition
of Adamnan; of these, nine or ten, though now obsolete, occur frequently in Irish MSS., and have been
in use down to recent times; the remainder exist at
the present day, and are still applied to the localities.

It will not be necessary to detail the numerous
writers, whose works are still extant, that flourished

at different periods from Adamnan down to the time
of Colgan and the O'Clerys; or the ancient MSS.
that remain to us, enumerating or describing Irish
localities. It will be enough to say that in the
majority of cases the places they mention are still
known by the same names, and have been identified
in our own day by various Irish scholars.

The conclusion naturally following from this is,
that the names by which all places of any note were
known in the sixth and succeeding centuries are,
with some exceptions, the very names they bear at
the present day.

A vast number of names containing the words *dun*,
rath, *lis*, *caher*, *carn*, *fert*, *cloon*, &c., are as old at least
as the advent of Christianity, and a large proportion
much older; for all these terms are of pagan origin,
though many of them were adopted by Christian missionaries. And in various parts of the book will be
found numbers of territorial designations, which were
originally tribe names, derived from kings and chieftains who flourished at different times from the foundation of the palace of Emania (300 years B.C.) to the
ninth century of the Christian era.

Those ecclesiastical designations that are formed
from the names of saints after such words as *kill*,
temple, *donagh*, *aglish*, *ti*, &c., were generally imposed
at various times from the fifth to the eighth or ninth
century; and among these may be enumerated the
greater number of our parish names. One example
will be sufficient to illustrate this, but many will be
found through the book, especially in the next three
or four chapters.

We have undoubted historic testimony that the
name of Killaspugbrone, near Sligo, is as old as the
end of the fifth century. It took its name from one

also a contemporary and friend of St. Brigid of Kildare, and became bishop of *Cassel Irra*, in the district of *Cuil Irra*, the peninsula lying south west of Sligo. In the Book of Armagh, and in the Tripartite Life, it is stated that after St. Patrick had passed from the *Forragh*, or assembly place, of the sons of Awly, he crossed the Moy at Bartragh, and built the church of *Cassel Irra* for his disciple, Bishop Bronus, the son of Icnus. Bronus died on the 8th June, 512, on which day he is commemorated in O'Clery's Calendar. And the name Killaspugbrone is very little altered from the original *Cill-easpuig-Bróin* (Four Mast.), the church of Bishop Bronus. A ruined little church still remains on the very spot, but it cannot be the structure erected by St. Patrick, for the style of masonry proves that it belongs to a very much later period.

The process of name-forming has continued from those early ages down to recent times. It was in active operation during the twelfth, thirteenth, fourteenth, and fifteenth centuries, for we have great numbers of names derived from English families who settled amongst us during these periods. It has never entirely ceased, and probably never will; for I might point to some names which have been imposed within our own memory.

The number of names given within the last two centuries is so small, however, that we may regard the process as virtually at an end, only making allowance for those imperceptibly slow changes incidental to language in its cultivated stage. The great body of our townland and other names are at least several hundred years old; for those that we find in the inquisitions and maps of the sixteenth and seventeenth centuries, which are numerous and minute, exist, with few exceptions, at the present day, and generally with very slight alterations of form.

PART II.

NAMES OF HISTORICAL AND LEGENDARY ORIGIN.

CHAPTER I.

HISTORICAL EVENTS.

HE face of the country is a book, which, if it be deciphered correctly, and read attentively, will unfold more than ever did the cuneiform inscriptions of Persia, or the hieroglyphics of Egypt. Not only are historical events and the names of innumerable remarkable persons recorded, but the whole social life of our ancestors—their customs, their superstitions, their battles, their amusements, their religious fervour, and their crimes—are depicted in vivid and everlasting colours. The characters are often obscure, and the page defaced by time, but enough remains to repay with a rich reward the toil of the investigator. Let us hold up the scroll to the light, and decipher some of these interesting records.

One of the most noted facts in ancient Irish and British history is the migration of colonies from the north of Ireland to the neighbouring coasts of Scot-

land, and the intimate intercourse that in consequence
existed in early ages between the two countries. The
first regular settlement mentioned by our historians
was made in the latter part of the second century,
by Cairbre Riada, son of Conary the second, king of
Ireland. This expedition, which is mentioned in
most of our Annals, is confirmed by Bede in the following words :—" In course of time, Britain, besides
the Britons and Picts, received a third nation, the
Scoti, who, issuing from Hibernia under the leader-
ship of Reuda, secured for themselves, either by
friendship or by the sword, settlements among the
Picts, which they still possess. From the name of
their commander they are to this day called Dal-
reudini; for in their language Dal signifies a part"
(Hist. Eccl., Lib. I. Cap. 1).

There were other colonies also, the most remarkable of which was that led by Fergus, Angus, and
Loarn, the three sons of Erc, in the year 506, which
laid the foundation of the Scottish monarchy. The
country colonized by these emigrants was known by
the name of *Airer-Gaedhil* [Arrer-gale], (Wars of
GG.), i.e. the territory of the Gael or Irish ; and the
name is still applied to the territory in the shortened
form of Argyle, a living record of these early colo-
nisations.

The tribes over whom Carbery ruled were, as Bede
and our own Annals record, called from him Dalriada, Riada's portion or tribe ; of which there were
two—one in Ireland, and the other and more illustrious in Scotland. The name has been long forgotten in the latter country, but still remains in
Ireland, though in such a worn down and fragmen-
tary state, that it requires the microscope of the
philologist and historian to recognise it.

The Irish Dalriada included that part of Antrim extending from the Ravel water northwards, and the same district is called at the present day the Route, or by Latin writers *Ruta*, which is considered by Ussher and O'Flaherty to be a corruption of the latter part of Dal-*Riada*. If this opinion be correct —and I see no reason to question it—there are few local names in the British islands more venerable for antiquity than this, preserving with little alteration, through the turmoil of seventeen centuries, the name of the first leader of a Scotic colony to the coasts of Alba.

The name of Scotland also commemorates these successive emigrations of Irishmen; it has, moreover, an interesting history of its own, and exhibits one of the most curious instances on record of the strange vicissitudes to which topographical names are often subjected, having been completely transferred from one country to another.

The name Scotia originally belonged to Ireland, and the Irish were called Scoti or Scots; Scotland, which was anciently called Alba, subsequently got the name of Scotia Minor, as being peopled by Scots from Ireland, while the parent country was for distinction often called Scotia Major. This continued down to about the eleventh century, when Ireland returned to the native name *Eire*, and "Scotia" was thenceforward exclusively applied to Scotland. The word "land" in both Ire-land and Scot-land was added by the English, the former being obviously a contraction for Eire-land.

That the Scoti were the inhabitants of Ireland would be sufficiently proved by the single quotation given above from Bede; but besides, we find it expressly stated by several other ancient authorities;

and the Irish are called Scoti in Cormac's Glossary,
as well as in other native writings. Adamnan often
uses Hibernia and Scotia synonymously : thus in
his Life of Columba we find the following passage :—"On a certain day the holy man ordered
one of his monks named Trenan of the tribe of
Mocuruntir, to go on a commission to Scotia (*ad
Scotiam*) : . . . . . . The saint answering him
' Go in peace ; you shall have a favourable and
good wind till you arrive in Hibernia (*ad Hiber-
niam*); you shall find a man coming to meet you
from a distance, who will be the first to seize the
prow of your ship in Scotia (*in Scotiá*) ; he will ac-
company you in your journey for some days in Hibernia." Lib. I., Cap. 18.

Many testimonies of this kind might be adduced
from other writers ; and if another clear proof were
necessary, we find it in an ode of the poet Claudian,
celebrating a victory of Theodosius over the three
nations of the Saxons, the Picts, and the Scots, in
which the following passage occurs :—" The Orcades
flowed with Saxon gore ; Thule became warm with
the blood of the Picts ; and icy Ierne wept her heaps
of (slaughtered) Scots."

The foundation of the celebrated palace of *Eamhuin*
or Emania, which took place about 300 years before the Incarnation, forms an important epoch ; it
is the limit assigned to authentic Irish history by the
annalist Tighernach, who asserts that all accounts of
events anterior to this are uncertain. The following
are the circumstances of its origin as given in the
Book of Leinster. Three Kings, Aedh-ruadh [Ay-
roo], Dihorba, and Ciombaeth [Kimbay], agreed to
reign each for seven years in alternate succession,
and they each enjoyed the sovereignty for three

periods, or twenty-one years, when Aedh-ruadh died. His daughter the celebrated Macha of the golden hair, asserted her right to reign when her father's turn came, and being opposed by Dihorba and his sons, she defeated them in several battles, in one of which Dihorba was killed, and she then assumed the sovereignty.

She afterwards married the surviving monarch, Kimbay, and took the five sons of Dihorba prisoners. The Ultonians proposed that they should be put to death :—"Not so," said she, "because it would be the defilement of the righteousness of a sovereign in me ; but they shall be condemned to slavery, and shall raise a rath around me, and it shall be the chief city of Ulster for ever." The account then gives a fanciful derivation of the name ; "And she marked for them the dun with her brooch of gold from her neck," so that the palace was called *Eomuin* or *Eamhuin*, from *eo*, a brooch, and *muin* the neck (see Armagh, p. 77, and O'Curry's Lectures, p. 527).

The remains of this great palace are situated about a mile and a half west of Armagh, and consist of a circular rath or rampart of earth with a deep fosse, enclosing about eleven acres, within which are two smaller circular forts. The great rath is still known by the name of the Navan Fort, in which the original name is curiously preserved. The proper Irish form is *Eamhuin*, which is pronounced *aven*, Emania, being merely a latinized form. The Irish article *an*, contracted as usual to *n*, placed before this, makes it *nEamhuin*, the pronunciation of which is exactly represented by Navan (see page 23, *supra*).

This ancient palace was destroyed in A.D. 332, after having flourished as the chief royal residence of Ulster for more than 600 years ; and it

would perhaps be difficult to identify its site with absolute certainty, were it not for the singular tenacity
with which it has retained its name through all the
social revolutions of sixteen hundred years.

The Red Branch Knights of Ulster, so celebrated
in our early romances, and whose renown has descended to the present day, flourished in the first
century, and attained their greatest glory in the reign
of Conor Mac Nessa.   They were a kind of militia in
the service of the monarch, and received their name
from residing in one of the houses of the palace of
Emania, called *Craebh-ruadh* [Creeveroe] or the Red
Branch, where they were trained in valour and feats
of arms.   The name of this ancient military college
is still preserved in that of the adjacent townland of
Creeveroe ; and thus has descended through another
medium, to our own time, the echo of these old
heroic days.

Another military organization not less celebrated,
of somewhat later date, was that of the Fians, or
Finians, or, as they are often called, the Fianna Erin.
They flourished in the reign of Cormac mac Art in
the third century, and formed a militia for the defence
of the throne; their leader was the renowned Finn
mac Cumhail [Finn mac Coole], who resided at the hill
of Allen in Kildare, and whom Macpherson attempted
to transfer to Scotland under the name of Fingal.
Finn and his companions are to this day vividly remembered in tradition and legend, in every part of
Ireland ; and the hills, the glens, and the rocks still
attest, not merely their existence, for that no one who
has studied the question can doubt, but the important
part they played in the government and military
affairs of the kingdom.

One of the principal amusements of these old

heroes, when not employed in war, was hunting; and
during their long sporting excursions, they had certain favourite hills on which they were in the habit
of resting and feasting during the intervals of the
chase. These hills, most of which are crowned by
carns or moats, are called *Suidhe-Finn* [Seefin],
Finn's seat or resting place, and they are found in
each of the four provinces; the name appears to
have belonged originally to the carns, and to have
extended afterwards to the hills.

There is one among the Dublin mountains, a few
miles south of Tallaght; another among the Galties;
and the fine mountain of Seefin terminates the Ballyhoura range towards the north east, three miles south
of Kilfinane in Limerick. Immediately under the
brow of this mountain, reposes the beautiful vale of
Glenosheen, whose name commemorates the great
poet and warrior, Oisin, the son of Finn; and in
several of the neighbouring glens there are rocks,
which are associated in the legends of the peasantry
with the exploits of these ancient warriors. There
are also places called Seefin in Cavan, Armagh (near
Newry), Down, King's County, Galway, Mayo, and
Sligo; while in Tyrone we find Seein, which is the
same name, with the *f* aspirated and omitted. Finn's
father, Cumhal [Coole], was slain by Gaul-mac-
Morna at the terrible battle of *Cnucha* or Castleknock,
near Dublin; he is believed to have had his residence
at Rathcoole (Cumhal's rath), now a small town nine
miles south west of the city; but I cannot find that
any vestige of his rath remains.

There are numerous places in every part of Ireland, where, according to tradition, Finn's soldiers
used to meet for various purposes; and many of

them still retain names that speak plainly enough of
these assemblies. In the county Monaghan we find
Lisnaveane, that is, *Lios-na-bhFiann,* the fort of the
Fianna; in Donegal, Meenavean, where on the *meen,*
or mountain flat, they no doubt rested from the
fatigues of the chase; near Killorglin in Kerry,
Derrynafeana (Derry, an oak wood), and in another
part of the same county is a river called Owenna-
feana; in Westmeath, Carnfyan and Skeanavean e
(Skea, a bush); and many other such names. ·

The name of Leinster is connected with one of the
most remarkable of the very early events recorded in
the history of Ireland. In the third century before
the Christian era, Coffagh Cael Bra murdered his
brother, Leary Lorc, monarch of Ireland, and the
king's son, Olioll Aine, and immediately usurped the
throne. Maen, afterwards called Labhradh Linshagh
(Lavra the mariner), son of Olioll, was banished by
the usurper; and having remained for some time
in the south of Ireland, he was forced to leave the
country, and crossed the sea to Gaul. He entered
the military service of the king of that country, and
after having greatly distinguished himself, he returned to his native land with a small army of
foreigners, to wrest the crown from the murderer of
his father and grandfather.

He landed at the mouth of the Slaney in Wexford,
and after having been joined by a number of followers, he marched to the palace of Dinn Righ [Din-
ree, the fortress of the kings], in which Coffagh was
then holding an assembly with thirty native princes
and a guard of 700 men. The palace was surprised
by night, set on fire, and all its inmates—king,
princes, and guards—burned to death. Maen then

assumed the sovereignty, and reigned for nineteen years.

The exact description of the annalists indentifies very clearly the position of this ancient palace, the great mound of which still exists, though its name has been long forgotten. It is now called Ballyknockan moat, and lies on the west bank of the Barrow, a quarter of a mile south of Leighlin-bridge.

Lavra's foreign auxiliaries used a peculiarly-shaped broad-pointed spear, which was called *laighen* [layen]; and from this circumstance, the province in which they settled, which had previously borne the name of *Galian*, was afterwards called *Laighen*, which is its present Irish name. The syllable "ster" (for which see further on) was added in after ages, and the whole word pronounced *Laynster*, which is the very name given in a state paper of the year 1515, and which naturally settled into the present form Leinster.

Lavra's expedition is mentioned by Tighernach, and by most of the other annalists who treat of that period; but as his adventures have been amplified into a romantic tale in the Book of Leinster, * which is copied by Keating and others, the whole story, if it were not confirmed, would probably be regarded as a baseless legend. The word *Gall* has, however, been used in the Irish language from the remotest antiquity to denote a foreigner. For some centuries before the Anglo-Norman invasion it was applied to the Danes, and since that period to the English—both applications being frequent in Irish manuscripts;—but it is obvious that it must have been originally ap-

* For which see O'Curry's Lectures, p. 252.

plied to a colony of *Gauls*, sufficiently numerous and important to fix the word in the language.

We find it stated in Cormac's Glossary that the word *Gall* was applied to pillar stones, because they were first erected in Ireland by the *Galli*, or primitive inhabitants of France ; which not only corroborates the truth of the ancient tradition of a Gaulish colony, but proves also that the word *Gall* was then believed to be derived from this people.   Thus the story of Lavra's conquest is confirmed by an independent and unsuspicious circumstance ; and as it is recorded by the accurate Tighernach, and falls within the limits of authentic Irish history as fixed by that annalist (about 300 years B. C.), there seems no sufficient reason to doubt its truth.

The little island of Inchagoill in Lough Corrib, midway between Oughterard and Cong, is one of the few examples we have remaining, in which the word *Gall* is applied in its original signification, i. e. to a native of Gaul ; and it corroborates, moreover, an interesting fragment of our ancient ecclesiastical history. The name in its present form is anglicised from *Inis-an-Ghoill*, the island of the *Gall*, or foreigner, but its full name, as given by O'Flaherty and others, is *Inis-an-Ghoill-chraibhthigh* [crauvy], the island of the devout foreigner. This devout foreigner was Lugnat or Lugnæd, who, according to several ancient authorities, was the *lumaire* or pilot of St. Patrick, and the son of his sister Liemania.   Yielding to the desire for solitude, so common among the ecclesiastics of that early period, he established himself, by permission of his uncle, on the shore of Lough Mask, and there spent his life in prayer and contemplation.

This statement, which occurs in the of St. Patrick, as well as others rel history of the saint, was by many impugned as unworthy of credit, till it received an unexpected confirmation in the discovery on the island of Lugnaed's headstone by Dr. Petrie. It is a small pillar stone, four feet high, and it bears in old Roman characters this inscription:—"LIE LUGNAEDON MACCLMENUEH," the stone of Lugnaed the son of Limenueh, which is the oldest Roman letter inscription ever discovered in Ireland.* Near it is the ruin of a small stone church called Templepatrick, believed—and with good reason according to Petrie—to have been founded by St. Patrick: if this be so, it is probable that it is the very church in which Lugnaed worshipped.

In several old authorities, this saint's name is written Lugna [Loona], in which form we find it preserved in another locality. Four miles north-north-east from Ballinrobe, in the demense of Ballywalter, is an ancient church, which is believed, in the traditions of the inhabitants, to be the third church erected in Ireland. Near the burial ground, is a holy well now known by the name of Toberloona, but which is called *Tobar-Lugna* in Mac Firbis's Poem in the Book of Lecan, i. e. Lugna's well. It is well known that among St. Patrick's disciples, his own nephew was the only one that bore the name of Lugna, and as this well is in the very neighbourhood where he settled, it appears quite clear that it was dedicated to him, and commemorates his name.

* I find that Dr. W. Stokes, in his recent edition of Cormac's Glossary, has given a somewhat different reading of this inscription, viz.:—"LIE LUGUÆDON MACCI MENUEH," the stone of Luguæd, the son of Menueh. Whether this reading is inconsistent with the assumption that the stone marks the grave of Lugnat, St. Patrick's nephew, I will not now undertake to determine; but the matter deserves investigation.

We have at least two interesting examples of local names formed by the word Gall as applied to the Danes—Fingall and Donegal. A colony of these people settled in the district lying north of Dublin, between it and the Delvin river, which, in consequence, is called in our authorities (O'C. Cal., Wars of GG., &c.), *Fine-Gall*, the territory or tribe of the Galls or Danes; and the same territory is still well known by the name of Fingall, and the inhabitants are locally called Fingallians.

Donegal is mentioned in several of our Annals, and always in the form of *Dun-na-nGall*, the fortress of the foreigners. These foreigners must have been Danes, and the name was no doubt applied to an earthen *dun* occupied by them anterior to the twelfth century; for we have direct testimony that they had a settlement there at an early period, and the name is older than the Anglo-Norman invasion. Dr. Petrie quotes an ancient Irish poem (Irish Penny Journal, p. 185), written in the tenth century, by the Tyroonnellian bard, Flann mac Lonan, in which it is stated that Egnaghan, the father of Donnel, from whom the O'Donnells derive their name, gave his three beautiful daughters, Duvlin, Bebua, and Bebinn, in marriage to three Danish princes, Caithis, Torges, and Tor, with the object of obtaining their friendship, and to secure his territory from their depredations; and the marriages were celebrated at Donegal, where Egnaghan then resided. There are places in other parts of Ireland called Donegal and Donegall; but some or all of these may have received their names from English settlers.

The Annals of Ulster relate that the Danish fortress was burned in 1159, by Murtough M'Loughlin, king of the Northern Hy Niell : not a vestige of it now remains, but O'Donovan considers it likely, that it was situated at a ford which crossed the river Esk, immediately west of the old castle, and which the Four Masters at 1419 call *Ath-na-nGall,* the ford of the foreigners.

There are several other places through the country called Donegal or Dungall, having the same general meaning ; we have no evidence to show whether the foreigners were Danes or English ; possibly they were neither.

There are great numbers of names in all parts of Ireland, in which this word Gall commemorates English settlements. Galbally in Limerick is called in the Four Masters, *Gallbhaile,* English-town, and it probably got its name from the Fitzgeralds, who settled there at an early period ; and there are besides, a dozen other places of the same name, ten of them being in Tyrone and Wexford. Galwally in Down, Galvally in Derry, and Gallavally in Kerry are all the same name, but the *b* is aspirated as it ought to be.

Ballynagall, Ballynagaul, and Ballygall, all townland names of frequent occurrence, mean also the town of the Englishmen ; and I am of opinion that Gaulstown, a name common in Kilkenny and Meath, is a translation of Ballynagall. The terminations *gall, nagall, gill,* and *guile,* are exceedingly common all over Ireland ; the two former generally mean "of the Englishmen," and the two latter " of the Englishman ;" Clonegall in Carlow, and Clongall in Meath, signify the Englishmen's meadow ; Moneygall in King's County, the shrubbery of the strangers ; Clongill in Meath, the Englishman's meadow ; Ballinguile and Ballyguile in Cork and Wicklow, the town of the Englishman.

8

Gallbhuaile [Galvoola] is a name that often occurs in different anglicised forms, meaning English-booley, i. e. a booley or dairy place belonging to English people. In Tipperary it gives name to the parish of Galbooly ; in Donegal it is made Galwolie ; while in other places we find it changed to Galboley and Galboola.

The mouth of the Malahide river, near Dublin, is called by the strange name of Muldowney among the people of the locality, a name which, when fully developed under the microscope of history, will remind us of a colony still more ancient than those I have mentioned. The Firbolgs, in their descent on Ireland, divided themselves into three bodies under separate leaders, and landed at three different places. The men of one of these hordes were called *Firdom-nainn* [Firdownan], or the men of the deep pits, and the legendary histories say that they received this name from the custom of digging deeply in cultivating the soil.

The place where this section landed was for many ages afterwards called *Inver-Domnainn* (Book of Leinster), the river mouth of the *Domnanns*, and it has been identified, beyond all dispute, with the little bay of Malahide ; the present vulgar name Muldowney, is merely a corruption of *Macil-Domnainn*, in which the word *macil*, a whirlpool, is substituted for the *inbher* of the ancient name. Thus this fugitive-looking name, so little remarkable that it is not known beyond the immediate district, with apparently none of the marks of age or permanency, can boast of an antiquity "beyond the misty space of twice a thousand years," and preserves the memory of an event otherwise forgotten by the people, and regarded by many as mythological ; while, at the same time, it affords a most instructive illustration of the tenacity with which loose fragments of language often retain the footmarks of former generations.

According to our early histories, which in this particular are confirmed by Bede (Lib. I., Cap. I.), the Picts landed and remained some time in Ireland, on their way to their final settlement in Scotland.   In the Irish Annals, they are usually called *Cruithne* [Cruhnĕ], which is also the term used by Adamnan, and which is considered to be synonymous with the word Picti, i. e. painted, from *cruith*, colour.   After their establishment in Scotland, they maintained intimate relations with Ireland, and the ancient Dalaradia, which extended from Newry to the Ravel Water in Antrim, is often called in our Annals the country of the Crutheni.   It is probable that a remnant of the original colony settled there; but we know besides that its inhabitants were descended through the female line, from the Picts; for Irial Glunmore (son of Conall Carnagh), the progenitor of these people, was married to the daughter of Eochy, king of the Picts of Scotland.

Several places in the north of Ireland retain the name of this ancient people.   Duncrun, in the parish of Magilligan, Derry, was in old days a place of some notoriety, and contained a church erected by St. Patrick, and a shrine of St. Columba ; it must have originally belonged to a tribe of Picts, for it is known in the Annals by the name of *Dun-Cruithne* (Four Masters), which Colgan (Tr. Th., p. 181, n. 187), translates *Arx Cruthænorum*, the fortress of the Cruthnians.   In the parish of Macosquin, in the same county, there is a townland called Drumcroon, and one in the parish of Devenish, Fermanagh, with the name of Drumcroohen, both of which signify the Picts' ridge.

Q *

After the Milesian conquest of Ireland, the vanquished races, consisting chiefly of Firbolgs and Tuatha De Dananns, were kept in a state of subjection by the conquerors, and oppressed with heavy exactions, which became at last so intolerable, that they rose in rebellion, early in the first century, succeeded in overthrowing for a time the Milesian power, and placed one of their own chiefs, Carbery Kincat, on the throne. After the death of this king the Milesian monarchy was restored through the magnanimity of his son Moran. These helot races, who figure conspicuously in early Irish history, are known by the name of *Aitheach-Tuatha* [Ahathooha], which signifies literally, plebeian races; and they are considered by some to be the same as the Attacotti, a tribe who are mentioned by Ammianus Marcellinus and by St. Jerome, as aiding the Picts and Scots against the Britons.

In the barony of Carra, county of Mayo, there is a parish called Touaghty, preserving the name of the ancient territory of *Tuath-Aitheachta* [Thooahaghta], so written by M'Firbis in "Hy Fiachraoh," which received its name from having been anciently occupied by a tribe of Firbolgs: the name signifies the *tuath* or district of the Attacotti or plebeians.

To travellers on the Great Southern and Western railway, the grassy hill of Knocklong, crowned by its castle ruins, forms a conspicuous object, lying immediately south of the Knocklong station. This hill was, many ages ago, the scene of a warlike gathering, the memory of which is still preserved in the name.

In the middle of the third century, Cormac mac Art, monarch of Ireland, undertook an expedition against Fiacha Muilleathan [Mullahan], king of

Munster, to reduce him to submission, and lay
the province under additional tribute; and his army
marched from Tara unopposed, till they pitched
their tents on this hill, which was up to that time
called *Druim-damhghaire* [davary], the hill of the
oxen. The Munster king marched to oppose him,
and encamped on the slope of the opposite hill, then
called *Sliere Claire*, but now Slievereagh (grey mountain), lying south of Knocklong, and north east of
Kilfinane.

After a protracted struggle, and many combats in
the intervening plain, Cormac, defeated and baffled,
was forced to retreat without effecting his object. He
was pursued, with great loss, as far as Ossory, and
obliged by Fiacha to give security that he would
repair the injury done to Munster by this expedition.
And from this event the hill of Knocklong received
its name, which is in Irish, *Cnoc-luinge*, the hill of
the encampment.

These are the bare historical facts. In the Book
of Lecan there is a full narrative of the invasion and
repulse; and it forms the subject of a historical tale
called the Forbais or Siege of *Druim-damhghaire*, a
copy of which is found in the Book of Lismore.
Like all historical romances, it is embellished by
exaggeration, and by the introduction of fabulous
circumstances; and the druids of both armies are
made to play a conspicuous part in the whole transaction, by the exercise of their magical powers.

It is related that Cormac's druids dried up, by their
incantations, the springs, lakes, and rivers of the district, so that the men and horses of the Munster army
were dying of thirst. Fiacha, in this great distress,
sent for Mogh-Ruith [Mō-rih], the most celebrated
druid of his time, who lived at *Dairbhre* [Darrery],

now Valentia island in Kerry; and he came, and the
men of Munster besought him to relieve them from
the plague of thirst.

Mogh-Ruith called for his disciple Canvore, and
said to him, " Bring me my magical spear; " and
his magical spear was brought, and he cast it high
in the air, and told Canvore to dig up the ground
where it fell. " What shall be my reward ?" said
Canvore ; " Your name shall be for ever on the
stream," said Mogh-Ruith. Then Canvore dug the
ground, and the living water burst asunder the spells
that bound it, and gushed forth from the earth, in a
great stream ; and the multitudes of men and horses
and cattle threw themselves upon it, and drank
till they were satisfied. Cormac was then attacked
with renewed valour, and his army routed with great
slaughter.

I visited this well a few years ago. It lies on the
road side, in the townland of Glenbrohane, near
the boundary of the parish of Emlygrennan, three
miles to the south of Knocklong ; and it springs from
a chasm, evidently artificial, dug in the side of Slievereagh, forming at once a very fine stream. It is still
well known in the district by the name of Tober
Canvore, Canvore's well, as I found by a very
careful inquiry ; so that Canvore has received his
reward.

That the Munster forces may have been oppressed
by an unusual drought which dried up the springs
round their encampment, is nothing very improbable ; and if we only suppose that the druid possessed some of the skill in discovering water with
which many people in our own day are gifted, we
shall not find it difficult to believe that this marvellous narrative may be in the main true ; for

all unusual occurrences were in those days accounted supernatural. And this view receives some confirmation from the prevalence of the tradition at the present day, as well as from the curious circumstance, that the well is still called Tober Canvore.

There is a village on the east side of the river Moy, a kind of suburb of Ballina, called Ardnarea, a name which discloses a dark tale of treachery and murder; it was originally applied to the hill immediately south of the village, which is now called Castle Hill, from a castle that has long since disappeared. The event that gave origin to this name is very fully related by Mac Firbis in his account of the Tribes and Customs of the Hy Fiachrach, and the same story is told in the Dinnsenchus. The persons concerned are all well known characters, and the event is far within the horizon of authentic history.

Guairĕ Aidhne [Ainy] was king of Connaught in the seventh century—a king whose name has passed into a proverb among the Irish for his hospitality. Though a powerful and popular monarch, he was not the true heir to the throne; the rightful heir was a man who in his youth had abandoned the world, and entered the priesthood, and who was now bishop of Kilmore-Moy; this was Cellach, or Kellagh, the son of the last monarch, Owen Bel, and fourth in descent from the celebrated Dathi. Cellach was murdered at the instigation of Guary, by four ecclesiastical students—the four Maols, as they were called, because the names of all began with the syllable Mael—who were under the bishop's tuition, and who, it appears by another account, were his own foster-brothers. The bishop's brother, however, soon after pursued and captured the murderers, and brought them in chains to the hill overlooking the Moy, which was up to that time called *Tulach-na-faircsiona* [Tullanafark-shina], the hill of the prospect, where he hanged them all ; and from this circumstance the place took the name of *Ard-na-riaghadh* [Ardnarea], the hill of the executions.

They were buried at the other side of the river, a little south of the present town of Ballina, and the place was called *Ard-na-Mael*, the hill of the (four) Maels. The monument erected over them remains to this day ; it is a cromlech, well known to the people of Ballina, and now commonly called the Table of the Giants. The name *Ard-na-Mael* is obsolete, the origin of the cromlech is forgotten, and bishop Cellach and his murderers have long since ceased to be remembered in the traditions of the people.

When we consider how prominently the Danes figure in our history, it appears a matter of some surprise that they have left so few traces of their presence. We possess very few structures that can be proved to be Danish ; and that sure mark of conquest, the change of local names, has occurred in only a very few instances : for there are little more than a dozen places in Ireland bearing Danish names at the present day, and these are nearly all on or near the east coast.

Worsae (p. 71) gives a table of 1373 Danish and Norwegian names in the middle and northern counties of England, ending in *thorpe, by, thwaite, with, toft, beck, næs, ey, dale, force, fell, tarn,* and *haugh.* We have only a few Danish terminations, as *ford,* which occurs four times ; *ey,* three times : *ster,* three times ; and *ore,* which we find in one name, not noticed at all by Worsae; and in contrast with 1373 names in one part of England, we have only about fifteen in Ireland, almost all confined to one particular district. This appears to me to afford a complete answer to the statement which we sometimes see made, that the Danes conquered the country, and that their chiefs ruled over it as sovereigns.

The truth is, the Danes never, except in a few of the maritime towns, had any permanent settlements in Ireland, and even there their wealth was chiefly derived from trade and commerce, and they seem to have had only very seldom any territorial possessions. Their mission was rather to destroy than to build up; wherever they settled on the coast, they were chiefly occupied either in predatory inroads, or in defending their fortresses against the neighbouring Irish; they took no permanent hold on the country; and their prominence in our annals is due to their fierce and dreadful ravages, from which scarcely any part of the country was free, and the constant warfare maintained for three hundred years between them and the natives.

The only names I can find that are wholly or partly Danish are Wexford, Waterford, Carlingford, Strangford (Lough), Olderfleet, Carnsore Point, Ireland's Eye, Lambay Island, Dalkey, Howth, Leixlip and Oxmantown; to these may be added the Laxweir on the Shannon, the termination *ster* in the names of three of the provinces, the second syllables of such names as Fingall and Donegal; probably Wicklow and Arklow, and the *s* prefixed to some names near the eastern coast (for which see p. 65).

The termination *ford*, in the first four names is the well-known northern word *fiord*, an inlet of the sea. Waterford, Wexford, and Strangford are pro-

bably altogether Danish; the first two are called
respectively by early English writers Vadrefiord
and Weisford. The Danes had a settlement somewhere near the shore of Strangford Lough, in the
ninth and tenth centuries, and the Galls of *Lough
Cuan* (its ancient and present Irish name) are frequently referred to in our Annals. It was these who
gave it the very appropriate name of Strangford,
which means *strong-fiord*, from the well-known tidal
currents at the entrance, which render its navigation
so dangerous.

The usual Irish name of Carlingford, as we find
it in our Annals, is *Cairlinn*; so that the full name,
as it now stands, signifies the *fiord* of *Cairlinn*.
In O'Clery's Calendar it is called *Snamh-ech*, the
swimming-ford of the horses; while in " Wars of
GG," and several other authorities, it is called
Snamh-Aighnech.

The last syllable of the name of Olderfleet Castle,
which stands on the little neck of land called the
Curran, near Larne in Antrim, is a corruption of
the same word *fiord*; and the name was originally
applied, not to the castle, but to the harbour. One
of the oldest known forms of the name is Wulfrich-
ford; and the manner in which it gradually settled
down to "Olderfleet" will be seen from the following
forms, found in various records:—Wulvricheford,
Wokingis-fyrth, Wolderfrith, Wolverflete, Ulder-
fleet, Olderfleet. It is probable, as Dr. Reeves
remarks, that in the first part of all these, is disguised the ancient Irish name of the Larne water,
viz., *Ollorbha* [Ollarva]; and that the various forms
given above were only imperfect attempts at representing the sound of *Ollarra-fiord*.

Carnsore Point in Wexford, is known in Irish by

the simple name *Carn*, i. e. a monumental heap.
The meaning of the termination will be rendered
obvious by the following passage from Worsae :—
"On the extremity of the tongue of land which borders on the north the entrance of the Humber, there
formerly stood a castle called Ravensöre, raven's
point. *Öre* is, as is well known, the old Scandinavian name for the sandy point of a promontory"
(p. 65). The *ore* in Carnsore, is evidently the same
word, and the name written in full would be *Carn's
öre*, the "ore" or sandy point of the Carn.

Ptolemy calls this cape, *Hieron Akron*, i. e. the
Sacred Promontory ; and Camden ("Britannia," Ed.
1594, p. 659), in stating this fact, says he has no
doubt but that the native Irish name bore the same
meaning. This conjecture is probably well founded,
though I cannot find any name now existing near
the place with this signification. Camden, however,
in order to show the reasonableness of his opinion,
states that Bannow, the name of a town nearly
twenty miles from it, where the English made their
first descent, signifies sacred in the Irish language.
The Irish participle *beannuighthe* [bannihĕ] means
blessed, and this is obviously the word Camden had
in view ; but it has no connection in meaning with
Bannow. The harbour where Robert Fitzstephen
landed was called in Irish *Cuan-an-bhainbh* (O'Flaherty, Iar Connaught) the harbour of the *bonnive* or
sucking pig ; and the town has preserved the latter
part of the name changed to Bannow.

"It is doubtful whether Wicklow derives its name
from the Norwegians, though it is not improbable
that it did, as in old documents it is called Wy-
kynglo, Wygyngelo, and Wykinlo, which remind us
of the Scandinavian *vig*, a bay, or *Viking*" (Worsae,

p. 325). Its Irish name is Kilmantan, St. Mantan's church. This saint, according to Mac Geoghegan (Annals of Clonmacnoise), and other authorities, was one of St. Patrick's companions, who had his front teeth knocked out by a blow of a stone from one of the barbarians who opposed the saint's landing in Wicklow ; hence he was called Mantan, or the toothless, and the church which was afterwards erected there was called after him, *Cill-Mantain* (Four Mast.). It is worthy of remark that the word *mantach* [mounthagh]—derived from *mant*, the gum—is still used in the south of Ireland to denote a person who has lost the front teeth.

Leixlip is wholly a Danish name, old Norse *Lax-hlaup*, i. e. salmon leap : this name (which is probably a translation from the Irish), it derived from the well known cataract on the Liffey, still called the Salmon Leap, a little above the village. Giraldus Cambrensis (Top. Hib. II., 41), after speaking of the fish leaping up the cataract, says ;—" Hence the place derives its name of *Saltus Salmonis* (Salmon Leap)." From this word *saltus*, a leap, the baronies of Salt in the county Kildare have taken their name. According to Warsae, the word *lax*, a salmon, is very common in the local names of Scotland, and we have another example of it in the *Lax-weir*, i. e. Salmon weir, on the Shannon, near Limerick.

The original name of Ireland's Eye was *Inis-Ereann;* it is so called in Dinnsenchus, and the meaning of the name is, the island of Eire or Eria, who, according to the same authority, was a woman. It was afterwards called *Inis-mac-Nessan* (Four Mast.), from the three sons of Nessan, a prince of the royal family of Leinster, namely, Dicholla, Munissa, and Nadsluagh, who erected a church on it in the seventh century, the ruins of which remain to this day. They are commemorated in O'Clery's Calendar, in the following words :—" The three sons of Nesan, of *Inis Faithlenn*, i. e. Muinissa, Nesslugh, and Duichoill Derg ;" from which it appears that *Inis Faithlenn*, or, as it would be now pronounced, Innisfallen, was another ancient name for the island ; this is also the name of a celebrated island in the lower lake of Killarney (*Inis Faithlenn*, Book of Leinster); and in both cases it signifies the Island of Fathlenn, a man's name, formerly of common occurrence.

The present name, Ireland's Eye, is an attempted translation of *Inis-Ereann*, for the translators understood *Ereann* to be the genitive case of *Eire*, Ireland, as it has the same form ; accordingly they made it Ireland's *Ey* (*Ireland's* island, instead of *Eria's* island), which in modern times has been corrupted to Ireland's *Eye*. Even Ussher was deceived by this, for he calls the island *Oculus Hiberniæ*. The name of this little island has met with the fate of the Highlander's ancestral knife, which at one time had its haft renewed, and at another time its blade : one set of people converted the name of Eire, a woman, to Ireland, but correctly translated *Inis* to *ey ;* the succeeding generations accepted what the others corrupted, and corrupted the correct part ; between both, not a vestige of the ancient name remains in the modern.

Eire or Eri was formerly very common in this country as a woman's name, and we occasionally find it forming part of other local names ; there are, for instance, two places in Antrim called Carnearny, in each of which a woman named Eire must have been buried, for the Four Masters write the name *Carn-Ercann*, Eire's monumental mound.

Lambay is merely an altered form of *Lamb-ey*, i. e. Lamb-island; a name which no doubt originated in the practice of sending over sheep from the mainland in the spring, and allowing them to yean on the island, and remain there, lambs and all, during the summer. Its ancient Irish name was *Rechru*, which is the form used by Adamnan, as well as in the oldest Irish documents; but in later authorities it is written *Rechra* and *Reachra*. In the genitive and oblique cases, it is *Rechrinn*, *Reachrainn*, &c., as for example in Leabhar Breac:—"*Fothaighis Colam-cille eclais irrachraind oirthir Bregh*," "Columkill erects a church on *Rachra* in the east of *Bregia*" (O'Don. Gram., p. 155). So also in the poem on the history of the Picts printed from the Book of Ballymote by Dr. Todd (Irish Nennius, p. 127) :—

> "From the south (i. e. from near the mouth of the Slaney) was Ulfa sent,
> After the decease of his friends;
> In *Rachra* in *Bregia* (*In Rachrand im Breagaibh*)
> He was utterly destroyed."

Though the name Rachra, as applied to the island, is wholly lost, it is still preserved, though greatly smoothed down by the friction of long ages, in the name of Portraine, the parish adjoining it on the mainland. In a grant to Christ Church, made in the year 1308, the island is called *Rechen*, and the parish to which it belonged, *Port-rahern*, which is merely an adaptation of the old spelling *Port-Rachrann*, and very well represents its pronunciation; in the lapse of 500 years *Port-rahern* has been worn down to Portraine (Reeves). The point of land there was, in old times, a place of embarkation for the island and elsewhere, and this is the tradition of the inhabitants to the present day, who still show some remains of the old landing place ; hence the name *Port-Rachrann* ; the *port* or landing place of *Rachra*.

Other islands round the coast were called *Rachra*, which are now generally called Rathlin, from the genitive form *Rachrann*, by a change from r to *l* (see pages 34 and 48). The use of the genitive for the nominative must have begun very early, for in the Welsh, " Brut y Tywysogion" or Chronicle of the Chieftains, we read "Ac y distrywyd Rechrenn," " and (the Danes) destroyed *Rechrenn*" (Todd, Wars of GG., Introd., p. xxxii).

The best known of these is Rathlin on the Antrim coast, which Ptolemy calls *Rikina*, and whose name has been modified in various ways by foreign and English writers; but the natives still call it Raghery, which correctly represents the old nominative form. Ussher (Br. Ecc. Ant., c. 17) says : " our Irish antiquaries call this island *Ro-chrinne*," and he states further, that it was so called from the great quantity of trees with which it was formerly covered. The island, however, was never called *Rochrinne*, but *Rachra*, in which no *n* appears, which puts out of the question its derivation from *crann* a tree.

Dalkey is called in Irish, *Delginis* (O'Cl. Cal., Four Mast., &c.), thorn island. The Danes who had a fortress on it in the tenth century, called it *Dalk-ei*, which has the same meaning as the Irish name, for the Danish word *dalk* signifies a thorn : the present name Dalkey is not much changed from *Delginis*, but the *l*, which is now silent, was formerly pronounced. It is curious that there has been a fortress on this island from the remotest antiquity to the present day. Our early chronicles record that Scadhgha [shā], one of the chiefs of the Milesian colony, erected the Dun of *Delginis;* this was succeeded by the Danish fort; and it is now occupied by a martello tower.

Oxmantown or Ostmantown, now a part of the city of Dublin, was so called because the Danes or Ostmen (i. e. eastmen) built there a town of their own, and fortified it with ditches and walls.

According to Worsae (p. 230), the termination *ster* in the names of three of the provinces is the Scandinavian *stadr,* a place which has been added to the old Irish names. Leinster is the *place* (or province) of *Laighen* or *Layn;* Ulster is contracted from *Ula-ster,* the Irish name *Uladh* being pronounced *Ulla;* and Munster from *Moon-ster,* or *Mounster* (which is the form found in a State paper of 1515), the first syllable representing the pronunciation of the Irish *Mumhan.*

Many of the acts of our early apostles are preserved in imperishable remembrance, in the names of localities where certain remarkable transactions took place, connected with their efforts to spread the Gospel. Of these I will give a few examples, but I shall defer to another chapter the consideration of those places which commemorate the names of saints.

Saul, the name of a village and parish near Downpatrick, preserves the memory of St. Patrick's first triumph in the work of conversion. Dichu, the prince of the district, who hospitably entertained the saint and his companions, was his first convert in Ireland; and the chief made him a present of his barn, to be used temporarily as a church. On the site of this barn a church was subsequently erected, and as its direction happened to be north and south, the church was also placed north and south, instead of the usual direction, east and west. On this transaction the following are Ussher's words :—" Which place, from the name of that church, is called in Scotic to this day, *Sabhall Patrick*; in Latin, *Zabulum Patricii* vel *Horreum Patricii*" (Patrick's barn). It is still called in Irish *Sabhall*, which is fairly represented in pronunciation by the modern form Saul.

It is highly probable that several churches were erected in other districts, in imitation of St. Patrick's primitive and favourite church at Saul, which were also placed north and south, and called by the same name. We know that among the churches of Armagh, one, founded probably by the saint himself, was in this direction, and called by the same name, *Sabhall*, though this name is now lost. And it is not unlikely that a church of this kind gave name to Saval, near Newry, to Drumsaul in the parish of Ematris, county Monaghan, and to Sawel, a lofty mountain in the north of Tyrone. This supposition supersedes the far-fetched explanation of the last name, given in the neighbourhood, which for several reasons I have no hesitation in pronouncing a very modern fabrication.

Very similar in the circumstances attending its origin is the name of Elphin, in the county Roscommon. In the Tripartite Life of St. Patrick (Lib. II. c. 38), we are told that a noble Druid named Ona, lord of the ancient district of *Corcaghlan* in Roscommon, presented his residence, called Emlagh-Ona (Ona's marsh) to St. Patrick, as a site for a church. The church was built near a spring, over which stood a large stone, and from this the place was called *Ail-finn*, which Colgan interprets "the rock of the clear

9

spring ;" the stone is now gone, but it remained standing in its original position until forty or fifty years
ago.   The townland of Emlagh, near Elphin, still
preserves the name of Ona's ancient residence.

The manner in which St. Brigid's celebrated establishment was founded is stereotyped in the name of
Kildare.   According to a tale in the Book of Leinster, quoted by O'Curry (Lectures, p. 487), the place
was called *Druim-Criaidh* [Drumcree] before the time
of St. Brigid ; and it received its present name from
" a goodly fair oke" under the shadow of which the
saint constructed her little cell.

The origin and meaning of the name are very
clearly set forth in the following words of Animosus,
the writer of the fourth Life of St. Brigid, published
by Colgan :—" That cell is called in Scotic, *Cill-dara*,
which in Latin sounds *Cella-quercûs* (the church of
the oak).   For a very high oak stood there, which
Brigid loved much, and blessed it ; of which the
trunk still remains (i. e. up to the close of the tenth
century, when Animosus wrote) ; and no one dares
cut it with a weapon."   Bishop Ultan, the writer of
the third Life, gives a similar interpretation, viz.,
Cella roboris.

If we may judge by the number of places whose
names indicate battle scenes, slaughters, murders,
&c., our ancestors must have been a quarrelsome
race, and must have led an unquiet existence. Names
of this kind are found in every county in Ireland ;
and various terms are employed to commemorate the
events.   Moreover, in most of these places, traditions
worthy of being preserved, regarding the occurrences
that gave origin to the names, still linger among the
peasantry.

The word *cath* [cah] signifies a battle, and its

presence in many names points out, with all the certainty of history, the scenes of former strife. We see it in Ardoath in Meath, and Mullycagh in Wicklow, both signifying battle height; in Dooncaha in Kerry and Limerick, the fort of the battle; Derrycaw and Derryhaw, battle-wood, in Armagh; and Drumnagah in Clare, the ridge of the battles.

One party must have been utterly defeated, where we find such names as Ballynarooga (in Limerick), the town of the defeat or rout (*ruag*); Greaghnaroog near Carrickmacross, and Maulnarouga in Cork, the marshy flat and the hillock of the rout; Rinuarogue in Sligo, and Ringarogy, the name of an island near Baltimore, on the south coast of Cork, both signifying the *rinn* or point of the defeat. And how vivid a picture of the hideousness of a battle-field is conveyed by the following names :—Meenagorp in Tyrone, in Irish *Min-na-gcorp*, the mountain flat of the corpses; Kilnamarve near Carrigallen, Leitrim, the wood of the dead bodies (*Coill-na-marbh*); Ballinamara in Kilkenny, the town of the dead (*Baile-na-marbh*), where the tradition of the battle is still remembered; Lisnafulla near Newcastle in Limerick, the fort of the blood; *Cnamhchoill* [knawhill] (Book of Leinster), a celebrated place near the town of Tipperary, now called Cleghile (by a change of *n* to *l*—see p. 49), whose name signifies the wood of bones : the same Irish name is more correctly anglicised Knawhill in the parish of Knocktemple, Cork.

Many of these sanguinary encounters, in which probably whole armies were almost annihilated, though lost to history, are recorded with perfect clearness in names like the following, numbers of

which are found all over the country :—Glenanair, a
fine valley near the boundary of Limerick and Cork,
five miles south of Kilfinane, the glen of slaughter,
where the people still preserve a vivid tradition of a
dreadful battle fought at a ford over the river ; and
with the same root word (*ár*, slaughter), Drumar
near Ballybay in Monaghan, Glasbare, a parish in
Kilkenny, the ridge, and the streamlet, of slaughter ;
and Coumanare (*Coum* a hollow), in the parish of
Ballyduff, a few miles from Dingle in Kerry, where
numbers of arrow heads have been found, showing
the truthfulness of the name ; which is also corroborated by a local tradition of a great battle fought in
the valley.   In Cork they have a tradition that a
great and bloody fight took place at some distant
time on the banks of the little river Ownanare (river
of slaughter), which joins the Dalua one mile above
Kanturk.

The murder of any near relative is termed in Irish
fionghal [finnal] which is often translated *fratricide ;*
and the frequent occurrence of names containing this
word, while affording undeniable evidence of the
commission of the crime, demonstrates at the same
time the horror with which it was regarded by the
people.   We have, for instance, Lisnafinelly in Monaghan, and Lisfennell in Waterford, where in both
cases the victim met his doom in one of the lonely
forts so common through the country ; Cloonnafin-
neola near Kilflyn in Kerry (*cloon*, a meadow) ;
Tattanafinnell near Clogher in Tyrone, the field
(*tate*) of the fratricide ; Drumnafinnila in Leitrim,
and Drumnafinnagle near Kilcar in Donegal, the
ridge of the fratricide, in the last of which places
there is a vivid tradition accounting for the name:—
that one time long ago, the clan of MacGilla Carr

(now called Carr), fell out among themselves, and slaughtered each other almost to annihilation ("Donegal Cliff Scenery" by "Kinnfaela," pp. 60, 61). And occasionally the murdered man's name is commemorated by being interwoven with the name of the spot, as may be seen in Gortmarrahafineen, near Kenmare in Kerry, which represents the Irish *Gort-marbhtha-Finghin*, the field of Fineen's murder. A name of this kind is recorded in the annals of Lough Key (II., 368), viz., *Ath-Marbhtha-Cathail*, the ford of the killing of Cathal, which in the anglicised form Aghawaracahill, is now the name of a townland in the parish of Kilmore in Roscommon, south of the village of Drumsna. But no one knows who this unfortunate *Cathal* was. We have also in the parish of Clones in Fermanagh, Cornamramurry, the round hill of the dead woman—*Cor-na-mna-mairbhe* (*bean*, a woman ; genitive *mna*).

In "A Tour through Ireland, by two English Gentlemen" (Dublin, 1748), we read:—"The poorer sort of *Irish* Natives are mostly *Roman Catholicks*, who make no scruple to assemble in the open Fields. As we passed Yesterday in a Bye-road, we saw a Priest under a Tree, with a large Assembly about him, celebrating Mass in his proper Habit ; and, though at a great Distance from us, we heard him distinctly. These sort of People, my Lord, seem to be very solemn and sincere in their devotion" (p. 163).

The Irish practice of celebrating Mass in the open air appears to be very ancient. It was more general, however, during the period preceding the above tour than at other times, partly because there were in many places no chapels, and partly because, during the operation of the penal laws, the celebration of Mass was declared illegal. And the knowledge of this, if we be wise enough to turn it to right account, may have its use, by reminding us of the time in which our lot is cast, when the people have their chapel in every parish, and those prohibitory enactments are made mere matters of history, by wise and kind legislation.

Even in our own day. we may witness the celebration of Mass in the open air; for many will remember the vast crowds that congregated on the summit of Brandon hill in Kerry, on the 28th of June, 1868, to honour the memory of Saint Brendan. The spots consecrated by the celebration of the sacred mysteries are at this day well known, and greatly revered by the people; and many of them bear names formed from the word *Aiffrion* (Affrin), the Mass, that will identify them to all future time.

Places of this kind are found all over Ireland, and many of them have given names to townlands; and it may be further observed, that the existence of such a name in any particular locality, indicates that the custom of celebrating Mass there must have continued for a considerable time.

Sometimes the lonely side of a hill was chosen, and the people remember well, and will point out to the visitor, the very spot on which the priest stood, while the crowd of peasants worshipped below. One of these hills is in the parish of Kilmore, county Roscommon, and it has left its name on the townland of Ardanaffrin, the height of the Mass; another in the parish of Donaghmore, county Donegal, called Corraffrin (*cor*, a round hill); a third in the parish of Kilcommon, Mayo, namely, Drumanaffrin; a fourth in Cavan, Mullanaffrin (*mullach*, a summit); and still another, Knockanaffrin, in Waterford, one of the highest hills of the Cummeragh range.

Sometimes again the people selected secluded dells and mountain gorges; such as Clashanaffrin in the parish of Desertmore, county of Cork (*clash*, a trench or fosse), and Lugganaffrin in the county of Galway, the hollow of the Mass. And occasionally they took advantage of the ancient forts of their pagan ancestors, places for ages associated with fairy superstitions; and while they worshipped, they were screened from observation by the circumvallations of the old fortress. The old palace of Greenan-Ely near Londonderry was so used; and there is a fort in the townland of Rahanane, parish of Kilcummin in Kerry, which still bears the name of Lissanaffrin, the fort of the Mass.

Many other names of like formation are to be met with, such as Glenanaffrin, Carriganaffrin, Lough Anaffrin, &c. Occasionally the name records the simple fact that Mass was celebrated, as we find in a place called Effrinagh, in the parish of Kiltoghert, Leitrim, a name which signifies simply " a place for Mass." And sometimes a translated name occurs of the same class, such as Mass-brook in the parish of Addergoole, Mayo, which is a translation of the Irish *Sruthan-an-Aiffrinn.*

There are other words also, besides *Affrin*, which are used to commemorate these Masses; such as *altóir*, an altar, which gives name to a townland, now called Altore, in the parish of Kiltullagh, Roscommon; and to another named Oltore, in the parish of Donaghpatrick, Galway. There is also a place called " Altore cross-roads," near Inchigeelagh, Cork; and we find Carrownaltore (the quarter land of the altar) in the parish of Aglish, Mayo.

CHAPTER II.

HISTORICAL PERSONAGES.

OUR annals generally set forth with great care the
genealogy of the most remarkable men — kings,
chieftains, or saints—who flourished at the different
periods of our history ; and even their character and
their personal peculiarities are very often given with
much minuteness. These annals and genealogies,
which are only now beginning to be known and
studied as they deserve, when examined by the in-
ternal evidence of mutual comparison, are found to
exhibit a marvellous consistency ; and this testimony
of their general truthfulness is fully corroborated by
the few glimpses we obtain of detached points in the
long record, through the writings of English and
foreign historians, as well as by the still severer test
of verifying our frequent records of natural occurrences.

Nor are these the only testimonies. Local names
often afford the most unsuspicious and satisfactory
evidences of the truth of historical records, and I
may refer to the preceding chapter for instances. It
is with men as with events. Many of the characters
who figure conspicuously in our annals have left
their names engraven in the topography of the country, and the illustration of this by some of the most
remarkable examples will form the subject of the
present chapter.

Before entering on this part of the subject, it will
be necessary to make a few remarks on the origin of
the names of our ancient tribes and territories, and

to explain certain terms that are often used in their
formation.

"It is now universally admitted that the ancient
names of tribes in Ireland were not derived from the
territories they inhabited, but from certain of their
distinguished ancestors. In nine cases out of ten,
names of territories and of the tribes inhabiting
them are identical"* (the former being derived from
the latter). The names of tribes were formed from
those of their ancestors, by prefixing certain words
or postfixing others, the most important of which are
the following :—

Cinel [kinel], kindred, race, descendants; *Cinel-
Aedha* [Kinelea : O'Heerin], the race of Aedh [Ay]
or Hugh, a tribe descended from Aedh (father of
Failbhe Flann, king of Munster in A.D. 636), who
were settled in the county Cork, and gave name to
the barony of Kinalea. Kinelarty, a barony in
Down, *Cinel-Fhaghartaigh* (Four Mast.), the race of
Fagartagh, one of the ancestors of the Mac Artans.

Clann, children, descendants, race; in the Zeuss
MS. it is given as the equivalent of *progenies*. The
barony of Clankee in Cavan derives its name from
a tribe who are called in Irish *Clann-an-Chaoich*
[Clanankee : Four Mast.], the descendants of the
one-eyed man; and they derived this cognomen from
Niall *Caoch* O'Reilly (*caoch* [kee], i. e. one-eyed,
Lat. *cæcus*), who was slain in 1256. The baronies
of Clanwilliam in Limerick and Tipperary, from the
clann or descendants of William Burke; Clanmaurice,
a barony in Kerry, so called from the Fitzmaurices,
the descendants of Maurice Fitzgerald. Besides

* From O'Donovan's Introduction to the "Topographical
Poems of O'Dugan and O'Heeren," where the reader will find
a valuable essay on tribe and family names.

several historic districts, this word gives name to
some ordinary townlands ; such as Clananeese Glebe
in Tyrone, from the race of Aengus or Æneas ; Clanhugh Demesne in Westmeath, the descendants of
Aedh or Hugh.

Corc, corca, race, progeny. Corcomohide, the name
of a parish in Limerick, is written in Irish *Corca-
Muichet* (Book of Lismore), the race of Muichet, who
in the " Forbais Dromadamhghaire" are stated to
have been descended from Muichet, one of Mogh
Ruith's disciples (see p. 101, *supra*).

Muintir, family, people ; Muntermellan and Mun-
terneese in Donegal, the family of Miallan and Aengus ; Munterowen in Galway, the family of Eoghan
or Owen ; Munterloney, now the name of a range of
mountains in Tyrone, from the family of *O'Luinigh*
or O'Looney, who were chiefs of the surrounding
district.

Siol [shiel], seed, progeny. Shillelagh, now a
barony in Wicklow, was so called from the tribe of
Siol-Elaigh (O'Heerin), the descendants of Elach :
this district was formerly much celebrated for its oak
woods, a fact that has given origin to the well-known
word *shillelagh* as a term for an oak stick. Shelburne
in Wexford, from the tribe of *Siol-Brain* (O'Heerin),
the progeny of Bran ; Shelmaliere in the same county,
the descendants of Maliere or Maelughra.

Tealach [tellagh], family. The barony of Tully-
haw in Cavan was so called from the Magaurans, its
ancient proprietors, whose tribe name was *Tealach-
Echach* (O'Dugan), i. e. the family of Eochy.

Ua signifies a grandson, and, by an extension of
meaning, any descendant : it is often written *hua* by
Latin and English writers, and still oftener *O*, which
is the common prefix in Irish family names.   The

nominative plural is *ui* [ee : often written in Latin
and English, *hui* or *hy*], which is applied to a tribe,
and this word still exists in several territorial designations. Thus Offerlane, now a parish in Queen's
County, was the name of a tribe, called in Irish
Ui-Foircheallain [Hy Forhellane : Four Mast.], the
descendants of Foircheallan ; Ida, now the name of
a barony in Kilkenny, which represents the sound of
Ui-Deaghaigh, the descendants of *Deaghadh ;* Imaile,
a celebrated district in Wicklow, *Ui-Mail* (O'Heeren),
the descendants of Mann *Mal*, brother of Cahirmore,
king of Ireland in the second century.

The ablative plural of *ua* is *uibh* [iv], and this
form is also found occasionally in names (see p. 34,
VII.). Thus Iverk, now a barony in Kilkenny, which
O'Heeren writes *Ui-Eire* (ablat. *Uibh-Eirc*), the descendants of Erc ; Iveleary in Cork (the descendants
of Laeghaire), taking its name from the O'Learys, its
ancient proprietors ; Iveruss, now a parish in Limerick, from the tribe of *Uibh-Rosa*.

That the foregoing is the proper signification of
this word in its three cases, we have authorities that
preclude all dispute ; among others that of Adamnan, who, in several passages of his Life of Columba,
translates *ua* by *nepos*, *ui* by *nepotes*, and *uibh* by *ne-
potibus*.

The word *tuath* [tua] meant originally *populus*
(people), which it glosses in the Wb MS. of Zeuss ;
but, in accordance with the custom of naming the
territory after its inhabitants, it came ultimately to
signify district, which is now the sense in which it
is used. Near Sheephaven in Donegal is a well-
known district called the Doe : its ancient name, as
given by O'Heeren, is *Tuath Bladhach ;* but by the
Four Masters and other authorities it is usually

called *Tuatha*, i. e. districts.   It was the inheritance
of the Mac Sweenys, the chief of whom was called
Mac Sweeny *na dTuath*, or, as it is pronounced and
written in English, *na Doe*, i. e. of the districts ; and
it is from this appellation that the place came to be
corruptly called Doe.

With the preceding may be enumerated the word
Fir or *Feara*, men, which is often prefixed to the
names of districts to form tribe names.   The old tribe
called *Fir-tire* (the men of the territory), in Wicklow,
is now forgotten, except so far as the name is preserved in that of the river Vartry.   The celebrated
territory of Fermoy in Cork, which still retains its
name, is called in Irish *Feara-muighe-Feine*, or more
shortly, *Feara-muighe* (O'Heerin), the men of the
plain.   It is called in the Book of Rights *Magh Fian*,
the second part of which was derived from the Fians
or ancient militia (p. 90) ; and the full name *Feara-
muighe-Feine* means the men of the plain of the
Fians.

There are also a few words which are suffixed to
men's names, to designate the tribes descended from
them ; such as *raidhe* [ree], in the word *Calraidhe*.
There were several tribes called *Calraidhe* or Calry
(the race of Cal), who were descended from Lewy
Cal, the grand-uncle of Maccon, king of Ireland in
the third century.   The names of some of these are
still extant : one of them was settled in the ancient
Teffia, whose name is preserved by the mountain of
Slievegolry, near Ardagh, county Longford, *Sliabh
gCalraidhe*, the mountain of the (people called) Calry.
There is a townland called Drumhalry (*Druim-Chal-
raidhe*, the ridge of the Calry), near Carrigallen in
Leitrim ; and another of the same name in the parish
of Killoe, county Longford ; which shows that Calry

of north Teffia extended northward as far as these two townlands. Calry in Sligo and Calary in Wicklow also preserve the names of these tribes.

The monarch Hugony the Great, who reigned soon after the foundation of Emania, divided Ireland into twenty-five parts among his twenty-five children; and this division continued for about three centuries after his time. Several of these gave names to the territories allotted to them, but all those designations are now obsolete, with a single exception. To one of his sons, Lathair [Laher], he gave a territory in Ulster, which was called from him *Latharna* [Laharna: Book of Rights], a name which exists to this day, shortened to Larne. Though now exclusively applied to the town, it was, in the time of Colgan, the name of a district which extended northwards along the coast towards Glenarm: the town was then called *Inver-an-Laharna*, the river-mouth of (the territory of) *Laharna*, from its situation at the mouth of the *Ollarbha*, or Larne Water. In the Down Survey Map it is called "Inver alias Learne;" and the former name is still retained in the adjacent parish of Inver.

Many of the remarkable persons who flourished in the reign of Conor mac Nessa, king of Ulster in the first century, still live in local names. The descendants of Beann, one of Conor's sons, were called from him *Branntraighe* [Bantry: Book of Rights], i. e. the race of Beann; a part of them settled in Wexford, and another part in Cork, and the barony of Bantry in the former county, and the town of Bantry in the latter, retain their name.

When the three sons of Usnagh were murdered at the command of Conor, Fergus mac Roy, ex-king of Ulster, who had guaranteed their safety, "indignant at the violation of his safe conduct, retired into exile, accompanied by Cormac Conlingas, son of Conor, and by three thousand warriors of Uladh. They received a hospitable welcome at *Cruachan* from Maev [queen of Connaught], and her husband Ailill, whence they afterwards made many hostile incursions into Ulster,"* taking part in that seven years' war between Ulster and Connaught, so celebrated by our historians and romancers as the "Tain bo Cuailnge," the cattle spoil of Cooley (near Carlingford).

Fergus afterwards resided in Connaught, and Maev bore him three sons, Ciar [Keer], Conmac, and Modhruadh [Mōroo], who became the heads of three distinguished tribes. Ciar settled in Munster, and his descendants possessed the territory west of Abbeyfeale, and lying between Tralee and the Shannon; they were called *Ciarraidhe* [Keery : Book of Rights], i. e. the race of Ciar, and this name was afterwards applied to the district; it was often called *Ciarraidhe Luachra*, from the mountain tract of *Sliabh Luachra* (rushy mountain, now Slievelougher), east of Castleisland. This small territory ultimately gave the name of *Ciarraidhe* or Kerry to the entire county.

The descendants of Conmac were called *Conmaicne* [Conmacne : *ne*, a progeny]; they were settled in Connaught, where they gave their name to several territories. One of these, viz., the district lying west of Lough Con and Lough Mask, from its situation near the sea, was called, to distinguish it from the others, *Conmaicne-mara* (O'Dugan : *muir*, the sea, gen. *mara*), or the sea-side *Conmaicne;* which name is still applied to the very same district, in the slightly contracted and well-known form Connemara.

* From "The Irish before the Conquest," by M. C. Ferguson.

The posterity of the third son, Modhruadh, were called *Corca-Modhruadh*, or *Corcomruad* (Book of Leinster), the race of Modhruadh; they settled in the north of the county of Clare, and their territory included the present baronies of Burren and Corcomroe, the latter of which retains the old name.

Another son of Fergus (not by Maev), was Finn or Cufinn (fair-haired hound), from whom were descended the tribe of the *Dál-Confinn* (*dál*, a tribe), who afterwards took the family name of O'Finn. They inhabited a district in Connaught, which was called from them *Cuil-O'bhFinn* [Coolovin: Four Mast.], the corner of the O'Finns; and the same name in the modernized form of Coolavin is still applied to the territory which now forms a barony in Sligo.

When the Connaught forces under Maev marched to invade the territory of Conor, the task of defending the different fords they had to cross was allotted to Cuchullin, the great Ulster champion; and the various single combats with the Connaught warriors, in all of which he was victorious, are described with great minuteness in the heroic romance of "Tain bo Cuailnge." One of these encounters took place at a ford of the little river *Nith* (now called the Dee, in Louth), where afterwards grew up the town of Ardee; and Cuchullin's antagonist was his former friend, the youthful champion Ferdia, the son of Daman, of the Firbolgic tribe Gowanree, who inhabited Erris. After a long and sanguinary combat Ferdia was slain, and the place was ever after called *Ath-Fhirdia* [Ahirdee: Leabhar na hUidhre], Ferdia's ford. The present form Ardee is a very modern contraction; by early English writers it is generally called Atherdee, as by Boate (Chap. I. Sect. vi.),

which preserves, with little change, the original Irish
pronunciation.

In the reign of Felimy the Lawgiver (A. D. 111
to 119), the men of Munster seized on Ossory, and
all the Leinster territories, as far as Mullaghmast.
They were ultimately expelled, after a series of
battles, by an Ulster chief, Lughaidh Laeighseach
[Lewy Leeshagh], son of Laeighseach Canvore, son
of the renowned Conall Cearnach, chief of the Red
Branch Knights of Ulster in the first century (see
p. 90). For this service the king of Leinster granted
Lewy a large territory in the present Queen's County;
and as his descendants, the O'Moores, were called
from him by the tribe name *Laeighis* [Leesh], their
territory took the same name, which in English is
commonly written Leix—a district that figures conspicuously in Irish and Anglo-Irish chronicles.

The name of this principality has altogether disappeared from modern maps, except so far as it is
preserved in that of the town of Abbeyleix, i. e. the
abbey of the territory of Leix, which it received
from a monastery founded there in 1183 by Conor
O'Moore.

The first battle between the Munstermen and the
forces of Lewy was fought at *Ath-Truisden*, a ford on
the river Greece, near Mullaghmast, and the former
retreated to the Barrow, where at another ford there
was a second battle, in which a Munster chief, Ae,
the foster-father of Ohy Finn Fohart (p. 131), was
slain; and from him the place was called *Ath-I*
(Wars of GG.), the ford of Ae, now correctly anglicised Athy.

From Fiacha Raidhe [Ree], grandson of king
Felimy, descended the tribe named *Corca-Raeidhe*
(O'Dugan), whose name is still borne by the barony

of Corkaree in Westmeath, their ancient patrimony.
This territory is mentioned by Adamnan (Lib. I.
cap. 47), who calls it *Korkureti;* and in the Book of
Armagh the name is translated *Regiones Roide,* i. e.
the territories of Raidhe or Ree.

The fanciful creations of the ancient Irish story-
tellers have thrown a halo of romance round the
names of many of the preceding personages; nevertheless I have treated of them in the present chapter,
because I believe them to be historical. As we de-
scend from those dim regions of extreme antiquity,
the view becomes clearer, and the characters that
follow may, with few exceptions, be considered as
standing out in full historical distinctness.

Cahirmore was monarch of Ireland from A. D. 120
to 123; he is well known in connection with the
document called the "Will of Cahirmore," which
has been translated and published by O'Donovan in
the Book of Rights. According to our genealogical
writers (see O'Flaherty's Ogygia, Part III. o. 59),
he had thirty sons, but only ten are mentioned in
the Will, two of whom are commemorated in well-
known modern names.

His eldest son was Ros-failghe [faly], i. e. Ros of
the rings (*fáill,* a ring, pl. *fáilghe*), whom the monarch
addresses as "my fierce Ros, my vehement Failghe."
His descendants were called *Hy Failghe* (O'Dugan),
i. e. the descendants of Failghe; they possessed a
large territory in Kildare and in King's and Queen's
Counties, to which they gave their tribe name; and
it still exists in the form of Offaly, which is now applied to two baronies in Kildare, forming a portion
of their ancient inheritance.

Another son, Ceatach, also named in the Will, was
probably the progenitor of the tribe that gave name

10

to the barony of Ikeathy, in Kildare—*Hy Ceataigh*,
the race of Ceatach. Others of Cahirmore's sons were
the ancestors of tribes, but their names have been
long extinct.

The barony of Idrone in Carlow, perpetuates the
memory of the tribe of *Hy Drona* (Book of Rights),
who formerly possessed this territory, and whose family name was O'Ryan; their ancestor, from whom
they derived their tribe name, was Drona, fourth in
descent from Cahirmore.

The county Fermanagh was so called from the
tribe of the *Fir-Monach* (O'Dugan), the men of Monach, who were originally a Leinster tribe, so named
from their ancestor Monach, fifth in descent from
Cahirmore, by his son, *Daire Barrach*. They had to
fly from Leinster in consequence of having killed
Enna, the son of the king of that province; one part
of them was located in the county of Down, where
the name is extinct; another part settled on the
shore of Lough Erne, where they acquired a territory extending over the entire county Fermanagh.

Enna Kinsellagh, king of Leinster in the end of
the fourth century, was fourth in descent from Cahirmore. He had a son named Felimy, from whom
descended the sept of *Hy Felimy* (Four Mast.); one
branch of them settled in the county Carlow, and
their name is still preserved in that of the parish of
Tullow-Offelimy, or Tullowphelim (which was also
applied to the town of Tullow), i. e. the *tulach* or
hill of the territory of *Hy Felimy*, which included
this parish.

Cahirmore was slain by the celebrated Conn of the
Hundred Battles, who ascended the throne in A. D.
123. After a reign of thirty-five years, Conn's two
brothers, Fiacha and Eochy Finn Fothart, betrayed

him into the hands of Tibraido Tireach, king of Ulster, who murdered him as he was making prepara-
tions to celebrate the Feis or convention of Tara.

Conary II., his successor (from A. D. 158 to 165),
had three sons—the three Carberys—who are renowned in Irish history :—Carbery Musc, Carbery
Baskin, and Carbery Riada. From Carbery Musc
were descended and named all the tribes called *Muscraidhe* [Muskerry: O'Heerin], i. e. the race of Musc;
of which, according to O'Heerin, there were six, all
in Munster. The names of all these have recently
disappeared except that of one, *Muscraidhe Mitaine,*
or *Muscraidhe O'Flynn,* which now forms the two
baronies of Muskerry in Cork. From Carbery Baskin
was named the ancient territory of Corcobaskin in
the south west of Clare, but the name has become
obsolete. Carbery Riada was the most celebrated
of the three, for whom see page 86. Carbery Musc
had a son named Duibhne [Divne], whose descendants gave name to the district of *Corca-Duibhne*
(O'Heerin), i. e. Duibhne's race; and a portion of
this territory still retains the name, though somewhat corrupted, viz., the barony of Corkaguiny (*dh*
changed to *g;* p. 56), in Kerry, which comprises the
peninsula between Tralee and Dingle bays.

Art, the son of Conn of the Hundred Battles, succeeded Conary, and immediately on his accession he
banished his uncle, Ohy Finn Fothart [Fohart],
from Munster. Eochy proceeded to Leinster, and
the king of that province bestowed on him and his
sons certain districts, the inhabitants of which were
afterwards called *Fotharta* [Foharta: Book of Rights],
from their ancestor. Of these, the two principal still
retain the name, viz., the baronies of Forth in Wexford and Carlow; the former called in the Annals,

for distinction, *Fotharta* of the Carn, i. e. of Carnsore Point; and the latter, *Fotharta Fea*, from the plain anciently called *Moy Fea*, lying east of the town of Carlow.

After Art, the son of Conn, had reigned thirty years, he was slain in the year 195, in the battle of *Magh Mucruimhe* [Muckrivĕ] near Athenry, by Lewy Maccon and his followers. It is stated in the "History of the Cemeteries" in Leabhar na hUidhre, that Art believed in the Faith the day before the battle, and predicted the spread of Christianity. It would appear also that he had some presentiment of his death; for he directed that he should not be buried at Brugh on the Boyne, the pagan cemetery of his forefathers, but at a place then called *Dumha Dergluachra* (the burial mound of the red rushy-place), "where *Treoit* is at this day" (Trevet in the county Meath). "When his body was afterwards carried eastwards to *Dumha Dergluachra*, if all the men of Erin were drawing it thence, they could not, so that he was interred at that place, because there was a Catholic church to be afterwards at the place where he was interred, for the truth and the Faith had been revealed to him through his regal righteous-ness" (Hist. of Cemeteries; see Petrie's R. Towers, p. 100).

In the historical tale called "The Battle of *Magh Mucruimhe*," it is stated that, when Art was buried, *three sods* were dug in honour of the Trinity; and that hence the place, from that time forward, got the name of *Tre-foit* (O'Clery's Cal., &c.), i. e. three *fóds* or sods, which is very little changed in the present name Trevet.

The celebrated Mogh Nuadhat [Mŏ Nuat], or Owen More, was king of Munster during the reign of Conn of the Hundred Battles ; he contended with that monarch for the sovereignty of all Ireland, and after defeating him in ten battles, he obliged him to divide the country equally between them—the well-known ridge of sand hills called Esker Riada, extending from Dublin to Galway, being adopted as the boundary. From Owen descended a long line of kings, and he was the ancestor of the most distinguished of the great Munster families.

He spent nine years in Spain, and the king of that country gave him his daughter Beara in marriage : on his return to Ireland, accompanied by Spanish auxiliaries, to make war against Conn, he landed on the north side of Bantry bay, and he called the harbour *Beara* in honour of his wife. It is now called Bearhaven ; the island that shelters it is called Great Bear Island ; and the barony is also known by the name of Bear.

Owen derived his *alias* name of Mogh Nuadhat (which signifies Nuadhat's slave) from his foster-father Nuadhat, king of Leinster. From this king, according to O'Donovan (Cambr. Evers., note, q. 473, Vol. I.), Maynooth derives its name :—*Magh-Nuadhat*, i. e. Nuat's plain.

Olioll Olum, the son of Owen, succeeded him as king of Munster, and was almost as renowned as his father ; he is usually taken as the starting-point in tracing the genealogies of the Munster families. Three of his sons—Owen, Cormac Cas, and Cian [Kean]—became very much celebrated.

In the year 226 was fought the battle of Crinna in Meath, between Cormac mac Art, king of Ireland, and the Ulstermen, under Fergus, son of Imchadh ; Cormac defeated the Ulster forces, by the assistance of Tadg [Teige], son of Cian ; and for this service

the king bestowed on him a large territory, extending from the Liffey northwards to Drumiskin in
Louth. Tadg's descendants were called *Cianachta*
[Keenaghta: O'Dugan], i. e. the race of Cian, from
his father; and the territory was afterwards known
by this name. It is forgotten in Leinster, but in
Ulster it is still the name of a barony in the north
west of Londonderry, called Keenaght, from the
O'Conors of Glengiven, who formerly ruled over it,
and who were a branch of the tribe of Keenaghta,
having been descended from Connla the son of Tadg.
The name is also preserved in Coolkeenaght, in the
parish of Faughanvale, Derry; *Cunille-Cianachta*
(Four Mast.), the bare tree or pole of Keenaght.

The barony of Ferrard in Louth indirectly keeps
up the memory of this ancient tribe. The range
of heights called Slieve Bregh, running from near
Collon in Louth, eastwards to Clogher Head, was
anciently called *Ard-Cianachta* (Four Mast.; *Ard-
Ceanachte*, Adamnan), the height of the territory of
Keenaght, and the inhabitants were called *Feara-
Arda-Cianachta,* or more shortly *Feara-Arda* (Four
Mast.), i. e. the men of the height, from which the
modern name Ferrard has been formed.

Tadg, the son of Cian, had a son named Cormac
Gaileng (Cormac of the dishonoured spear); see
Knockgrean, (2nd. Ser.), who, having fallen under
the displeasure of his father, fled from Munster to
Connaught, where he obtained from Cormac mac
Art, king of Ireland, a district which had previously
been inhabited by the Firbolgs or "Attacots." The
descendants of Cormac Gaileng and his son Luigh,
or Lowy, were known by the two names *Gailenga*
(O'Dugan), or the race of Gaileng, and *Luighne*
[Leyny: O'Dugan], the posterity (*ne*) of Luigh.

These were originally only various names for the
same tribe, but they are at the present day applied
to different districts—one, in the modern form of
Gallen, to a barony in Mayo, and the other to a
barony in Sligo, now called Leyny.

A branch of the same tribe settled in Leinster,
where there were two territories, called respectively
Mor-Gailenga and *Gailenga-beag* (O'Dugan), or the
great and little *Gailenga;* the latter is obsolete, but
the former is still retained in the name of the modern
barony of Morgallion in Meath.

Eile, the seventh in descent from Cian, was the
ancestor of the tribes called Eile or Ely, who gave
name to several districts, all in the ancient *Mumha*
or Munster, and of which O'Carroll was king. The
only one of these whose name has held its ground
is Ely O'Fogarty, so called from its ancient possessors, the O'Fogartys; and the name is now applied
to a barony in Tipperary, in the shortened form of
Eliogarty.

Eochy Liathanach [Lehanagh] was fifth in descent from Oliol Olum, and from him the tribe of
O'Liathain, who now call themselves O'Lehane or
Lyons, are derived. Castlelyons in Cork was situated in their territory, and still retains its name—
Caislen-ui-Liathain [Cashlan-ee-Leehan], the castle
of the territory of *Hy-Liathain.*

Settled in different parts of Connaught and Leinster were formerly seven tribes—three in the former
province, and four in the latter—all with the same
tribe name of *Dealbhna* [Dal'vŭna]; they were an
offshoot of the Dalcassians of north Munster, and
were descended from Lewy Dealbhaeth [Dalway],
who was the son of Cas mac Tail (seventh in descent
from Oliol Olum), the ancestor of the Dalcassians

They derived their tribe name from Lewy Dealbhaeth :—*Dealbhna*, i. e. the descendants of Dealbhaeth.   None of these tribes have left their name
in our present territorial nomenclature except one,
namely, *Dealbhna mor*, or the great *Dealbhna*, which
is now the barony of Delvin in Westmeath.

From Conall, the ninth from Olioll Olum, descended the tribe of *Hy Conaill Gabra* (Book of
Leinster), who possessed a territory in the county of
Limerick, a part of which still retains the name, viz.,
the baronies of Upper and Lower Connello.

I have already mentioned (p. 89) the destruction
of the palace of Emania, in the year 332, by the
three Collas; these were Colla Uais, Colla Meann,
and Colla da Chriooh, who were the ancestors of
many noble families in Ulster and Scotland, and the
first of whom reigned as king of Ireland from A.D.
323 to 326.   He was the progenitor of the several
tribes known by the name of *Ui mic Uais* [Ee-mic-
oosh], one of which was seated somewhere in the
north of Ireland, another in East Meath, near Tara,
and a third in Westmeath.   This last is the only one
of the three whose name has survived ; whose territory is now a barony, and known by the name of
Moygoish, which is an attempt at pronouncing the
original *Ui mic Uais*.

Caerthann [Kieran], the great-grandson of Colla
Uais, was the ancestor, through his son Forgo, of
the tribe called *Hy Mic Caerthainn* (Four Mast.) ; the
territory they inhabited, which was situated in the
west of the present county of Derry, was called from
them *Tir-mic-Caerthainn* (the land of Kieran's son),
or more shortly, *Tir-Chaerthainn*, which is still the
name of a barony, now called Tirkeeran.

The barony of Cremorne in Monaghan preserves the name of the ancient district of *Crioch-Mughdhorn* [Cree-Mourne], i. e. the country (*crioch*) of the people called *Mughdhorna*, who were descended and named from Mughdhorn [Mourne], the son of Colla Meann. About the middle of the 12th century, a tribe of the Mac Mahons emigrated from Cremorne, and settled in the south of the present county of Down, to which they gave their tribe name of *Mughdhorna*, and which is now known as the barony of Mourne.

The Mourne mountains owe their name to the same event, having been previously called *Beanna-Boirche* [Banna borka]. The shepherd Boirche, according to the Dinnsenchus, herded on these mountains the cattle of Ross (son of Imchadh), king of Ulster in the third century, and the account states that his favourite look-out point was the summit of Slieve Slanga, now Slieve Donard, the highest peak in the range; hence these mountains received the very appropriate name of *Beanna-Boirche*, Boirche's peaks.

Niallan, descended in the fourth degree from Colla Da Chrioch [Cree], was the progenitor of the tribe called *Hy Niallain* (i. e. Niallan's race); and their ancient patrimony forms the two baronies of Oneilland in Armagh, which retains the name.

The descendants of Eochy Moyvane, king of Ireland from A. D. 358 to 365, branched into a vast number of illustrious families, the earlier members of which have left their names impressed on many localities. The following short genealogical table exhibits a few of his immediate descendants, viz., those concerned in the present inquiry, and it will render

what I have to say regarding them more easily un-
stood.

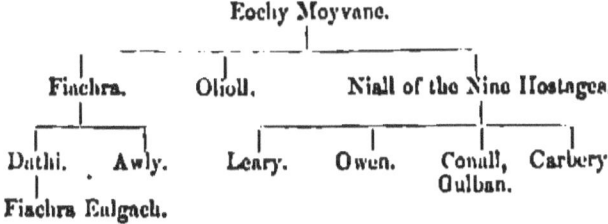

Fiachra [Feecra], son of Eochy Moyvane, was the
ancestor of the *Hy Fiachrach*, which branched into a
great number of families. Amhalgaidh [Awly], his
son, brother of the monarch Dathi [Dawhy], was
king of Connaught, and gave name to *Tir-Amhal-
gaidh*, i. e. Awly's district, now the barony of Tir-
awly in Mayo.

Fiachra Ealgach, son of Dathi, gave his name to
Tir-Fhiachrach (Four Masters), Fiachra's district;
and the sound is very well preserved in the modern
name Tireragh, which is applied to a barony in
Sligo. The barony of Tirerrill in the same county
was possessed by the descendants of Olioll, son of
Eochy Moyvane, and from him it got the name of
Tir-Oliolla (Hy Fiachrach), which, by a change of *l*
to *r*, has been corrupted to the present name.

The great monarch Niall of the Nine Hostages,
king of Ireland from A.D. 379 to 405, had fourteen
sons, eight of whom had issue, and became the
ancestors of many great and illustrious families: of
these eight, four remained in Meath, viz., Laeghaire
[Leary], Conall Crifan, Fiacha, and Maine; and
four settled in Ulster—Eoghan or Owen, Conall
Gulban, Carbery, and Enna Finn. The posterity

of Niall are usually called *Hy Neill*, the southern *Hy Neill* being descended from the first four, and the northern *Hy Neill* from the others.

Laeghaire was king of Ireland from A. D. 428 to 458, and his reign was rendered illustrious by the arrival of St. Patrick ; he erected one of the forts at Tara, which still exists, and retains the name *Rath-Laeghaire;* and the old name of Kingstown—Dunleary, Laeghaire's Dun—was, in the opinion of some, derived from him.

Owen and Conall Gulban are renowned in Irish history as the heads of two great branches of the northern *Hy Neill*, the *Kinel Owen* and *Kinel Connell*. Owen, who died in A. D. 465, was the ancestor of the O'Neills, and his descendants possessed the territory extending over the counties of Tyrone and Londonderry, and the two baronies of Raphoe and Inishowen in Donegal ; all this district was anciently called *Tir-Eoghain* (Wars of GG.), Owen's territory, which is now written Tyrone, and restricted to one county. The peninsula between Lough Foyle and Lough Swilly received also its name from him, Inishowen, i. e. Owen's island.

Conall, who received the cognomen Gulban from having been fostered near the mountain *Binn-Gulbain* (Gulban's peak ; now Binbulbin) in Sligo, died in 464 ; he was the ancestor of the O'Donnells, and his posterity ultimately possessed the county of Donegal, which from him was called Tirconnell, Conall's district.

One of the sons of Conall Gulban was Enna Boghaine [Boana], and he became the ancestor of a tribe called *Kinel Boghaine ;* the district they inhabited was called *Tir-Boghaine* (Four Mast.), and frequently *Baghaincach* [Bawnagh], i. e. Boghaine's

territory; and this latter still holds its place in the
form of Banagh, which is the name of a modern
barony, a portion of the ancient district.

Baeighill [Boyle], who was tenth in descent from
Conall Gulban, was the ancestor of the O'Boyles,
and the district they possessed was called from them
Baeighellach (Four Mast.), or Boylagh, which is
still the name of a barony in the south west of
Donegal.

Flaherty, also descended from Conall Gulban, was
king of Ireland from A. D. 723 to 729: fifth in
descent from him was Cannanan, from whom is
derived the family of O'Cannanan (or, as they now
call themselves, Cannon), who were anciently chiefs
or kings of Tirconnell, till they ultimately sank
under the power of the O'Donnells.   From this
family Letterkenny in Donegal received its name,
which is a shortened form of *Letter-Cannanan*, the
O'Cannanans' hill-slope.

Carbery, another of Niall's sons, was the ancestor
of the Kinel-Carbery; a part of them settled in the
north of the present county of Longford, where the
mountain Slieve-Carbury retains their name; and
another portion took possession of a territory in the
north of Sligo, which is now known as the barony of
Carbury.   The baronies of Carbery in Cork derive
their name from a different source. When Cathal
O'Donovan left his native district, *Cairbre-Aebhdha*
in Limerick, in the beginning of the 14th century,
and settled in the south of Cork, he called his newly
acquired territory Cairbre, the tribe name of his
family; and it has retained this name ever since.

CHAPTER III.

EARLY IRISH SAINTS.

Our early ecclesiastical writers have left us ample records of the most remarkable of those illustrious men and women, who in the fifth and succeeding centuries devoted their lives to the conversion of the Irish nation. There are, on the other hand, great numbers, of whom we possess only meagre details, sometimes obscure and conflicting, and often very perplexing to the student of those early times. And many passed silently to their reward, leaving their names, and nothing more, to attest their participation in the good work.

Most of these saints settled in particular districts, and founded churches, monasteries, or schools, which continued for ages to be centres of civilization, and of knowledge both secular and religious. Whoever understands the deep religious feeling of our people, and the fidelity with which they cling to the traditions of their ancestors, will not be surprised that in most cases they retain to this day in the several localities, a vivid recollection of the patron saints, and cherish their memory with feelings of affection and veneration.

These churches generally retain the names of their founders, suffixed to such words as *Kill*, and *Temple* (a church), *Tee*, *Ti* or *Ty*, (a house), &c. Names of this kind abound in every part of the country; and in all Ireland there are probably not less than ten thousand that commemorate the names of the founders, or of the saints to whom the churches were

dedicated, or that in some other way indicate ecclesiastical origin.

To attempt an enumeration of even the principal
saints that adorned our country from the fifth to the
eight or ninth century, and who are commemorated
in local names, would far exceed the limits of a
chapter; but I shall here select a few for illustration, passing over, however, some of the great
saints, such as Patrick, Brigid, and Columba, whose
lives, and the religious establishments that retain
their names, are generally speaking sufficiently well-
known.

Soon after St. Patrick's arrival in Ulster, and
while he was in the neighbourhood of Downpatrick,
he met and converted a young man named Mochaei
[Mohee], whose mother was Bronach, daughter of
the pagan chief Milcho, with whom the saint had
spent seven years of his youth in captivity. After
having baptized him, he tonsured and dedicated
him to the Church; and according to O'Clery's
Calendar he was the first of the Irish saints to
whom St. Patrick presented a crozier and a book of
the Gospels.

This Mochaei, who was also called Caelan (i. e.
a slender person), became afterwards very much distinguished, and ultimately attained the rank of
bishop: he died in the year 497. He built a church
and established a school at a place called *Naendruim*,
or Nendrum, in Strangford Lough, which was long
a puzzle to topographers, and was generally confounded with Antrim, till Dr. Reeves, in his "Description of Nendrum," identified the place, and
corrected the long-established error. It forms the
eastern portion of Ballinakill parish, and in memory
of the saint it was also called *Inis Mochaei* or Mahee

island, which last name it retains to this day. Even
yet this place retains the relics of its former distinction, namely, the remains of a round tower, and of a
triple cashel or wall surrounding the foundations of
the old church. The name *Naendruim* signifies " nine
ridges;" for so it is explained in MS. II. 3. 18 :—
" Naendruim, i. e. the name of a church, i. e. nine
hillocks in the island in which it is" (see Naendruim
in App. to O'R. Dict.).

Another of St. Patrick's disciples was St Domhanghart [Donart], bishop, son of Eochy, king of Ulidia. He founded two churches—one at a place
called *Rath-murbhuilg*, near the foot of Slieve Donard,
and the other "on the very summit of the mountain itself, far from all human habitation" (Colgan,
A.SS., p. 743). The ruins of this little church existed
down to a recent period on Slieve Donard ; and
the name of the mountain stands as a perpetual
memorial of the saint, who is still held in extraordinary veneration among the Mourne mountains,
and of whom the peasantry tell many curious
legends.

The ancient name of this mountain was *Slieve
Slainge*, so called from the bardic hero Slainge, the
son of Parthalon, who was buried on its summit; and
the great carn raised over him still exists, and forms
a very conspicuous object. Giraldus Cambrensis,
writing in the twelfth century, records the two names
of the mountain, but St. Domhanghart's name he
latinizes *Dominicus* :—" A very high mountain which
hangs over the sea flowing between Britain and
Ireland, is called Salanga, from the second [son of
Bartholanus, namely, Salanus, i. e. Slainge]; but because St. Dominicus many ages afterwards built a
noble monastery at its base, it is now more usually

called the mountain of St. Dominicus" [i. e. Slieve
Donard : Top. Hib., Dist., III. Cap. II.].

The "noble monastery" of Cambrensis is the
church mentioned by Colgan (A. SS., p. 743) as
"formerly called *Rath-murbhuilg,* now called *Machaire-ratha,*" and which he states is at the foot of the
mountain. This identifies it with Maghera, now
the name of a village and parish, north of the mountain ; *Machaire-ratha* (the plain of the fort) being
pronounced *Maghera-raha,* which was shortened to
Maghera. The old name *Rath-murbhuilg* (which signifies the rath of the sea-inlet), was of course originally applied to a fort, but it was afterwards transferred to the church, and thence to the parish. The
change of name was effected by first dropping *mur-
bhuilg,* and afterwards prefixing *machaire ;* and the
intermediate stage appears in the taxation of 1306,
in which the church is called simply *Rath.*

The *murbholg* from which it took its original name
is the small inlet near it, entering from Dundrum
Bay ; and it is a curious confirmation of the authenticity of the foregoing history of the name, that on
its shore there are still two townlands (originally
one) called Murlough, which is the anglicised form
of *Murbholg.*

There is a village in Derry called Maghera, which
is also contracted from *Machaire-ratha.* It was anciently called *Rath-Luraigh* (Four Mast.), i. e. the
fort of St. Lurach, or, as he is now called, Lowry, the
patron saint, whom O'Clery's Calendar, at the 17th
of February, designates as "Lurach of the Poems,
son of Cuana, of the race of Colla Uais, monarch of
Ireland :" he is well remembered in the place, and
his church, grave, and holy well are still to be seen.
From this church, the level land where the town

stands took the name of *Machaire-Ratha-Luraigh* (the plain of Rathlowry), contracted to *Machaire-ratha*, and modernized to Maghera.

The patron of Kinawly in Fermanagh is St. Natalis, or, as he is called in Irish, Nailě [Nawly], and from him the place is called *Cill-Naile* (O'Cl. Cal.), which ought to have been anglicised *Kilnawly*. In O'Clery's Calendar, the following notice of him occurs at the 27th of January:—"Naile of *Inbher-Naile*, in *Tir-Baghuine* in *Cinel-Connill* (the barony of Banagh in Donegal), and afterwards abbot of *Cill-Naile*, and *Daimhinis* in *Feara-Manach*" (Devenish in Fermanagh). *Inbher-Naile* (Naile's river mouth, is the present village of Inver, west of Donegal, of which he is also the patron, and where he is still remembered; and his name is preserved in that of Legnawly Glebe (Naile's hollow), near the village.

Another Natalis or Naile is the patron saint of Kilmanagh, west of Kilkenny (*Cill-Manach*, Mart. Taml., the church of the monks); and it may be assumed that the church of Killenaule in Tipperary (which is not far from Kilmanagh), was dedicated to, and named from him.

Some, and among others Colgan, are of opinion that the two Nailěs are identical, but this is disputed by Dr. Lanigan. The O'Clerys make them different, and state that Naile of Kinawly was the son of Aengus, that king of Munster, of whom is told the celebrated anecdote, that, when he was baptized by St. Patrick in Cashel, his foot was accidentally pierced by the crozier, and so deep was his fervour that he bore it without a word, thinking it was a part of the ceremony. Whoever tries to disentangle this question by referring to the calendars, will find it involved in much confusion: but it seems certain that they

11

were two different persons; that Naile of Kilmanagh was really the son of Aengus; and that the other Naile flourished somewhat later, for it is stated that he died in 564.

Ardbraccan (Brecan's height) in Meath, was founded by St. Brecan, about whose history, although he was a very remarkable man, there hangs considerable obscurity. The most probable accounts represent him as the son of Eochy Ballderg, prince of Thomond, who was baptized by St. Patrick at Singland near Limerick. Brecan, after having erected a church at Ardbraccan, removed to the Great Island of Arran, where he fixed his principal establishment; and here are still to be seen the ruins of his church, and his tombstone, inscribed with his name, in very ancient Roman characters (see Petrie's R. Towers, p. 138). He is also venerated at Kilbreokan (Brecan's church), in the parish of Doora in Clare (O'Cl. Cal., p. 117).

St. Ité, or Idé, virgin, who is often called the Brigid of Munster, was one of the most illustrious saints in an age abounding in illustrious men and women. She was born about the year 480, of the noble race of the Desii in Waterford, being descended from Fiacha, the son of Felim the Lawgiver. She was from her earliest years filled with the spirit of piety, and when she came of age, obtained her parents' consent to devote herself to a religious life. After having received the veil, she proceeded to the territory of *Hy Conaill* in Limerick, where she selected a spot called *Cluain Credhuil* [Clooncrail] for her residence. She was soon visited by great numbers of pious maidens, who placed themselves under her direction; and in this manner sprang up her nunnery, which was the first in that part of the country, and which

afterwards attained to great celebrity. The name of
the place was changed to *Cill-Ide* (O'Cler. Cal.), or
as it is now called, Küleedy, which gives name to a
parish; and at the present day the place contains the
ruins of a very ancient, and exquisitely beautiful
little church.

This virgin saint is remembered with intense veneration all over Munster, and especially in Limerick.
Her name is sometimes changed to Midé (by prefixing *Mo**), and in this form we find it in the names of
churches dedicated to her, of which there are several,
and which are now called Kilmeedy; one of them
giving name to a village in Limerick.

St. Brendan of Clonfert, or as he is often called
Brendan the navigator, was the son of Finlogh of
the race of Ciar (see p. 126); and was born near
Tralee in Kerry in the year 484. He received the
rudiments of his education under a bishop Erc, and
was an intimate friend of St. Ite of Killeedy. After
having studied with St. Iarlath at Tuam, and with
St. Finnian at Clonard, he visited Brittany, where
he founded a monastery. It was previous to this
last visit that he undertook his famous voyage, in
which he is said to have spent seven years sailing
about on the western sea, and to have landed on
various strange shores.

He founded the monastery of Clonfert in Galway.

* The syllables *mo* (my) and *do* or *da* (thy), were often prefixed to the names of Irish saints as terms of endearment or
reverence; thus Conna became Mochonna, and Dachonna. The
diminutives *án*, *ín*, and *óg* were also often postfixed; as we find
in Ernan, Ernog, Baeithin, Baethan, &c. Sometimes the names
were greatly changed by these additions; thus *Aedh* is the same
name as *Maedhog* (Mo-Aedh-óg, my little Aedh), though when
pronounced they are quite unlike, *Aedh* being pronounced *Ai*,
and *Maedhog*, *Mogue*: Ai = Mogue! (See 2nd Ser., c. II.)

11 *

about the year 553, where he drew together a vast
number of monks; it soon became one of the most
celebrated religious establishments in Ireland; and in
memory of the founder the place is generally called
in the Annals *Clonfert Brendain.* He also founded
the monastery of Ardfert, in his native county (which
is also called *Ardfert Brendain*), where a beautiful
ancient church still remains.   There are several
places in Ireland called Clonfert, which name is
written in the Book of Leinster *Cluain-ferta*, the
meadow of the grave; and Ardfert is written by the
Four Masters *Ard-ferta*, the height of the grave.
There is a parish in King's County called Kilclon-
fert (the church of the meadow of the grave: St.
Colman patron), the ancient name of which as given
in O'Clery's Cal., is *Cluain-ferta-Mughaine.*

There are two remarkable mountains in Ireland
called Brandon Hill from this saint.   One is near
Inistioge in Kilkenny; and the other is the well-
known mountain—one of the highest in Ireland—
west of Tralee in Kerry, on the summit of which are
the ruins of his oratory, with an ancient stone-paved
causeway leading to it, which are probably coeval
with St. Brendan himself.

There were many saints named Ciaran or Kieran,
but two of them were distinguished beyond the
others; St. Ciaran of Clonmacnoise, of whom I shall
not speak here, and St. Ciaran of Ossory.   Regarding the exact period when the latter flourished, there
is much uncertainty; but according to the most reliable accounts he became a bishop about the year
538. He was born in the island of Cape Clear; but
his father, Lugueus, was a native of Ossory, and of
kingly descent.

Ciaran was one of the numerous band of saints

who attended St. Finnian's school at Clonard ; and having retired to a solitary place called *Saighir* [Sair], in the territory of *Eile* in Munster, he after some time erected a monastery there, which gradually grew and became the nucleus of a town. He subsequently employed himself partly in the care of his monastery, and partly in preaching the Gospel to the Ossorians and others, of whom he converted great numbers.

According to a gloss in the Felire of Aengus at the 5th of March (Ciaran's festival day), *Saighir* was the name of a fountain ; after the saint's time it was called *Saighir-Ciarain*, which is now contracted to Seirkieran, the name of a parish near Parsonstown. Ciaran is also the patron of Rathkieran in Kilkenny, where he probably built his church near a pagan rath, which took his name.

On the island of Cape Clear, traditions of St. Ciaran still flit among the peasantry. An ancient little church retains the name of Kilkieran ; and a strand in one part of the island is called Trakieran (Ciaran's strand), on which stands a primitive stone cross, said to have been made by the saint's own hands.

St. Ciaran established a nunnery near Seirkieran for his mother Liadhan [Leean], or Liedania ; and from her the place has since borne the name of Killyon (Liadhan's church). It is highly probable that it is from her also that the parish of Killyon in Meath, and the townland of Killyon in the parish of Dunfierth, Kildare, received their names. The parish of Killinn in Galway, which is written Killithain in the Register of Clonmacnoise, took its name from some saint of this name, but whether from St. Ciaran's mother or another Liedania, is uncertain.

There were several saints called Baeithin [Bwee-heen], of whom the most distinguished was Baeithin of Iona, so called because he was a companion, relative, and disciple of St. Columba, and governed the monastery for four years after that saint's death: he died the 9th of June, 600. This saint, whom Columba very much loved, is often mentioned by Adamnan; and in O'Clery's Calendar he is spoken of in these words:—"Baeithin, abbot of Icolum-kille after Columkille himself; and *Tech-Baeithin* (Baeithin's house), in *Cinel-Conaill* (Donegal), was his chief church, for he was of the race of Conall Gulban, son of Niall of the Nine Hostages." His memory is still revered at this church, which is now called Taughboyne, and gives name to a parish in Donegal.

There is another *Tech-Baeithin* in the ancient territory of *Airteach* in Roscommon, which also gives name to a parish, now called Tibohine, the patron saint of which is a different Baeithin. He is mentioned in O'Clery's Calendar at the 19th of February (his festival day):—"Baeithin, bishop (son of Cunna) of *Tech-Baeithin* in Airteach, or in the west of *Midhe* (Meath). He was of the race of Enda, son of Niall" [of the Nine Hostages]. He was one of the ecclesiastics to whom the apostolic letter was written in the year 640, on the subject of the time for celebrating Easter (see Bede, Hist. Eccl., Lib. II. Cap. xix.).

The church "in the west of *Midhe*," mentioned above, is Taughboyne, in the parish of Churchtown, Westmeath, where he is also patron. He built another church near an ancient rath, not far from Kells in Meath, and the rath remains, while the church has disappeared; hence it was called *Rath-Baeithin*, and

in recent times Balrathboyne, the town of Baeithin's
rath, which is now the name of a parish.

Another Baeithin, son of Finnach, of the race of
Laeighsech Ceannmhor (see p. 128), built a church
at Ennisboyne (Baeithin's island or river holm), in
the parish of Dunganstown, Wicklow, where there is
still an interesting church ruin. He is supposed to
have flourished about the beginning of the seventh
century. Crossboyne in Mayo is called in " Hy
Fiachrach," *Cros-Baeithin*, i. e. St. Baeithin's cross;
but who this Baeithin was I have not been able to
ascertain.

St. Ninny, the patron of Inishmacsaint in Fermanagh, is commemorated in O'Clery's Calendar at the
17th of January, in the following words:—"Ninnidh,
bishop of *Inis-muighe-samh*, in Loch-Erne; and he
was Ninnidh Saebhruise (*saebhruisc*, i. e. *torri oculi*),
who was of the race of Enda, son of Niall" [of the
Nine Hostages]; and at the 16th of January he is
mentioned in the Mart. Taml. as "Ninnid Lethderc"
(i. e. one-eyed).   He was a disciple of St. Finnian of
Clonard, and was a contemporary of St. Columba.

Knockninny, a hill in the south of Fermanagh,
which gives name to a barony, is called *Cnoc-Ninnidh*
(Ninny's hill) by the Four Masters; and though we
have no written record of St. Ninny's connection with
it, the uniform tradition of the place is, that the hill
derived its name from him.

St. Molaga, or, as he is sometimes called, Lochein,
was born in the territory of Fermoy in Cork, where
he also received his education; and after distinguish-
ing himself by piety and learning, he established a
monastery at a place called *Tulach-Min* (smooth little
hill), in the same district.

He visited Connor, in Ulster, and thence proceeded

to North Britain and Wales. On his return he settled for some time in Fingal, north of Dublin, where he kept a swarm of bees, a portion of the bees brought over from Wales by St. Modomnoc of Tibberaghny in Kilkenny. From this circumstance the place was called *Lann-beachoire* [backera : O'Clery's Cal.], the church of the bee-man.[*] This is the ruined church and cemetery of Bremore, a little north of Balbriggan, now nameless, but which in the Reg. Alani of the see of Dublin is called *Lambeecher.* He returned to *Tulach-min,* and died there on the 20th of January, some short time after the year 664.

He is the patron saint of Templemolaga near Mitchelstown in Cork, where on the bank of the Funcheon, in a sequestered spot, is situated his church ; it is called in the Book of Lismore, *Eidhnen Molaga*—Molaga's little ivy (church), a name which most truly describes the present appearance of this venerable little ruin. It is now called Templemolaga, and gives name to the parish ; and near it is situated the saint's well, Tober-Molaga. About four miles north-east of Templemolaga is the ruined church of Labbamolaga, Molaga's *bed* or grave, which gives name to a townland. The place called *Tulach-min* was obviously identical with, or in the immediate neighbourhood of, Templemolaga ; but the name is now obsolete.

[*] Giraldus, among others, relates this circumstance of the importation of bees by St. Modomnoc, or Domnoc, or as he calls him, Dominicus :—" S. Dominicus of Ossory, as some say, introduced bees into Ireland, long after the time of Solinus" (Top. Hib., Dist. I., c. v.). Some records say that these were the first bees brought to Ireland, but Lanigan (Vol. II. p. 321) shows that there were bees in the country before St. Domnoc's time. It is evident that he merely imported hive or domesticated bees.

Timoleague, in the south of Cork, is called by the
Four Masters, *Teach-Molaga*, Molaga's house; we
have no record of St. Molaga's connection with this
place, but there can be little doubt that he built a
church there, from which the name is derived; and
the place is still well known for its fine abbey ruins.

St. Mocheallog [Mohallog] or Dacheallog flourished in the beginning of the seventh century.
According to Lanigan, he spent some time under
the instruction of St. Declan of Ardmore, and died
between the years 639 and 656. He founded a
church at Kilmallock in Limerick, which the same
author says is supposed to be a contraction of *Cill-
Mocheallog*; but there can be no doubt at all that it
is so, and for two sufficient reasons:—first, because
in the Felire of Aengus it is stated at the 26th of
March, St. Mocheallog's festival day, that *Cill-Da-
cheallog* is in the territory of Hy Carbery in Munster,
which identifies it with Kilmallock, as Hy Carbery
included the barony of Coshma; and, secondly, the
inhabitants at this day, when speaking Irish, always call the town *Cill-Mocheallog*, St. Mocheallog's
Church.

Finan was the name of many saints, of whom
Finan surnamed *Lobhar*, or the leper, because for
thirty years he was afflicted with some kind of lep-
rosy, was the most remarkable. He was a native of
Ely O'Carroll in King's County, then forming part of
Munster, and governed for some time as abbot the
monasteries of Swords near Dublin, and Clonmore-
Mogue in Leinster. He is mentioned in O'Clery's
Calendar at the 16th of March, in the following
words:—" Finan the leper of *Sord*, and of *Cluain-
mór* in Leinster; and of *Ard-Fionain* in Munster;

he was of the race of Cian, son of Olioll Olum." He died between the years 675 and 695.

He founded a monastery in the island of Innis-fallen (see p. 109), in the lower lake of Killarney; and that of Ardfinnan in Tipperary (mentioned above), which preserves his name. Kilfinane in Limerick doubtless owes its foundation to this Finan also, being called in Irish *Cill-Fhionain*, i. e. Finan's church; his well still exists, and his festival was formerly celebrated there, but all memory of the exact day is lost.

Another Finan, who was surnamed Cam, i. e. crooked, because, as the Mart. Taml. has it, "there was an obliquity in his eyes," flourished in the sixth century. He was a native of Corkaguiny in Kerry, and was descended from Carbery Musc. He is the patron of Kinnitty, in King's County—*Ceann-Eitigh*, Etech's head—so called according to a gloss in the Felire of Aengus at the 7th of April, the saint's festival day, because the head of Etech, an ancient Irish princess, was buried there. Derrynane, the well-known seat of the O'Connell family, took its name from him—*Doire-Fhionáin* (*Fh* silent)—Finan's oak grove; and his house, one of the beehive-shaped structures, is still to be seen on Church Island, in Currane Lough, four miles north of Derrynane. His name is also preserved in Rahinnane, Finan's fort, now a townland near Ventry, so called from a fine rath, in the centre of which stand the ruins of a castle.

One of the brightest ornaments of the Irish Church in the seventh and eighth centuries was the illustrious Adamnan, abbot of Iona, and the writer of the well-known Life of St. Columba; whom the Venerable

Bede designates as "a wise and good man, and most eminently learned in the science of the Holy Scriptures" (Hist. Eccl., Lib. V., Cap. xv.). We have no direct record of the exact place or time of his birth, but there is good reason to believe that he was a native of Donegal, and that he was born about the year 627. He was elected abbot of Iona in the year 679. In 685 he was sent to Alfrid, king of the Northumbrian Saxons, to solicit a restoration of some captives that had been carried off the previous year from the territory of Meath by Saxon pirates; and in this mission he was eminently successful. About the year 703 he visited Ireland for the last time, and succeeded in inducing most of the northern Irish to adopt the Roman method of computing the time for Easter. He returned to Iona in 704, in which year he died, in the 77th year of his age.

The name Adamnan is, according to Cormac's Glossary, an Irish diminutive of Adam. It is generally pronounced in three syllables, but its proper Irish pronunciation is *Awnaun*, the *d* and *m* being both aspirated (Adhamhnan). The saint's name is commemorated in several places in Ireland, and always, as might be expected, in this phonetic form.

He is the patron of Raphoe, where he was called Eunan, but no place there retains the name. He is also patron of Ballindrait in the parish of Clonleigh, Donegal, the Irish name of which is *Droichet-Adhamhnain*, St. Adamnan's bridge. The modern designation has not preserved the name of the saint; Ballindrait is contracted from the Irish *Baile-an-droichit*, the town of the bridge.

Errigal in Londonderry has Adamnan also for its patron, and hence it was called in Irish *Airecal-Adhamhnain*, Adamnan's habitation. The old church was situated in the townland of Ballintemple (the town of the *church*); south of which is the only local commemoration of the saint's name, viz., a large stone called "Onau's rock."

In the life of St. Farannan, published by Colgan, we are informed that Tibraide, lord of *Hy Fiachrach*, bestowed on St. Columba a place called *Cnoc-na-maoile*; but that it was subsequently called *Scrin-Adhamhnain* from a shrine of that saint afterwards erected there. From this shrine the parish of Skreen in Mayo derived its name. He is there called Awnaun, and his well, Toberawnaun (which gives name to a townland), lies a little south of the old church.

There is a townland called Syonan in the parish of Ardnurcher in Westmeath, which, according to the Annals of Clonmacnoise, received its name from him. The tradition of the place is, that Adamnan in one of his visits to Ireland preached to the multitude on the hill there, which has ever since been called *Suidhe-Adhamhnain* [Syonan], Adamnan's seat. Killonan in the parish of Derrygalvin in Limerick, may also have been called so from him, but of this we have no evidence.[*]

The Martyrology of Tallaght, at the 3rd of March, mentions St. Moshacra, the son of Senan, of *Teach-Sacra*; and in O'Clery's Calendar we find, "Mosha-cra, abbot of Clonenagh, and of *Teach Sacra*, in the vicinity of Tallaght."

This Moshacra or Sacra was one of the fathers who composed the synod held at Armagh about the year 696, at which Adamnan attended from Iona. He was the founder and abbot of the monastery at *Teach-*

---

[*] See the Rev. William Reeves' Edition of Adamnan's Life of St. Columba, from which the above account has been taken.

Sacra (Sacra's house), a name afterwards changed to Tassagard (Grace's Annals), and subsequently contracted to Saggart, which is now the name of a village and parish near Tallaght in Dublin.

One of the most remarkable among the early saints of Ireland was St. Moling, bishop of Ferns. He was descended from Cahirmore, monarch of Ireland in the second century; his mother was Nemhnat, a native of Kerry, and he is therefore often called Moling Luachra, from the district of *Luachair*, on the borders of Cork, Kerry, and Limerick. At his intercession, and in opposition to the advice of St. Adamnan, Finaghty, king of Ireland, remitted the Borumha or cow-tribute to the Leinstermen, which had been exacted for centuries, and which was reimposed many years afterwards, by Brian Borumha. He died on the 17th of May, 697.

He is mentioned in O'Clery's Calendar as " Moling Luachra, bishop and confessor, of *Tigh-Moling*." This place is situated on the Barrow, in the south of the county of Carlow, and was originally called *Rosbroc*, badger wood; but the saint erected a church there about the middle of the seventh century, and it was afterwards called *Tigh-Moling* [Tee-Moling], i. e. St. Moling's house, which is now reduced to St. Mullins. The village of Timolin in Kildare, took its name from a church erected there by him, and it preserves more correctly the original form, *Tigh-Moling*.

St. Aengus the Culdee—or, as he is often called, Aengus the Hagiologist—embraced a religious life in the monastery of Clonenagh, in Queen's County; and having made great progress in learning and holiness, he entered the monastery of Tallaght, near Dublin. There he spent several years under St.

Maelruain, whom he assisted to compile a Calendar
of saints, which is well known as the Martyrology of
Tallaght. He was the author of a still more celebrated work, which is now commonly known as the
Felirĕ of Aengus, a metrical calendar, in which the
saints of each day are commemorated in a stanza of
four lines. He died, according to the most probable
accounts, about the year 824.*

He built a cell for himself in a lonely spot near
Clonenagh, to which he frequently retired for medi-
tation and prayer. It was called from him *Disert-
Aengusa,* Aengus's hermitage, now modernized to
Dysartenos; and it is the only place I know that
commemorates the name of this venerable man.

CHAPTER IV.

LEGENDS.

MANY of the legends with which the early history of
our country abounds are no doubt purely fabulous,
the inventions of the old shanachies or story tellers.
Great numbers, on the other hand, are obviously
founded on historical events; but they have been so
distorted and exaggerated by successive generations
of romancers, so interwoven with strange or supernatural circumstances, or so far removed from their
true date into the regions of antiquity, that they
have in many cases quite lost the look of probability.
It is impossible to draw an exact line of demarcation

* See the Life of St. Aengus the Culdee, by the Rev. John
O'Hanlon.

between what is partly real and what is wholly ficti-
tious; but some of these shadowy relations possess
certain marks, and are corroborated by independent
circumstances, which render it extremely probable
that they have a foundation of truth.

It must be carefully borne in mind that the correctness of the interpretations given in this chapter is
not at all affected by the truth or falsehood of the
legends connected with the names. It is related in
the Dinnsenchus, that Conall Cearnach, one of the
most renowned of the Red Branch knights of Ulster
in the first century, lived in his old age at *Cruachan*,
the royal palace of Maev, queen of Connaught. Olioll
More, Maev's husband, was slain by the old warrior
with a cast of a javelin; and the men of Connaught
pursued and overtook him at a ford over a river in the
present county of Cavan, where the village of Bally-
connel now stands. There they slew him, so that
the place was ever after called *Bel-atha-Chonaill*
[Bellaconnell]; and this event is still remembered
in the traditions of the neighbourhood.

The reader may or may not believe this story;
nevertheless the name signifies Conall's ford-mouth,
for we find it always written in Irish authorities,
and pronounced at this day by the natives, *Bel-atha-
Chonaill;* and it is certain that it took its name from
some man named Conall, whether it be Conall Cearnach or not.

The accounts handed down to us of the early
colonies belong to the class of historical legends.
I have included some of them in the chapter on historical events, and others I shall bring in here; but
in this case too it is difficult, and sometimes impossible, to determine the line of separation. They have
been transmitted from several ancient authorities, and

always with remarkable consistency; many of them
are reflected in the traditions of the peasantry; and
the truth of several is confirmed by present existing
monuments. But to most of them the old historians
have assigned an antiquity so incredible or absurd,
that many reject them on this account as a mass of
fables.

The first who led a colony to Ireland, according to
our bardic histories, was a woman named Ceasair or
Casar, who came *forty days before the deluge*, with
fifty young women and three men—Bith [Bih], Ladh-
ra [Lara], and Fintan. Ceasair and the three men
died soon after their arrival, and gave names to four
different places; but they are all now forgotten, with
one exception. Bith was buried on a mountain,
which was called from him *Sliabh Beatha* [Slieve-
baha]. It is well known and retains the very same
name in Irish; but it is called in English Slieve
Beagh—a range situated on the confines of Monaghan,
Fermanagh, and Tyrone. Bith's carn still exists, and
is a large and conspicuous monument on the top of a
hill, in the townland of Carnmore (to which it gives
name), parish of Clones, Fermanagh; and it may be
seen from the top of the moat of Clones, distant about
seven miles north west.*

The first leader of a colony after the flood was
Parthalon, who, with his followers, ultimately took
up his residence on the plain anciently called *Sean-
mhagh-Ealta-Eduir* [Shan-va-alta-edar], the old plain
of the flocks of Edar, which stretched along the coast
by Dublin, from Tullaght to *Edar*, or Howth. The
legend—which is given in several very ancient authorities—relates that after the people of this colony

* See O'Donovan's Four Masters, Vol. I., p. 3.

had lived there for 300 years, they were destroyed by
a plague, which in one week carried off 5,000 men
and 4,000 women; and they were buried in a place
called, from this circumstance, *Taimhleacht-Mhuin-
tirc-Parthaloin* (Four Mast.), the *Taclaght* or plague-
grave of Parthalon's people. This place, which lies
about five miles from Dublin, still retains the name
Taimhleacht, modernized to Tallaght; and on the hill,
lying beyond the village, there is to be seen at this
day a remarkable collection of ancient sepulchral
tumuli, in which cinerary urns are found in great
numbers.

The word *Taimhleacht,* a plague-monument—a
place where people who died of an epidemic were
buried—is pretty common as a local appellative in
various parts of Ireland, under different forms: it is
of pagan origin, and so far as I know is not applied
to a Christian cemetery, except by adoption, like
other pagan terms. In the northern counties it is
generally made Tamlaght and Tamlat, while in other
places it takes the forms of Tawlaght, Towlaght, and
Toulett.

In combination with other words, the first *t* is
often aspirated, which softens it down still more.
Thus Derryhowlaght and Derryhawlagh in Fermanagh, is the oak grove of the plague-grave; Doonam-
lat in Monaghan, and Dooballat in Cavan, black
grave. Magherahamlet in Down, is called on the
Down Survey, *Magherehowlett,* and in a patent of
James I., *Magherhamlaght,* both of which point to
the Irish *Machaire-thaimhleachta* [Mahera-havlaghta],
the field of the plague-grave.

The Fomorians—a race of pirates who infested
the coasts of Ireland, and oppressed the inhabitants
—are much celebrated in our histories. They came

to Ireland in the time of Nevvy (who led another
colony, thirty years after the destruction of Parthalon's people) ; and their principal stronghold was
Tory island. Balor of the great blows was their
chief, and two of the tower-like rocks on the east side
of Tory are still called Balor's castle and Balor's
prison.

His wife, Cethlenn (Kehlen), seems to have been
worthy of her husband. She fought at the second
battle of Moyturey, and inflicted a wound on the
Dagda, the king of the Tuatha De Dananns, of which
he afterwards died. It is stated in the Annals of
Clanmacnoise, that Enniskillen received its name
from her : in the Irish authorities it is always called
Inis-Cethlenn, Cethlenn's island.

At this time there lived on the mainland, opposite
Tory, a chieftain named Mac Kineely, who was the
owner of the Glasgavlen, a celebrated cow, remembered in tradition all over Ireland. Balor possessed
himself of the *Glas* by a stratagem, and carried her
off to Tory; and then Mac Kineely, acting on the
directions of a fairy called Biroge of the mountain,
concerted a plan of revenge, which many years after
led to the death of Balor. When Balor became
aware of this, he landed with his band on the mainland coast, and seized on Mac Kineely ; and, placing
his head on a large white stone, he cut it clean off
with one blow of his sword.

Hence the place was called *Cloch-Chinnfhaelaidh*,
which is the name used by the Four Masters and
other authorities, signifying Kinfaela's or Kineely's
stone ; and the pronunciation is well preserved in the
present name of the place, Cloghineely. The stone
is still to be seen, and is very carefully preserved ; it
is veined with red, which is the stain of Mac Kineely's

blood that penetrated to its centre; and the tourist
who is a lover of legend may indulge his taste among
the people, who will tell endless stories regarding
this wonderful stone.*

From the same people the Giant's Causeway has
derived its name.   It is called in Irish *Clochan-na-
bhFomharaigh*, [Clohanavowry: O'Brien's Dict. voce
Fomhar]—the *cloghan*, or stepping-stones, or causeway of the Fomorians; and as those sea rovers
were magnified into giants in popular legend, the
name came to be translated "Giant's Causeway."

The celebrities of the Tuatha de Danann colony
have left their names on many localities.   From the
princess Danann some suppose they derive their
name; and from her also two remarkable mountains
in Kerry were called *Da-chich-Danainne*, the two
paps of Danann, now well known as The Paps.

One of the most celebrated characters among this
people was Manannan Mac Lir, of whom we are told
in Cormac's Glossary and other ancient authorities,
that he was a famous merchant who resided in, and
gave name to *Inis Manann*, or the Isle of Man;
that he was the best merchant in western Europe;
and that he used to know, by examining the heavens,
the length of time the fair and the foul weather
would last.

He was also called Orbsen; and he was killed by
Ullin, grandson of Nuad of the silver hand, in a
battle fought at Moycullen near Lough Corrib, in
which the two chiefs contended for the sovereignty
of Connaught; "and when his grave was dug, it was

* See O'Donovan's Four Masters, Vol. I., p. 18, for a very
full version of this legend.

then *Loch Orbsen* burst [out of the grave] over
the land, so that it is from him that *Loch Orbsen*
is named. (Yellow Book of Lecan, quoted by
O'Curry, Atlantis, VII., p. 228). This lake is
called *Loch Orbsen* (Orbsen's lake) in all our authorities; and this was changed to the present name,
Lough Corrib, by omitting the final syllable, and
by the attraction of the *c* sound from *Loch* to
Orbsen; Boate has it in the intermediate form, *Lough
Corbes*.

Many of the legendary heroes of the Milesian
colony are also remembered in local names. When
the sons of Milesius came to invade Ireland, a storm
was raised by the incantations of the Tuatha De
Dananns which drove them from *Inver Sceine*, or
Kenmare bay, where they had attempted to land,
scattered their fleet along the coast, and drowned
many of their chiefs and people. Donn, one of the
brothers, and all the crew of his ship were lost on a
range of rocks off Kenmare bay, afterwards called in
memory of the chief, *Teach-Dhoinn*, i.e. Donn's House,
which is the name used by the Irish-speaking peasantry at the present day; but they are called in
English, the Bull, Cow, and Calf.

Colpa the swordsman, another of the brothers, was
drowned in attempting to land at the mouth of the
Boyne; and that part of the river was called from
him *Inver Colptha* [Colpa: Four Mast.], Colpa's
river mouth. This name is no longer applied to it;
but the parish of Colp, lying on its southern bank,
retains the name with little change.

Eimher [Eiver], son of Milesius, landed with his
followers at *Inver Sceine*, and after three days they
fought a battle against a party of the Tuatha De Da-

nanns at Slieve Mish, near Tralee, where fell Scota, the wife of Milesius, and Fas, wife of Un. Fas was interred in a glen, called from her *Gleann-Fuisi* (Four Mast.); it is now called Glenofaush, and is situated at the base af Caherconree mountain about seven miles west of Tralee. The Four Masters state that "the grave of Scota is to be seen between Slieve Mish and the sea;" it is still well known by the name of Scota's grave, and is situated by the Finglas stream; the glen is called Glenscoheen, Scotina's or Scota's glen; and the monument, which was explored some years ago by a party of antiquaries, still remains.

A decisive battle was afterwards fought at *Tailltenn* or Teltown in Meath, in which the Tuatha De Dananns were finally routed; in following up the pursuit, two distinguished Milesian chieftains were slain; namely, Fuad and Cuailnge, the sons of Brogan, grandfather of Milesius. The former fell at *Sliabh Fuaid* (Four Masters: Fuad's mountain), near Newtownhamilton in Armagh, which still retains the name of Slieve Fuad; it is the highest of the Fews range; but the two words, *Fuad* and *Fews*, have no connection, the former being much the more ancient.

The place where Cuailnge [Cooley] fell was called *Sliabh Cuailnge* (Four Masters); it is the mountainous peninsula lying between the bays of Dundalk and Carlingford, and the range of heights still bears the name of the Cooley Mountains. From Bladh [Blaw], another of Brogan's sons, was named *Sliabh Bladhma* (Slieve-Blawma; Four Masters), now called Slievebloom. Whether this is the same person who is commemorated in Lickbla in Westmeath, I cannot tell; but the name signifies "Bladh's flagstone," for the Four Masters write it *Liag-Bladhma*.

Fial, the wife of Lewy (son of Ith, the uncle of Milesius), gave name to the river Feale in Kerry: the legend says that her husband unexpectedly came in sight, while she stood naked after bathing in the stream; and that she, not recognising him, immediately died through fear and shame. An abbey, built in later ages on its banks, was called in Irish *Mainistir-na-Feile*, i. e. the abbey of the river Feale, which is now called Abbeyfeale, and gives name to the town.

Legends about cows are very common. Our Annals relate that Breasal Boidhiobhadh [Bo-yeeva] son of Rury, ascended the throne of Ireland, A. M. 5001. He received his cognomen, because there was a great mortality of cows in his reign: *bo*, a cow, *diobhadh*, death. The Annals of Clonmacnoise mention this event in the following words:—"In his time there was such a morren of cows in this land, as there were no more then left alive but one Bull and one Heiffer in the whole kingdom, which Bull and Heiffer lived at a place called *Gleann Sawasge*." This glen is situated in the county of Kerry, in the parish of Templenoe, north-west of Kenmare, and near the valley of Glencare; and it is still called *Gleann-samhaisce* [sowshkĕ], the valley of the heifer. The tradition is well remembered in the county, and they tell many wonderful stories of this bull and heifer, from which, they maintain, the whole race of Irish cows is descended.

There is a small lake in the island of Inishbofin, off the coast of Connemara, in which there lives an enchanted white cow, or *bo-finn*, which appears above the waters at certain times; hence the lake is called *Loch-bo-finne*, the lake of the white cow, and it has given name to the island. Bede calls the island *Inis-*

bo-finde, and interprets it "the island of the white cow."

There is another Inishbofin in Lough Ree on the Shannon, which in Colgan's Life of St. Aidus is similarly translated; and another off the coast of Donegal, south of Tory island. We find also several lakes in different parts of Ireland called Lough Bofin, the white cow's lake; Lough Boderg (of the red cow), is a lake on the Shannon south of Carrick-on-Shannon; Corrabofin near Ballybay in Monaghan (properly Carrowbofin, the quarter-land of the white cow); Gortbofinna (Gort, a field), near Mallow in Cork, Drombofinny (Drom, a ridge) in the parish of Desertserges, same county; Lisbofin in Fermanagh and Armagh; Lisboduff (the fort of the *black* cow), in Cavan, and many others. It is very probable that these names also are connected with legends.

There are several places in Ireland whose names end with *urcher,* from the Irish word *urchur,* a throw, cast, or shot. In every such place there is a legend of some remarkable cast of a weapon, memorable for its prodigious length, for killing some great hero, a wild animal, or infernal serpent, or for some other sufficient reason. For example, Urcher itself is the name of three townlands in Armagh, Cavan, and Monaghan; and in the last-mentioned county, in the parish of Currin, there is a place called Drumurcher, the ridge of the cast.

The most remarkable of these mighty casts is commemorated at the place now called Ardnurcher, in Westmeath—a cast that ultimately caused the death of Conor Mac Nessa, king of Ulster in the first century. The name Ardnurcher is a corruption, and the proper form would be Athnurcher; the Four Masters, in recording the erection of the castle in 1192, whose

ruins are still there, call it *Ath-an-urchair ;* and the
natives still call it in Irish *Baile-atha-an-urchair,*
which they pronounce *Bluanurcher.*

Conall Cearnach, on a certain occasion, slew in
single combat a Leinster chieftain named Mesgedhra
[Mesgëra], whose brains—according to the barbarous
custom then prevalent—he mixed with lime, and
made of them a hard round ball, which he kept both
as a weapon and as a trophy. There was at this time
a war raging between Ulster and Connaught, and
Ceat [Keth] mac Magach, a Connaught chief, having
by stratagem obtained possession of the ball, kept it
always slung from his girdle ; for it had been pro-
phesied that Mesgëra would be revenged of the
Ulstermen after his death, and Ceat hoped that this
prophecy would be fulfilled by means of the ball.

Ceat went one time with his band, to plunder some
of the Ulster territories, and returning with a great
spoil of cattle, he was pursued and overtaken by an
army of Ulstermen under the command of Conor,
and a battle was fought between them. The Connaught chief contrived to separate the king from his
party, and watching his opportunity, he cast the ball
at him from his *tabhall* or sling ; and the ball struck
the king on the head, and lodged in his skull. His
physician, Fingen, was brought, and he declared that
the king would die immediately if the ball were removed ; but that if it were left so, and provided the
king kept himself free from all inquietude, he would
live.

And his head was stitched up with a golden thread,
and he lived in this state for seven years, till the day of
our Lord's Crucifixion ; when observing the unusual
darkness, he sent for Bacrach, his druid, and asked
him what it meant. Bacrach told him that the Son

of God was on that day crucified by the Jews. "That is a pity," said Conor ; " were I in his presence, I would slay those who were around my king, putting him to death." And with that he rushed at a grove that stood near, and began hewing it with his sword, to show how he would deal with the Jews ; and from the excessive fury which seized him, the ball started from his head, and some of his brain gushed out ; and in that way he died.

The place where Conor was wounded was called *Ath-an-urchair*, the ford of the cast ; which Michael O'Clery, in a fly-leaf note in O'Clery's Calendar, identifies with *Ath-an-urchair* or Ardnurcher in Westmeath (see O'Curry's Lect., p. 636).

Many other legendary exploits of the heroic times are commemorated in local names, as well as casts of a spear. A favourite mode of exhibiting physical activity among the ancients, as well as the moderns, was by a leap ; but if we are to believe in the prodigious bounds ascribed by legend to some of our forefathers, the members of our athletic clubs may well despair of competing with them. The word *leim*, a leap, will be discussed hereafter, but I may remark here that it is generally applied to these leaps of the ancient heroes.

The legend that gave name to Loop Head in Clare is still well remembered by the people. Cuchullin [Cuhullin], the chief of the Red Branch knights of Ulster, endeavouring once to escape from a woman named *Mal*, by whom he was pursued, made his way southwards to the extremity of the county of Clare, where he unhappily found himself in a *cul-de-sac*, with the furious termagant just behind him. There is a little rock called *Bullán-na-léime* (leap rock), rising over the waves, about twenty-five feet beyond

the cape, on which the chief alighted with a great
bound from the mainland ; and the woman, nothing
daunted by the raging chasm, sprang after him ;
when, exerting all his strength, he leaped back again
to the mainland—a much more difficult feat than
the first—and his pursuer, attempting to follow him,
fell short into the boiling sea.   Hence the cape was
called *Leim-Chonchuillinn*, Cuchullin's Leap, which is
the name always used by ancient Irish writers, as for
instance by the Four Masters ; afterwards it was more
commonly called, as it is at the present day in Irish,
Ceann-Leime [Canleama], the head of the leap, or
Leap Head, which seems to have been modified into
the present name *Loop* Head by the Danes of the
lower Shannon : Danish *hlaup*, a leap.   The woman's
body was swept northwards by the tide, and was
found at the southern point of the cliffs of Moher,
which was therefore called *Ceann caillighe* [Cancallee]
or Hag's Head : moreover the sea all along was dyed
with her blood, and it was called *Tonn-Mal* or Mal's
Wave, but it is now known by the name of Mal
Bay.   *Ceann-Leime* is also the Irish name of Slyne
Head in Galway ; but I do not know the legend, if
there be one (see page 82, *supra*).

There are several places whose names contain this
word *leim* in such a way as to render it probable that
they are connected with legends.   Such for example
is Leamirlea in the parish of Kilmalkedar, Kerry,
Leim-fhir-leith, the leap of the grey man ; Leamy-
doody and Leamyglissan in Kerry, and Lemybrien
in Waterford ; which mean, respectively, O'Dowd's,
O'Gleeson's, and O'Brien's leap ; Carrigleamleary
near Mallow, which is called in the Book of Lismore,
Carraig-leme-Laeguiri, the rock of Laeghaire's or
Leary's leap.   Leap Castle in King's County, near

Roscrea, the ruins of which are still to be seen, is
called by the Four Masters *Leim-ui-Bhanain* [Leamy-
vannan], O'Banan's leap.

The name of Lough Derg, on the Shannon, reminds
us of the almost unlimited influence of the bards in
old times, of the merciless way in which they often
exercised it, and the mingled feelings of dread and
reverence with which they were regarded by all,
both nobles and people. This great and long continued power, which some of the Irish monarchs found
it necessary to check by severe legislation, is an undoubted historic fact; and the legend transmits a very
vivid picture of it, whether the circumstance it records happened or not. It is one of the incidents
in an ancient tale called *Talland Etair*, or the Siege
of Howth (see O'Curry's Lect., p. 266).

Aithirne [Ahirny], a celebrated Ulster poet of the
time of Conor mac Nessa, once undertook a journey
through Ireland, and of every king through whose
territories he passed, he made the most unreasonable
and outrageous request he could think of, none of
whom dared refuse him. Eochy mac Luchta was at
that time king of south Connaught and Thomond, and
had but one eye. The malicious poet, when leaving
his kingdom, asked him for his eye, which the king
at once plucked out and gave him; and then desiring
his attendant to lead him down to the lake, on the
shore of which he had his residence, he stooped down
and washed the blood from his face. The attendant
remarked to him that the lake was red with his blood;
and the king thereupon said:—"Then *Loch-Derghderc*
[Dergerk] shall be its name for ever;" and so the
name remains. The lake is called by this name, which
signifies "the lake of the red eye," in all our old

authorities, and the present name Lough Derg is
merely a contraction of the original.

In the parish of Kilgobban in Kerry, about eight
miles west of Tralee, is situated the beautiful valley
of Glannagalt; and it was believed not only in Kerry,
but over the whole of Ireland, wherever the glen was
known, that all lunatics, no matter in what part of
the country, would ultimately, if left to themselves,
find their way to this glen to be cured.   Hence the
name, *Gleann-na-ngealt*, the valley of the lunatics.
There are two wells in the glen, called Tobernagalt,
the lunatics' well, to which the madmen direct their
way, crossing the little stream that flows through the
valley, at a spot called Ahagaltaun, the madman's
ford, and passing by Cloghnagalt, the standing stone
of the lunatics; and they drink of the healing waters,
and eat some of the cresses that grow on the margin;
—the water and the cress, and the secret virtue
of the valley will restore the poor wanderers to sanity.

The belief that gave origin to these strange pil-
grimages, whatever may have been its source, is of
great antiquity.   In the ancient Fenian tale called
Cath Finntragha, or "The battle of Ventry," we are
told that Dairĕ Dornmhar, "The monarch of the
world," landed at Ventry to subjugate Erin, the only
country yet unconquered;   and Finn-mac-Cumhail
and his warriors marched southwards to oppose him.
Then began a series of combats, which lasted for a
year and a day, and Erin was successfully defended
against the invaders.   In one of these conflicts, Gall,
the son of the king of Ulster, a youth of fifteen, who
had come to Finn's assistance, "having entered the
battle with extreme eagerness, his excitement soon
increased to absolute frenzy, and after having per-

formed astounding deeds of valour, he fled in a state
of derangement from the scene of slaughter, and
never stopped till he plunged into the wild seclusion
of this valley (O'Curry, Lect., p. 315). O'Curry
seems to say that Gall was the first lunatic who
went there, and that the custom originated with him.

There is another Fenian legend, well known in
Donegal, which accounts for the name of Lough
Finn, and of the river Finn, which issues from it
and joins the Mourne near Lifford. The following
is the substance, as taken down from the peasantry
by O'Donovan; but there is another and somewhat
different version in "The Donegal Highlands."
Finn Mac Cumhail once made a great feast in the
Finn Valley, and sent two of his heroes, Goll and
Fergoman, to bring him a fierce bull that grazed
on the borders of the lake. On their way they fell
in with a litter of young pigs, which they killed
and left there, intending to call for them on their
way back, and bring them for the feast; but Finn,
who had a foreknowledge of some impending evil,
ascended a hill, and with a mighty voice, called to
the heroes to return by a different route.

They returned each with his half of the bull; Goll
obeyed Finn's injunction, but Fergoman, disregard-
ing it, approached the spot where he had left the
litter, and saw an enormous wild sow, the mother of
the brood, standing over their bodies. She immediately rushed on him to revenge their death, and a
furious fight began, the sow using her tusks, the
warrior his spear.

Fergoman had a sister named Finn, who was as
warlike as himself; and after long fighting, when
he was lacerated by the sow's tusks and in danger of
death, he raised a great shout for his sister's help.

She happened to be standing at the same side of the
lake, but she heard the echo of the shout from the
cliffs on the opposite side; she immediately plunged
in, and swam across, but as she reached the shore,
the voice came from the side she had left, and when
she returned, the echo came resounding again from
the opposite cliffs. And so she crossed and recrossed,
till the dreadful dying shouts of Fergoman so overwhelmed her with grief and terror, that she sank in
the middle of the lake and was drowned. Hence it
was called *Loch Finne*, the lake of Finn, and gave
also its name to the river.

The place where the heroes killed the young pigs,
and where Fergoman met his fate, is still called
Meenanall, in Irish *Min-an-áil*, the *meen* or mountain flat of the litter; and the wild sow gave name
to Lough Muck, the lake of the pig, lying a little
south of Lough Finn.

Whatever may be thought of this wild legend, it is
certain that the lake received its name from a woman
named Finn, for it is always called in Irish *Loch
Finne*, which bears only one interpretation, Finn's or
Finna's lake; and this is quite consistent with the
name given by Adamnan to the river, namely *Finda*.
The suggestion sometimes put forth, that the name
was derived from the word *finn*, white or clear, is
altogether out of the question; for the waters of
both, so far from being clear, are from their source
all the way down to Lifford, particularly remarkable
for their inky blackness.

Among the many traditions handed down by the
Irish people, none are more universal than that of
the bursting forth of lakes. Almost every considerable lake in Ireland has its own story of an enchanted
well, which by the fatal neglect of some fairy in-

junction, or on account of an affront offered to its
guardian spirit, suddenly overflowed the valley, and
overwhelmed the inhabitants with their cattle and
their houses in one common ruin.

Nor is this tradition of recent origin, for we find
lake eruptions recorded in our most ancient annals;
and nearly all the principal lakes in Ireland are
accounted for in this manner. There is one very
remarkable example of an occurrence of this kind—
an undoubted fact—in comparatively recent times,
namely, in the year 1490; at which year the Four
Masters record :—" There was a great earthquake
(*maidhm talmhan*, an eruption of the earth) at *Sliabh
Gamh* (the Ox Mountains), by which a hundred
persons were destroyed, among whom was the son of
Manus Crossagh O'Hara. Many horses and cows
were also killed by it, and much putrid fish was
thrown up; and a lake in which fish is [now] caught
sprang up in the place." This lake is now dried up,
but it has left its name on the townland of Moym-
lough, in Irish *Maidhm-loch*, the erupted lake, in the
parish of Killoran, county of Sligo; and a vivid tradition of the event still prevails in the county. (See
O'Donovan's Four Masters, Vol. IV., p. 1185).

I will digress here for a moment to remark that
the word *madhm* [maum or moym] is used in the
western counties from Mayo to Kerry, and especially
in Connemara, to denote an elevated mountain pass
or chasm; in which application the primary sense of
breaking or bursting asunder is maintained. This
is the origin of the several places called Maum in
these counties, some of which are well known to
tourists—such as Maum Hotel; Maumturk, the pass
of the boars; Maumakeogh, the pass of the mist,
&c. In Mayo we find Maumnaman, the pass of the

women; in Kerry Maumnahaltora, of the altar; and
in Fermanagh Mullanvaum, the summit of the elevated pass.

The origin of Lough Erne in Fermanagh, is pretty
fully stated in the Annals of the Four Masters; and
it is also given in the Book of Invasions, and in
O'Flaherty's Ogygia. Fiacha Labhruinne [Feeha
Lavrinna] was king of Ireland from A. M. 3727 to
3751; and it is related that he gained several battles
during his reign, in one of which he defeated the
Ernai, a tribe of Firbolgs, who dwelt on the plain
now covered by the lake. "After the battle was
gained from them, the lake flowed over them, so that
it was from them the lake is named [*Loch Eirne*],
that is, a lake over the Ernai."

Our most ancient records point to the eruption of
Lough Neagh as having occurred in the end of the
first century. From the universality of the tradition, as well as its great antiquity, it seems highly
probable that some great inundation actually occurred
about the time mentioned, and the well-known shal-
lowness of the lake lends some corroboration to the
truth of the records. Giraldus, who evidently borrowed
the story from the native writers, relates that it was
formed by the overflowing of a fairy fountain, which
had been accidentally left uncovered; and mentions
what the people will tell you to this day, that the
fishermen sometimes see the lofty and slender *eccle-
siasticæ turres*, or round towers, beneath its waters—
a belief which Moore has embalmed in the well-
known lines:—

> "On Lough Neagh's banks as the fisherman strays,
>   When the clear cold eve's declining,
> He sees the round tower of other days
>   In the waves beneath him shining."

The ancient name of the territory now covered by the lake, was *Liathmhuine* [Leafony: grey shrubbery], and it was taken possession of by a Munster chieftain named Eochy Mac Maireda, after he had expelled the previous inhabitants. He occupied the plain at the time of the eruption, and he and all his family were drowned, except one daughter and two sons. Hence the lake was called *Loch-nEchach* [Lough Nchagh], i. e. Eochy's lake, which is its name in all our ancient writings, and of which the present name has preserved the sound, a little shortened. The *N* which now forms the first letter does not belong to the word; it is what is sometimes called the prosthetic *n*, and is a mere grammatical accident. The name often occurs without it; for instance in the Book of Leinster it is given both ways—*Loch-nEthach*, and *Loch-Echach;* and we find it spelled *Lough Eaugh* in Camden, as well as in many of the maps of the 16th and 17th centuries.

This eruption is mentioned in an ancient poem, published by Dr. Todd (Irish Nennius, p. 267) from the Book of Leinster; and from this also it appears that *Linnmhuine* [Linwinny], the *linn* or lake of the shrubbery, in allusion to the old name of the territory, was another name for the lake :—

> " Eochy Maireda, the rebellious son,
>   Of wonderful adventure,
>   Who was overwhelmed in lucid *Linnmhuine*,
>   With the clear lake over him."

Eochy's daughter, Liban, is the subject of an exceedingly wild legend, for which see Reeves's Ecclesiastical Antiquities, p. 376.

CHAPTER V.

FAIRIES, DEMONS, GOBLINS, AND GHOSTS.

IT is very probable that the belief in the existence of fairies, so characteristic of the Keltic race of these countries, came in with the earliest colonies.   On this question, however, I do not intend to enter: it is sufficient to observe here, that the belief, in all its reality, is recorded in the oldest of our native writings, and that with a distinctness and circumstantiality that prove it to have been, at the time of which they treat, long established and universally received.

It was believed that these supernatural beings dwelt in habitations in the interior of pleasant hills, which were called by the name of *sidh* or *sith* [shee]. Colgan's explanation of this term is so exact, and he gives such an admirable epitome of the superstition respecting the *sidh* and its inhabitants, that I will here translate his words:—" Fantastical spirits are by the Irish called men of the *sidh*, because they are seen as it were to come out of beautiful hills to infest men ; and hence the vulgar belief that they reside in certain subterraneous habitations within these hills ; and these habitations, and sometimes the hills themselves, are called by the Irish *sidhe* or *siodha*."

In Colgan's time the fairy superstition had descended to the common people—the *vulgus*; for the spread of the Faith, and the influence of education, had disenthralled the minds of the better classes. But in the fifth century, the existence of the *Duine sidhe* [dinna-shee; people of the fairy mansions],

was an article of belief with the high as well as with
the low; as may be inferred from the following
curious passage in the Book of Armagh, where we
find the two daughters of Laeghaire [Leary], king of
Ireland, participating in this superstition:—" Then
St. Patrick came to the well which is called *Clebach*,
on the side of *Cruachan* towards the east; and before sunrise they (Patrick and his companions) sat
down near the well. And lo! the two daughters of
king Laeghaire, Ethnea the fair and Fedelma the
ruddy, came early to the well to wash, after the
manner of women; and they found near the well a
synod of holy bishops with Patrick. And they knew
not whence they came, or in what form, or from
what people, or from what country; but they supposed them to be *Duine sidhe*, or gods of the earth,
or a phantasm" (Todd's Life of St. Patrick, p. 452).
Dr. Todd adds in a note:—" *Duine sidhe*, the men of
the *sidhe*, or phantoms, the name given by the Irish
to the fairies—men of the hills; the word *sidhe* or
soidha signifies the habitations supposed to belong to
these aerial beings, in the hollows of the hills and
mountains. It is doubtful whether the word is cognate with the Lat. *sedes*, or from a Celtic root, *side*,
a blast of wind."

The belief of king Laeghaire's daughters regarding these aerial beings, as related in a MS. copied in
the year 807, is precisely the same as it was in the
time of Colgan, and the superstition has descended
to our own time in all its integrity. Its limits are
indeed further circumscribed; but at the present day
the peasantry in remote districts believe that the
fairies inhabit the *sidhe*, or hills, and that occasionally
mortals are favoured with a view of their magnificent
palaces.

13*

To readers of modern fairy lore, the banshee is a
well-known spirit :—Irish *bean-sidhe*, woman of the
fairy mansions. Many of the old Milesian families
are attended by a banshee, who foretells and laments
the approaching death of a member of the favoured
race by *keening* round the house in the lonely night.
Numberless banshee stories are related with great
circumstantiality, by the peasantry all over Ireland,
several of which are preserved in Crofton Croker's
fairy legends.

In our old authorities it is very often stated that
the fairies are the Tuatha De Danann; and the
chiefs of this race—such as the Dagda, Bove Derg,
&c.—are frequently referred to as the architects and
inhabitants of the *sidhe*. For example, in the copy
of the " History of the Cemeteries " contained in the
MS. H. 3. 17, T. C. D., the following statement
occurs relating to the death of Cormac mac Art :—
" Or it was the *siabhra* [shoevra] that killed him,
i. e. the Tuatha de Danann, for they were called
siabhras." In some cases, however, the *sidhe* were
named after the chiefs of the Milesian colony, as in
case of *Sidh-Aedha* at Ballyshannon (see page 182) ;
and at present the Tuatha De Danann origin of these
aerial beings seems to be quite forgotten ; for almost
all raths, cashels, and mounds—the dwellings, forts,
and sepulchres of the Firbolgs and Milesians, as well
as those of the Tuatha De Danann—are considered
as fairy haunts.

Of this ancient Tuatha De Danann people our
knowledge is very scant indeed ; but, judging from
many very old tales and references in our MSS.,
and from the works supposed to be executed by this
race, of which numerous remains still exist—sepulchral
mounds, gracefully formed slender spearheads, &c.—

we may conclude that they were a people of superior intelligence and artistic skill, and that they were conquered and driven into remote districts, by the less intelligent but more warlike Milesian tribes who succeeded them. Their knowledge and skill procured for them the reputation of magicians; and the obscure manner in which they were forced to live after their subjugation, in retired and lonely places, gradually impressed the vulgar with the belief that they were supernatural beings.

It is not probable that the subjugation of the Tuatha De Danann, with the subsequent belief regarding them, was the origin of Irish fairy mythology. The superstition, no doubt, existed long previously; and this mysterious race, having undergone a gradual deification, became confounded and identified with the original local gods, and ultimately superseded them altogether.

The most ancient and detailed account of their final dispersion is found in the Book of Fermoy, a MS. of the year 1463; where it is related in the tale of Curchog, daughter of Manannan Mac Lir, that the Tuatha De Danann, after the two disastrous battles of *Tailleann* and *Druim Lighean*, held a meeting at *Brugh* on the Boyne, under the presidency of Manannan; and by his advice they distributed and quartered themselves on the pleasant hills and plains of Erin. Bodhbh [Bove] Derg, son of the Dagda, was chosen king; and Manannan, their chief counsellor, arranged the different places of abode for the nobles among the hills.

Several of the *sidhs* mentioned in this narrative are known, and some of them are still celebrated as fairy haunts. *Sidh Buidhbh* [Boov], with Bove Derg for its chief, was on the shore of Lough Derg,

somewhere near Portumna. Several hills in Ireland,
noted fairy haunts, took their names from this chief,
and others from his daughter, Bugh [Boo]. One of
the former is Knockavoe near Strabane. The Four
Masters mention it at A.D. 1522, as " *Cnoc-Buidhbh*,
commonly called *Cnoc-an-Bhogha ;* " which shows
that the former was the correct old name, and that it
had been corrupted in their time to *Cnoc-an-Bhogha*,
which is its present Irish name, and which is represented in sound by the anglicised form, Knockavoe.
They mention it again at 1557 ; and here they give
it the full name *Cnoc-Buidhbh-Derg*, Bove-Derg hill.
It was probably the same old chief who left his name
on Rafwee in the parish of Killeany in Galway;
which, in an ancient authority quoted by Hardiman
(Iar C. 370), is called *Rath-Buidhbh*, Bove's fort.
From his daughter is named Canbo, in the parish of
Killummod, Roscommon, which Duald M'Firbis
writes *Ceann-Bugha*, i.e. Bugh's head or hill.

Sidh Truim, under the guardianship of Midir, was
situated a little to the east of Slane, on the Boyne,
but its name and legend are now forgotten. *Sidh
Neannta*, under Sidhmall, is now called Mullaghshee
or Fairymount, and is situated in the parish of Kil-
geffin, near Lanesborough, in the county Roscommon. *Sidh Meadha* [Mū], over which presided Finn-
bharr [Finvar], is the well-known mountain now
called Knockma, five miles south-west of Tuam ; the
tradition respecting it is still preserved in all its
vividness ; and the exploits of Finvara, its guardian
fairy, are celebrated all over Ireland.

Sidh Aedha Ruaidh, another of these celebrated
fairy resorts is the hill now called Mullaghshee, on
which the modern church is built, at Ballyshannon in
Donegal. The Book of Leinster and other ancient

authorities relate that Aedh-Ruadh [Ay-roo], the
father of Macha, founder of Emania (see p. 88), was
drowned in the cataract at Ballyshannon, which was
thence called after him, *Eas-Ruaidh*, or *Eas-Aedha-
Ruaidh* [Assroo, Assayroo], Aedh Ruadh's waterfall,
now shortened to Assaroe. He was buried over the
cataract, in the mound which was called from him
Sidh-Aedha—a name still partly preserved in Mullaghshee, the hill of the *sidh* or fairy palace.

This hill has recently been found to contain sub-
terranean chambers, which confirms our ancient legendary accounts, and shows that it is a great sepulchral mound like those on the Boyne. How few of
the people of Ballyshannon know that the familiar
name Mullaghshee is a living memorial of those dim
ages when Aedh Ruadh held sway, and that the
great king himself has slept here in his dome-roofed
dwelling for more than two thousand years!

These are a few illustrations of the extent to which
the fairy mythology was accepted in Ireland in remote ages. But, even if history were wholly silent
regarding the former prevalence of this belief, it
would be sufficiently attested by the great numbers
of places, scattered all over the country, whose
names contain the word *sidh*, or, as it is usually
modernized, *shee*. It must be borne in mind that
every one of those places was once firmly believed
to be a fairy mansion, inhabited by those mysterious beings, and that in case of many of them, the
same superstition lurks at this day in the minds of
the peasantry.

Sidh, as we have seen, was originally applied to a
fairy palace, and it was afterwards gradually transferred to the hill, and ultimately to the fairies themselves; but this last transition must have begun at a

very early period, for we find it expressly stated in a
passage in the Leabhar-na-hUidhre, that the ignorant called the faries *side*. At the present day, the
word generally signifies a fairy, but the diminutive
sidheóg [sheeoge] is more commonly employed. When
sidh forms part of a name, it is often not easy to determine whether it means the fairies themselves or
their habitations.

Shee and its modifications constitute or begin the
names of about seventy townlands, which are pretty
equally distributed over the four provinces, very few
being found, however, in the counties of Louth,
Dublin, and Wicklow. Besides these, there are
many more places whose names contain this word in
the middle or end; and there are innumerable fairy
hills and forts through the country, designated by
the word *shee*, which have not communicated their
names to townlands.

Sidh-dhruim [Sheerim], fairy ridge—the old name
of the Rock of Cashel and of several other ancient
fairy haunts—is still the name of six townlands in
Armagh under the modern form Sheetrim; the change
from *d* to *t* (in *druim*) must have begun a long time
ago, for *Sidh-druim* is written *Sith-truim* in Torna
Eigas's poem ("Hy Fiachrach," p. 29) : Sheerev-
agh, in Roscommon and Sligo, grey *shee*; Shee-
gorey near Boyle, the fairy hill of Guaire or Gorey,
a man's name. There is a townland in the parish of
Corbally, Tipperary, called the Sheehys, or in Irish
Na sithe [na sheeha], i. e. the fairy mounts ; and a
range of low heights south of Trim in Meath, is
well known by the name of the Shee hills, i. e. the
fairy hills.

There is a famous fairy palace on the eastern
shoulder of Slievenaman mountain in Tipperary.

According to a metrical romance contained in the Book of Lismore and other authorities, the Tuatha De Danann women of this *sidh* enchanted Finn mac Cumhail and his Fianna : and from these women the mountain took its name. It is now called in Irish, *Sliabh-na-mban-fionn*, which would signify the mountain of the fair-haired women ; but O'Donovan shows that the true name is *Sliabh-na-mban-Feimhinn* [Slievenamon Fevin], the mountain of the women of *Feimheann*, which was an ancient territory coextensive with the barony of Iffa and Offa East ; and this was shortened to the present name, *Sliabh-na-mban*, or Slievenaman.

The word occurs still more frequently in the end of names ; and in this case it may be generally taken to be of greater antiquity than the part of the name that precedes it.   There is a parish in Longford called Killashee, which was probably so called because the church was built near or on the site of one of these mounts.   Killashee in Kildare has, however, a different origin.   Cloonshee near Elphin in the county Roscommon, is called by the Four Masters *Cluain-sithe*, fairy meadow ; and there are several other places of the same name.   Rashee in Antrim, where St. Patrick is recorded to have founded a church, is in Irish *Rath-sithe* (Four Masters), the fort of the fairies ; and the *good people* must have often appeared, at some former period, to the inhabitants of those places now called Ballynashee and Ballynasheeoge, the town of the fairies.

The word *sidh* undergoes several local modifications ; for example Knocknasheega near Cappoquin in Waterford, is called in Irish *Cnoc-na-sige*, the hill of the faries ; and the name of Cheek Point on the Suir below Waterford, is merely an adaptation from

Sheega point; for the Irish name is *Póinte-na-síge* [Pointa-na-sheega], the point of the fairies. The townland of Sheegys (i. e. fairy hills) in the parish of Kilbarron, Donegal, was once no doubt a favourite resort of fairies; and on its southern boundary, near high water work, there is a mound called Mulnashcefrog, the hill of the fairy dwellings. In the parish of Aghanagh, Sligo, there are two townlands, called Cuilsheeghary, which the people call in Irish, *Coillsoithchaire*, the fairies' wood, for a large wood formerly stood there.

While *sidheóg* means a fairy, the other diminutive *sidheán* [sheeawn] is always applied to a fairy mount. The word is used in this sense all over Ireland, but it is particularly common in Connaught, where these *sheeauns* are met with in great numbers; they are generally beautiful green round hillocks, with an old fort on the summit. Their numbers would lead one to believe that in old times, some parts of Connaught must have been more thickly peopled with fairies than with men.

Great numbers of places have taken their names from these haunted hills; and the word assumes various forms, such as Sheaun, Shechaun, Sheean, and Shean, which give names to about thirty townlands scattered through the four provinces. It is not unfrequently changed to Sion, as in the parish of Laraghbryan in Kildare, where the place now so called evidently took its name from a *sheeaun*, for it is written *Shiane* in an Inquisition of James I.; and there are several other instances of this odd corruption. Near Ballybay in Monaghan, is a place called Shane, another form of the word; and the plural Shanes, fairy hills, occurs in the parish of Loughguile, Antrim. Sheena in Leitrim, Sheeny in Meath and Fermanagh, and Sheeana in Wicklow, are different forms of the Irish plural *sidhne* [sheena], fairy hills.

The sound of the *s* is often eclipsed by *t* (p. 23), and this gives rise to further modifications. There is a castle called Ballinteean giving name to a town-land in the parish of Ballysakeery, Mayo, which is written by M'Firbis, *Baile-an-tsiodhain*, the town of the fairy hill; the same name occurs near Ballinrobe in the same county, and in the parish of Kilglass, Sligo: in Down and Kildare it takes the form of Ballintine; and that this last name is derived from *sidhean* is shown by the fact that Ballintine near Bla-ris in Down is written Shiane in an Inquisition of James I. Aghintain near Clogher in Tyrone, would be written in the original, *Achadh-an-tsiadhain* [Aghanteean], the field of the fairy mount.

Most of the different kinds of fairies, so well known at the present day to those acquainted with the Irish peasantry, have also been commemorated in local names. A few of those I will here briefly mention, but the subject deserves more space than I can afford.[*]

The Pooka—Irish *púca*—is an odd mixture of merriment and malignity; his exploits form the subject of innumerable legendary narratives; and every literary tourist who visits our island, seems to consider it a duty to record some new story of this capricious goblin. Under the name of Puck, he will be recognized as the "merry wanderer of the night," who boasts that he can "put a girdle round about the earth in forty minutes;" and the genius of Shak-

speare has conferred on him a kind of immortality
he never expected.

There are many places all over Ireland where the
Pooka is still well remembered, and where, though he
has himself forsaken his haunts, he has left his name
to attest his former reign of terror.   One of the best
known is Pollaphuca in Wicklow, a wild chasm
where the Liffey falls over a ledge of rocks into
a deep pool, to which the name properly belongs,
signifying the pool or hole of the Pooka.   There are
three townlands in Clare, and several other places in
different parts of the country, with the same name;
they are generally wild lonely dells, caves, chasms in
rocks on the sea shore, or pools in deep glens like
that in Wicklow—all places of a lonely character,
suitable haunts for this mysterious sprite.   The original name of Puckstown in the parish of Mosstown
in Louth, and probably of Puckstown, near Artaine
in Dublin, was Pollaphuca, of which the present
name is an incorrect translation.   Boheraphuca (*boher*, a road) four miles north of Roscrea in Tipperary,
must have been a dangerous place to pass at night, in
days of old.   Carrigaphooca (the Pooka's rock) two
miles west of Macroom, where on the top of a rock
overhanging the Sullane, stand the ruins of the
M'Carthy's castle, is well known as the place whence
Daniel O'Rourke began his adventurous voyage to
the moon on the back of an eagle; and here for many
a generation the Pooka held his "ancient solitary
reign," and played pranks which the peasantry will
relate with minute detail.

About half way between Kilfinane in Limerick,
and Mitchelstown in Cork, the bridge of Ahaphuca
crosses the Ounageeragh river at the junction of its
two chief branches, and on the boundary of the two

counties. Before the erection of the bridge, this was a place of evil repute, and not without good reason, for on stormy winter nights, many a traveller was swept off by the flood in attempting to cross the dangerous ford; these fatalities were all attributed to the malice of the goblin that haunted the place; and the name—the Pooka's ford—still reminds us of his deeds of darkness.

He is often found lurking in raths and lisses; and accordingly there are many old forts through the country called Lissaphuca and Rathpooka, which have, in some cases, given names to townlands. In the parish of Kilcolman in Kerry, are two townlands called Rathpoge on the Ordnance map, and Rathpooke in other authorities—evidently *Rathpuca*, the Pooka's rath. Sometimes his name is shortened to *pook*, or *puck;* as, for instance, in Castlepook, the goblin's castle, a black, square, stern-looking old tower, near Doneraile in Cork, in a dreary spot at the foot of the Ballyhoura hills, as fit a place for a pooka as could be conceived. This form is also found in the name of the great moat of Cloghpook in Queen's County (written Cloyth-an-puka in a rental book of the Earl of Kildare, A. D. 1518), the stone or stone fortress of the pooka; and according to O'Donovan, the name of Ploopluck near Naas in Kildare, is a corruption—a very vile one indeed—of the same name.

The word *siabhra* [sheevra] is now very frequently employed to denote a fairy, and we have found it used in this sense in the quotation at page 180 from the "History of the Cemeteries." This term appears in the names of several places: there is, for example, a townland called Drumsheaver, in the parish of Tedavnet, Monaghan, but which is

written in several modern authorities, Drumshevery,
the ridge of the *sheerras ;* and they must have also
haunted Glennasheevar, in the parish of Inishmacsaint in Fermanagh.

Nor is the leprechaun forgotten—the merry sprite
" Whom maids at night, Oft meet in glen that's
haunted," who will give you the *sparán scillinge*, an
inexhaustible fairy purse, if you can only manage to
hold him spell-bound by an uninterrupted gaze.
This lively little fellow is known by several different
names, such as *luprachaun, luricane, lurrigadane, cluri-
cane, luppercadane, loughryman,* &c. The correct original designation from which all these have been
corrupted, is *luchorpán,* or as we find it in the MS.
H. 2, 16 (col. 120), *lucharban ;* from *lu,* "everything
small " (Cor. Gl., *voce* "luda"), and *corpán,* a diminutive of *corp,* a body, Lat. *corpus;* so that *luchorpán*
signifies " an extremely little body " (see Stokes's
Cor. Gl. p. 1).

In the townland of Creevagh, near Cong in Mayo,
there is a cave called Mullenlupraghaun, the leprechauns' mill, " where in former times the people left
their *caskeens* of corn at nightfall, and found them
full of meal in the morning" (Wilde's Lough Corrib)—ground by the leprechauns. And it is certain
that they must have long chosen, as favourite haunts,
Knocknalooricaun (the hill of the looricauns), near
Lismore in Waterford, and Poulaluppercadaun (*poul,*
a hole), near Killorglin in Kerry.

Every one knows that fairies are a merry race and
that they enjoy immensely their midnight gambols;
moreover, it would seem that they indulge in many
of the ordinary peasant pastimes. The fairy fort of
Lisfarbegnagommaun stands in the townland of
Knocknagraigue East, four miles from Corrofin in

Clare; and whoever cautiously approaches it on a calm moonlight night, will probably see a spectacle worth remembering—the little inhabitants, in all their glory, playing at the game of *coman*, or hurley. Their favourite amusement is told clearly enough in the name *Lios-fear-beg-na-gcomán*, the fort of the little hurlers. Sam Lover must have been well acquainted with their pastimes when he wrote his pretty song, " The fairies are dancing by brake and by bower;" and indeed he probably saw them himself, " lightly tripping o'er the green," in one of the many forts, where they indulge in their nightly revelry, and which are still called Lissarinka, the fort of the dancing.

Readers of Crofton Croker will recollect the story of the rath of Knockgraffon, and how the little man, Lusmore, sitting down to rest himself near the fort, heard a strain of wild music from the inside. Knockgraffon is not the only " airy " place where the *ceól-sidhe*, or fairy music, is heard; in fact this is a very common way of manifesting their presence; and accordingly certain raths in the south of Ireland are known by the name of Lissakeole, the fort of the music. Neilson (Irish Gram., page 55) mentions a hill in the county of Down, called Knocknafeadalea, whistling hill, from the music of the fairies which was often heard to proceed from it; and the townland of Lisnafeddaly in Monaghan, and Lisnafeedy in Armagh, both took their names (signifying the fort of the whistling: *fead* or *fid*, a whistle) from *lisses*, with the same reputation.

The life of a fairy is not, however, all merriment. Sometimes the little people of two neighbouring forts quarrel, and fight sanguinary battles. These encounters always take place by night; the human inhabit-

ants are terrified by shrill screams and other inde-
scribable noises; and in the morning the fields are
strewn with drops of blood, little bones, and other
relics of the fight.   Certain forts in some of the
northern counties, whose inhabitants were often engaged in warfare, have, from these conflicts, got
the name of Lisnascragh, the fort of the screeching.

Very often when you pass a lonely fort on a dark
night, you will be astonished to see a light shining
from it; the fairies are then at some work of their
own, and you will do well to pass on and not disturb
them.   From the frequency of this apparition, it has
come to pass that many forts are called Lisnagannell
and Lisnagunnell, the fort of the candles; and in
some instances they have given names to townlands,
as, for example, Lisnagonnell in the county Down;
Lisnageculy in Tipperary; Lisgonnell in Tyrone;
and Liscunnell in Mayo.   We must not suppose that
these fearful lights are always the creation of the
peasant's imagination; no doubt they have been in
many instances actually seen, and we must attribute
them to that curious phenomenon, *ignis fatuus*, or
Will-o'-the-wisp.   But the people will not listen to
this, for they know well that all such apparitions are
the work of the good people.

Fairies are not the only supernatural beings let
loose on the world by night; there are ghosts, phantoms, and demons of various kinds; and the name of
many a place still tells the dreaded scenes nightly
enacted there.   The word *dealbh* [dalliv], a shape or
image (*delb*, effigies, Zcuss, 10) is often applied to a
ghost.   The townland of Killeennagallive in the
parish of Templebredon, Tipperary, took its name
from an old churchyard, where the dead must have
rested unquietly in their graves; for the name is

a corruption (p. 56) of *Cillin-na-ndealbh*, the little church of the phantoms. So also Drumnanaliv in Monaghan, and Clondallow in King's County, the ridge and the meadow of the spectres. And in some of the central counties, certain clusters of thorn bushes, which have the reputation of being haunted, are called by the name of Dullowbush (*dullow*, i.e. *dealbh*), i. e. the phantom bush.

There is a hideous kind of hobgoblin generally met with in churchyards, called a dullaghan, who can take off and put on his head at will—in fact you generally meet him with that member in his pocket, under his arm, or absent altogether; or if you have the fortune to light on a number of them you may see them amusing themselves by flinging their heads at one another, or kicking them for footballs. Ballindollaghan in the parish of Baslick, Roscommon, must be a horrible place to live in, if the dullaghan that gave it the name ever shows himself now to the inhabitants.

Every one knows that a ghost without a head is very usual, not only in Ireland, but all over the world; and a little lake in the parish of Donaghmore in Donegal, four miles south of Stranorlar, is still called Lough Gillagaucan, the headless man's lake, from having been haunted by one of these visitants. But I suppose it is only in Ireland you could meet with a ghost without a shirt. Several of these tasteless fellows must have at some former period roamed nightly at large in some of the northern counties, where there are certain small lakes, which are now called Lough Gillagauleny, the lake of the shirtless fellow: one for instance, two miles east of the northern extremity of Lough Eask, near the

14

town of Donegal; and another in the parish of Rossinver in Leitrim, five miles from Manorhamilton
(*Gilla*, a fellow; *gan*, without; *leine*, a shirt).

Glennawoo, a townland in the parish of Kilmacteige, Sligo, must have been, and perhaps is still, a
ghastly neighbourhood, for the name *Gleann-na-
bhfuath* [Glennawoo] signifies the glen of the spectres;
and in the parish of Aghavea, Fermanagh, is a place
which was doubtless almost as bad, viz., Drumarraght,
the ridge of the *arraght* or apparition. Near the
church of Kilnamona in Clare, there is a well called
Toberatasha; it is in the form of a coffin, and its
shape is not more dismally suggestive than its name,
Tobar-a'-taise, the well of the *fetch* or ghost. What
kind of malignant beings formerly tormented the
people of Drumahaire in Leitrim, it is now impossible to tell; and we should be ignorant of their
very existence if our annalists had not preserved
the true form of the name—*Druim-da-ethair* [Drum-
a-ehir; Four Masters], the ridge of the two air-
demons.

Besides the celebrated fairy haunts mentioned at
p. 182, there are several other places in different parts
of Ireland, presided over, each by its own guardian
spirit, and among them several female fairies, or *ban-
shees*. Some of these are very famous, and though
belonging to particular places, are celebrated by the
bards over the whole of Ireland.

Cliodhna [Cleena] is the potent banshee that rules
as queen over the fairies of South Munster; and you
will hear innumerable stories among the peasantry,
of the exercise of her powerful spells. Edward Walsh
makes his lover of " O'Donovan's Daughter " thus
express himself:—

" God grant 'tis no fay from Knockfierna that woos me ;
God grant 'tis not Cleena the queen that pursues me ;
That my soul, lost and lone, has no witchery wrought her,
While I dream of dark groves and O'Donovan's daughter."

In the Dinnsenchus there is an ancient poetical
love story, of which Cleena is the heroine ; wherein
it is related that she was a foreigner, and that she
was drowned in the harbour of Glandore, near Skibbereen in Cork. In this harbour the sea, at certain
times, utters a very peculiar, deep, hollow, and me-
lancholy roar among the caverns of the cliffs, which
was formerly believed to foretell the death of a king
of the south of Ireland ; and this surge has been
from time immemorial called *Tonn-Cleena*, Cleena's
wave. Cleena had her palace in the heart of a great
rock, situated about five miles south-south-west from
Mallow ; it is still well known by the name of Carrig-
Cleena, and it has given name to two townlands.

Aeibhell [Eevil], or more correctly Aebhinn [Ee-
vin], whose name signifies "beautiful," was another
powerful banshee, and presided over north Munster :
she was in an especial manner the guardian spirit of
the Dalcassians. When the Dalcassian hero, Dunlang
or Dooling O'Hartigan, the friend and companion of
Murchadh [Murraha], Brian Boru's eldest son, was
on his way to the battle of Clontarf, she met him and
tried to dissuade him from fighting that day. For
she told him that he would fall with Murchadh : and
she offered him the delights and the immortality of
Fairyland, if he would remain away. But he replied
that nothing could induce him to abandon Murchadh
in the day of battle, and that he was resolved to go,
even to certain death. She then threw a magical
cloak round him which made him invisible, warning

14*

him that he would certainly be slain if he threw it off.

He rushed into the midst of the battle, and fought for some time by the side of Murchadh, making fearful havoc among the Danes. Murchadh looked round him on every side, and at last cried out, " I hear the sound of the blows of Dunlang O'Hartigan, but I cannot see him !" Then Dunlang could no longer bear to be hidden from the eyes of Murchadh; and he threw off the cloak, and was soon after slain according to the fairy's prediction.

The aged king, Brian, remained in his tent during the day. And towards evening the tent was left unguarded in the confusion of the battle; and his attendant urged him to mount his horse and retire, for he was in danger from straggling parties of the Danes. But he answered—" Retreat becomes us not, and I know that I shall not leave this place alive. For Aeibhell of Craglea came to me last night, and told me that I should be killed this day " (see Wars of GG., p. 201).

Aeibhell had her palace two miles north of Killaloe, in a rock called Crageevil, but better known by the name of Craglea, grey rock. The rock is situated in a silent glen, under the face of a mountain; and the peasantry affirm that she forsook her retreat, when the woods which once covered the place were cut down. There is a spring in the face of the mountain, still called Tobereevil, Aeibhell's well.

There is a legend common over all Ireland, connected generally with lakes, that there lives at the bottom, a monstrous serpent or dragon, chained there by a superior power. The imprisonment of these demoniac monsters is commonly attributed to St. Patrick, who, when he cleared the country of demons, chose this mode of disposing of some of the most ferocious:—and there they must remain till the day of judgment. In some places it is said that they are permitted to appear above the waters at certain times, generally every seven years; and then the inhabitants hear the clanking of chains, or other unearthly noises.

During the period of St. Patrick's sojourn in Connaught, he retired on the approach of Lent to the mountain of Croaghpatrick, and there spent some time in fasting and prayer. To this historical fact has been added a fabulous relation, which Jocelin in his life of St. Patrick, written in the twelfth century, appears to have been the first to promulgate, but which is now one of Ireland's most celebrated legends; namely, that the saint brought together on the top of the mountain all the serpents and venomous creatures and *demons* of Ireland, and drove them into the sea. There is a deep hollow on the northern face of the mountain, called to this day Lugnademon, the *lug* or hollow of the demons, into which they all retreated on their way to final banishment.

This story, however, is not found in the early authentic lives of the saint; and that it is a comparatively recent invention is evident from the fact, that Ireland's exemption from reptiles is mentioned by Solinus, who wrote in the third century; and Bede mentions the same fact, but without assigning any cause; whereas, if such a remarkable occurrence had been on record, doubtless he would not fail to notice it.

Legends of aquatic monsters are very ancient among the Irish people. We find one mentioned by Adamnan (Lib. II., cap. 27), as infesting Loch Ness,

in Scotland. In the life of St. Mochua of Balla, it
is related that a stag which was wounded in the chase
took refuge in an island in Lough Ree ; but that no
one dared to follow it, "on account of a horrible
monster that infested the lake, and was accustomed
to destroy swimmers." A man was at last prevailed
on to swim across, "but as he was returning, the
beast devoured him." O'Flaherty (Iar Connaught,
c. 19) has a very circumstantial story of an "Irish
crocodil," that lived at the bottom of Lough Mask ;
and in O'Clery's Calendar (p. 145) we read about
the upper lake of Glendalough :—"They say that
the lake drains in its middle, and that a frightful
serpent is seen in it, and that from fear of it no one
ever durst swim in the lake."

This legend assumes various forms in individual
cases, and many are the tales the people can relate of
fearful encounters with a monster covered with long
hair and a mane ; moreover, they are occasionally
met with in old castles, lisses, caves, &c., as well as
in lakes. The word by which they are most commonly designated in modern times, is *piast ;* we find
it in Cormac's Glossary in the old Irish form *béist,*
explained by the Lat. *bestia,* from which it has been
borrowed ; and it is constantly used in the Lives of
the Irish saints, to denote a dragon, serpent, or monster. Several lakes in different parts of the country
are called Loughnapiast, or, more correctly, *Loch-na-
peiste,* each of which is inhabited by a demoniacal
serpent ; and in a river in the parish of Banagher,
Derry, there is a spot called *Lig-na-peiste* (Lig, a
hollow or hole), which is the abode of another.

When St. Patrick was journeying westward, a
number of them attempted to oppose his progress at
a place in the parish of Ardcarn in Roscommon,

which is called to this day Knocknabenat; or, in Irish, *Cnoc-na-bpiast*, the hill of the serpents. In the parish of Drumhome in Donegal, stands a fort which gives name to a townland called Lisnapaste; there is another with a similar name in the townland of Gullane, parish of Kilconly, Kerry, in which the people say a serpent used to be seen; and near Freshford in Kilkenny, is a well called 'Tobernapeastia, from which a townland takes its name.

Sometimes the name indicates directly their supernatural and infernal character; as, for instance, in Pouladown near Watergrasshill in Cork, i. e. *Poll-a'-deamhain*, the demon's hole. There is a pool in the townland of Killarah, parish of Kildallan, Cavan, three miles from Ballyconnell, called Loughandoul, or, in Irish, *Loch-an-diabhail*, the lake of the devil; and Deune Castle, in the parish of Kilconly in Kerry, is the demon's castle, which is the signification of its Irish name, *Caislen-a'-deamhain*.

CHAPTER VI.

CUSTOMS, AMUSEMENTS, OCCUPATIONS.

THE pagan Irish divided their year, in the first instance, into two equal parts, each of which was afterwards subdivided into two parts or quarters. The four quarters were called *Earrach, Samhradh, Foghmhar,* and *Geimhridh* [Arragh, Sowra, Fowar, Gevrĕ]: Spring, Summer, Autumn, and Winter, which are the names still in use; and they began on the first days of February, May, August, and November, respectively. We have historical testimony that games were celebrated at the beginning of Summer, Autumn, and Winter; and it may be reasonably inferred that Spring was also ushered in by some sort of festivity.

The first day of May, which was the beginning of the summer half year, was called *Bealltaine* [Beltany]; it is still the name always used by those speaking Irish; and it is well known in Scotland, where *Beltane* has almost taken its place as an English word:—

> " Ours is no sapling, chance sown by the fountain,
> Blooming at *Beltane* in winter to fade."

Tuathal [Thoohal] the Acceptable, king of Ireland in the first century, instituted the feast of Bealltaine at *Uisneach*, now the hill of Usnagh in Westmeath, where, ever after, the pagan Irish celebrated their festivities, and lighted their Druidic fires on the first of May; and from these fires, according to Cormac's Glossary, the festival derived its name:—
" *Bealltaine*, i.e. *bil-tene*, i.e. *tene-bil*, i.e. the goodly fire (*tene*, fire), i.e. two goodly fires which the Druids were used to make, with great incantations on them, and they used to bring the cattle between them against the diseases of each year."

While Usnagh was regarded as the chief centre of these rites, there were similar observances on the same day in other parts of Ireland; for Keating informs us that "upon this occasion they were used to kindle two fires in every territory in the kingdom, in honour of the pagan god." Down to a very recent period these fires were lighted, and the May-day games celebrated both in Ireland and Scotland; and even at this day, in many remote districts, some relics of the old druidic fire superstitions of May morning still linger among the peasantry.[*]

The May-day festivities must have been formerly celebrated with unusual solemnity, and for a long succession of generations, at all those places now called Beltany, which is merely the anglicised form of *Bealltaine*. There are two of them in Donegal—one near Raphoe, and the other in the parish of Tulloghobegly; there is one also near Clogher in Tyrone, and another in the parish of Cappagh in the same county. In the parish of Kilmore, Armagh, we find Tamnaghvelton, and in Donegal, Meenabaltin, both signifying the field of the Beltane sports; and in Lisbalting, in the parish of Kilcash, Tipperary, the old *lis* where the festivities were carried on is still to be seen. There is a stream joining the river Galey near Athea in Limerick, called Glasheennabaultina, the *glasheen* or streamlet of the May-day games.

One of the Tuatha De Danann kings, Lewy of the long hand, established a fair or gathering of the people, to be held yearly on the 1st day of August, at a place on the Blackwater in Meath, between Navan and Kells; in which various games and pastimes, as well as marriages, were celebrated, and which were continued in a modified form down to the beginning of the present century. This fair was instituted by Lewy in commemoration of his foster-mother Taillte, who was daughter of the king of Spain; and in honour of her he called the place *Taillteun* (*Taillte*, gen. *Taillteun*), which is the present Irish name, but corrupted in English to Teltown.

[*] See Wilde's Irish Popular Superstitions; Petrie's Round Towers; and O'Donovan's Introduction to the Book of Rights.

The place still exhibits the remains of raths and
artificial lakes; and according to tradition, marriages
were celebrated in one particular hollow, which is
still called *Lag-an-acnaigh* [Laganeany, the hollow
of the fair]. Moreover, the Irish-speaking people
all over Ireland still call the first of August *Lugh-
Nasadh* [Loonasa], i. e. Lewy's fair.

The first of November was called *Samhuin* [savin
or sowan], which is commonly explained *samh-fhuin*,
i. e. the end of *samh* or summer; and, like *Bealltaine*,
it was a day devoted by the pagan Irish to religious
and festive ceremonials. Tuathal also instituted the
feast of Samhuin (as well as that of Belltaine—see p.
200); and it was celebrated on that day at *Tlachtga*,
now the Hill of Ward near Athboy in Meath, where
fires were lighted, and games and sports carried on.
It was also on this day that the *Feis* or convention
of Tara was held; and the festivities were kept up
three days before and three days after Samhuin.
These primitive celebrations have descended through
eighteen centuries; and even at the present time, on
the eve of the first of November, the people of this
country practise many observances which are undoubted relics of ancient pagan ceremonials.

While the great festival established by Tuathal
was celebrated at Tlachtga, minor festivities were, as
in case of the Belltaine, observed on the same day in
different places through the country; and in several
of these the name of *Samhuin* has remained as a perpetual memorial of those bygone pastimes. Such a
place is Knocksouna near Kilmallock in Limerick.
The Four Masters, who mention it several times, call
it *Samhuin*—a name exactly analogous to Beltany:
while in the Life of St. Finnchu, in the Book of Lismore, it is called *Cnoc-Samhna*, the hill of *Samhuin*,

which is exactly represented in pronunciation by
Knocksouna. According to this last authority, the
hill was more anciently called *Ard-na-rioghraidhe*
[reery], the hill of the kings; from all which we
may infer that it was anciently a place of great
notoriety. In the parish of Kiltoghert, county Leitrim, there is a place with a name having the same
signification, viz., Knocknasawna; and a hill two
miles from Raphoe in Donegal, is called Mulla-
sawny, the hill-summit of *Samhain.*

It would appear from the preceding names, as well
as from those that follow, that these meetings were
usually held on hills; and this was done no doubt
in imitation of the original festival; for *Tlachtga* or
the hill of Ward, though not high, is very conspicuous over the flat plains of Meath. Drumhawan
near Ballybay in Monaghan, represents the Irish
Druim-Shamhain, the ridge of *Samhain;* and in the
parish of Donaghmoyne in the same county, is another place called Drumhaman, which is the same
name, for it is written Drumhaven in an old map of
1777; in the parish of Kilcronaghan, Londonderry,
we find a place called Drumsamney, and the original
pronunciation is very well preserved in Drumsawna,
in the parish of Magheraculmoney, Fermanagh.
Carrickhawna [*Carrick,* a rock], is found in the
parish of Toomour in Sligo; and Gurteenasowna
(*Gurteen,* a little field), near Dunmanway in Cork.

An assembly of the people, convened for any purpose whatever, was anciently called *aenach* [ēnagh];
and it would appear that these assemblies were often
held at the great regal cemeteries. For, first, the
names of many of the cemeteries begin with the
word *aenach,* as *Aenach-Chruachain, Aenach-Tailltenn,
Aenach-in-Broga,* &c.; and it is said in the "History

of the Cemeteries" (Petrie, R. Towers, p. 106), that
" there are fifty hills [burial mounds] at each *Acnach*
of these." Secondly, the double purpose is shown
very clearly in the accounts of the origin of *Carn-
Amhalgaidh* [Awly] near Killala :—" *Carn-Amhal-
gaidh*, i. e. of Amhalgaidh, son of Fiachra Ealgach,
son of Dathi, son of Fiachra. It was by him that
this carn was formed, for the purpose of holding a
meeting (*acnach*) of the Hy Amhalgaidh around it
every year, and to view his ships and fleets going
and coming, and as a place of interment for himself"
(Book of Lecan, cited in Petrie's R. Towers, p. 107.
See p. 138, *supra*).

In modern times and in the present spoken language, the word *acnach* is always applied to a cattle
fair. It is pretty certain that in some cases the present cattle fairs are the representatives of the ancient
popular assemblies, which have continued uninter-
ruptedly from age to age, gradually changing their
purposes to suit the requirements of each succeeding
generation. This we find in the case of Nenagh in
Tipperary, which is still celebrated for its great fairs.
Its most ancient name was *Acnach-Thete ;* and it
was afterwards called—and is still universally called
by speakers of Irish—*Acnach-Urmhumhan* [Enagh-
Urooan], the assembly or assembly-place of *Ur-
mhumhan* or Ormond, which indicates that it was at
one time the chief meeting-place for the tribes of
east Munster. The present name is formed by the
attraction of the article *'n* to *Acnach*, viz., *nAcnach*,
i. e. the fair, which is exactly represented in pronunciation by Nenagh (see p. 24).

This word forms a part of a great number of
names, and in every case it indicates that a fair was
formerly held in the place, though in most instances

these fairs have been long discontinued, or transferred to other localities. The usual forms in modern names are *-eeny, -eena, -enagh,* and in Cork and Kerry, *-eanig.* Monasteranenagh in Limerick, where the fine ruins of the monastery founded by the king of Thomond in the twelfth century, still remain, is called by the Four Masters, *Mainister-an-aenaigh,* the monastery of the fair. But the fair was held there long before the foundation of the monastery, and down to that time the place was called *Aenach-beag* (Four Mast.), i. e. little fair, probably to distinguish it from the great fair of Nenagh.

The simple word Enagh is the name of about twenty townlands in different counties, extending from Antrim to Cork; but in some cases, especially in Ulster, this word may represent *eanach* a marsh. The Irish name for Enagh, in the parish of Clonlea, county Clare, is *Aenagh-O'bhFloinn* [Enagh-O-Vlin], the fair or fair-green of the O'Flynns.

Ballinenagh is the name of a place near Newcastle in Limerick, and of another in Tipperary, while the form Ballincanig is found in Kerry, and Ballynenagh in Londonderry—all meaning the town of the fair: Ardaneanig (*ard,* a height), is a place near Killarney; and in Cork and Sligo we find Lissaneena and Lissaneeny, the fort of the fair. The plural of *eanach* is *aentaigh;* and this is well represented in pronunciation by Eanty (–beg and –more), in the parish of Kilcorney in Clare.[*]

In the Tripartite Life of St. Patrick, we have an interesting notice of one of the ancient tribe assem-

[*] See Mr. W. M. Hennessy's paper "On the Curragh of Kildare," for much valuable information on the subject of the ancient *aenachs.*

blies. In the saint's progress through Connaught,
he visited the assembly place of the tribe of Amhalgaidh (Awley: brother of Dathi: see p. 138), and
preached to a very great multitude; and on that
occasion ho converted and baptized the seven sons
of Amhalgaidh, and 12,000 persons. This place
was called *Forrach-mac-nAmhalgaidh* [Forragh-mac-
nawley], i. e. the assembly place of Amhalgaidh's
clan; the word *Forrach*, which Tireclian latinizes
Forrgea, signifying the piece of ground on which a
tribe were accustomed to hold their meetings. According to O'Donovan, this name survives, and preserves the identity of this interesting spot. About
a mile and a half south west from Killala, there are
two townlands, adjoining one another, one called
Farragh, which is little changed from the old form
Forrach, as given in the Tripartite Life; and the
other—which is on a hill—called Mullafarry, i. e.
Mullach-Forraigh, the hill of the meeting place.
There is also a hill in the same neighbourhood,
called Knockatinnole, *Cnoc-a'-tionóil*, the hill of the
assembly, which commemorates gatherings of some
kind; but whether in connection with the meetings
at Farragh, or not, it is hard to say, for it lies about
five miles distant to the south east, on the shore of
the Moy.

The word *Forrach* or *Farrach* was employed to
designate meeting places in other parts of Ireland
also; and we may be pretty sure that this was the
origin of such names as Farragh in the parishes of
Denn and Kilmore in Cavan; Farra in the parish
of Drumcree, Armagh; Farrow in Westmeath and
Leitrim; Fury in Wexford; Furrow near Mitchelstown in Cork; Gortnafarra in the vale of Aherlow

in Tipperary, the field of the assembly place; Far-raghroe in Longford, and Forramoyle in Galway, the red, and the bald or bare, meeting place.

Nás [nawce] is a word of similar acceptation to *aenach;* Cormac's Glossary explains it a fair or meet-ing-place. This term is not often used, but there is one place celebrated in former ages, to which it has given name, viz., Naas in Kildare. It was the most ancient residence of the kings of Leinster; having been founded, according to bardic history, by Lewy of the long hand, who also founded *Tuilltenn* in Meath (see p. 201); it continued to be used as a royal residence till the tenth century; and the great mound of the palace still remains, just outside the town. This word is also found in a few other names, all in Leinster; such as Nash in the parish of Owenduff, Wexford, which is still a fair green; and Ballynaas in the parish of Rathmacnee in the same county.

The word *sluagh* [sloo], usually translated host, signifies any multitude, but in the Annals it is com-monly applied to an army; it occurs in the Zeuss MSS., where it glosses *agmen,* i. e. a host on march.

This word forms a part of the names of several places, where great numbers of people must have been formerly in the habit of congregating, for some purpose. One of the best known is Ballinasloe, on the Galway side of the river Suck. Its Irish name as used by the Four Masters, is *Bel-atha-na-sluaigheadh* [Bellanaslooa], the ford-mouth of the hosts; and it is very probable that these gatherings, whatever may have been their original purpose, are represented by the present great horse fairs.

Very often the *n* is replaced by *t,* by eclipse (see page 23). Srahatloe, in the parish of Aghagower,

Mayo, is an instance, the Irish name being *Srath-a'-tsluaigh*, the river-holm of the host. So also Tullin-tloy in Leitrim ; Knockatloe in Clare, and Knocka-tlowig near Castleventry in Cork, all signifying the hill of the host.

Meetings or meeting-places are sometimes desig-nated by the word *pobul*, which signifies people. This is not, as might be supposed from its resem-blance to the English word, of modern introduction ; for it occurs in the most ancient Irish MSS., as for instance in those of Zeuss, where it glosses *populus*. It is ofted used to denote a congregation, and from this it is sometimes employed in the sense of "parish;" but its primary sense seems to be *people* simply, with-out any reference to assemblies.

The barony of Pubblebrien in Limerick, is called in Irish *Pobul-ui-Bhriain* [Pubble-ee-vreen], O'Brien's people, for it was the patrimony of the O'Briens ; and on the confines of Limerick, Cork, and Kerry, is an extensive wild district, well known by the name of Pobble O'Keeffe, O'Keeffe's people.

There is a townland near Enniskillen, containing the remains of an old church, and another near Ard-straw in Tyrone, both called Pubble, i. e. a congre-gation or parish. The word occurs in combination in Reanabobul in the parish of Ballyvourney, Cork, *Reidh-na-bpobul*, the mountain-flat of the congrega-tions; in Lispopple in Dublin and Westmeath (*lis*, a fort) ; and in Skephubble, near Finglas, Dublin, the *skeagh* or bush of the congregation, where prob-ably the young people were formerly accustomed to assemble on a Sunday after Mass, to amuse them-selves round an ancient whitethorn tree.

So far as conclusions may be drawn from the evi-dence of local names, we must believe that the pastime meetings of the peasantry were much more common formerly than now. In every part of the country, names are found that tell of those long forgotten joyous assemblies; and it is interesting to note the various contrivances adopted in their formation.

The word *bouchail* [boohil], a boy, is of frequent occurrence in such names; for example, Knockannamohilly, in the parish of Youghalarra, Tipperary, in Irish *Cnocan-na-mbouchaillidhe*, the hill of the boys, indicates the spot where young men used to assemble for amusement; and with the same signification is Knocknamohill in the parish of Castlemacadam, Wicklow; Knocknabohilly, the name of a place near Cork city, and of another near Kinsale; and Knockanenabohilly, in the parish of Kilcrumper, Cork— the two last names being less correctly anglicised than the others. We find names of similar import in the north: Edenamohill is a townland in the parish of Donaghmore, Donegal; and there is another place of the same name in the parish of Magheraculmoney in Fermanagh, both anglicised from *Eudan-na-mbouchail*, the hill-brow of the boys; and Ardnamoghill (*ard*, a height), is the name of a place in the parish of Killea, Donegal.

Sometimes the same idea is expressed by the word *óg* [oge], which literally signifies young, but is often applied to a young person. Tullyhog, or Tullahogue, near Stewartstown in Tyrone, where the O'Hagans resided, and where they inaugurated the chiefs of the O'Neills, is very often mentioned in the Annals, always by the name of *Tulach-óg* or *Tealach-óg*, the hill of the youths; and the name indicates that the place was used for the celebration of games, as well as for the inauguration of the chieftains. The fine old fort

15

on which the ceremonies took place in long past ages,
still remains on the top of the *tulach* or hill; and
from time immemorial up to fifty or sixty years ago,
a yearly gathering of young people was held on it,
the representative of the ancient assemblies. In
Tipperary we find Glennanoge and Ballnghoge, the
glen and the road of the youths. The synonymous
term *oglach* occurs in Coolnanoglagh, in the parish of
Monagay, Limerick, the hill-back of the young persons; while in the parish of Grange, Armagh, we
find Ballygassoon, the town of the *gossoons* (young
boys), or in the Munster dialect, *gorsoons*.

Others terms are employed to designate the places
of these meetings, which will be understood from a
few examples. There can be little doubt that Bally-
sugagh near Saul in Down, has its name from some
such merry-makings; for its name, *Baile-sugach*,
merry-town, indicates as much. Knockaunavogga, in
the parish of Bourney, Tipperary, shows a similar
origin, as is seen by its Irish name, *Cnocan-a'-
mhagaidh*, the hill of the joking or pleasantry; and
this termination is found in many other names, such
as Ardavagga (*ard*, a height), in the parish of Kil-
murry-ely, King's County; and Cashlaunawogga,
the castle of the merriment, a ruined fortress near
Kilfenora in Clare. So also Knockannavlyman, in the
parish of Ballingarry, Limerick, *Cnocan-a'-bhladh-
mainn*, the hill of the boasting; Ardingary near Letterkenny, which the Four Masters call *Ard-an-ghaire*,
the hill of the shouting or laughter; Knocknaclogha
near Pomeroy in Tyrone, the seat of Macdonnell,
the commander of O'Neill's galloglasses, *Cnoc-an-
chluiche* (Four Masters), the hill of the game.

Not unfrequently the same idea is expressed by
the word *diomhaoin* [deeveen], which signifies idle

or vain—a term imposed, we may be sure, by wise old people, who looked upon these pastime meetings as mere idleness and vanity. We see this in such names as Drumdeevin, near Kilmacrenan in Donegal, and Dromdeeveen, west of Dromcolliher in Limerick, both signifying idle ridge ; Coomdeeween in Kerry (*coom*, a hollow) ; Tievedeevan in Donegal, idle hill-side (*taebh*).

By an examination of local names, we are enabled not only to point out the spots where the peasant assemblies were held, but also often to get a glimpse of the nature of the amusements. Dancing has from time immemorial been a favourite recreation with our peasantry ; and numbers of places have taken their names from the circumstance that the young people of the neighbourhood were accustomed to meet there in the summer evenings, to forget in the dance the fatigue of the day's labour.

The word for dance is *rince* or *rinceadh* [rinka] ; and it is curious that, of all the Indo-European languages, the Irish and Sanscrit have alone preserved the word, and that with little change, the Sansc. *rinkha* being almost identical with the Irish.

Those who have visited the great cave near Mitchelstown, county Cork, will remember the name of the townland in which it is situated—Skeheenarinky, or in Irish *Sceithin-a'-rinceadh*, the little bush of the dancing ; the bush no doubt marking the trysting-place, under which sat the musician, surrounded by the merry juveniles. A large stone (*cloch*) must have served a similar purpose in Clogharinka in the parish of Muckalee, Kilkenny ; and we have Clasharinka, the trench or hollow of the dance, near Castlemartyr in Cork. A mill is generally a place of

15 *

amusement ; and that it was sometimes selected for dance meetings, we see by Mullenaranky, the mill of the dance, in the parish of Lisronagh in Tipperary. A merry place must have been Ballinrink in the parish of Killeagh, Meath, since it deserved the name of *dancing town;* and this was the original name of Ringstown in the parish of Faughalstown in Westmeath.

When deer roamed wild through every forest, when wild boars and wolves lurked in the glens and mountain gorges, and various other beasts of chase swarmed on the hills and plains, hunting must have been to the people both an amusement and a necessary occupation. Our forefathers, like most ancient people, were passionately fond of the chase ; and our old tales and romances abound in descriptions of its pleasures and dangers, and of the prowess and adventures of the hunters. That they sometimes had certain favourite spots for this kind of sport, we have sufficient proof in such names as Drumnashaloge in the parish of Clonfeacle, Tyrone ; and Drumashellig near Ballyroan in Queen's County, in Irish *Druim-na-scalg,* the ridge of the chase. The word *scalg,* [shallog], hunting occurs in many other names, and as it varies little in form, it is always easy to recognise it. Derrynashallog (*Derry,* an oak wood) is in the parish of Donagh in Monaghan ; and Ballynashallog, the town of the hunting, lies near the city of Londonderry.

The very spot where the huntsman wound his horn to collect his dogs and companions, is often identified by such names as Tullynahearka near Aughrim in Roscommon, *Tulaigh-na-hadhairce,* the hill of the horn ; Killeenerk in Westmeath (*Killeen,* a little wood), and Drumnaheark in Donegal (*Drum*, a ridge); Knockerk near Slane in Meath, and Lismahirka in Roscommon, the hill and the fort of the horn.

Another favourite athletic exercise among the ancient Irish, and which we find very often mentioned in old tales, was hurling; and those who remember the eagerness with which it was practised in many parts of Ireland twenty-five years ago, can well attest that it had not declined in popularity. Down to a very recent period, it was carried on with great spirit and vigour in the Phœnix Park, Dublin, where the men of Meath contended every year against the men of Kildare; and it still continues, though less generally than formerly, to be a favourite pastime among the people.

The hurley or curved stick with which the ball was struck, corresponding with the bat in cricket, is called in Irish *coman*, signifying literally a little crooked stick, from *com* or *cam*, curved. It is by this word that the game itself is commonly designated; and it is called *coman* in most parts of Ireland, even by the English-speaking people. It forms a part of several names, but the initial *c* is commonly made *g* by eclipse (see p. 22); and in every case it serves to identify the places where the game was played. Aughnagomaun, in the parish of Ballysheehan, Tipperary, is written in Irish *Achadh-na-gcoman*, the hurling-field; there is a townland near Belfast called Ballygammon, which, as it is written *Ballygoman* in a grant of James I., obviously represents *Baile-na-gcoman*, the town of the hurling; and we have Gortgommon in Fermanagh, and Lisnagommon in Queen's County, the field and the fort, of the *comans*.

Look-out points, whether on the coast to com-

mand the sea, or on the borders of a hostile territory
to guard against surprise, or in the midst of a pastoral
country to watch the flocks, are usually designated
by the word *coimhead* [covade]. This word signifies
watching or guarding, and it is generally applied
to hills from which there is an extensive prospect.
Mullycovet and Mullykivet in Fermanagh must
have been used for this purpose, for they are both
modern forms of *Mullaigh-coimheada*, the hill of the
watching; and Glencovet the name of a townland
in Donegal, and of another near Enniskillen, and
Drumcovet in Derry, have a similar origin. Sometimes the *m* is fully pronounced, and this is generally
the case in the south, and occasionally in the north;
as in Cloontycommade near Kanturk in Cork, *Cluain-
lighe-coimheada*, the meadow of the watching house;
and Slieve Commedagh, a high mountain near Slieve
Donard in Down, the mountain of the watching.

The compound *Deagh-choimhead* [Deacovade] signifies "a good reconnoitering station" (*deagh*, good);
and it gives name to Dechommed or Decomet in
Down, Deechomade in Sligo, Dehomad in Clare,
and a few other places.

In old Irish writings these reconnoitering stations
are often mentioned. For instance, in the ancient
tale of the Battle of Moyrath, Congal Claen speaks
to the druid, Dubhdiadh :—"'Thou art to go therefore from me, to view and reconnoitre the men of
Erin [i. e. the Irish army under King Domhnall];
and it shall be according to thy account and description of the chiefs of the west, that I will array my
battalions, and arrange my forces.' Then Dubhdiadh went to *Ard-na-hiomfhaireese* [Ard-na-himark-
ehn, i. e. the hill of the reconnoitering], and from it
he took his view" (Battle of Moyrath, p. 179).

Elevated stations that command an extensive view often received names formed from the word *radharc* [ryark in the south; rayark or rawark in the north]. The Mullaghareirk mountains lie to the south east of Abbeyfeale in Limerick, and the name *Mullach-a-radharc* signifies the summit of the prospect. The same word is found in Lisrearke, in the parish of Currin, Monaghan (*Lis*, a fort); and in Knockan-aryark, two miles east of Kenmare, prospect hill. There is a residence near Dalkey in Dublin, with the name Rarkanillin, which represents the Irish *Radharc-an-oilcain*, the view of the Island, i.e. Dalkey Island.

In an early stage of society in every country, signal or beacon fires were in common use, either for the guidance of travellers or to alarm the country in any sudden emergency. Fires were lighted also on certain festival days, as I have stated (p. 200); and those lighted on the eve of St. John, the 24th of June, are continued to the present day through the greater part of Ireland. The tradition is, that the May-day festival was transferred by St. Patrick to the 24th of June, in honour of St. John, but for this we have no written authority. The spots where signal or festival fires used to be lighted, are still, in many cases, indicated by the names, though in almost all these places the custom has, for ages, fallen into disuse. The words employed are usually *teine* and *solas* [tinnĕ, sullas].

Teine is the general word for fire, and in modern names it is usually found forming the termination *tinny*. It is found in Kiltinny near Coleraine, the wood of the fire; Duntinny in Donegal (*dun*, a fort); Mullaghtinny near Clogher in Tyrone, the summit of the fire. Tennyphobble near Granard in Long-

ford, *Teine-phobail*, the fire of the parish or congregation, plainly indicates some festive assembly round a
fire. Cloghaunnatinny, in the parish of Kilmurry,
Clare, was anciently, and is still called in Irish,
Clochàn-bile-teine, the stepping stones of the fire tree,
from a large tree which grew near the crossing, under
which May fires used to be lighted. These fires were
no doubt often lighted under trees, for the Four
Masters mention a place called *Bile-teineadh* [Billa-
tinnĕ], the old tree of the fire; which O'Donovan
identifies with the place near Moynalty in Meath,
now called in Irish, *Coill-a'-bhile*, the wood of the
bile, or old tree, and in English, Billywood. And
in the parish of Ardnurcher, Westmeath, there is a
place now called Creeve, but anciently *Craebh-teine*
[Creeve-tinnĕ: Four Mast.] the branchy tree of the
fire.

The plural of *teine* is *teinte* [tintĕ], and this is also
of frequent occurrence in names, as in Clontinty near
Glanworth, Cork, the meadow of the fires; Molly-
nadinta, in the parish of Rossinver, Leitrim; *Mullaigh-
na-dteinte*, the summit of the fires. This word, with
the English plural added (p. 32), gives names to
Teuts (i. e. fires), three townlands in Cavan, Fermanagh, and Leitrim; and the English is substituted
for the Irish plural in Tinnies in Valentia island.
The diminutive is found in Clontinteen in Westmeath, and in Tullantintin in Cavan, the meadow
and the hill of the little fire.

Solus is the word in general use for light in the
present spoken language; there is another form,
soillse, which is sometimes used in modern Irish, and
which is also found in the Zeuss MSS., where it
glosses *lumen* (Zeuss, gram. Celt., p. 257); and its
diminutive *soillsean* (silcshaun) is often found in local

names. *Solus* gives name to Ardsollus, the hill of light, in Clare; in Antrim there is a place called Drumnasole, the ridge of the lights; Sollus itself is the name of a townland in Tyrone; while we find Rossolus in Monaghan, and Rostollus in Galway (s eclipsed by *t*; see p. 23), the wood or the promontory of light.

There are similar names formed from *soillsean*; as for instance, Mullaghsclsana in the parish of Errigal Trough, Monaghan, the hill of the illuminations; and Corhelshinagh in the same county, the round hill of the fires. Sileshaun, the name of a place in the parish of Inagh, Clare, exactly represents the pronunciation of the word; and this same name is shortened to Selshan on the eastern shore of Lough Neagh, north of Lurgan.

In former days, when roads were few, and bridges still fewer, a long journey was an undertaking always arduous, and generally uncertain and dangerous. Rivers were crossed by fords, and to be able to strike exactly on the fordable point, was to the traveller always important; while at night, especially on a dark, wet, and stormy night, it became not unfrequently a matter of life or death. To keep a light of some kind burning on the spot would suggest itself as the most natural and effectual plan for directing travellers; and except in a state of society downright barbarous, it is scarcely conceivable that some such expedient would not at least occasionally be adopted.

The particular kind of light employed, it would now probably be vain to speculate; a taper or splinter of bogwood in a window pane, if a house lay near, a lantern hung on the bough of a tree, a blaze of dried furze or ferns kept up till the expected arrival

—some or all of these we may suppose would be adopted, according to circumstances. That this custom existed appears very probable from this fact, that many fords—now generally spanned by bridges—in different parts of Ireland, still go by the name of *Ath-solais*, the ford of the light, variously modernized according to locality; and some of them have given names to townlands. At the same time, it must be observed, that the brightness of the water may have originated some of the names quoted below; for we find the word *solus* sometimes applied to water in this sense. Thus in a poem in the Book of Lecan, a certain district is designated "*Fir-tire na sreb solus*," " Fir-Tire of the bright streams " (IIy F. 24); and near the lake of Coumshingane in the Comeragh Mountains in Waterford, a stream flows down a ravine, which, after a heavy shower, is a brilliant foaming torrent that can be seen several miles off; and this is called *An tuisge solais*, the water of light, or bright water.

A ford on the river Aubeg, three miles east of Kanturk in Cork, has given name to the townland of Assolas; there is a ford of the same name, where the road from Bunlahy in Longford, to Scrabby, crosses a little creek of Lough Gowna; another on the Glennanair river near Doneraile, on the confines of Limerick and Cork; and Athsollis bridge crosses the Buingea river, just beside the railway, four miles south east from Macroom. Several small streams in different parts of the country have names of this kind, from a ford somewhere on their course—one for instance, called Aughsullish, in the parish of Doon, Tipperary. The name of Lightford bridge, two miles south east from Castlebar, is a translation from the Irish name which is still used, *Ath-a'-solais*;

and Ballynasollus in Tyrone should have been made
Bellnnasollus, for its Irish name is *Bel-atha-na-solus*,
the ford mouth of the lights. Ballysoilshaun bridge
spans the Nenagh river four miles south east from
Nenagh; its Irish name is *Bel-atha-soillsedin*, which
was originally the name of the ford before the bridge
was built, and which has the same meaning as the
last name. There is a ford on the river Swilly, two
miles west of Letterkenny, which, judging from its
position and its being defended by a castle, as well
as from its frequent mention in the Annals, must
have been in former days one of the principal passes
across the river; and as such was no doubt often sig-
nalled by lights. The Four Masters write the name
Scairbh-sholais, the *scariff* or shallow ford of the light;
it is now called Scarriffhollis, and the castle, which
has disappeared, was called Castlehollis.

Places of execution have been at all times, and in
all countries, regarded by the people with feelings
of awe and detestation; and even after the discon-
tinuance of the practice, the traditions of the place
preserve the memory of it from one generation to
another. A name indicative of the custom is almost
certain to fix itself on the spot, of which we have
instances in the usual English names Gallows-hill,
Gallows-green, &c.; and such names, from the peculiarity of their history, retain their hold, when many
others of less impressive signification, vanish from the
face of the country.

Several terms are used in Ireland to denote such
places, the principal of which are the following :—
croch signifies literally a cross, but is almost always
understood to mean a cross as an instrument of execution, or a gallows. It is of long standing in the
language, and is either cognate with or borrowed

from the Latin *crux*, which it glosses in the Zeuss
MSS. We find it in Knocknacrohy, the name of
three townlands in Limerick, Kerry, and Waterford,
in Irish *Cnoc-na-croiche*, the hill of the gallows; and
in Ardnacrohy in Limerick, with the same meaning.
The instrument of death must have been erected in
an ancient fort, in Ranacrohy in Tipperary. The
word often takes the forms of *crehy* and *creha* in
modern names, as in Cappanacreha (*Cappa*, a plot of
ground), in Galway; and Raheenacrehy near Trim
in Meath, the little fort of the gallows.

Crochaire [crohera] signifies a hangman; and it is
in still more frequent use in the formation of names
than *croch*, usually in the forms *croghery* and *croghera*.
Knockaroghery, the hangman's hill, is a village in
Roscommon, where there is a station on the Midland
Railway; and there are places of the same name in
Cork and Mayo. Mullaghcroghery, with a similar
meaning, occurs three times in Monaghan; and in
Cork, Glenacroghery and Ardnagroghery, *Ard-na-
gcrochaire* (p. 22), the hill of the hangmen.

Scalan [shallan] signifies the rope used by an exe-
cutioner; and it is sometimes used to designate the
place where people were hanged. It gives name to
Shallon, a townland near Finglas in Dublin; there
is another place of the same name near Swords, and
a third near Julianstown in Meath. Shallany in
the parish of Derryvullen, Fermanagh, is the same
name slightly altered; and Drumshallon in Louth
and Armagh, signifies the ridge of the gallows.

There is another mode of designating places of
execution, from which it appears that criminals were
often put to death by decapitation; an inference
which is corroborated by various passages in Irish
authorities. Names of this kind are formed on the

Irish word *ceann*, a head, which is placed in the end of words in the genitive plural, generally taking the forms *nagin*, *nagan*, &c.

There is a place called Knocknagin near Balrothery in Dublin, where quantities of human remains were found some years ago, and this is also the name of a townland in the parish of Desertmartin, Derry : Irish form *Cnoc-na-gceann*, the hill of the heads. The termination is modified in accordance with the Munster pronunciation in Knocknagown in Cork, and in Knockaunnagown in Waterford, both having the same meaning. Loughnagin occurs in Donegal, and Gortinagin, the little field of the heads, in the parish of Cappagh, Tyrone.

In a state of society when war was regarded as the most noble of all professions, and before the invention of gunpowder, those who manufactured swords and spears were naturally looked upon as very important personages. In Ireland they were held in great estimation ; and in the historical and legendary tales, we find the smith was often a powerful chieftain, who made arms for himself and his relations. We know that Vulcan was one of the most powerful of the Grecian gods, and the ancient Irish had their Goban, the Tuath De Danann smith-god, who figures in many of the ancient romances.

The land possessed by smiths, or the places where they resided, may in many cases be determined by the local names. *Gobha* [gow] is a smith, old Irish form *goba* ; old Welsh *gob*, now *gof* ; Cornish and Breton *góf*. The usual genitive form is *gobhan* [gown], but it is often the same as the nominative ; and both forms are reproduced in names, the former being commonly made *gowan* or *gown*, and the latter *gow*. Both terminations are very common, and may be generally translated "of the smith," or if it be *nagowan*, " of the smiths."

Ballygowan, Ballygow, and Ballingowan, the town of the smith, are the names of numerous places through the four provinces; and there are several townlands in Ulster and Munster called Ballynagowan, the town of the smiths. Occasionally the Irish genitive plural is made *goibhne*, which in the west of Ireland is anglicised *guirnia*, *girna*, &c.; as in Carrownaguivna and Ardgivna in Sligo, the quarter-land, and the height, of the smiths.

Sometimes the genitive singular is made *goe* or *go* in English; as we find in Athgoo near Newcastle in Dublin, the smith's ford; Kinego in Tyrone and Donegal, the smith's head or hill (*ceann*); Ednego near Dromore in Down, the hill brow (*cudan*) of the smith. It takes a different form in Clongowes in Kildare, the smith's meadow, where there is now a Roman Catholic college—the same name as Cloongown in Cork.

Ceard signifies an artificer of any kind; it occurs in the Zeuss MSS. in the form of *cerd* or *cert*, and glosses *aerarius*. In Scotland, it has held its place as a living word, even among speakers of English, but it is applied to a tinker:—

> " Her charms had struck a sturdy caird,
>   As weel as poor gut scraper."   BURNS.

Aerarius, which according to the glossographer of a thousand years ago, is equivalent to *cerd*, signifies literally a worker in brass; and curiously enough, this corresponds exactly with the description the *caird* gives of himself in Burns's poem:—

> " My bonnie lass,
>   I work in brass,
>   A tinker is my station."

This word usually enters into names with the *c* eclipsed (p. 22), forming the termination *nagarde* or *nagard*, "of the artificers." Thus there are several places in Antrim, Derry, Limerick, and Clare, called Ballynagarde, in Irish *Baile-na-gceard*, the town of the artificers : the same name is corrupted to Bally-nacaird in the parish of Racavan in Antrim, and to Ballynacard in King's County. Castlegarde and Gortnagarde in Limerick, the castle, and the field, of the artificers.

Cearda or *ceardcha* denotes a workshop of any kind, but it is now generally applied to a forge : old Irish *cerddchae*, officina (Zeuss). It enters very often into names as a termination, under several forms, indicating the spots where forges formerly stood. It is very often contracted to *cart*, as in Coolnacart in Monaghan, which would be correctly written in Irish *Cul-na-ceardcha*, the hill-back of the forge. A final *n* is often added, in accordance with the fifth declension ; as in Coolnacartan in Queen's County, the same name as the last ; Ballycarton in Derry ; Mullaghcarton in Antrim (*mullach*, a summit) ; Shronacarton and Rathnacarton in Cork, the nose or point, and the fort, of the forge. Other forms are exhibited in Farranacardy in Sligo, forge land ; and Tully-nagardy near Newtownards in Down, *Tulaigh-na-gceardcha*, the hill of the forges.

Saer, a builder or carpenter, appears in modern names generally in the form *seer* ; as in Rathnaseer in Limerick, the fort of the carpenters ; Derrynascer (Derry, an oakwood), the name of several townlands in Leitrim and the Ulster counties ; Farranseer in Cavan and Londonderry, carpenter's land. Sometimes the *s* becomes *t* by eclipse (page 23) ; as in Ballinteer, the name of a place near Dundrum in

Dublin, and of another place in Londonderry, in Irish *Baile-an-tsaeir*, the town of the carpenter or builder.

The ancient Keltic nations navigated their seas and lakes in the *currach* or hide-covered wicker boat; and it is very probable that it was in fleets of these the Irish made their frequent descents on the coasts of Britain and Gaul. Canoes hollowed out of a single tree were also in extensive use in Ireland, especially on the rivers and lakes, and they are now frequently found buried in lakes and dried-up lake beds.

Cobhlach [cowlagh] means a fleet; but the term was applied to a collection of boats, such as were fitted out for lake or river navigation, as well as to a fleet of ships. In Munster the word is pronounced as if written *cobhallach* [cōltagh], and it is preserved according to this pronunciation in the names of several places, the best known of which is Carrigaholt, a village in Clare, at the mouth of the Shannon. The Four Masters write it *Carraig-an-chobhlaigh* [Carrigahowly], the rock of the fleet; and the rock from which it took its name rises over the bay where the fleets anchored, and is crowned by the ruins of a castle. The present Irish pronunciation is *Carraig-a'-chobhallaigh* (Carrigahōlty), which by the omission of the final syllable, settled into the modern name. Another place of the same name, also well known, and which preserves the correct Irish pronunciation, is Carrigahowly on Newport bay in Mayo, the castle of the celebrated Grace O'Malley, the Connaught chieftainess, who paid a visit to Queen Elizabeth. The word, with its Munster pronunciation, appears in Ringacoltig in Cork harbour, opposite Hawlbowline island, the *rinn* or point of the fleet.

Most of the various terms employed to designate

ships and boats, also find their way into local names. According to the Book of Lecan and other authorities, Ceasair and her people (see p. 160) landed at a place called *Dun-na-mbarc*, the fortress of the barks or ships, which O'Donovan (Four Mast., vol. i., p. 3) believes is the place now called Dunnamark, near Bantry. And this word *barc* is not, as might be thought, a loan word from English, for it is used in our oldest MSS. (as in L. na hUidhre: see Kilk. Arch. Jour. 1870, p. 100). *Long* signifies a ship. According to Cormac's Glossary, it is derived from the Saxon word *lang*, long; it appears more likely, however, that both the Saxon and Irish words are cognate with the Lat. *longus*, for we find the Irish word in the Zeuss MSS. (*forlongis - narigatione*). It occurs occasionally in local names, as in Tralong near Ross Carbery in Cork, the strand of the ships; Dunnalong on the Foyle, five miles south of Derry, the name of which is Irish as it stands, and signifies the fortress of the ships; Annalong on the coast of the county Down, *Ath-na-long*, the ford of the ships, a name which shows that the little creek at the village was taken advantage of to shelter vessels, in ancient as well as in modern times.

Many places take their names from *bád*, a boat; several of which spots, we may be pretty certain, were ferries, in which a boat was always kept, little or nothing different from the ferries of the present day. Such a place was Rinawade on the Liffey, near Celbridge, above Dublin—*Rinn-a'-bháid*, the point of the boat; and Donabate near Malahide, the church (*domhnach*) of the boat.

"The Irish made use of another kind of boat in their rivers and lakes, formed out of an oak wrought hollow (i. e. one oak), which is yet used in some

16

places, and called in Irish *coiti*, English *cott*" (Harris's Ware, p. 179). The correct Irish word is *cot*, of which *coiti* or *coite* is the genitive, and it is still in constant use for a small boat or canoe. From it is derived the name of Annacotty, now a small village on the river Mulkear, east of Limerick, called in Irish *Ath-na-coite*, the ford of the *cot* or small boat : as well as that of Ayleacotty in Clare, the cliff of the boat : the name of Carrickacottia on the shore of the river Erne, a mile below Belleck, indicates that the *cot* for the conveyance of passengers across, used to be moored to the *carrick* or rock. A diminutive form appears in the name of a well-known lake near Killarney, Lough Guitane, which the people pronounce *Loch-coiteáin*, the lake of the little *cot* ; a name exactly the same as Loughacutteen in the parish of Whitechurch near Caher in Tipperary, only that a different diminutive is used.

CHAPTER VII.

AGRICULTURE AND PASTURAGE.

THE inhabitants of this country were, from the earliest antiquity, engaged in agriculture and pasturage. In our oldest records we find constant mention of these two occupations ; and the clearing of plains is recorded as an event worthy of special notice, in the reigns of many of the early kings.

It has been remarked by several writers, and it is still a matter of common observation, that many places, especially hill sides, now waste and wild, show plain traces of former cultivation. Boate (Nat. Hist. Chap. X., Sect. iii.), writes:—"It hath been observed in many parts of Ireland, chiefly in the county of Meath, and further northward, that upon the top of great hills and mountains, not only at the side and foot of them, to this day the ground is uneven, as if it had been plowed in former times. The inhabitants do affirm, that their forefathers being much given to tillage, contrary to what they are now, used to turn all to plowland." The Archbishop of Dublin, in a letter inserted in the same book says: · "For certain Ireland has been better inhabited than it is at present: mountains that now are covered with boggs, have formerly been plowed; for when you dig five or six feet deep, you discover a proper soil for vegetables, and find it plowed into ridges and furrows." And Smith (Hist. of Cork, I., 198), speaking of the mountains round the source of the river Lee, tells us:—"Many of the mountains have formerly been tilled, for when the heath that covers them is pulled up and burned, the ridges and furrows of the plough are visible."

These facts tend to confirm the opening statement of this chapter, that the Irish have from all time lived partly by tillage. Many have come to the same conclusion as the Archbishop of Dublin, that "Ireland has been better inhabited than it is at present" (about 1645). But I think Boate gives the true solution in the continuation of the passage quoted above:—"Others say that it was done for want of arable, because the champain was most everywhere beset and overspread with woods, which by degrees are destroyed by the wars."

There are several terms entering into local names, which either indicate directly, or imply, agricultural

operations, the enclosure of the land by fences, or its
employment as pasture; and to the illustration of
those that occur most frequently I will devote the
present chapter.

Ceapach [cappagh] signifies a plot of land laid out
for tillage; it is still a living word in Connaught,
and is in common use in the formation of names, but
it does not occur in Ulster so frequently as in the
other provinces. Cappagh and Cappa are the most
usual anglicised forms; and these, either alone or in
combination, give names to numerous places. It has
been often asserted, and seems generally believed,
that Cappoquin (county Waterford) means "The
head of the house of Conn;" but this is a mere guess:
the name is a plain Irish compound, *Ceapach-Chuinn*,
signifying merely Conn's plot of land, but no one can
tell who this Conn was.

Cappaghwhite in Tipperary, is called after the
family of White; Cappaghcreen near Dunboyne in
Meath, withered plot; Cappanageeragh near Geashill
in King's County, the plot of the sheep; Cappatee-
more in Clare, near Limerick city, is in Irish
Ceapach-a'-tighe-mhoir, the plot of the great house;
Cappanalarabaun in Galway, the plot of the white
mare; Cappaghmore and Cappamore, great tillage
plot. The word is sometimes made Cappy, which is
the name of a townland in Fermanagh; Cappy-
donnell in King's County, Donnell's plot; and the
diminutive Cappog or Cappoge (little plot), is the
name of several places in Ulster, Leinster, and
Munster.

Garrdha [gara], a garden; usually made *garry* or
garra in modern names. About half a mile from
Banagher in King's County, are situated the ruins of
Garry Castle, once the residence of the Mac Coghlans,

the chiefs of the surrounding territory. This castle
is called in the Annals, *Garrdha-an-chaislein* [Garran-
cashlane], i. e. the garden of the castle; and from this
the modern name Garrycastle has been formed, and
has been extended to the barony. The literal meaning of the old designation is exactly preserved in the
name of the modern residence, Castle-Garden, situated near the ruins.

Garry, i. e. the garden, is the name of a place near
Ballymoney in Antrim; and the parish of Myross,
west of Glandore in Cork, is called the Garry, from
its fertility compared with the surrounding district.
The well-known Garryowen, near Limerick, signifies
Owen's garden; Garrysallagh in Cavan and other
counties, dirty garden, and sometimes, willow garden;
Garryvicleheen near Thurles in Tipperary, Mac
Leheen's garden; Ballingarry, the town of the garden, is the name of a town on the borders of Limerick
and Tipperary, and of fourteen townlands. The word
Garry begins the names of about ninety townlands
scattered over the four provinces.

Gort, a tilled field: in the Zeuss MSS. it occurs
in the form *gart*, and glosses *hortus*, and Colgan
translates it *prædium*. It is obviously cognate with
Fr. *jardin*, Sax. *geard*, Eng. *garden*, Lat. *hortus*. It
is a very prolific root word, for there are more than
1200 townlands whose names are formed by, or begin
with Gort and Gurt, its usual modern forms. Gort-
naglogh, or as it would be written in Irish, *Gort-
na-gcloch*, the field of the stones, is the name of a
dozen townlands, some of them in each of the four
provinces; Gortmillish in Antrim, sweet field, so
called probably from the abundance of honeysuckle;
Gortaganniff near Adare in Limerick, the field of the
sand; Gortanure and Gortinure, in several counties,

the field of the yew. The town of Gort in Galway, is called by the Four Masters *Gort-innsi-Guaire*, and this is also its present Irish name; it signifies the field of the island of Guary, and it is believed that it took its name from Guairĕ Aidhne, king of Connaught in the seventh century (see p. 103).

Gorteen, Gortin, and Gurteen (little field), three different forms of the diminutive, are exceedingly common, and are themselves the names of about 100 townlands and villages. The ancient form *gart* is preserved in the diminutive Gartan, the name of a parish in Donegal, well-known as the birth place of Saint Columba; which is written *Gortan* in some ancient Irish authorities, and *Gartan* in others.

Tamhnach [tawnagh] signifies a green field which produces fresh sweet grass. This word enters very generally into names in Ulster and Connaught, especially in the mountainous districts: it is found occasionally, though seldom, in Leinster, and still more seldom in Munster. In modern names it usually appears as Tawnagh, Tawny, and Tonagh, which are themselves the names of several places; in the north of Ulster the aspirated *m* is often restored (see p. 44), and the word then becomes Tamnagh and Tamny. In composition it takes all the preceding forms, as well as Tawna and Tamna.

Saintfield in Down is a good example of the use of this word. Its old name, which was used to a comparatively late period, and which is still well known, was Tonaghneeve, the phonetic representative of *Tamhnach-naemh*, the field of saints. There is a townland near the town which still retains the name of Tonaghmore, great field; originally so called to distinguish it from Tonaghneeve.

The forms *Tawnagh* and *Tawna* are found in Taw-

naghlahan near Donegal, broad field ; Tawnagha-
knaff in the parish of Bohola, Mayo, the fields of the
bones (*cnamh*, a bone), which probably points out the
site of a battle ; Tawnakeel near Crossmolina, narrow
field. Tawny appears in Tawnyeely near Mohill in
Leitrim, the field of the lime (*Tamhnach-aelaigh*) ;
and Tawnybrack in Antrim, speckled field. Tamnagh and its modifications give names to Tamnagh-
bane in Armagh, white field ; Tamnaficarbet and
Tamnafiglassan, both in Armagh—the first *Tamh-
nach-feadha-carbait*, the field of the wood of the chariot, and the second the field of Glassan's wood ;
Tamnymartin near Maghera in Derry, Martin's
field.

Rathdowney, the name of a village and parish in
Queen's County, signifies as it stands, the fort of the
church (*domhnach*) ; but the correct name would be
Rathlowney, representing the Irish *Rath-lamhnaigh*,
as the Four Masters write it—the fort of the green
field. This was the old pagan name, which the
people corrupted (by merely changing *t* to *d*) under
the idea that *domhnach* was the proper word, and that
the name was derived from the church, which was
built on the original rath.

There is a form *Tavnagh*, used in some of the
Ulster counties, especially in Antrim and Monaghan;
such as Tavnaghdrissagh in Antrim, the field of the
briers; Tavanaskea in Monaghan, the field of the
bushes. In composition the *t* is sometimes aspirated,
as in Corhawnagh and Corhawny, the rough field,
or the round hill of the field, the names of several
places in Cavan and the Connaught counties.

Achadh [aha], a field : translated *campulus* by
Adamnan. It is generally represented in modern
names by *agha*, *agh*, or *augh* ; but in individual cases

the investigator must be careful, for these three
words often stand for *ath*, a ford.

The parish of Agha in Carlow, takes its name from
a very old church ruin, once an important religious
foundation, which the Four Masters call *Achadh-ar-
ghlais*, the field of the green tillage. Aghinver on
Lough Erne in Fermanagh, is called in the Annals
Achadh-inbhir, the field of the *inver*, or river mouth.
Aghmacart in Queen's County, is in Irish *Achadh-
mic-Airt*, the field of Art's son; Aghindarragh in
Tyrone, the field of the oak; Aghawoney near Kilmacrenan in Donegal, written by the Four Masters
Achadh-mhona, bogfield. Achonry in Sligo is called
in the Annals, *Achadh-Chonaire* [Ahaconnary],
Conary's field. Ardagh is the name of numerous
villages, townlands, and parishes through the four
provinces; several of these are often mentioned in
the Annals, the Irish form being always *Ard-achadh*,
high field. In a few cases the modern form is
Ardaghy.

Cluain [cloon] is often translated *pratum* by Latin
writers, and for want of a better term it is usually
rendered in English by "lawn" or "meadow." Its
exact meaning, however, is a fertile piece of land, or
a green arable spot, surrounded or nearly surrounded by bog or marsh on one side, and water on
the other.

The word forms a part of a vast number of names
in all parts of Ireland; many of the religious establishments derived their names from it; and this has
led some writers into the erroneous belief that the
word originally meant a place of religious retirement.
But it is certain that in its primitive signification it
had no reference to religion; and its frequent occurrence in our ecclesiastical names is sufficiently ex-

plained by the well-known custom of the early Irish
saints, to select lonely and retired places for their
own habitations, as well as for their religious establishments.

The names of many of the religious *cloons* are in
fact of pagan origin, and existed before the ecclesiastical foundations, having been adopted without
change by the founders :—among these may be
reckoned the following.   Clones (pronounced in two
syllables) in Monaghan, where a round tower remains to attest its former religious celebrity ; its
name is written in the Annals *Cluain-Eois*, [Cloo-
noce] Eos's meadow ; and it is not improbable that
Eos was the pagan chief who raised the great fort,
the existence of which proves it to have been a place
of importance before the Christian settlement.

Clonard in Meath, where the celebrated St. Finian
had his great school in the sixth century, is called
in all the Irish authorities, *Cluain-Eraird*, from which
the present name has been contracted.   Many have
translated this "The retirement on the western
height;" but this is a mere guess, and at any rate
could not be right, for the site of the establishment
is a dead flat on the left bank of the Boyne.   According to Colgan, Erard was a man's name signifying
" noble, exalted, or distinguished, and it was formerly
not unfrequent among the Irish " (A. SS., p. 28).
He then states that this place was so called from some
man named Erard, so that *Cluain-Eraird* or Clonard
signifies Erard's meadow ; and since, as in case of
Clones, a moat still remains there, Erard may have
been the pagan chief who erected it, ages before the
time of St. Finian.   It is worthy of remark that
Erard is occasionally met with as a personal name
even at the present time.   There are several other

places in Leinster and Munster called Clonard and
Cloonard, but in these the Irish form of the name is
probably *Cluain-ard*, high meadow.

We find the names of some of the religious establishments formed by suffixing the name of a saint
or some other Christian term to the word *cluain* ; and
in these cases, this *cluain* may be a remnant of the
previous pagan name, which was partly changed
after the ecclesiastical foundation. Clonallan, now
a parish near Newry in Down, is mentioned by
Keating, Colgan, and others, who call it *Cluain-Dal-
lain*, Dallan's meadow ; the *d* is omitted by aspiration (see p. 20) in the modern name, but in the
Taxation of 1306 it is retained, the place being
called *Clondalan*. It received its name from Dallan
Forgall, who flourished about the year 580 ; he was
a celebrated poet, and composed a panegyric in verse
on St. Columba, called *Amhra-Choluimcille*, of which
we possess copies in a very old dialect of the Irish.
From him also the church of Kildallan in Cavan,
and some other churches, derived their names (see
Reeves, Eccl. Ant., p. 114).

Except in a very few cases, *cluain* is represented in
the present names by either *clon* or *cloon;* and there
are about 1800 places in Ireland whose names begin
with one or the other of these syllables. *Clon* is found
in the following names :— Clonmellon in Westmeath
is written by the Four Masters, *Cluain-Milain*, Milan's
Meadow. Clonmel in Tipperary, they write *Cluain-
meala*, which is the Irish name always used at the
present time : this name, which it bore long before
the foundation of the town, originated, no doubt,
from the abundance of wild bees' nests. There is
also a Clonmel near Glasnevin, Dublin, and another
in King's County. Clonmult, the meadow of the

wethers, is the name of a village and parish in Cork, and of a townland in Cavan.

With *cloon* are formed Cloontuskert in Roscommon, which is written in the Annals *Cluain-tuaiscert*, the northern meadow ; Cloonlogher, the name of a parish in Leitrim, *Cluain-luachra*, the meadow of rushes ; Cloonkeen, a very common townland name, *Cluain-caoin*, beautiful meadow, which is also very often anglicised Clonkeen. Clonkeen in Galway is written *Cluain-cain-Cairill* in "Hy Many," from Cairell, a primitive Irish saint : and it is still very usually called Clonkeen-Kerrill. Sometimes the word is in composition pronounced *clin*, as we see in Bracklin, the same as Brackloon, both townland names of frequent occurrence, derived from *Breac-chluain* (Four Mast.), speckled meadow; and of similar formation are Mucklin Mucklone and Muck-loon, pig meadow.

Two forms of the diminutive are in use ; one, *Cluainin* [Clooneen], occurs in the Four Masters, and in the form Clooneen (little meadow), it gives name to a great many townlands, chiefly in the west of Ireland. The other diminutive, *Cluaintin*, in the anglicised form Cloonteen, is the name of several places in Connaught and Munster. The plural of *cluain* is *cluainte* [cloonty], and this also enters into names. It is sometimes made *cloonta*, as in Cloontabonniv in Clare, the meadows of the *bonnives* or young pigs; Cloontakillew and Cloontakilla in Mayo, the meadows of the wood. But it is much oftener made Cloonty, or with the double plural Cloonties ; which are themselves the names of several places. Occasionally it is made *clinty* in Ulster, as in Clinty in the parish of Kirkiuriola in Antrim ; Clintycracken in Tyrone, *Cluainte-croiceann*, the meadows of the skins, so called probably from being used as a place for tanning.

Tuar[toor]signifies a bleach green; in an extended sense it is applied to any place where things were spread out to dry, and very often to fields along small streams, the articles being washed in the stream, and dried on its banks; and it was sometimes applied to spots where cattle used to feed and sleep. The word is used in Munster, Connaught, and Leinster, but does not occur at all in the Ulster counties.

Toor is the almost universal anglicised form, and this and Tooreen or Tourin (little bleach green) are the names of more than sixty townlands in the three provinces: as a part of compounds, it helps to give names to a still larger number. Toornageeha in Waterford and Kerry, signifies the bleach green of the wind; Toorfune in Tipperary, fair or white coloured bleach green; Toorcennablauha in Kerry, the little bleach green of the flowers (*bláth*); Tooreennagrena in Cork, sunny little bleach green.

It occasionally exhibits other forms in the Leinster counties. The Irish name of Ballitore, a village in Kildare, is *Bel-atha-a'-tuair* [Bellatoor], the ford-mouth of the bleach green, and it took this name from a ford on the river Greece; Monatore (*mon a* bog) occurs in Wicklow and Kildare; Tintore in Queen's County is in Irish *Tigh-an-tuair* [Teentoor], the house of the bleach green; and the same name without the article becomes Tithewer, near Newtown-mountkennedy in Wicklow.

The peasantry in most parts of Ireland use a kind of double axe for grubbing or rooting up the surface of coarse land; it is called a *grafán* [graffaun], from the verb *graf*, to write, engrave, or scrape, cognate with Greek *graphō*. Lands that have been grubbed or *graffed* with this instrument have in many cases received and preserved names, formed on the verb *graf*, that indicates the operation. This is the origin of those names that begin with the syllable *graf*; such as Graffa, Graffan, Graffoe, Graffoge, Graffin, and Graffy, which are found in the four provinces, and all of which signify grubbed land.

Ploughing by the horsetail, and burning corn in the ear, were practised in Ireland down to a comparatively recent period; Arthur Young witnessed both in operation less than a hundred years ago; but at that time they had nearly disappeared, partly on account of acts of Parliament framed expressly to prevent them, and partly through the increasing intelligence of the people. *Loisgreán* [lusgraun] is the term applied to corn burnt in the ear; and the particular spots where the process was carried on are in many cases indicated by names formed on this word.

The modern forms do not in general depart much from what would be indicated by the original pronunciation; it is well represented in Knockaluskraun and Knockloskcraun in Clare, each the name of a hill (*knock*) where corn used to be burned. The simple term gives name to Loskeran near Ardmore in Waterford.

Sometimes the word is pronounced *lustraun*; and this form is seen in Caherlustraun near Tuam in Galway, where the corn used to be burned in an ancient *caher* or stone fort; in Lugalustran in Leitrim, and Stralustrin in Fermanagh, the hollow, and the river holm of the burnt corn.

Land burnt in any way, whether by accident or design for agricultural purposes—as, for instance, when heath was burnt to encourage the growth of

grass, as noticed by Boate (Nat. Hist. XIII., 4)—
was designated by the word *loisgthe* [luskĕ], burnt;
which in modern names is usually changed to *lusky*,
losky or *lusk*. Ballylusky and Ballylusk, i. e. *Baile-
loisgthe*, burnt town, are the names of several townlands, the former being found in the Munster counties,
and the latter in Leinster; while it is made Bally-
losky in Donegal: Molosky in Clare, signifies burnt
plain:—*Mo* = *magh*, a plain.

Sometimes the word *teotán* [totaun], a burning, is
employed to express the same thing, as in Knockato-
taun in Mayo and Sligo, *Cnoc-a'-teotáin*, the hill of
the burning: Parkatotaun in Limerick, the field of
the burning.

It was formerly customary with those who kept
cattle, to spend a great part of the summer wandering
about with their herds among the mountain pastures,
removing from place to place, as the grass became
exhausted. During the winter they lived in their
lowland villages, and as soon as they had tilled a
spot of land in spring, they removed with their herds
to the mountains till autumn, when they returned to
gather the crops. (See 2nd Ser. chap. xxvi.).

The mountain habitations where they lived, fed
their cattle, and carried on their dairy operations
during the summer, were called in Irish *buaile*
[booly], a word evidently derived from *bo*, a cow.
This custom existed down to the sixteenth century;
and the poet Spenser describes it very correctly, as
he witnessed it in his day:—"There is one use
amongst them, to keepe their cattle, and to live themselves the most part of the yeare in boolies, pastur-
ing upon the mountaine, and waste wilde places;
and removing still to fresh land, as they have de-
pastured the former" (View of the State of Ireland;

Dublin edition, 1809, p. 82). O'Flaherty also notices the same custom :—"In summer time they
drive their cattle to the mountaines, where such as
looke to the cattle live in small cabbins for that season " (Iar-Connaught, o. 17). The term *looley* was
not confined to the mountainous districts; for in
some parts of Ireland it was applied to any place
where cattle were fed or milked, or which was set
apart for dairy purposes.

Great numbers of places retain the names of these
dairy places, and the word *buaile* is generally represented in modern names by the forms Booley, Boley,
Boola, and Boula, which are themselves the names of
many places, and form the beginning of a still larger
number. In Boleylug near Baltinglass in Wicklow,
they must have built their " cabbins " for shelter in
the *lug* or mountain hollow; Booladurragha in Cork,
and Booldurragh in Carlow, dark booley (*Buaile-
dorcha*), probably from being shaded with trees;
Booleyglass, a village in Kilkenny, green booley.

The word is combined in various other ways, and
it assumes other forms, partly by corruption and
partly by grammatical inflexion. Farranboley near
Dundrum in Dublin, is booley land; Aughvolyshane
in the parish of Glenkeen, Tipperary, is in Irish *Ath-
bhuaile-Sheain*, the ford of John's booley. Ballyboley,
the name of some townlands in Antrim and Down,
Ballyvooly in the parish of Layd, Antrim, and
Ballyvool near Inistioge, Kilkenny, are all different
forms of *Baile-buaile*, the town of the dairy place;
Ballynaboley, Ballynaboola, and Ballynabooley, have
the same meaning, the article *na* being inserted; and
Boulabally near Adare in Limerick, is the same
name with the terms reversed. On Ballyboley hill
near the source of the Larne water in Antrim, there

are still numerous remains of the old "cabbins," extending for two miles along the face of the hill; they are called *Boley houses*, and the people retain the tradition that they were formerly used by the inhabitants of the valley when they drove up their cattle in summer to pasture on the heights (see Reeves, Ecol. Ant., p. 268).

The diminutive *buaillin* [boolteen], and the plural *buailte* [boolty], occur occasionally: Boolteens and Boolteeny (see p. 32, vi.), in Kerry and Tipperary, both signify little dairy places; Boultypatrick in Donegal, Patrick's booleys.

CHAPTER VIII.

SUBDIVISIONS AND MEASURES OF LAND.

AMONG a people who followed the double occupation of tillage and pasturage, according as the country became populated, it would be divided and subdivided, and parcelled out among the people; boundaries would be determined, and standards of measurement adopted. The following was the old partition of the country, according to Irish authorities:—There were five provinces: Leinster, Ulster, Connaught, Munster, and Meath, each of which was divided into *tricha-céds* (thirty hundreds) or *trichas*, Meath containing 18, Connaught 30, Ulster 36, Leinster 31, and Munster 70; each *tricha* contained 30 *baile-bia-taighs* (victualler's town), and each *Baile-biatagh*, 12 *seisreachs*. The division into provinces is still retained with some modification, but the rest of the old distribution is obsolete. The present subdivision is into provinces, counties, baronies, parishes, and townlands; in all Ireland there are 325 baronies, 2422 parishes, and about 62,000 townlands. Various minor subdivisions and standards of measurement were adopted in different parts of the country; and so far as these are represented in our present nomenclature, I will notice them here.[*]

The old term *tricha* or *triucha* [truha], is usually rendered by "cantred" or "district," and we find it giving name to the barony of Trough in Monaghan; to the townland of Trough near O'Brien's Bridge in Clare; and to True in the parish of Killyman in Tyrone. *Seisreach* [sheshragh] is commonly translated "plowland;" it is said to be derived from *seisear*, six, and *each*, a horse, and it was used to denote the extent of land a six-horse plough would turn up in one year. We find the term in Shesheraghmore and Shesheraghscanlan near Borrisokane in Tipperary: in Shesheraghkeale (*keale*, narrow) near Nenagh, the same name as Sistrakeel (see p. 60, v.) in the parish of Tamlaght Finlagan, Derry; and in Drumsastry in Fermanagh, the ridge of the plowland.

The terms in most common use to denote portions of land or territory, were those expressing fractional parts, of which there are five that occur very fre-

* For further information the reader is referred to Dr. Reeves's paper "On the Townland Distribution of Ireland" (Proc. R. L. Academy, Vol. VII., p. 473), from which much of the information in this chapter has been derived; and to a paper "On the Territorial Divisions of the Country," by Sir Thomas Larcom, prefixed to the "Relief Correspondence of the Commissioners of Public Works."

quently. The word *leath* [läh] signifies half, and we
find it forming part of names all over Ireland. Thus
when a *seisreach* was divided into two equal parts,
each was called *leath-sheisreach* [lahesheragh], half
plowland, which gives name to Lahesheragh in
Kerry, to Lahesseragh in Tipperary, and to Bally-
nalahessery near Dungarvan in Waterford, which
signifies the town of the half-plowland. In like
manner, half a townland was denoted by the term
Leath-bhaile, pronounced, and generally anglicised,
Lavally and Levally, which are the names of about
thirty townlands scattered through the four provinces. Laharan, the name of many places in Cork
and Kerry, signifies literally, half land, Irish *Leath-
fhearann*, the initial *f* in *fearann* (land) being rendered
silent by aspiration (see p. 20).

The territory of Lecale in Down, now forming
two baronies, is called in the Irish authorities *Leth-
Cathail*, Cathal's half or portion. Cathal [Cahal],
who was fifth in descent from Deman, king of Ulidia
in the middle of the sixth century, flourished about
the year 700; and in a division of territory this district was assigned to him, and took his name. It
had been previously called *Magh-inis*, which Colgan
translates *Insula campestris*, the level island, being a
plain tract nearly surrounded by the sea.

Trian [treen] denotes the third part of anything;
it was formerly a territorial designation in frequent
use, and it has descended to the present time in the
names of several places. A tripartite division of territory in Tipperary gave origin to the name of the
barony of Middlethird, which is a translation from the
Irish, *Trian-meadhanach* [munagh] as used by the
Four Masters. There was a similar division in Waterford, and two of the three parts—now two baronies—

are still known by the names of Middlethird and
Upperthird. The barony of Dufferin in Down, is
called by the Four Masters *Dubh-thrian* [Duvreen],
the black third, the sound of which is very well represented in the present name; the same as Diffreen
in Leitrim, near Glencar lake.

Trian generally takes the forms of Trean and Trien,
which constitute or begin the names of about 70
townlands in the four provinces. Treanamullin
near Stranorlar in Donegal, signifies the third part
or division of the mill, i. e. having a mill on it;
Treaufohanaun in Mayo, the thistle-producing third;
Treanlaur in Galway and Mayo, middle third;
Treanmanagh in Clare, Kerry, and Limerick, same
meaning; Trienaltenagh in Londonderry, the third
of the precipices or cliffs.

Ceathramhadh [carhoo or carrow] signifies a quarter, from *ceathair* [cahir] four. The old townlands
or ballybetaghs, were very often divided into quarters,
each of which was commonly designated by this word
ceathramhadh, which, in the present names generally
takes one of the two forms *carrow*, and *carhoo;* the
former being the more usual, but the latter occurring
very often in Cork and Kerry. Carrow forms or
begins the names of more than 700 townlands, and
Carhoo, of about 30; and another form Carrive,
occurs in some of the northern counties.

The four quarters into which the townland was
divided were generally distinguished from one another by adjectives descriptive of size, position, shape,
or quality of the land, or by suffixing the names of
the occupiers. Thus, there are more than 60 modern
townlands called Carrowkeel, *Ceathramhadh-cael,*
narrow quarter; Carrowgarriff and Carrowgarve,
rough (*garbh*) quarter, is the name of sixteen; there
17*

are 25 called Carrowbane and Carrowbaun, white quarter; 24 called Carrowbeg, little quarter; and more than 60 called Carrowmore, great quarter. Lecarrow, half-quarter, gives name to about 60 townlands, the greater number of them in Connaught.

A fifth part is denoted by *coigeadh* [cōga]: the application of this term to land is very ancient, for in the old form *coiced* it occurs in the Book of Armagh, where it is translated *quinta pars*. In later times it was often used in the sense of " province," which application evidently originated in the division of Ireland into *fire* provinces. In its primitive signification of a fifth part—probably the fifth part of an ancient townland—it has given names to several places. Cooga, its most usual modern form, is the name of several townlands in Connaught and Munster; there are three townlands in Mayo called Coogue; and Coogaquid in Clare, signifies literally " fifth part;—*cuid*, a part.

Sriscadh [shesha] the sixth part; to be distinguished from *seisreach*. As a measure of land, it was usual in Ulster and north Connaught, where in the forms Sess, Sessia, Sessingh, it gives names to about thirty townlands. It occurs also in Munster, though in forms slighty different; as in the case of Sheshia in Clare, and Sheshiv in Limerick; Shesharoe in Tipperary, red sixth; Sheshodonnell in Clare, O'Donnell's sixth part.

Several other Irish terms were employed; such as Ballyboe or " cow-land," which prevailed in some of the Ulster counties, and which is still a very common townland name in Donegal. In some of the counties of Munster, they had in use a measure called *gniomh* [gneeve], which was the twelfth part of a plowland; and this term occurs occasionally in the other provinces. It has given name to about twenty townlands now called Gneeve and Gneeves, the greater number of them in Cork and Kerry. There is a place in the parish of Kilmacabea, Cork, called Three-gneeves; and in the same county there are two townlands, each called Two-gneeves.

In many parts of Ireland the Anglo-Norman settlers introduced terms derived from their own language, and several of these are now very common as townland names. *Cartron* signifies a quarter, and is derived through the French *quarteron* from the mediæval Lat. *quarteronus;* it was in very common use in Connaught as well as in Longford, West-meath, and King's County; and it was applied to a parcel of land varying in amount from 60 to 100 acres. There are about 80 townlands called Cartron, chiefly in Connaught, and 60 others of whose names it forms the beginning. The terms with which it is com-pounded are generally Irish, such as Cartronganny near Mullingar, *Cartron-gainimh,* sandy cartron; Cartronnagilta in Cavan, the cartron of the reeds; Cartronrathroe in Mayo, the cartron of the red fort.

Tate or *tath* appears to be an English word, and meant 60 native Irish acres. It occurs chiefly in Fer-managh, Monaghan, and Tyrone, generally in the forms *tat, tatt,* and *tatty;* and, as in the case of *cartron,* it usually compounds with Irish words. Tattyna-geeragh in the parish of Clones in Fermanagh, the *tate* of the sheep; Tattintlieve in Monaghan, the *tate* of the *sliere* or mountain.

In Cavan, certain measures of land were called by the names *poll, gallon,* and *pottle.* Thus Pollakeel is the narrow *poll;* Pollamore, great *poll,* &c. In most

other counties, however, *poll* is an Irish word signifying a hole.   Pottlebane and Pottleboy in Cavan,
signify white and yellow *pottle*, respectively ; Gallon-
nambraher the friars' *gallon*, &c.

CHAPTER IX.

NUMERICAL COMBINATIONS.

While names involving numerical combinations are
found all over the world, a careful examination
would be pretty sure to show that each people had a
predilection for one or more particular numbers.
During my examination of Irish proper names, I
have often been struck with the constant recurrence
of the numbers two and three ; and after having
specially investigated the subject, I have found, as I
hope to be able to show, that names involving these
two numbers are so numerous as to constitute a
distinct peculiarity, and that this is the case most
especially with regard to the number two.
I never saw it stated that the number two was in
Ireland considered more remarkable than any other ;
but from whatever cause it may have arisen, certain
it is that there existed in the minds of the Irish
people a distinctly marked predilection to designate
persons or places, where circumstances permitted it,
by epithets expressive of the idea of duality, the epithet being founded on some circumstance connected
with the object named ; and such circumstances were
often seized upon to form a name in preference to
others equally or more conspicuous.   We have, of

course, as they have in all countries, names with
combinations of other numbers, and those containing
the number three are very numerous ; but the number two is met with many times more frequently
than all the others put together.

The Irish word for two that occurs in names is *dá*
or *dhá*, both forms being used ; *dá* is pronounced
daw; but in the other form, *dh*, which has a peculiar
and rather faint guttural sound, is altogether suppressed in modern names ; the word *dhá* being generally represented by the vowel *a*, while in many cases
modern contraction has obliterated every trace of a
representative letter. It is necessary to bear in mind
that *dá* or *dhá* generally causes aspiration, and in
a few cases eclipses consonants and prefixes *n* to
vowels (see pp. 19 and 21, *supra*).

We find names involving the number two recorded
in Irish history, from the most ancient authorities
down to the MSS. of the seventeenth century, and
they occur in proportion quite as numerously as at
the present day; showing that this curious tendency
is not of modern origin, but that it has descended,
silent and unnoticed, from ages of the most remote
antiquity.

There is a village and parish in the north west of
Tipperary, on the shore of Lough Derg, now called
Terryglass; its Irish name, as used in many Irish
authorities, is *Tir-da-ghlas*, the territory of the two
streams; and the identity of this with the modern
Terryglass is placed beyond all doubt by a passage
in the "Life of St. Fintan of Clonenagh," which describes *Tir-da-glas* as "in the territory of Munster,
near the river Shannon." The great antiquity of this
name is proved by the fact that it is mentioned by
Adamnan in his "Life of St. Columba" (Lib. II., Cap.

xxxvi.), written in the end of the seventh century; but according to his usual custom, instead of the Irish name, he gives the Latin equivalent : in the heading of the chapter it is called *Ager duorum rivorum,* and in the text *Rus duum riculorum,* either of which is a correct translation of *Tir-da-ghlas.** There is a subdivision of the townland of Clogher in the parish of Kilnoe, Clare, called Terryglass, which has the same Irish form and meaning as the other.

In the Book of Leinster there is a short poem, ascribed to Finn Mac Cumhail, accounting for the name of *Magh-da-ghéisi,* in Leinster, the plain of the two swans ; and the Dinnsenchus gives a legend about the name of the river Owendalulagh, which rises on the slope of Slieve Aughty, and flows into Lough Cooter near Gort in Galway. This legend states, that when Echtghe (Ektĕ], a Tuatha De Danann lady, married Fergus Lusca, cupbearer to the king of Connaught, she brought with her two cows, remarkable for their milk-bearing fruitfulness, which were put to graze on the banks of this stream ; and from this circumstance it was called *Abhainn-da-loilgheach,* the river of the two milch cows. According to the same authority, Slieve Aughty took its name from this lady—*Sliabh-Echtghe,* Echtghe's mountain. Several other instances of names of this class, mentioned in ancient authorities, will be cited as I proceed.

Though this peculiarity is not so common in personal as in local names, yet the number of persons mentioned in Irish writings whose names involve the number two, is sufficiently large to be very remark-

---

* See Reeves's Adamnan, where *ager duorum rivorum* is identified with Terryglass.

able. The greater number of these names appear to be agnomina, which described certain peculiarities of the individuals, and which were imposed for the sake of distinction, after a fashion prevalent among most nations before the institution of surnames.

One of the three Collas who conquered Ulster in the fourth century (see p. 136) was called *Colla-da-Chrich*, Colla of the two territories. *Da-chrich* was a favourite sobriquet, and no doubt, in case of each individual, it records the fact of his connection, either by possession or residence, with two countries or districts; in case of Colla, it most probably refers to two territories in Ireland and Scotland, in the latter of which he lived some years in a state of banishment before his invasion of Ulster. In the Martyrology of Donegal there are nine different persons mentioned, called Fer-da-chrich, the man of the two territories.

The word Dubh applied to a dark-visaged person is often followed by *da;* thus the Four Masters mention two persons named Dubh-da-bharc, the black (man) of the two ships; four named Dubh-da-chrich; eight, Dubh-da-bhoireann (of the two stony districts?); two, Dubh-da-inbher, of the two estuaries; one, Dubh-da-ingean, of the two daughters; four, Dubh-da-leithe, of the two sides or parties; and two, Dubh-da-thuath, of the two districts or cantreds. In the " Genealogy of *Corcaluidhe*" we find Dubh-da-mhagh, of the two plains; and in the Martyrology of Donegal, Dubh-da-locha, of the two lakes.

Fiacha Muilleathan, king of Munster in the third century, was called Fer-da-liach, the man of the two sorrows, because his mother died and his father was killed in the battle of Magh Mucruimhe on the day of his birth. The father of Máine Mor, the ancestor of the *Hy Many*, was Eochaidh, surnamed Fer-da-ghiall, the man of the two hostages. Many more names might be cited, if it were necessary to extend this list; and while the number two is so common, we meet with few names involving any other number, except three.

It is very natural that a place should be named from two prominent objects forming part of it, or in connection with it, and names of this kind are occasionally met with in most countries. The fact that they occur in Ireland would not be considered remarkable, were it not for these two circumstances— first, they are, beyond all comparison, more numerous than could be reasonably expected; and secondly, the word *dá* is usually expressed, and forms part of the names.

Great numbers of places are scattered here and there through the country whose names express position between two physical features, such as rivers, mountains, lakes, &c., those between two rivers being the most numerous. Killederdaowen in the parish of Duniry, Galway, is called in Irish, *Coill-eder-da-abhainn*, the wood between two rivers; and Killa-drown, in the parish of Drumcullen, King's County, is evidently the same word shortened by local corruption. Dromderaown in Cork, and Dromdiraowen in Kerry, are both modern forms of *Druim-'dir-dhá-abhainn*, the ridge between two rivers, where the Irish *dhá* is represented by *a* in the present names. In Cloonederown, Galway — the meadow between two rivers—there is no representative of the *dha*, though it exists in the Irish name; and a like remark applies to Ballyederown (the townland between two rivers), an old castle situate in the angle where the rivers Funcheon and Araglin in Cork, mingle their waters. Coracow in the parish of Killaha, Kerry, is a name much shortened from its original *Comhrac-dhá-abha*, the meeting of the two streams. The Four Masters at A.D. 528, record a battle fought at a place called *Luachair-mor-etir-da-inbhir*, the large rushy place between two river mouths, otherwise called *Ailbhe* or *Cluain-Ailbhe* (Ailbhe's meadow), now Clonalvy in the county Meath.

With *glaise* (a stream) instead of *abhainn*, we have Ederdaglass, the name of two townlands in Fermanagh, meaning (a place) between two streams; and Drumederglass in Cavan, the ridge between two streams. Though all trace of *da* is lost in this name, it is preserved in the Down Survey, where the place is called Drumaderdaglass.

Ederdacurragh in Fermanagh, means (a place) between two marshes; Aderavoher in Sligo, is in Irish *Eadar-dha-bhothair* (a place) between two roads, an idea that is otherwise expressed in Gouldavoher near Mungret, Limerick, the fork of the two roads. Dromdiralough in Kerry, the ridge between two lakes, and Drumederalena in Sligo, the ridge between the two *lenas* or meadows; Inchideraille near Inchigeelagh, is in Irish *Inis-idir-dha-fháill*, the island or river holm between two cliffs; a similar position has given name to Derdaoil or Dariel, a little village in the parish of Kilmastulla, Tipperary, which is shortened from the Irish *Idir-da-fhaill*, between two cliffs; Cloonderavally in Sligo, the *cloon* or meadow between the two *ballies* or townlands.

Crockada in the parish of Clones, Fermanagh, is only a part of the Irish name, *Cnoc-edar-da-ghreuch*, the hill between the two marshy flats; and the true form of the present name would be Knockadder. Mogh, the name of a townland in the parish of Rath-

lynin, Tipperary, is also an abbreviation of a longer
name; the inhabitants call it *Magh-idir-dha-abhainn*,
the plain between two rivers.

The well-known old church of Aghadoe, near Killarney, which gives name to a parish, is called by the
Four Masters, at 1581, *Achadh-da-eó*, the field of
the two yew trees, which must have been growing
near each other, and must have been sufficiently
large and remarkable to attract general attention.
Part of the townland of Drumharkan Glebe in the
parish of Cloone, Leitrim, is called Cooldao, the back
of the two yews.   In the townland of Cornagee,
parish of Killinagh, Cavan, there is a deep cavern,
into which a stream sinks; it is called Polladaossan,
the hole of the two *dossans* or bushes.

Near Crossmolina in Mayo, is a townland called
Glendavoolagh, the glen of the two boolies or dairy
places.   In the parish of Killashee, Longford, there
is a village and townland called Cloondara, containing the ruins of what was once an important ecclesiastical establishment; it is mentioned by the Four
Masters at 1323, and called *Cluain-da-rath*, the meadow of the two raths; and there is a townland of the
same name in the parish of Tisrara, Roscommon.

The parish of Donagh in Monaghan, takes its name
from an old church, the ruins of which are still to be
seen near the village of Glasslough; it is mentioned
twice by the Four Masters, and its full name, as
written by them, is *Domhnach-maighe-da-chlaoine*,
[Donagh-moy-da-cleena], the church of the plain of
the two slopes. Dromdaleague or Dromaleague, the
name of a village and parish in Cork, signifies the
ridge of the two stones.   Ballydehob in the south of
the same county, took its name from a ford which is
called in Irish *Bel-atha-da-chab*, the ford of the two

cabs or mouths; the *two mouths*, I suppose, describing some peculiarity of shape.

Several places derive their names from two plains: thus Damma, the name of two townlands in Kilkenny, is simply *Da-mhagh* two plains; Rosdama in the parish of Grange, same county, the wood of the two plains. That part of the King's County now occupied by the baronies of Warrenstown and Cooles-town, was anciently called *Tuath-da-mhaighe*, the district of the two plains, by which name it is frequently mentioned in the annals, and which is sometimes anglicised Tethmoy; the remarkable hill of Drumcaw, giving name to a townland in this neighbourhood, was anciently called *Druim-da-mhaighe*, from the same district; and we find Glendavagh, the glen of the two plains, in the parish of Aghaloo, Tyrone.

The valley of Glendalough, in Wicklow, takes its name from the two lakes so well known to tourists; it is called in Irish authorities *Gleann-da-locha*, which the author of the Life of St. Kevin translates "the valley of the two lakes;" and other glens of the same name in Waterford, Kerry, and Galway, are also so called from two lakes near each other. There is an island in the Shannon, in the parish of Killady-sert, Clare, called Inishdadroum, which is mentioned in the "Wars of GG." by the name of *Inis-da-dromand*, the island of the two *drums* or backs, from its shape; and a similar peculiarity of form has given name to Inishdavar in the parish of Derryvullan, Fermanagh (of the two *barrs* or tops); to Cornadarum, Fermanagh, the round hill of the two *drums* or ridges; and to Corradeverrid in Cavan, the hill of the two caps (*barred*). Tuam in Galway, is called in the annals *Tuaim-da-ghualann*, the tumulus of the two shoulders, evidently from the shape of the ancient sepulchral mound from which the place has its name.

Desertcreat, a townland giving name to a parish in Tyrone, is mentioned by the Four Masters as the scene of a battle between the O'Neills and the O'Donnells, in A.D. 1281, and it is called by them *Diseart-da-chrioch*, the desert or hermitage of the two territories; they mention also a place called *Magh-da-chairneach*, the plain of the two carns; *Magh-da-ghabhal*, the plain of the two forks; *Ailiun-da-bhernach*, the island of the two gaps; *Magh-da-Chainneach*, the plain of the two Cainneachs (men). The district between Lough Conn and the river Moy was anciently called *An Da Bhac*, the two bends, under which name it is frequently mentioned in the annals.

There is a townland in the parish of Rossinver, Leitrim, called Lisdarush, the fort of the two promontories; and on the side of Hungry Hill, west of Glengariff in Cork, is a small lake which is called Coomadavallig, the hollow of the two roads; in Roscommon we find Cloondacarra, the meadow of the two weirs; the Four Masters mention *Clar-atha-dacharadh*, the plain (or footboard) of the ford of the two weirs; and Charlemont in Tyrone was anciently called *Achadh-au-da-charadh*, the field of the two weirs. Gubbacrock in the parish of Killesher, Fermanagh, is written in Irish *Gob-dha-chnoc*, the beak or point of the two hills.

Dundareirke is the name of an ancient castle in Cork, built by the M'Carthys, signifying the fortress of the two prospects (*Dun-da-radharc*), and the name is very suitable; for, according to Smith, "it is on a hill and commands a vast extended view as far as

Kerry, and east almost to Cork;" there is a townland of the same name, but written Dundaryark, in
the parish of Danesfort, Kilkenny.

The preceding names were derived from conspicuous physical features, and their origin is therefore
natural enough, so far as each individual name is
concerned; their great number, as already remarked,
is what gives them significance. But those I am now
about to bring forward admit in general of no such
explanation, and appear to me to prove still more con-
clusively the existence of this remarkable disposition
in the minds of the people, to look out for groups of
two. Here also, as in the preceding class, names
crowd upon us with remarkable frequency, both in
ancient authorities and in the modern list of townlands.

Great numbers of places have been named from
two animals of some kind. If we are to explain these
names from natural occurrences, we must believe that
the places were so called because they were the favourite haunt of the two animals commemorated;
but it is very strange that so many places should be
named from just two, while there are very few from
one, three, or any other number—except in the general way of a genitive singular or a genitive plural.
Possibly it may be explained to some extent by the
natural pairing of male and female; but this will not
explain all, nor even a considerable part, as any one
may see from the illustrations that follow. I believe
that most or all of these names have their origin in
legends or superstitions, and that the two animals
were very often supernatural, viz., fairies, or ghosts,
or human beings transformed by Tuatha De Danann
enchantment.

We very frequently meet with two birds—*dá-én.*

A portion of the Shannon near Clonmacnoise was anciently called *Snamh-dá-én* [Snauv-da-ain], the *snauv*
or swimming-ford of the two birds. The parish of
Duneane in Antrim, has got its present name by a
slight contraction from *Dún-dá-én*, the fortress of the
two birds, which is its name in the Irish authorities,
among others, the Felire of Aengus. There is a
mountain stretching between Lough Gill and Col-
looney, Sligo, which the Four Masters mention at
1196 by the name of *Sliabh-dá-én*, the mountain of
the two birds, now called Slieve Daeane; it is curious
that a lake on the north side of the same mountain is
called Lough Dagea, the lake of the two geese, which
are probably the two birds that gave name to the
mountain. There is a townland in the parish of
Kinawly, Fermanagh, called Rossdanean, the peninsula of two birds; Balladian near Ballybay in Mo-
naghan, is correctly|*Bealach-a'-da-én* (*bealach*, a pass);
and Colgan (A. SS., p. 42, note 9) mentions a place
near Lough Neagh, called *Cluain-dá-én*, the meadow
of the two birds.

Two birds of a particular kind have also given
their names to several places, and among these, two
ravens seem to be favourites. In the parish of Kinawly,
Fermanagh, is a townland called Aghindaiagh, in Irish
Achadh-an-da-fhiach, the field of the two ravens; in
the townland of Kilcolman, parish of same name,
Kerry, is a pit or cavern called *Poll-da-fhiach*, the
hole of the two ravens; we find in Cavan, Neddaiagh,
the nest of the two ravens; in Galway, Cuilleen-
daeagh, and in Kerry Glandaeagh, the little wood,
and the glen, of the two ravens. The parish of Bal-
teagh in Down is sometimes written in old documents, Ballydaigh, and sometimes Boydafeigh,
pointing to *Baile-da-fhiach* or *Both-da-fhiach*, the

town or the hut of the two ravens "preserving the
tradition that two ravens flew away with the plumb-
line from the cemetery Rellick in the townland of
Kilhoyle, where the parishioners were about to erect
their church, to Ardmore, the townland where the
site was at length fixed" (Reeves: Colt. Vis. 133).
With *Branóg*, another name for the same bird, we
have Brannock Island, near Great Aran Island, Galway bay, which is called in Irish *Olican-da-bhranóg*
(O'Flaherty, Iar Connaught), the island of the two
ravens.   Aghadachor in Donegal, means the field of
the two herons or cranes.   There is a townland in the
parish of Killinvoy, Roscommon, whose name is im-
properly anglicised Lisdaulan; the Four Masters at
1380, call it *Lios-da-lon*, the fort of the two black-
birds.

Several places get their names from two hounds;
such as Moyacomb in Wicklow (see p. 52); Cahiracon,
two townlands in Clare, which are called to this day
in Irish *Cathair-dhá-chon*, the *caher* or stone fortress
of the two hounds; and Lisdachon in Westmeath.
In the parish of Devenish, Fermanagh, there are
two conterminous townlands called Big Dog and
Little Dog; these singular appellations derive their
origin from the modern division into two unequal
parts, of an ancient tract which is called in the annals, *Sliabh-dá-chon*, the mountain of the two hounds.
We find also Cloondacon in Mayo, the meadow of the
two hounds.

In several other places we have two oxen commemorated, as in Cloondadauv in Galway, which the
annalists write *Cluain-dá-damh*, the meadow of the
two oxen; Rossdagamph in Fermanagh, and Augh-
adanore, Armagh, the promontory and the field of
the two oxen; in the first, *d* is changed to *g* (see p.

56), and in the second, *da* prefixes *n* to the vowel. At the year 636, the Four Masters mention a lake in which a crannoge was built, situated in Oriel, but not now known, called *Loch-da-damh*, the lake of the two oxen.

Two bucks are commemorated in such names as Ballydavock, Cappadavock, Glendavock, Lisdavock, (town, plot, glen, fort), and Attidavock, the site of the house of the two bucks. The parish of Clonyhurk in King's County, containing the town of Portarlington, takes its name from a townland which the Four Masters call *Cluain-da-thorc*, the meadow of the two boars; Glendahurk in Mayo is the glen of the two boars; and Lisdavuck in King's County, the fort of the two pigs (*muc*, a pig).

Cloondanagh in Clare is in Irish *Cluain-da-neach*, the meadow of the two horses; we find the same two animals in Tullyloughdaugh in Fermanagh, and Aghadaugh in Westmeath; the second meaning the field, and the first the hill of the lake, of the two horses; and Clondelara, near Clonmacnoise, is the meadow of the two mares. Clondalee in the parish of Killyon, Meath, is called in Irish *Cluain-da-laegh*, the meadow of the two calves. Aghadavoyle in Armagh is the field of the two *maels*, or hornless cows; two animals of the same kind have given name to a little island in Mayo, viz., Inishdaweel, while we have two yellow cows in Inishdauwee, the name of two townlands in Galway.

There is a legend concerning the origin of Clondagad in Clare, the cloon of the two *gads* or withes, and another accounting for the name *Dun-da-leth-glas*, anciently applied to the great rath at Downpatrick, the fortress of the two broken locks or fetters. The two remarkable mountains in Kerry now called the

Paps, were anciently called, and are still, in Irish, *Da-chich-Danainne* [Da-kee-Dannina], the two paps of Danann (see p. 163) ; and the plain on which they stand is called *Bun-a'-da-chich*, the bottom or foundation of the two Paps : Drumahaire, the name of a village in Leitrim, signifies the ridge of the two air-spirits or demons (see p. 194).

In this great diversity it must be supposed that two persons would find a place ; and accordingly we find Kildaree, the church of the two kings, the name of two townlands in Galway (for which see Sir William Wilde's "Lough Corrib"), and of another near Crossmolina, Mayo. There is a fort one mile south of the village of Killoscully, Tipperary, called Lis-davraher, the fort of the two friars ; and there is another of the same name in the south of Ballymoylan townland, parish of Youghalarra, in the same county. In both these cases the friars were probably ghosts.

There is a parish called Toomore in the county of Mayo, taking its name from an old church standing near the river Moy ; it is also the name of a townland in the parish of Aughrim, Roscommon, and of a townland and parish in Sligo. This is a very curious and a very ancient name. Toomore in Mayo is written *Tuaim-da-bhodhar* by Duald Mac Firbis and the Four Masters ; and *Tuaim-da-bhodar* in a poem in the "Book of Lecan." The pronunciation of the original is *Tooma-our*, which easily sank into Toomore ; and the name signifies the tomb of the two deaf persons ; but who they were, neither history nor tradition records.

The memory of the two venerable people who gave name to Cordalea in the parish of Kilmore, Cavan, has quite perished from the face of the earth, except only so far as it is preserved in the name *Cor-da-liath*, the hill of the two grey persons. Two people of a different complexion are commemorated in Glendaduff in Mayo, the glen of the two black visaged persons. Meendacalliagh in the parish of Lower Fahan, Donegal, means the *meen* or mountain flat of the two *calliaghs* or hags, probably a pair of those old witches who used to turn themselves, on Good Friday, into hares, and suck the cows.

It must occur to any one who glances through these names to ask himself the question—what was the origin of this curious custom ? I cannot believe that it is a mere accident of language, or that it sprang up spontaneously without any particular cause. I confess myself wholly in the dark, unable to offer any explanation : I have never met anything that I can call to mind in the whole range of Irish literature tending in the least degree to elucidate it. Is it the remnant of some ancient religious belief, or some dark superstition, dispelled by the light of Christianity ? or does it commemorate some widespread social custom, prevailing in times beyond the reach of history or tradition, leaving its track on the language as the only manifestation of its existence ? We know that among some nations certain numbers were accounted sacred, like the number seven among the Hebrews. Was two a sacred number with the primitive people of this country ? I refrain from all conjecture, though the subject is sufficiently tempting ; I give the facts, and leave to others the task of accounting for them.

The number three occurs also with remarkable frequency in Irish proper names, so much so that it would incline one to believe that the Irish had a predilection for grouping things in triads like the

Welsh.   Dr. Reeves has observed that the old chro-
niclers often enumerate rivers in threes; such as the
three *Uinseanna;* the three Sucks; the three Finns;
the three *Coimdes;* the three rivers, *Siúir, Feil,* and
Erere; the three, *Fleasc, Mand,* and *Labhrann;* the
three black rivers, *Fubhna, Torann* and *Callann;* the
nine *Brosnachs* (3 × 3); the nine *Righes,* &c.—all
these taken from the Four Masters.

Mr. Hennessy has directed my attention to a great
number of triple combinations; such as the three
Tuathas or districts in Connaught; the places called
three castles in Kilkenny and Wicklow; *Bearna-tri-
carbad* the gap of the three chariots, a place in the
county Clare; the carn of the three crosses at Clonmacnoise; several places called three plains; three
Connaughts; and many others.   He has also given
me a long list, taken from the annals, of names of
persons distinguished by three qualities (such as *Fear-
na-dtri-mbuadh,* the man of the three virtues, a cognomen of Conary More), which would enable me to
extend this enumeration of triplets much farther;
but as I am at present concerned only about *local*
names, I shall content myself with simply noting
the fact, that names of this kind occur in great numbers in our old writings.

Many of these combinations were no doubt adopted
in Christian times in honour of the Trinity, of which
the name Trevet (see p. 132) is an example; and
it is probable that the knowledge of this mystery
disposed men's minds to notice more readily combinations of three, and to give names accordingly,
even in cases where no direct reference to the Trinity
was intended.

We learn the origin of Duntryleague near Galbally
in Limerick, from a passage in the Book of Lismore,

which states that "Cormac Cas (king of Munster),
son of Oilioll Olum (see p. 133, *supra*) fought the
battle of Knocksouna (near Kilmallock) against
Eochy Abhradhruadh [Ohy-Avraroo], king of Ulster, in which Eochy was slain ; and Cormac was
wounded (in the head), so that he was three years
under cure, with his brain continually flowing from
his head." Then a goodly *dun* was constructed for
him, "having in the middle a beautiful clear spring,
and a great royal house was built over the well, and
three *liagáns* (pillar stones) were placed round it, on
which was laid the bed of the king, so that his
head was in the middle between the three pillars.
And one of his attendants stood constantly by him
with a cup, pouring the water of the well on his
head. He died there after that, and was buried in
a cave within the dun ; and from this is (derived)
the name of the place, *Dun-tri-liag*, the fortress of
the three pillar stones."

The erection of three stones like those at Duntryleague must have been usual, for we find several
names containing the compound *tri-liag*, three pillar
stones. It occurs simply in the form of Trillick, as
the name of a village in Tyrone, and of two townlands, one in Donegal and the other in Fermanagh.
In the parish of Ballymacormick, Longford, there
are two townlands called respectively, Trillickacurry
and Trillickatemple, the *trillick* or three stones of
the marsh, and of the church. Near Dromore in
Down, we find Edentrillick, and in the parish of
Tynan, Armagh, Rathtrillick, the first the hill brow,
and the second the fort, of the three pillar stones.

Several places take their names from three persons,
who were probably joint occupiers. In the parish of
Kilbride, Meath, there is a townland called Ballintry,

Baile-an-tri, the town of the three (persons). The
more usual word employed in this case, however, is
triur [troor], which means, not three in the abstract,
but three persons; and it is not improbable that in
the last mentioned name, a final *r* has been lost.
Ballintruer in the parish of Donaghmore, Wicklow,
has the same meaning as Balliutry. In the parish
of Ramoan, Antrim, is a hill called Carntroor, where
three persons must have been buried under a carn;
and in the parish of Templecorran, same county, is
another hill called Slieveatrue, which name appears
to be a corruption from Slieveatroor, the mountain
of the three persons.

Cavantreeduff in the parish of Cleenish, Fermanagh, has probably some legendary story connected
with it, the Irish name being *Cabhan-tri-damh*, the
round hill of the three oxen. The celebrated castle
of Portnatrynod at Lifford, of which the name is
now forgotten, and even its very site unknown, is repeatedly mentioned in the Annals, and always called
Port-na-dtri-namhad [Portnadreenaud], the *port* or
bank of the three enemies; who these three hostile
persons were, history does not tell, though the people
of Lifford have a legend about them.

There is a place in the parish of Gartan, Donegal,
called Dunnatreesruhan, the mouth of the three
streamlets. A fort with three circumvallations is
often called Lisnatreeclee, or more correctly Lisna-
dreeglee, i. e. in Irish, *Lios-na-dtri-geladh*, the *lis* of
the three mounds. Ballytober in the Glens of Antrim is a shortened form of the correct Irish name,
Baile-na-dtri-dtobar, the town of the three springs.

We find occasionally other numbers also in names.
At the year 872, the Four Masters mention a place
called *Rath-aru-bo*, the fort of the one cow. There

is a place of this name, now called Raheanbo, in the
parish of Churchtown, Westmeath, but whether it is
the *Rath-aen-bo* of the annals is uncertain.   In the
parish of Maghcross, Monaghan, is a townland called
Corrinenty, in Irish *Cor-an-aen-tighe*, the round hill
of the one house ; and Boleynoendorrish is the name
of a place near Ardrahan, Galway, signifying the
booly or dairy place of the one door.   The island of
Inchenagh in the north end of Lough Ree, near
Lanesborough, is called by the Four Masters, *Inis-
endaimh*, the island of the one ox.   In the parish of
Rathronan, Limerick, is a townland called Kerry-
kyle, *Ceithre-choill*, four woods.   A townland in the
parish of Tulla, Clare, is called Derrykeadgran, the
oak wood of the hundred trees ; and there is a parish
in Kilkenny called Tullahaught, or in Irish *Tulach-
ocht*, the hill of the eight (persons).

PART III.

NAMES COMMEMORATING ARTIFICIAL STRUCTURES.

CHAPTER I.

HABITATIONS AND FORTRESSES.

EFORE the introduction of Christianity, buildings of all the various kinds erected in Ireland, whether domestic, military, or sepulchral, were round, or nearly round, in shape. This is sufficiently proved by the numerous forts and mounds that still remain all over the country, and which are almost universally circular. We find, moreover, in our old manuscripts, many passages in which the strongholds of the chiefs are described as of this shape; and in the ancient Life of St. Patrick written by St. Evin, there is an Irish stanza quoted as the composition of a druid named Con, in which it is predicted, that the custom of building houses narrow and quadrangular would be introduced among other innovations by St. Patrick.

The domestic and military structures in use among the ancient Irish were denoted by the words, *lios, rath, dun, cathair, brugh,* &c.; and these terms are still in use and applied to the very same objects. A notion very generally prevails, though much less so now than formerly, that the circular forts which still exist in great numbers in every county in Ireland, were erected by the Danes; and they are hence very often called "Danish raths." It is difficult to trace the origin of this opinion, unless we ascribe it to the well-known tendency of the peasantry to attribute almost every remarkable ancient work to the Danes. These people had, of course, fortresses of some kind in the maritime towns where they were settled, such as Dublin, Limerick, Waterford, Donegal, &c. In the "Wars of GG." (p. 41), we are told that they "spread themselves over Munster, and they built *duns* and *daingeans* (strongholds) and *caladh-phorts*" (landing ports); the Chronicon Scotorum at the year 845, records the erection of a *dun* at Lough Ree, by the Danish king Turgesius, from which he plundered Connaught and Meath; and it is not unlikely that the Danes may have taken, and for a long time occupied, some of the strongholds they found in the country. But that the *raths* and *lisses* are not of Danish origin would be proved by this fact alone, that they are found in every part of Ireland, and more plentiful in districts where the Danes never gained any footing, than where they had settlements.

There is abundance of evidence to show that these structures were the dwellings of the people of this country before the adoption of houses of a rectangular form; the larger *raths* belonging to the better classes, and the great fortified *duns* to the princes and chieftains. The remains still to be seen at the historic sites—Tara, The Navan, Rathcroghan, Bruree, &c.—places celebrated for ages as royal residences—afford striking testimony to the truth of this; for here we find the finest and most characteristic specimens of the Irish circular forts in all their sizes and varieties.

But besides, in our ancient writings, they are constantly mentioned as residences under their various names of *dun*, *rath*, *lios*, &c.—as constantly as houses and castles are in books of the last two or three centuries. To illustrate this, I will give a few passages, which I might extend almost indefinitely, if it were necessary. In the " Feast of *Dun-na-ngedh* " (" Battle of Moyrath "), Congal Claen thus addresses his foster father, king Domhnall:—" Thou didst place a woman of thine own tribe to nurse me in the garden of the *lios* in which thou dwelledst." On which O'Donovan remarks:—"The Irish kings and chieftains lived at this period (A.D. 637) in the great earthen *raths* or *lisses* the ruins of which are still so numerous in Ireland." In the same tale we read of two visitors that " they were conducted into the *dun*, and a dinner sufficient for a hundred was given to them " (p. 22); and in another place, king Domhnall says to Congal:—" Go to view the great feast which is in the *dun* " (p. 24).

In the " Forbais Dromadambghaire " (see p. 101, *supra*), we read that when Cormac sent to demand tribute from the men of Munster, they refused; but as there was a great scarcity in Cormac's dominions, they offered to relieve him by a gift of " a cow out of each *lios* in Munster;" and in the poem of Dubhthach-ua-Lugair in the Book of Leinster, celebrating the triumphs of Enna Kinsellagh, king of Leinster, it is stated that the tribute which was paid to Enna out of Munster, was " an *uinge* of gold from every *lios*."

In many cases, too, we find the building of *raths* or *lisses* recorded. Thus in the passage quoted from the Book of Leinster (p. 89, *supra*), queen Maev sentences the five sons of Dihorba to "raise a *rath*" around her, which should be "the chief city of Ulster for ever." In the "Battle of Moylena" (p. 2), it is stated that Nuadhat, the foster father of Owen Moro (see p. 133, *supra*), "raised a kingly *rath* on Magh Feimhin." In the Book of Armagh, and in several of the ancient Lives of St. Patrick, it is stated that on a certain occasion, the saint heard the voices of workmen who were building a *rath ;* and Jocelin, in relating the same circumstance, says that the work in which they were engaged was "*Rayth*, i. e. *murus*."

The houses in which the families lived were built within the enclosed area, timber being, no doubt, the material employed, in accordance with the well-known custom of the ancient Irish ; and the circum-vallations of the rath served both for a shelter and a defence. I might adduce many passages to prove this, but I will content myself with two—one from the MS. Harl. 5,280, Brit. Mus., quoted by O'Curry (Lect., p. 618) :—"They then went forward until they entered a beautiful plain. And they saw a kingly *rath*, and a golden tree at its *door* ; and they saw a splendid house in it, under a roof-tree of *findruine* ; thirty feet was its length." And the other from the tale of "The fate of the Children of Usnagh" (Atlantis, No. VI.), in which we find it stated that as Deirdre's mother "was passing over the floor of the house, the infant shrieked in her womb, so that it was heard all over the *lis*."

The circular form was not discontinued at the introduction of Christianity. The churches indeed were universally quadrangular, but this form was adopted only very slowly in the strongholds and dwellings of the chiefs and people. Even in ecclesiastical architecture the native form to some extent prevailed, for it seems evident that the shape of the round towers was suggested by that of the old fortresses of the country. Circular *duns* and raths, after the ancient pagan fashion, continued to be erected down to the twelfth or thirteenth century. It is recorded in the "Wars of GG.," that Brian Borumha fortified or erected certain *duns*, fastnesses, and islands (i. e. *crannoges*), which are enumerated; and the remains of several of these are still to be seen, differing in no respect from the more ancient forts. Donagh Cairbreach O'Brien, the sixth in descent from Brian Borumha, erected, according to the "Cathreim Thoirdhealbhaigh" (compiled in 1459 by John M'Grath), "a princely palace of a circular form, at Clonroad" (near Ennis); and the same authority states that Conchobhair na Siudainë, the son of Donagh, built at the same place a *longphort* of earth, as a residence for himself.

It is highly probable that originally the words *lios, rath, dun,* &c., were applied to different kinds of structures: but however that may be, they are at present, and have been for a long time, especially the two first, confounded one with another, so that it seems impossible to make a distinction. The *duns* indeed, as I shall explain further on, are usually pretty well distinguished from the *lisses* and *raths*; but we often find, even in old authorities, two of these terms, and sometimes the whole three, applied to the very same edifices.

In the following passage for instance, from the annotations of Tirechan, in the Book of Armagh, the terms *lios* and *dun* appear to be applied synonymously : —"Cummen and Breathán purchased *Ochter-uAchid* (upper field, supposed to be Oughteragh, a parish in the county Leitrim),with its appurtenances, both wood, and plain, and meadow, together with its *lius* and its garden. Half of this wood, and house and *dun*, was mortmain to Cummen " (Petrie, R. Towers, p. 218). And some other terms also are used in the same manner; as for example, in case of the great enclosure at Tara, which is known by the two names, *Rath*-na-riogh, and *Cathair*-Crofinn.

In another passage* from the Book of Ballymote, the word *rath* is used to denote the circular entrenchment, and *les* the space enclosed by the *raths*, while the whole quotation affords another proof that houses were built on the interior :—(a person who was making his way towards the palace) "leaped with that shaft over the three *raths*, until he was on the floor of the *les;* and from that until he was on the floor of the king-house."

Lios. The word *lios* [lis] and *rath* were applied to the circular mound or entrenchment, generally of earth, thrown up both as a fortification and a shelter round the level space on which the houses were erected; and accordingly they are often translated *atrium* by Latin writers. But though this is the usual application of these terms, both—and especially *rath*—were, and are, not unfrequently applied to the great high entrenched mounds which are commonly

* Quoted by Mr. J. O'Beirne Crowe, in an article in the Journal of the Hist. and Arch. Assoc. of Ireland, January, 1869, p. 222.

designated by the word *dun*. These forts are still
very numerous through the country, and they are
called *lisses* and *raths* to the present day. Their
great numbers, and the very general application of
the terms, may be judged of from the fact, that there
are about 1400 townlands and villages dispersed
through all parts of Ireland, whose names begin with
the word *Lis* alone; and of course this is only a very
small fraction of all the *lisses* in Ireland.

The name of Lismore in Waterford, affords a good
illustration of the application of this word; and its
history shows that the early saints sometimes surrounded their habitations with circular *lisses*, after
the fashion of their pagan ancestors. In the Life of
St. Carthach, the founder, published by the Bolland-
ists at the 14th of May, we are told that when the
saint and his followers, after his expulsion from Rahan, arrived at this place, which had previously been
called *Maghsciath* (Ma-skee), the plain of the shield,
they began to erect a circular entrenchment. Then
a certain virgin, who had a little cell in the same field,
came up and inquired what they were doing; and St.
Carthach answered her that they were preparing to
construct a little enclosure or *lis* around their goods,
for the service of God. And the holy virgin said,
" It will not be little, but great." "The holy father,
Mochuda (i. e. Carthach) answered—'Truly it will
be as thou sayest, thou handmaid of Christ; for from
this name the place will be always called in Scotic,
Liasamor, or in Latin *Atrium-magnum*,'" i. e. great
lis or enclosure. There are altogether eleven places
in Ireland called by this name Lismore; all with the
same meaning.

Many local names are formed by the union of the
term *lios* with a personal name; the individual com-

memorated being either the builder of the *lis*, or one
of its subsequent possessors. Listowel in Kerry is
called by the Four Masters, *Lios-Tuathail*, Tuathal's
or Thoohal's fort; Liscarroll in Cork, Carroll's or
Cearbhall's ; Liscahane in the parish of Ardfert,
Kerry, called in the Annals, *Lios-Cathain*, Cathan's
or Kane's *lis*.   The parish of Lissonuffy in Roscommon, took its name from an old church built by the
O'Duffys within the enclosure of a fort ; it is called
by the Four Masters *Lios-O-nDubhthaigh*, the fort of
the O'Duffys, the pronunciation of which is exactly
preserved in the present name.

Or if not by name, we have a person commemorated in some other way : as, for instance, in Lisal-
banagh in Londonderry, the Scotchman's *lis* ; Lisa-
taggart in Cavan, of the priest ; Lisnabantry in
the same county, the *lis* of the widow (*Lios-na-bain-
treabhaighe*, pron. Lisnabointry) ; Lissadill in the
parish of Drumcliff, Sligo, which the Four Masters
write *Lios-an-doill*, the fort of the blind man, the
same name as Lissadoill in Galway ; Lissancarla
near Tralee, the earl's fort.

The old form of this word is *les*, genitive *lis* ; but
in the modern language a corrupt genitive *leasa*
[lassa] is often found. All these are preserved in
modern names ; and the word is not much subject to
change in the process of anglicisation.   Different
forms of the genitive are seen in the following :—
Drumlish, the ridge of the fort, the name of a village
in Longford, and of some townlands in the northern
counties ; Moyliss, Moylish, and Moylisha (Moy, a
plain) ; Gortalassa, the field of the *lis* ; Knockalassa
(hill) ; Ballinlass, Ballinliss, Ballinlassa, and Ballin-
lassy, the town of the fort ; all widely-spread townland names.

The two diminutives *liosán* and *lisín* [lissaun, lish-een], little fort, are very common. The latter is usually made Lisheen, which is the name of twenty townlands, and helps to form many others. It assumes a different form in Lissen or Lissen Hall, the name of a place near Swords in Dublin, and of another in the parish of Kilmore, Tipperary. *Liosán* appears in Lissan and Lissane, which are the names of several townlands and parishes. The Irish plural appears in Lessanny (little forts) in Mayo; and the English in Lessans, near Saintfield in Down. It occurs in combination in Mellison in Tipperary, which is called in Irish, *Magh-liosain*, the plain of the little *lis*, and in Ballylesson in Down and Antrim, the town of the little fort.

With the adjective *dur* prefixed, signifying "strong," the compound *durlas* is formed, which means, according to O'Donovan, strong fort (Sup. to O'Reilly's Dict. in *voce*). Several great forts in different parts of the country are called by this name, one of the finest of which is situated in the parish of Kilruan, Tipperary; it is surrounded by three great entrenchments, and contains within it the ruins of a small ancient church. It is now called *Rath-durlais* in Irish, and gives name to the townland of Rathurles. Several places derive their names from this word *durlas*, the best known of which is the town of Thurles in Tipperary, which was often called *Durlas-O'Fogarty*, from its situation in O'Fogarty's country; but whether the fort remains or not, I cannot tell. Durless, another form, is the name of a townland in Mayo, and of two others in Tyrone.

Rath. This term has been explained in conjunction with *lios*, at page 270; in the Book of Armagh, *rath* is translated *fossa*. In a great number of cases this

word is preserved in the anglicised names exactly as
it is spelled in Irish; namely, in the form of *rath*,
which forms or begins the names of about 700 townlands. The townland of Rathurd near Limerick, is
now called in Irish *Rath-tSuird*, but by the annalists
Rath-arda-Suird, the fort of Sord's height, Sord being
probably a man's name. The Four Masters record the
erection of this *rath* by one of Heber's chieftains, in
A.M. 3501; and its remains are still to be seen on
the top of Rathurd hill, near the old castle. Rathnew in Wicklow, is called in Irish authorities *Rath-
Naoi*, the latter part of which is a man's name,
possibly the original possessor. Rathdrum, also in
Wicklow, means the rath of the *drum* or long hill,
and there are several other places of the same name
in different parts of Ireland; for raths were often
built on the tops of low hills.

Rathmore, great fort, is the name of forty townlands in different counties. In many of these the
forts still remain, as at Rathmore, four miles east of
Naas in Kildare. The great fortification that gave
the name to Rathmore near the town of Antrim,
still exists, and is famous for its historical associations. It is the *Rath-mor-Muighe-Line* (great
rath of Moylinny) of our historians; Tighernach
notices it as existing in the second century; and
in the seventh it was the residence of the princes
of Dalaradia. It was burned in the year 1315 by
Edward Bruce, which shows that even then it was an
important residence (Reeves, Eccl. Ant. p. 280).
Magh-Line (plain of Line), from which this great fort
took its name, was a district of the present county of
Antrim, anciently very much celebrated, whose name
is still retained by the townland of Moylinny near
the town of Antrim. The old name is also partly

retained by the parish of Ballylinny (town of Linĕ) lying a few miles eastward.

Rath is in Irish pronounced *raw*, and in modern names it takes various phonetic forms, to correspond with this pronunciation, such as *ra, rah, ray*, &c., which syllables, as representatives of *rath*, begin the names of about 400 townlands. Raheny near Dublin is called by the annalists *Rath-Enna*, the fort of Enna, a man's name formerly common in Ireland; the circumvallations of the old fort are still distinctly traceable round the Protestant church, which was built on its site. The village of Ardara in Donegal, takes its name from a conspicuous rath on a hill near it, to which the name properly belongs, in Irish *Ard-a'-raith*, the height of the rath. Drumragh, a parish in Tyrone, containing the town of Omagh, is called in the Inquisitions, Dromrathe, pointing to the Irish *Druim-ratha*, the ridge or hill of the rath. The word occurs singly as Raigh in Galway and Mayo; Raw, with the plural Raws, in several of the Ulster counties; and Ray in Donegal and Cavan.

Other modern modifications and compounds are exhibited in the following names:—Belra in Sligo, Belragh near Carnteel in Tyrone, and Belraugh in Londonderry, al meaning the mouth or entrance of the fort; Corray, in the parish of Kilmacteige, Sligo, *Cor-raith*, the round hill of the rath. Roemore in the parish of Breaghwy, Mayo, is called *Ruhemore* in an Inquisition of James I., which shows it to be a corruption of *Rathmore*, great fort; and there is another Roemore in the parish of Kilmeena, same county. Raharney in Westmeath preserves an Irish personal name of great antiquity, the full name being *Rath-Athairne*, Aharny's fort.

The diminutive Raheen (little fort), and its plural

19 *

Raheens, are the names of about eighty townlands, and form part of many others. There are six town-lands called Raheenroe, little red rath : the little fort which gave name to Raheenroe near Ballyorgan in the south of Limerick, has been levelled within my own memory.

Dun. The primary meaning of the word *dun* is "strong" or "firm," and it is so interpreted in Zeuss, page 30 :—"*Dun*, firmus, fortis." In this sense it forms a part of the old name of Dunluce castle, near the Giant's Causeway—*Dunlios* as it is called in all Irish authorities. *Dunlios* signifies strong *lis* or fort —the word is used by Keating, for instance, in this sense (see Four M., V. 1324f)—and this name shows that the rock on which the castle ruins stand was in old times occupied by a fortified *lis*. It has the same signification in *Dunchladh* [Dunclaw], i. e. fortified mound or dyke, the name of the ancient boundary rampart between Brefny and Annaly, extending from Lough Gowna to Lough Kinclare in Longford; a considerable part of this ancient entrenchment is still to be seen near Granard, and it is now well known by the anglicised name of Duncla.

As a verb, the word *dun* is used in the sense of "to close," which is obviously derived from its adjec-tival signification ; and this usage is exemplified in Corragunt, the name of a place in Fermanagh, near Clones, which is a corruption from the Irish name, *Corradhunta* (change of *dh* to *g*, page 56), i. e. closed or shut up weir.

Dun, as a noun, signifies a citadel, a fortified royal residence ; in the Zeuss MSS. it glosses *arx* and *castrum ;* Adamnan translates it *munitio ;* and it is rendered "pallace " by Mageoghegan in his transla-lation of the Annals of Clonmacnoise:—" He builded

seven downes or pallaces for himself." It is found in
the Teutonic as well as in the Keltic languages—
Welsh, *din;* Anglo-Saxon, *tún;* old high German,
zun. It is represented in English by the word *town;*
and it is the same as the termination *dunum,* so common in the old Latinised names of many of the cities
of Great Britain and the Continent.

This word was anciently, and is still, frequently
applied to the great forts, with a high central mound,
flat at top, and surrounded by several—very usually
three—earthen circumvallations. These fortified *duns,*
so many of which remain all over the country, were
the residences of the kings and chiefs; and they are
constantly mentioned as such in the Irish authorities.
Thus we read in the Feast of *Dun-na-ngedh* (Battle of
Maghrath, p. 7), that Domhnall, son of Aedh, king
of Ireland from A. D. 624 to 639, "first selected
Dun-na-ngedh, on the banks of the Boyne, to be his
habitation, ... and he formed seven very great
ramparts around this *dun,* after the model of the
houses of Tara." And other passages to the same
effect are cited at page 267 *et seq.*

In modern names, *dun* generally assumes the forms
dun, doon, or *don;* and these syllables form the beginning of the names of more than 600 townlands,
towns, and parishes.

There are twenty-seven different places called
Doon; one of them is the village and parish of Doon
in Limerick, where was situated the church of St.
Fintan; the fort from which the place received the
name, still remains, and was anciently called *Dun-
blesque.* Dunamon, now a parish in Galway, was so
called from a castle of the same name on the Suck;
but the name, which the annalists write *Dun-Iomgain,*
Imgan's fort, was anciently applied to a *dun,* which

is still in part, preserved. Dundonnell, i. e. Donall's
or Domhnall's fortress, is the name of a townland in
Roscommon, and of another in Westmeath; and
Doondonnell is a parish in Limerick; in Down it is
modified, under Scottish influence, to Dundonald,
which is the name of a parish, so called from a fort
that stands not far from the church.

The name of Dundalk was originally applied, not to
the town, but to the great fortress now called the moat
of Castletown, a mile inland; there can be no doubt
that this is the *Dun-Dealgan* of the ancient histories
and romances, the residence of Cuchullin, chief of the
Red Branch Knights in the first century. In some
of the tales of the Leabhar na hUidhre, it is called
Dun-Delca, but in later authorities, *Dun-Dealgan*,
i. e. Delga's fort; and according to O'Curry, it received its name from Delga, a Firbolg chief who
built it. The same personal name appears in Kil-
dalkey in Meath, which in one of the Irish charters
in the Book of Kells, is written *Cill-Delga*, Delga's
church.

There is a townland near Lisburn, now called
Duneight, but written *Downeagh* in an Inquisition of
James I., which has been identified by Dr. Reeves
with the place called in the "Circuit of Ireland"
Dun-Eachdhach, Eochy's fortress: where the great
king Muircheartach of the leather cloaks, slept a
night with his men, when performing his circuit of
the country in the year 941. There is a parish in
Antrim, and also a townland, called Dunaghy, which
is the same name more correctly anglicised.

The celebrated Rock of Dunamase in Queen's
County is now covered by the ruins of the OM'ores'
castle, but it must have been previously occupied by
a *dun* or *caher*. In an Inquisition of Richard II., it

is called *Donemaske*, which is a near approach to its
Irish name as we find it in the Annals, viz., *Dun-
Masg*, the fortress of Masg, who was grandson of
Sedna Sithbhaic (Sedna-Sheevick), one of the ances-
tors of the Leinster people.

A great number of these *duns*, as will be seen from
the preceding, have taken their names from persons,
either the original founders or subsequent possessors.   But various other circumstances, in connection
with these structures, were seized upon to form names.
Doneraile in Cork, is called in the Book of Lismore,
Dun-air-aill, the fortress on the cliff, but whether the
dun is still there I cannot tell.   There is a parish in
Waterford whose name has nearly the same signification, viz., Dunhill; it is called in Grace's Annals
Dounoil, which very well represents the Irish *Dun-
aille*, the fortress of the cliff.   It is understood to have
taken its name from a rock on which a castle now
stands; but a dun evidently preceded the castle, and
was really the origin of the name.   Doonally in the
parish of Calry, Sligo (an ancient residence of the
O'Donnells), which the Four Masters write *Dun-aille*,
and which is also the name of several townlands in
Sligo and Galway, is the same name, but more correctly rendered.

Of similar origin to these is Dundrum in Down,
which the Four Masters mention by the name of *Dun-
droma*, the fort on the ridge or long hill; the original
fort has however disappeared, and its site is occupied
by the well-known castle ruins.   There are several
other places called Dundrum, all of which take
their name from a fort built on a ridge; the ancient
fort of Dundrum, near Dublin, was most probably
situated on the height where the church of **Taney**
now stands.

Although the word *dun* is not much liable to be
disguised by modern corruption, yet in some cases it
assumes forms different from those I have mentioned.
The town of Downpatrick takes its name from the
large entrenched *dun* which lies near the Cathedral.
In the first century this fortress was the residence of a
warrior of the Red Branch Knights, called *Celtchair*,
or Keltar of the battles; and from him it is variously
called in Irish authorities *Dunkeltar*, *Rathkeltar*, and
Araskeltar (*aras*, a habitation). By ecclesiastical writers it is commonly called *Dun-leth-glas*, or *Dun-
da-leth-glas;* this last name is translated, the *dun* of the
two broken locks or fetters (*glas*, a fetter), which
Jocelin accounts for by a legend—that the two sons
of Dichu (see p. 112), having been confined as hostages by king Leaghaire, were removed from the place
of their confinement, and the *two* fetters by which
they were bound were broken, by miraculous agency.
"Afterwards, for brevity's sake, the latter part of this
long name was dropped, and the simple word *Dun*
retained, which has past into the Latin *Dunum*,
and into the English *Down*" (Reeves Eccl. Ant., p.
143). The name of St. Patrick was added, as a kind
of distinctive term, and as commemorative of his connection with the place.

Down is the name of several places in King's
County and Westmeath; and the plural Downs (i. e.
forts) is still more common. The name of the Glen
of the Downs in Wicklow, is probably a translation
of the Irish *Gleann-na-ndún*, the glen of the *duns* or
forts. Downamona in the parish of Kilmore, Tipperary, signifies the fort of the bog.

Dooneen, little fort, and the plural Dooneens, are
the names of nearly thirty townlands in the south
and west; they are often made Downing and

Downings in Cork, Carlow, Wicklow, and Kildare; and Downeen occurs once near Ross Carbery in Cork.

The diminutive in *an* is not so common, but it gives name to some places, such as Doonan, three townlands in Antrim, Donegal, and Fermanagh; Doonane in Queen's County and Tipperary; and Doonane (little forts) in the parish of Armoy, Antrim.

There are innumerable names all over the country, containing this word as a termination. There is a small island, and also a townland, near Dungarvan, called Shandon, in Irish *Seandun*, old fort; and there is little doubt that the fortress was situated on the island. This name is better known, however, as that of a church in Cork, celebrated in Father Prout's melodious *chanson :—*

> " The bells of Shandon,
> 'That sound so grand on
> The pleasant waters of the river Lee."

The name reminds us of the time when the hill, now teeming with city life under the shadow of the church, was crowned by the ancient fortress, which looked down on St. Finbar's infant colony, in the valley beneath. Shannon in Donegal, near Lifford, is from the same original, having the *d* aspirated, for it is written *Shandon* in some old English documents; and Shannon in the parish of Calry, Sligo, is no doubt similarly derived.

We sometimes find two of the terms, *lios, rath,* and *dun,* combined in one name; and in this case, either the first is used adjectively, like *dun* in Dunluce (p. 276), or it is a mere explanatory term, used synonymously with the second. Or such a name might

originate in successive structures, like the old name
of Caher in Tipperary, for which see p. 284, *infra*. Of
the union of two terms, we have a good illustration
in Lisdoonvarna in the north west of Clare, well
known for its spa, which takes its name from a large
fort on the right of the road as you go from Bally-
vaghan to Ennistymon. The proper name of this
is Doonvarna (*Dun-bhearnach*), gapped fort, from its
shape; and the word *Lis* was added as a generic
term, somewhat in the same manner as "river," in
the expression "the river Liffey;" Lisdoonvarna,
i. e. the *lis* (of) Doonvarna. In this way came also
the name of Lisdown in Armagh, and Lisdoonan in
Down and Monaghan. The word *bearnach*, gapped,
is not unfrequently applied to a fort, referring, not
to its original form, but to its dilapidated appearance,
when the clay had been removed by the peasantry,
so as to leave breaches or gaps in the circumvallations.
Hence the origin of such names as Rathbarna in Roscommon, and Caherbarnagh in Clare, Cork, and Kerry.

One of the most obvious means of fortifying a fort
was to flood the external ditch, when the construction admitted it, and the water was at hand; and
whoever is accustomed to examine these ancient structures, must be convinced that this plan was often
adopted. In many cases the old channel many be
traced, leading from an adjacent stream or spring;
and not unfrequently the water still remains in its
place in the fosse.

The names themselves often prove the adoption of
this mode of defence, or rather the existence of the
water in its original position, long after the fort had
been abandoned. There are twenty-eight townlands
called Lissaniska and Lissanisky, chiefly in the southern half of Ireland—*Lios-an-uisge*, the fort of the

water. None of these are in Ulster, but the same
name occurs as Lisanisk in Monaghan, Lisanisky in
Cavan, and Lisnisk and Lisnisky in Antrim, Down,
and Armagh. With the same signification we find
Rathaniska, the name of a place in Westmeath ; Ra-
heenaniska and Raheenanisky in Queen's County ;
Rahaniska and Rahanisky in Clare, Tipperary, and
Cork; and in the last-mentioned county there is a
parish called Dunisky or Doonisky.

Long after the *lisses* and *raths* had been abandoned
as dwellings, many of them were turned to different
uses ; and we see some of the high *duns* and mounds
crowned with modern buildings, such as those at
Drogheda, Naas, and Castletown near Dundalk.
The peasantry have always felt the greatest reluctance
to putting them under tillage; and in every part of
Ireland, you will hear stories of the calamities that
befel the families or the cattle of the foolhardy
farmers, who outraged the fairies' dwellings, by removing the earth or tilling the enclosure.

They were, however, often used as pens for cattle,
for which some of them are admirably adapted ; and
we have, consequently, many such names as Lisna-
geeragh, Rathnageeragh, and Rakeeragh, the fort of
the sheep ; Lisnagree and Lisnagry (*Lios-na-ngroidh*),
of the cattle ; Lisnagowan, the *lis* of the calves, &c.

Cathair This word, which is pronounced *caher*,
appears to have been originally applied to a city, for
the old form *cathir* glosses *civitas* in the Wb. MS. of
Zeuss. It has been, however, from a very early
period—perhaps from the beginning—used to designate a circular stone fort ; it is applied to both in the
present spoken language.

These ancient buildings are still very common
throughout the country, especially in the south and

west, where the term was in most general use; and
they have given names to great numbers of places.
In modern nomenclature the word usually takes one
of the two forms, *caher* and *cahir*; and there are more
than 300 townlands and towns whose names begin
with one or the other of these two words, all in
Munster and Connaught, except three or four in
Leinster—none in Ulster.

Caher itself is the name of more than thirty townlands, in several of which the original structures are
still standing. The stone fort that gave name to
Caher in Tipperary, was situated on the rocky island
now occupied by the castle, which has of course obliterated every vestige of the previous edifice. Its
full name, as used by the Four Masters and other
authorities, was *Cathair-duna-iascaigh* [eesky], the
circular stone fortress of the fish-abounding *dun*, and
this name is still used by the Irish-speaking people;
from which it is obvious, "that an earthen *dun* had
originally occupied the site on which a *caher* or stone
fort was erected subsequently" (Petrie, "Irish Penny
Journal," p. 257). I think it equally evident that
before the erection of the *caher* its name was *Dun-
iascaigh* [Duneesky], the fish-abounding *dun*, and
indeed the Four Masters once (at 1581) give it this
appellation. Dr. Petrie goes on to say:—"The
Book of Lecan records the destruction of the *caher*
by Cuirreach, the brother-in-law of Felimy the Lawgiver, as early as the third century, at which time it
is stated to have been the residence of a female named
Badamar."

Cahersiveen in Kerry retains the correct pronunciation of the Irish name, *Cathair-Saidhbhin*, the stone
fort of *Saidhbhin* or Sabina. *Saidhbhin* is a diminutive of *Sadhbh* [Sauv], a woman's name formerly

in very general use, which in latter times has been
commonly changed to Sarah. Caherconlish in Limerick must have received its name, like Caher in
Tipperary, from the erection of a stone fort near an
older earthen one; its Irish name being *Cathair-
chinn-lis* (Annals of Innisfallen), the caher at the
head of the *lis*. The ruins of the orignal stone fort
that gave name to Cahermurphy in the parish of
Kilmihil, Clare, still remain : the Four Masters call it
Cathair-Murchadha, Murrough's *caher*. The whitish
colour of the stones has given the name of Cahergal
(*Cathair-geal*, white *caher*) to many of these forts,
from which again eleven townlands in Cork, Waterford, Galway, and Mayo, have derived their names.

Cahereen, little *caher*, is the name of a place near
Castleisland in Kerry. The genitive of *cathair* is
catharach [caheragh], and this forms the latter part
of a number of names; for example, there is a
place near Dunmanway, and another near Kenmare,
called Derrynacaheragh, the oak wood of the stone
fort.

Caiseal. Cormac Mac Cullenan, in his glossary,
conjectures that the name of Cashel in Tipperary, is
derived from *Cis-ail*, i. e. tribute-rent; the same derivation is given in the Book of Rights; while O'Clery
and other Irish authorities propose *Cios-ail*, rent-rock
—the rock on which the kings of Munster received
their rents ; for Cashel was once the capital city of
Munster, and the chief residence of its kings. There
can be no doubt that all this is mere fancy, for the
word *caiseal* is very common in Irish, and is always
used to signify a circular stone fort; it is a simple
word, and either cognate with, or, as Ebel asserts,
derived from the Latin *castellum;* and it is found in

the most ancient Irish MSS., such as those of Zeuss,
Cormac's Glossary, &c.

Moreover, in the modern form, Cashel, it is the
name of about fifty townlands, and begins the names
of about fifty others, every one of which was so
called from one of these ancient stone forts ; and
there is no reason why Cashel in Tipperary should
be different from the others. As a further proof that
this is its real signification, it is translated *ma-
ceria* in a charter of A. D. 1004, which is entered in
the Book of Armagh (Reeves's Adamnan, p. 75).
About the beginning of the fifth century, Core, king
of Munster, took possession of Cashel, and there can
be but little doubt that he erected a stone fort on the
rock now so well known for its ecclesiastical ruins,
for we are told that he changed its name from *sidh-
dhruim* [Sheedrum : fairy ridge] to *Caiseal.* The
cashels belong to the same class as cahors, raths, &c.,
and like them are of pagan origin ; but the name was
very often adopted in Christian times to denote the
wall with which the early saints surrounded their
establishments.

Cashels, and places named from them, are scattered over the four provinces, but they preponderate
in the western and north western counties. Cashel-
fean in Cork and Donegal, and Cashelnavean near
Stranorlar in the latter county, both signify the stone
fort of the Fianna or ancient Irish militia (see p. 90);
Cashelfinoge near Boyle in Roscommon, the fort of
the scald crows. Sometimes this word is corrupted
to *castle*, as we find in Ballycastle in Mayo, the
correct name of which would be *Ballycashel*, for it is
called in Irish, *Baile-an-chaisil*, the town of the *cashel* ;
but the name of Ballycastle in Antrim is correct,

for it was so called, not from a *cashel*, but from a *castle*. Castledargan in the parish of Kilross, Sligo, is similarly corrupted, for the Four Masters call it *Caiseal-Locha-Deargain*, the stone fort of Lough Dargan.

Brugh and *Bruighean*. *Brugh* [bru] signifies a palace or distinguished residence. This term was applied to many of the royal residences of Ireland ; and several of the places that have preserved the word in their names have also preserved the old *brughs* or *raths* themselves. Bruree on the river Maigue in Limerick, is a most characteristic example. Its proper name, as it is found in many Irish authorities, is *Brugh-righ*, the fort or palace of the king ; for it was the principal seat of Oilioll Olum, king of Munster in the second century (see p. 133), and afterwards of the O'Donovans, chiefs of Hy Carbery, i. e. of the level country round Bruree and Kilmallock. In the Book of Rights, it is mentioned first in the list of the king of Cashel's seats, and there are still remaining extensive earthen forts, the ruins of the ancient *brugh* or palace of Oilioll Olum and his successors. According to an ancient MS. quoted by O'Curry (Battle of Moylena, p. 72), the most ancient name of this place was *Dun-Cobhthaigh* or Duncoffy, Coffagh's *dun ;* which proves that it was a fortified residence before its occupation by Oilioll Olum.

The present name of Bruff in Limerick, is a corruption of *Brugh* (see p. 52). It is now called in Irish *Brubh-na-leise*, in which both terms are corrupted, the correct name being *Brugh-na-Deise* [Bru-na-daishĕ], i. e. the *brugh* or mansion of the ancient territory of *Deis*-beg ; and from the first part, *Brubh* [bruv], the modern form Bruff is derived. The *brugh* that gave name to this place still exists ; it is an earthen fort near the town called at the present residence, as the name sufficiently attests—*Cloch-grianain*, the stone castle of the *grianan*.

It will be perceived that *grianan* is a diminutive from *grian*; the other diminutive in *óg* sometimes occurs also, and is understood to mean a sunny little hill. We find Greenoge, a village and parish in Meath; and this is also the name of a townland near Rathcoole, Dublin, and of another near Dromore in Down (see, for these diminutives, 2nd Ser., chap. II.).

Aileach. The circular stone fortresses already described under the words *cathair* and *caiseal*, were often called by the name *aileach* [ellagh], a word which signifies literally a stone house or stone fort, being derived from *ail*, a stone. Michael O'Clery, in his Glossary of ancient Irish words, gives this meaning and derivation :—"*Aileach* or *ailtheach*, i. e. a name for a habitation, which (name) was given from stones." (See Second Series, chap. I.)

Aileach is well known to readers of Irish history as the name of the palace of the northern Hy Neill kings, which is celebrated in the most ancient Irish writing under various names, such as *Aileach Neid*, *Aileach Frighrinn*, &c. The ruins of this great fortress, which are situated on a hill, four miles north west from Derry, have been elaborately described in the Ordnance memoir of the parish of Templemore; they consist of a circular *cashel* of cyclopean masonry, crowning the summit of the hill, surrounded by three concentric ramparts. It still retains its old name, being called Greenan-Ely, i. e. the palace of *Aileach*, for *Ely* represents the pronunciation of *Ailigh*, the genitive of *Aileach*; and it gives name to the two adjacent townlands of Elaghmore and Elaghbeg.

Elagh is also the name of two townlands in Tyrone, and there are several places in Galway and Mayo

called Ellagh, all derived from a stone fort. In
Caherelly, the name of a parish in Limerick, there is
a union of two synonymous terms, the Irish name
being *Cathair-ailigh*, the *caher* of the stone fort. So
also in Cahernally near the town of Headford in
Galway, which is called *Cathair-na-hailighi*, the *caher*
of the stone-fort, in an ancient document, quoted by
Hardiman (Iar C. 371); and the old stone-built
fortress still remains there. A stone fort must have
existed on a ridge in Dromanallig, a townland near
Inchigeelagh in Cork; and another on the promontory called Ardelly in Erris, which Mac Firbis, in
" Hy Fiachrach," calls *Ard-Ailigh.*

Teamhair. The name of Tara, like that of Cashel,
has been the subject of much conjecture, and our old
etymologists have also in this instance committed the
mistake of seeking to decompose what is in reality a
simple term. The ancient name of Tara is *Teamhair*,
and several of our old writers state that it was so
called from Tea, the wife of Heremon, who was
buried there:—*Teamhair*, i. e. the *mur* or wall of
Tea. But this derivation is legendary, for *Teamhair*
was, and is still, a common local name.

Teamhair [Tawer] is a simple word, and has pretty
much the same meaning as *grianan* (see p. 290); it
signifies an elevated spot commanding an extensive
prospect, and in this sense it is frequently used as a
generic term in Irish MSS. In Cormac's Glossary
it is stated that the *teamhair* of a house is a *grianan*
(i. e. balcony), and that the *teamhair* of a country is
a hill commanding a wide view. This meaning applies to every *teamhair* in Ireland, for they are all
conspicuously situated; and the great Tara in Meath,
is a most characteristic example. Moreover, it must
be remembered that a *teamhair* was a residence, and

that all the *teamhairs* had originally one or more forts, which in case of many of them remain to this day.

The genitive of *teamhair* is *teamhrach* [taragh or towragh], and it is this form which has given its present name to Tara in Meath, and to every other place whose name is similarly spelled (see p. 34). By the old inhabitants, however, all these places are called in Irish *Teamhair*. Our histories tell us that when the Firbolgs came to Tara, they called the hill *Druim-caein* [Drumkeen], beautiful ridge ; and it was also called *Liathdhruim* [Leitrim], grey ridge. There is a place called Tara in the parish of Witter, Down, which has a fine fort commanding an extensive view ; another in the parish of Durrow, King's County ; and Tara is the name of a conspicuous hill near Gorey in Wexford, on the top of which there is a carn.

There was a celebrated royal residence in Munster, called *Teamhair-Luachra*, from the district of *Sliabh Luachra* or Slievelougher. Its exact situation is now unknown, though it is probable that the fort is still in existence ; but it must have been somewhere near Ballahantouragh, a ford giving name to a townland near Castleisland in Kerry, which is called in Irish *Bel-atha-an-Teamhrach*, the ford-mouth of the *Teamhair*. A similar form of the name is found in Knockauntouragh, a little hill near Kildorrery in Cork, on the top of which is a fort—the old *Teamhair*—celebrated in the local legends ; and in the parish of Kiltoom in Roscommon, north west of Athlone, there is a place called Ratawragh, the *rath* of the conspicuous residence.

There are many other places deriving their names from these *teamhairs*, and to understand the follow-

ing selection, it must be remembered that the word
is pronounced *tarrer*, *tawer*, and *tower*, in different
parts of the country. One form is found in Tower-
beg and Towermore, two townlands in the parish of
Devenish, Fermanagh ; and there is a Towermore
near Castlelyons in Cork. Taur, another modification, gives name to two hills (-more and -beg), in
the parish of Clonfert, same county. Tawran, little
Teamhair (*Teamhrán*), occurs in the parish of Kill-
araght, Sligo ; we find the same name in the slightly
different form Tavraun, in the parish of Kilmovee,
Mayo ; while the diminutive in *ín* gives name to
Tevrin in the parish of Rathconnell, Westmeath.

Faithche. In front of the ancient Irish residences,
there was usually a level green plot, used for various
purposes—for games and exercises of different kinds,
for the reception of visitors, &c. *Faithche* [faha] was
the name applied to this green ; the word is translated *platea* in Cormac's Glossary ; and it is constantly
used by ancient Irish writers, who very frequently
mention the *faithche* in connection with the king's or
chieftain's fort. For instance, in the feast of *Dun-na-
ngedh* it is related that a visitor reached "*Aileach
Neid* (see p. 292, *supra*), where the king held his residence at that time. The king came out upon the
faithche, surrounded by a great concourse of the men
of Erin ; and he was playing chess amidst the host"
(Battle of Moyrath, p. 36).

The word is, and has been, used to denote a hurling field, or fair green, or any level green field in
which meetings were held, or games celebrated, whether in connection with a fort or not; in the Irish
version of Nennius, for instance, it is applied to a
hurling green. In Connaught, at the present time,

it is universally understood to mean simply a level green field.

The word enters pretty extensively into names, and it is generally made Fahy and Faha, the former being more usual in Connaught, and the latter in Munster ; both together constitute the names of about thirty townlands. It enters into several compounds, such as Fahanasoodry near Ballylanders in Limerick, *Faithche-na-súduire*, the green of the tanners, where tanning must have been carried on ; Fahykeen in Donegal, beautiful green.

The word takes various other forms, of which the following names will be a sufficient illustration. Faheeran in the parish of Kilcomreragh, King's County, is a contraction of *Faithche-Chiarain* [Faha-Kieran : Four Masters], Ciaran's green plot ; Faiafannan near Killybegs, Donegal, Fannan's green. It is made Foy in several places, as, for instance, near Rathangan in Kildare ; in Armagh we find Foyduff, Foybeg, and Foymore (black, little, great), and in Donegal, Foyfin, fair or whitish *faithche*. Foygh occurs in Longford and Tyrone ; in Donegal we have Foyagh, and in Fermanagh, Fyagh, both meaning a place abounding in green plots.

The townland of Dunseverick in Antrim, which takes its name from the well-known castle, is also called Feigh, a name derived, no doubt, from the *faithche* of the ancient *dun*, which existed ages before the erection of the castle ; and we may conclude that the name of Rathfeigh in Meath (the fort of the *faithche* or green), was similarly derived. The name Feigh occurs also in the south, but it is not derived from *faithche*. Ballynafoy in Down, is the town of the green ; the same name is found in Antrim, in the

forms Ballynafeigh, Ballynafey, and Ballynafie;
and in Kildare we find it as Ballynafagh.

The word occurs with three diminutives. Fahan
in Kerry, and Fahane in Cork, both signify little
faithche. Faheens (little green plots), is found in
Mayo; and there is a lake not far from the town of
Donegal, called Lough Foyhin, the lake of the little
green. In Sligo we have Foyoges, and in Longford,
Fihoges, both having the same meaning as Faheens.

Mothar. The ruin of a *caher* or *rath* is often designated in Munster by the term *mothar* [möher]; and
sometimes the word is applied to the ruin of any
building. This is its usual meaning in Clare; but
its proper signification is "a cluster of trees or
bushes;" and in other parts of Ireland, this is probably the sense in which it should be interpreted
when we find it in local names. On a cliff near Hag's
Head, on the western coast of Clare, there formerly
stood, and perhaps still stands, an old *caher* or stone
fort called Moher O'Ruan, O'Ruan's ruined fort;
and this is the feature that gave name to the well-
known Cliffs of Moher.

The word is used in the formation of local names
pretty extensively in Munster and Connaught, and in
two of the Ulster counties, Cavan and Fermanagh;
while in Leinster I find only one instance in the
parish of Offerlane, Queen's County. Scattered over
this area, Moher is the name of about twenty-five
townlands, and it is found in combination in those of
many others.

The plural Mohera (clusters or ruined forts), is the
name of a townland near Castlelyons in Cork; and
we find the word in Moheracreevy in Leitrim, the
ruin or cluster of or near the *creeve* or large tree. In
Cork also, near Rathcormick, is a place called Mo-

hereen, little *moher;* and Moheragh, signifying a place abounding in *mohers*, occurs in the parish of Donohill, Tipperary. Moheranea in Fermanagh, signifies the *moher* of the horse; and Drummoher in Clare, and Drommoher in Limerick, the ridge of the ruined fort.

Crannóg. The word *crannóg*, a formation from *crann*, a tree, means literally a structure of wood. In former times the Anglo-Irish employed it very generally to signify a basket or hamper of a certain size for holding corn. In its topographical use—the only use that concerns us here—it is applied to wooden houses placed on artificial islands in lakes. These islands were formed in a shallow part, by driving stakes into the bottom, which were made to support cross beams; and on these were heaped small trees, brambles, clay, &c., till the structure was raised over the surface of the water. On this the family, and in many cases several families, lived in wooden houses, sufficiently protected from enemies by the surrounding lake, while communication with the land was carried on by means of a small boat. The word *crannóg* was very often, and is now generally understoood, to mean the whole structure, both island and houses.

These lake dwellings were used from the most remote ages down to the sixteenth or seventeenth century, and they are frequently mentioned in the annals. The remains of many of them have been recently discovered, and have been examined and described by several archæologists. There are various places through the country whose names contain the word *crannóg*, in most of which there was a lake, with an artificial island, though in some cases the lakes have disappeared.

Crannoge is the name of a townland near Pomeroy
in Tyrone; Cronoge, of another in Kilkenny; and
in the parish of Cloonclare, Leitrim, is a place called
Crannoge Island. Crannogeboy (yellow) in the
parish of Inishkeel, Donegal, was once the residence
of one of the O'Boyles. Coolcronoge, the corner or
angle of the wooden house, is the name of a place in
the parish of Ardagh, Limerick. There is a small
lake near Ballingarry in the north of Tipperary,
called Loughnahinch (the lake of the island), in
which there is a crannoge fifty feet in diameter, which
gave name both to the lake and to the townland of
Ballynahinch; and the parish of Ballynahinch in
Connemara, which gives name to a barony, was so
called from a crannoge on an island in Ballynahinch
Lake. The Four Masters mention eight crannoges
in as many different parts of Ireland.

Longphort. This term is in frequent use, and generally signifies a fortress, but sometimes an encampment. The word was applied both to the old circular
entrenched forts and to the more modern stone
castles; and the fortresses bearing this designation
have given name to all those places called Longford,
of which there are about twenty. The town of Longford is called in the annals Longford-O'Farrell, from
the castle of the O'Farrells, the ancient proprietors,
which, according to tradition, was situated where the
military barrack now stands. The barony of Longford in Roscommon, takes its name from Longford
castle in the parish of Tiranascragh. Longford
demesne in the parish of Dromard, county Sligo, west
of Ballysadare, now the property of the Crofton
family, was formerly the seat of the O'Dowds, from
whom it took the name of *Longphort-O'Dowda* ("Hy
Fiachrach"), O'Dowd's fortress.

In a few cases, the word is somewhat disguised in modern names, as in Lonart near Killorglin in Kerry, which is a mere softening of the sound of *Longphort*. Athlunkard is the name of a townland near Limerick, from which Athlunkard-street in the city derives its name; the correct anglicised form would be *Athlongford*, the ford of the fortress or encampment. And it sometimes takes such forms as Lonehort, Lonehurt, &c.

Teach. This word [pron. *tagh*] means a house of any kind, and is cognate with Lat. *tectum;* it was used both in pagan and Christian times, and has found its way extensively into local names. The best anglicised form is *tagh*, which is of frequent occurrence; as in Tagheen, a parish in Mayo, which is called in "Hy Fiachrach," *Teach-chaein*, beautiful house; and Taghboy, a parish in Meath, yellow house. Sometimes the final guttural was omitted, as in Taduff in Roscommon, black house.

The form *tigh* [tee] is however in more general use in the formation of names than the nominative (see p. 34); and it usually appears as *tee, ti,* and *ty.* Teebane and Teemore (white and great house), are the names of several townlands in the northern counties; Tibradden near Dublin, and Tyone near Nenagh, Braddan's and John's house.

When *tigh* is joined with the genitive of the article, it almost always takes the form of *tin* or *tinna*, which we find in the beginning of a great number of names. There is a small town in Carlow, and several townlands in Wicklow and Queen's County, called Tinnahinch, which represents the Irish *Tigh-na-hiunsé*, the house of the island or river holm; Tincurragh and Tincurry in Wexford and Tipperary, the house of the *curragh* or marsh; Tinnascart in Cork and Waterford, and Tinnascarty in Kilkenny, the house of the *scart* or cluster of bushes.

The site on which a house stood is often denoted by the combination *ait-tighe* [aut-tee], literally, "the place of a house;" in modern names it is almost always made *atti* or *atty*, which form the beginning of about sixty townland names, the latter part being very often the name of the former owner of the house. It occurs once in the Four Masters at 1256, where they mention a place called *Ait-tighe-Mic-Cuirrin*, the site of Mac Currin's house.

Attidermot near Aughrim in Galway, signifies the site of Dermot's house; Attykit near Cashel in Tipperary of Ceat's or Ket's house. In a few cases, the compound is followed by some term characterising the house, as in Attiduff in Monaghan and Sligo, the site of the black house; Attatantee in Donegal, in Irish *Ait-a'-tseau-tighe*, the site of the old house. The word *ait* is sometimes used alone, to denote the site of anything, as in Atshanboe in Tipperary, the site of the old tent (*both*, a tent); Attavally, the name of three townlands in Mayo, the site of the *bally* or village.

From the general meaning of house, *teach* or *tigh* came to be used frequently in Christian times to denote a church; and hence the word is often joined to the names of saints, to designate ecclesiastical foundations, which afterwards gave names to parishes and townlands. Examples of this occur in Chap. III. Part II.; and I will add a few more here.

Taghadoe, a parish in Kildare, takes its name from an old church, which, however, has wholly disappeared, though a portion of the round tower still stands in the churchyard; the name is written by Irish authorities, *Teach-Tuae*, St. Tua's church. Tia-

quin was originally the name of a primitive church
in Galway, and it is written in Irish *Tigh-Dachonna*
[Teaconna], St. Dachonna's house, from which the
present name was formed by contraction, and by the
aspiration of the *D* (see p. 20). A castle was erected
there long afterwards, from which the barony of Tia-
quin has been so called. Timahoe in Queen's County,
well known for its beautiful round tower, took its
name (*Tech-Mochua*, O'Clery's Cal.) from St. Mochua,
the original founder and patron, who flourished in
the sixth century. St. Munna or Fintan, who died
in A. D. 634, founded a monastery in Wexford, which
was called from him *Teach-Munna* (Book of Leinster),
St. Munna's house, now modernized to Taghmon;
and the parish of Taghmon in Westmeath derived its
name from the same saint. Tymon, the name of a
place near Dublin, containing an interesting castle
ruin, has the same signification as Taghmon, but
whether the Munna whom it commemorates, is the
same as St. Munna of Taghmon, I cannot tell.

This word enters into various other combinations
in local names. There is a townland in the parish of
Lower Bodoney, Tyrone, called Crockatanty, whose
Irish name is *Cnoc-a'-tscan-tighe* (see pp. 51 and 23,
supra), the hill of the old house; and we see the
same form in Tullantanty (*Tulach*, a hill) in Cavan,
which has also the same meaning. Edentiroory near
Dromore in Down, means the *edan* or hill brow of
Rory's house.

I have already mentioned (p. 65) that in some of
the eastern counties, *s* is sometimes prefixed to this
word; and in addition to the examples given there,
I may mention Staholmog in Meath, St. Colmoc's
or Mocholmoc's house; and Stamullen in the same
county, Maelan's house.

Both [bŏh]. This word signifies a tent, *booth*, or
hut, and it was applied not only to the huts erected
for human habitation, but also sometimes to cattle
houses. It is an old word in the language, and
exists also in the kindred Keltic dialects:—Welsh
bod, Cornish *bod* and *bos*. It occurs very often in
our ancient authorities; and the annals make mention of several places whose names were derived from
these huts.

Templeshanbo at the foot of Mount Leinster in
Wexford, was anciently called *Scanboth* [Shanbŏh],
old tent or hut, the prefix Temple having been added
in recent times. It was also called *Scanboth-Siné*,
and *Scanboth-Colmain*, from St. Colman O'Fiachra,
who was venerated there. *Scanboth-Siné* signifies
the old tent of Sín [Sheen] a woman's name belonging to the pagan ages; and it is very probable that
this was its original name, and that St. Colman, like
many other Irish saints, adopted it without change.
There is a Shanbo in Meath, a Shanboe in Queen's
County; and Shanbogh is the name of a parish in
Kilkenny—all different forms of the same word. It
also appears in Drumshanbo (the *drum* or ridge of
the old tent), the name of a village in the parish of
Kiltoghert, Leitrim, of a townland in the parish of
Cloone, same county, and of another in the parish of
Kildress, Tyrone. This name is popularly believed
—in my opinion erroneously—to signify " the ridge
of the old cow" (*bo*, a cow), from the resemblance of
the outline of the hill at each place, to a cow's back.

Bough, which is merely an adaptation of *Both*, is
the name of a townland in Carlow, and of another
in Monaghan. Raphoe in Donegal, is called in the
annals *Rath-both*, the fort of the huts. In the Tripartite Life it is related that while St. Patrick was

at Dagart, in the territory of Magdula, he founded seven churches, of which *Both-Domhnaigh* (the tent of the church) was one ; which name is still retained in the parish of Bodoney in Tyrone. There is an old church near Dungiven in Londonderry, which in various Irish authorities is called *Both-Mheidhbhe* [Vēva], Maev's hut, an old pagan name which is now modernised to Bovevagh. Bohola, a parish in Mayo, takes its name from a church now in ruins, which is called in "Hy Fiachrach," *Both-Thola*, St. Tola's tent ; and in the parish of Templeniry, Tipperary, there is a townland called Montanavoe, in Irish *Mointeán-a'-bhoith*, the boggy land of the tent.

We have the plural (*botha*) represented by Boho, a parish in Fermanagh, which is only a part of its name as given by the Four Masters, viz., the *Botha* or tents of *Muintir Fialain*, this last being the name of the ancient tribe who inhabited the district : Boha-boy in Galway, yellow tents.

Almost all local names in Ireland beginning with *Boh* (except the *Bohers*), and those also that end with *-boha* and *-bohy*, are derived from this word. Thus Bohullion in Donegal, represents the Irish *Both-chuillinn*, the hut of the holly, i. e. surrounded with holly trees. Knockboha, a famous hill in the parish of Lackan, Mayo, is called in "Hy Fiach-rach," *Cnoc-botha*, the hill of the hut ; and Knock-naboha in Limerick and Tipperary, has the same meaning.

There are two diminutives of this word, viz., *Bothán* and *Bothóg* [bohaun, bohoge]. both of which are in very common use in the south and west of Ireland, even among speakers of English, to denote a cabin or hut of any kind. Bohaun is the name of four townlands in Galway and Mayo ; and we find

Bohanboy (yellow little hut) in Donegal. The other, Bohoge, is the name of a townland in the parish of Manulla, Mayo.

Caislen. The word *caislen* or *caislean* [cashlaun] is applied to a castle ; and like *caiseal*, it is evidently a loan word—a diminutive formation from the Latin *castellum*. Like the older *duns*, *cahers*, &c., these more modern structures gave names to numerous places, and the word is almost always represented by the English word *castle*.

Of the names containing this word, far the greater number are purely Irish, notwithstanding the English look of the word *castle*. Castlereagh is a small town in Roscommon, which gives name to a barony. The castle, of which there are now no remains, stood on the west side of the town, and it is called by the Four Masters, *Caislen-riabhach*, grey castle. There is a barony in Down of the same name, which was so called from an old castle, a residence of a branch of the O'Neills, which stood on a height in the townland of Castlereagh near Belfast; and some half dozen townlands in different counties are called by this name, so descriptive of the venerable appearance of an ancient castle. Castlebar in Mayo belonged, after the English invasion, to the Barrys, one of whom no doubt built a castle there, though the name is the only record we have of the event. It is called in Irish authorities, *Caislen-an-Bharraigh* (Barry's castle); and Downing, who wrote a short description of Mayo in 1680, calls it *Castle-Barry*, which has been shortened to the present name.

In a few cases, the Irish form is preserved, as for example in Cashlan, the name of two townlands in Monaghan, and of one in Antrim ; Cashlaundarragh in Galway, the castle of the oak tree ; Cashlancran

21

in Mayo, the castle of the trees; Ballycushlane in Wexford, the town of the castle.

Daingean. The word *daingean* [dangan] as an adjective, means strong; as a noun it means a stronghold of any kind, whether an ancient circular fort, or a more modern fortress or castle; and it is obviously connected with the English words *dungeon* and *donjon*. Dangan, which is the correct English form, is the name of a village in Kilkenny, and of a number of townlands, including Dangan in Meath, once the residence of the Duke of Wellington. This was also the old name of Philipstown; the erection of "the castle of *Daingean*" is recorded by the Four Masters at 1546; but it is probable that the name is older than the castle, and that it had been previously borne by a circular fort. The name of Dundanion at Blackrock near Cork, is like that of Dunluce (p. 276, *supra*); for *dun* is here an adjective, and the name signifies strong *dangan* or fortress.

Occasionally this word is anglicised Dingin, which is the name of a townland in Cavan; Dinginavanty in the parish of Kildrumsherdan in this county, means Mantagh's fortress. It is this form which has given origin to the modern name of Dingle in Kerry, by the usual change of final *l* to *n* (Dingin, Dingell, Dingle: see p. 48). It is called in the annals, *Daingean-ui-Chuis*, now usually written Dingle-I-Coush, i. e. the fortress of O'Cush, the ancient proprietor before the English invasion. These people sometimes call themselves Hussey in English, and this is the origin of the mistaken assertion made by some writers, that the place received its name from the English family of Hussey.

In the north of Ireland the *ng* in the middle of the word *daingean*, is pronounced as a soft guttural, which as it is very faint, and quite incapable of being represented by English letters, is suppressed in modern spelling, thereby changing *daingean* to *dian* or some such form. There are some townlands called Dian and Dyan in Tyrone and Monaghan; two in Armagh and one in Down, called Lisadian, the *lis* of the stronghold. Even in Mayo, a pronunciation much the same is sometimes heard; and hence we have the name of Ballindine, a village in that county, the same as Ballindagny in Longford, Ballindaggan in Wexford, and Ballindangan near Mitchelstown in Cork, the town of the stronghold. Elsewhere in Mayo, however, the word retains its proper form as in Killadangan, the wood of the fortress.

Badhun, or *Badhbhdhun* [bawn]. Beside many of the old castles, there was a *bawn* or large enclosure surrounded by a strong fence or wall, which was often protected by towers; and into this enclosure the cattle were driven by night to protect them from wolves or robbers. It corresponds to the *faithche* of the old pagan fortresses (see p. 295), and served much the same purposes; for as Smith remarks, speaking of the castle of Kilcrea, west of Cork, " the bawn was the only appendage formerly to great men's castles, which places were used for dancing, goaling, and such diversions * * * and for keeping cattle at night."

O'Donovan writing in the " Ulster Journal of Archæology," says:—" The term *bawn*, which frequently appears in documents relating to Irish history since the plantation of Ulster, is the anglicised form of the Irish *badhun*, an enclosure or fortress for cows. It occurs seldom in Irish documents, the earliest mention of a castle so called being found in the ' Four

Masters' at 1547, viz., *Badhun-Riaganach.*[*] From this forward it is met with in different parts of Ireland. In the most ancient Irish documents, a cow fortress is more usually called *bo-dhaingean*, but *bo-dhun* or *ba-dhun* is equally correct. Sometimes written *Badhbh-dhun*, the fortress of *Badhbh* [Bauv], the Bellona of the ancient Irish, but this is probably a fanciful writing of it." This latter form, however, and its presumed derivation from the name of the old war goddess, receive some support from the fact, that in Ulster it is pronounced *bauran*, in which the *r* plainly points to a *bh* in the Irish original; and this pronunciation is perpetuated in Bavan, the name of three townlands in Down, Cavan, and Louth.[†]

The bawns may still be seen near the ruins of many of the old castles through the country; and in some cases the surrounding wall, with its towers, remains in tolerable preservation. The syllable *bawn* is of very usual occurrence in local names, but as this is also the anglicised form of *bán* a green field, it is often difficult to tell from which of the two Irish words it is derived, for *badhun* and *bán* are pronounced nearly alike. The townland of Bawn in the parish of Moydow, Longford, derives its name from the bawn of Moydow castle, whose ruins remain yet in the townland.

* The word occurs however, in the form of *bo-dhun* in the Annals of Loch Cé at the years 1199 and 1200.

† Duald Mac Firbis writes the word *badhbh-dhun* in "Hy-Fiachrach." Boa Island, in Lough Erne, is called by the Four Masters, *Badhbha*, while the natives call it *Inis-Badhbhan*, i. e. the island of *Badhbh*. Mr. W. M. Hennessy's paper—read a short time since—"On the War-Goddess of the Ancient Irish," is not yet published, and I regret not being able to avail myself of it to illustrate more fully this interesting subject.

Lathrach. The site of anything is denoted by the word *lathrach* [lauragh], but this word is usually applied to the site of some sort of building. *Lathrach senmuilind* (H. 3. 18, T. C. D.), the site of an old mill. There are many places scattered through the four provinces called Laragh and Lauragh, to which this word gives name; Laragh in the parish of Skreen in Sligo, is called *Lathrach* in the Book of Lecan, and the village of Laragh at the entrance to Glendalough is another well-known example. Laraghaleas in Londonderry means the site of the *lis* or fort; Laraghshankill in Armagh, the site of the old church (see Shankill); Laraghbryan near Leixlip in Kildare, Bryan's house site. Caherlarhig, the stone fort of the site, near Clonakilty in Cork, very probably derived its name from a *caher*, built on the site of a more ancient *dun*.

Lathair [lauher], from which *lathrach* is derived, and which literally means "presence," is itself sometimes used in Cork and Kerry to signify a site, and is found also forming a part of names in these counties. Laheratanvally near Skibbereen in Cork, the site of the old town (*Lathair-a'-tscanbhaile*); Lahertidaly in the same neighbourhood, the site of Daly's house. Laracor near Trim in Meath, once the residence of Dean Swift, is called in an Inq. of Jac. I., Laraghcorre, which points to the original Irish form *Lathrach-cora*, the site of the weir. We find the diminutive Lareen in Leitrim, and Lerhin in Galway; Lislarheen (-more and -beg) in Clare, signifies the fort of the little site.

Laragh in the parish of Kiloumreragh, Westmeath, takes its name from a castle of the Mageoghegans, whose ruins are yet there, and which the Four Masters call *Leath-rath* [Larra], i. e. half rath; and some of the other Laraghs are probably derived from this Irish compound, and not from *lathrach*. *Leath-rath* is also the Irish name of Lara or Abbeylara in Longford, for so it is written in the annals.

Suidhe [see]. This word means a seat or sitting-place, cognate with Lat. *sedes*; it is found in our oldest authorities; and among others, the MSS. of Zeuss (Gram. Celt. p. 60). It is frequently used in the formation of names, usually under the forms *see*, *sy*, *se*, and *sea*; and these four syllables, in the sense of "seat," begin the names of over thirty townlands. It is very commonly followed by a personal name, which is generally understood to mean that the place so designated was frequented by the person, either as a residence, or as a favourite resort. The names of men, both pagan and Christian, are found combined with it.

See, which exactly represents *suidhe* in pronunciation, is the name of a townland in Cavan. On the south shore of Lough Derg in Donegal, is the townland Seadavog, the seat of St. Davog, the patron of Termondavog, or as it is now called Termonmagrath. In this name the word *sea* is understood in its literal sense, for the people still show the stone chair in which the saint was wont to sit.

The parish of Seagoe in Armagh, is called in Irish *Suidhe-Gobha* [See-gow], the seat of St. Gobha (Gow) or Gobanus; Colgan calls him " Gobanus of *Teg-da-Goba*, at the bank of the river Bann;" from which expression it appears that the place was anciently called *Tech-Dagobha*, the house of St. Dagobha, this last name being the same as Gobanus (p. 147, note, *supra*; see Reeves's Eccl. Ant.p. 107); and the parish of Seapatrick in Down, is called in Trias. Thaum. *Suidhe-Padruic*, St. Patrick's sitting place.

Shinrone in the King's County is mentioned by the Four Masters, who call it *Suidhe-an-róin* [Seenrone], the seat of the *ron*, i. e. literally a seal, but figuratively a hirsute or hairy man. In the same authority we find Sceoran in Cavan, written *Suidhe-Odhrain*, Odhran's or Oran's seat. Secoonglass in Limerick, Cuglas's seat; Syunchin near Clogher in Tyrone, the seat of the ash, i. e. abounding in ash trees.

Suidheachán [seehaun] is a diminutive formation on *suidhe*, which we also find occasionally in names. For instance, there is a hill called Seaghane (the seat) near Tallaght in Dublin; Seehanes (seats) is the name of a place near Dromdaleague in Cork, so called because it was the seat of O'Donovan; and Seeaghandoo and Seeaghanbane (black and white), are two townlands in Mayo.

CHAPTER II.

ECCLESIASTICAL EDIFICES.

It is well known that most of the terms employed in Irish to designate Christian structures, ceremonies, and offices, are derived directly from Latin. The early missionaries, finding no suitable words in the native language, introduced the necessary Latin terms, which, in course of time, were more or less considerably modified according to the laws of Irish pronunciation. Those applied to buildings are no-

ticed in this chapter; but we have besides, such
words as *easpog,* old Irish *epscop,* a bishop, from *epis-
copus;* *sagart* or *sacart,* a priest, from *sacerdos;* *bean-
nacht,* old Irish *bendacht,* a blessing from, *benedictio;*
Aiffrionn or *Aiffrend,* the Mass, from *offerenda;* and
many others. (See Second Series, chap. vi. and xxvi.)

We know from many ancient authorities that the
early Irish churches were usually built of timber
planks, or of wattles or hurdles, plastered over with
clay; and that this custom was so general as to be
considered a national characteristic. Bede, for instance, mentions that when Finan, an Irish monk,
became bishop of Lindisfarne, "he built a church fit
for his episcopal see; he made it not, however, of
stone, but altogether of sawn oak, and covered it
with reeds, after the manner of the Scots" (Hist.
Eccl., III. 25); and many other authorities to the
same effect might be cited. In some of the lives of
the early saints, we have interesting accounts of the
erection of structures of this kind, very often by the
hands of the ecclesiastics themselves—accounts that
present beautiful pictures of religious devotion and
humility; for the heads of the communities often
worked with their own hands, in building up their
simple churches—men who were, for long ages
afterwards, and are still, venerated for their learning
and holiness.

These structures, often put up hastily to meet the
wants of a newly formed religious community, or
the recently converted natives of a district, we know
were generally very small and simple; and in some
cases the names preserve the memory of the primitive materials. Kilclief in the county of Down,
took its name from one of those rude edifices; for its
Irish name, as used by several authorities, is *Cill-*

cleithe [clĕha], the hurdle church (*cliath* a hurdle), from which the present form has been derived by the change of *th* to *f* (p. 52). The same name is found as Kilclay near Clogher in Tyrone ; and a parish in Westmeath, called Kilcleagh (Killcliathagh in Reg. Clon.), exhibits another, and still more correct form.

But timber was not the only material employed; for stone churches began to be erected from the earliest Christian period. It was believed indeed, until very recently, that buildings of stone and mortar were unknown in Ireland previous to the Anglo-Norman invasion; but Petrie has shown that churches of stone were erected in the fifth, sixth, and succeeding centuries; and the ruins of many of these venerable structures are still to be seen, and have been identified as the very buildings erected by the early saints.

Cill. The Irish words, *cill, eaglais, teampull, domhnach*, &c.—all originally Latin—signify a church. *Cill* [kill], also written *cell* and *ceall*, is the Latin *cella*, and next to *baile*, it is the most prolific root in Irish names. Its most usual anglicised form is *kill* or *kil*, but it is also made *kyle, keel*, and *cal ;* there are about 3,400 names beginning with these syllables, and if we estimate that a fifth of them represent *coill*, a wood, there remain about 2,700 whose first syllable is derived from *cill*. Of these the greater number are formed by placing the name of the founder or patron after this word, of which I give a few illustrative examples here, but many more will be found scattered through the book.

Colman was a favourite name among the Irish saints; O'Clery's Calendar alone commemorates about sixty of the name. It is radically the same as Colum or Columba, and its frequency is probably to be at-

tributed to veneration for the great St. Columba.
There are in Ireland seven parishes, and more than
twenty townlands (including Spenser's residence
in Cork) called Kilcolman (Colman's church); but
in many of these it is now difficult or impossible to
determine the individual saints after whom they were
called. St. Cainnech or Canioe, who gave name to
Kilkenny, and also to Kilkenny West in Westmeath,
was abbot of Aghabo in Queen's County, where he
had his principal church; he is mentioned by Adamnan in his Life of St. Columba; he was born in A. D.
517, and died in the year 600. He was a native
of the territory of Keenaght in Derry, and he is
much venerated in Scotland, where he is called
Kenneth; and several churches in Argyle and in the
Western Islands, now called Kilkenneth and Kil-
kenzie, were named from him. There are thirty-five
townlands and parishes scattered through the four
provinces, called Kilbride, in Irish *Cill-Bhrighde*,
Brigid's or Bride's church, most of which were dedicated to St. Brigid of Kildare; and Kilbreedy, the
name of two parishes in Limerick, has the same origin.
Kilmurry is the name of nearly fifty townlands, in
most of which there must have been churches dedicated to the Blessed Virgin, for the usual Irish name
is *Cill-Mhuire*, Mary's church; but some may have
been so called from persons named *Muireadhach*.

Besides the names of saints, this term is combined
with various other words, to form local names. Shankill, in Irish *Seincheall*, old church, is the name of
seventeen townlands and four parishes, among others
the parish which includes Belfast. There is a village
in Kildare called Kilcullen, which was much celebrated for its monastery; it is called by Irish writers
Cill-cuillinn, the church of the holly; and there are

several townlands in other counties of the same name. At Killeigh near Tullamore, there was once a great ecclesiastical establishment, under the patronage of St. Sincheall. Its original name, as used in Irish authorities, is *Cill-achaidh* [Killahy], the church of the field, which has been softened down to the present form. There was, according to Colgan, another place of the same name in East Breifny; and to distinguish them, Killeigh in King's County is usually called by the annalists *Cill-achaidh-droma-fada*, i. e. Killeigh of Drumfada, from a *long ridge* or hill which rises immediately over the village.

Kyle, a form much used in the south, is itself the name of more than twenty townlands, and constitutes the first syllable of about eighty others; a large proportion of these, however, probably half, are not churches but woods (*coill*). In some parts of the south, Kyle is used to denote a burial place for children, and sometimes for unbaptized infants, but this is a modern application.

The diminutive Killeen is the name of about eighty townlands, and its combinations are very numerous —all derived from a "little church," except about a fifth from "woods." Killeentierna in Kerry must have been founded by, or dedicated to, some saint named Tierna, or Tighernach. Killeens and Killeeny, little churches, are also often met with. Monagilleeny near Ardmore in Waterford, is in Irish *Moin-na-gcillinidhe*, the bog of the little churches.

Calluragh, or as it is written in Irish, *Ceallurach*, which is a derivative from *cill*, is applied in the southern counties, and especially in Clare, to an old burying ground; sometimes it means a burial place disused, except only for the interment of children; and occasionally it denotes a burial place for unbap-

tized infants, even where there never was a church;
as for example, in the parish of Kilcrohane in Kerry,
where the old forts or lisses are sometimes set apart
for this purpose, and called *Callooraghs*. In the anglicised form, Calluragh, this word has given name to
several townlands.

Cealtrach [caltragh], which is also a derivative
from *cill*, is used—chiefly in the western half of Ireland—to denote an old burying ground. It is commonly anglicised Caltragh, which is the name of a
great many places; and there is a village in Galway
called Caltra, another modification of the same word.
We find Cloonacaltry in Sligo and Roscommon, the
cloon or meadow of the burying ground. *Cealdrach*
[caldragh], another Irish form, gives name to eight
townlands, now called Caldragh, which are confined
to six counties, with Leitrim as centre; in one case
it is made Keeldra in the last county.

Eaglais. Another term for a church is *eaglais*
[aglish], derived, in common with the Welsh *ecclwis*,
the Cornish *eglos*, and the Armoric *ylis*, from the
Latin *ecclesia*. This term was applied to a great
many churches in Ireland; for we have a considerable
number of parishes and townlands called Aglish and
Eglish, the former being more common in the south,
and the latter in the north. There is a parish in
Tipperary called Aglishcloghane, the church of the
cloghaun or row of stepping-stones; another in Limerick called Aglishcormick, St. Cormac's church;
and a third in Cork, called Aglishdrinagh, the church
of the *dreens* or sloe bushes. Ballynahaglish, the
town of the church, is the name of a parish in Mayo,
and of another in Kerry; and near Ballylanders in
Limerick, is a place called Glennahaglish, the glen
of the church. In the corrupt form Heagles, it is the

name of two townlands near Ballymoney in Antrim ;
and in the same neighbourhood we find Drumaheglis,
the ridge or long hill of the church.

Teampull.   From the Latin *templum* is derived the
Irish *teampull.*   Like *cill, eaglais,* and *domhnach,* it
was adopted at a very early date, being found in the
oldest Irish MSS., among others those cited by Zeuss.
In anglicised names it is usually changed to *temple,*
which forms the beginning of about ninety townland
names ; and it is to be borne in mind that these,
though to all appearance at least partly English, are
in reality wholly Irish. A remarkably large proportion of parishes have taken their names from these
teampulls, there being no less than fifty parish names
beginning with the word *temple.*

There are four parishes in Cork, Longford, Tipperary, and Waterford, where the original churches
must have been dedicated to the Archangel Michael,
as they still bear the name of Templemichael ; Templebredon in Tipperary, is called in Irish *Teampull-
ui-Bhrideáin,* O'Bredon's church ; and Temple-etney
in the same county, was so called from St. Eithne,
whose memory is fast dying out there.   The original church of Templecarn, not far from Pettigo in
Donegal, must have been built near a pagan sepulchre, for the name signifies the church of the *carn*
or monument.   Templetuohy in Tipperary signifies
the church of the *tuath* or territory, and it received
this name as having been the principal church of
the *tuath* or district in which it was situated.   A
cathedral, or any large or important church, was
sometimes called, by way of distinction, Templemore,
great church ; and this is the name of three parishes
in Londonderry, Mayo, and Tipperary, the first in-

oluding the city of Derry, and the last the town of Templemore.

Domhnach. The Irish word *domhnach* [downagh], which signifies a church, and also Sunday, is from the Latin *Dominica*, the Lord's day. According to the Tripartite Life, Jocelin, Ussher, &c., all the churches that bear the name of *Domhnach*, or in the anglicised form, Donagh, were originally founded by St. Patrick; and they were so called because he marked out their foundations on Sunday. For example, in the Tripartite Life we are told that the saints " having remained for seven Sundays in *Cinnachta*, laid the foundations of seven sacred houses to the Lord; [each of] which he therefore called *Dominica*," i. e. in Irish *Domhach*. Shanonagh in the parish of Templeoran in Westmeath, is called Sendonagh, in Sir Robert Nugent's Patent, and explained in it " Old Sonday," but it properly means " Old Church."

In the year 439, while St. Patrick was in Connaught, his nephew, bishop Sechnall or Secundinus, arrived in Ireland in company with some others. He was the son of Restitutus the Lombard by St. Patrick's sister Liemania or Darerca (see p. 94, *supra*), and very soon after he was left by his uncle in Meath. The church founded for him, where he resided till his death in 448, was called from him *Domhnach-Sechnaill* [Donna-shaughnill : Leabhar Breac], the church of St. Sechnall, now shortened to Dunshaughlin, which is the name of a village and parish in the county Meath.

There are nearly forty townlands whose names are formed by, or begin with, Donagh, of which more than twenty are also parish names. In all those

places there must have been one of the primitive
Dominicas, and most of them have burial places and
ruins to this day; fourteen of the parishes are
called Donaghmore, great church. Donaghanie near
Clogherny in Tyrone, is called by the Four Masters,
Domhnach-an-eich, the church of the steed; according to the same authority, the proper name of
Donaghmoyne in Monaghan, is *Domhnach-maighin*
the church of the little plain; and there is a
place of the same name near Clogher in Tyrone.
The Irish name of Donaghedy in Tyrone, is *Domh-
nach-Chaeide* (O'C. Cal.); and it was so called from St.
Caeide or Caidoc, a companion of St. Columbanus.
The genitive form of the word (see p. 34) gives
name to Donnycarney, Cearnach's or Carney's
church, a village near Dublin, and another near
Drogheda.

Aireagal. This word (pronounced *arrigle*) means
primarily a habitation, but in a secondary sense, it
was often applied to an oratory, hermitage, or small
church. The word is obviously derived from the
Latin *oraculum*; for besides the similarity of form,
we know that in the Latin Lives of the Irish saints
who flourished on the continent, the oratories they
founded are often designated by the term *oraculum*
(Petrie, R. Towers, p. 349). It has been used in
Irish from the earliest times, for it occurs in our
oldest MSS., as for instance in the Leabhar na
hUidhre, where we find it in the form *airicul*.

Errigal, the usual English form, is the name of a
parish in Londonderry, and of a townland in Cavan.
The well-known mountain called Errigal in Donegal,
in all probability took its name from an oratory
somewhere near it. The church of Errigal Keer-
ogue, which gives name to a parish in Tyrone, was

once a very important establishment; it is often
mentioned by the annalists, and called by them
Aireagal-Dachiarog, the church of St. Dachiarog.
Errigal Trough in Monaghan, is called in Irish
Aireagal-Triucha, the church of (the barony of)
Trough. Duarrigle is the name of a place on the
Blackwater, near Millstreet in Cork, containing the
ruins of a castle built by the O'Keeffes; its Irish
name is *Dubh-aireagal*, black habitation or oratory;
there is another place of the same name near Kanturk;
and we have Coolnaharragill in the parish of Glan-
behy, west of Killarney, the corner or angle of the
oratory.

Urnaidhe. This word which is variously written
urnaidhe, ornaidhe, or *ernaidhe* [urny, erny], signifies
primarily a prayer, but in a secondary sense, it is
applied to a prayer-house: Latin *oratorium.* It
takes most commonly the form Urney, which is the
name of some parishes and townlands in Cavan,
Tyrone and King's County; Urney in Tyrone is
often mentioned by the Four Masters, and called
Ernaidhe or *Urnaidhe.* The word often incorporates
the article in English (see p. 23), and becomes Nur-
ney (*an Urnaidhe,* the oratory), which is the name of
several parishes, villages, and townlands, in Carlow
and Kildare. It occurs in combination in Temple-
nahurney in Tipperary, the church of the oratory.

Scrin. *Scrin* [skreen], which comes directly from
the Latin *scrinium,* signifies a shrine, i. e. an orna-
mented casket or box, containing the relics of a saint.
These shrines were very usual in Ireland; they were
held in extraordinary veneration, and kept with the
greatest care; and several churches where they were
preserved were known on this account by the Irish
name *Scrin,* or in English, Skreen or Skrine. The

most remarkable of these was Skreen in Meath, which is called in the annals *Scrin-Choluimcille*, St. Columkille's shrine, and it was so called because a shrine containing some of that saint's relics was preserved there.

Lann. *Lann*, in old Irish *land*, means a house or church. The word is Irish, but in its ecclesiastical application, it was borrowed from the Welsh, and was introduced into Ireland at a very early age; when it means simply "house," it is no doubt purely Irish, and not a loan word. It forms part of the terms *ith-lann* and *lann-iotha* [ihlan, lan-iha], both of which are used to signify a granary or barn, literally *house of corn* (*ith*, corn); the latter is often used by the English speaking people of some of the Munster counties, who call a barn a *linney*; and from the former we have Carrignahihilan, the name of a townland near Kenmare, the rock of the granary. *Lann* is found in our earliest MSS., among others in those of Zeuss; it occurs also in an ancient charter in the Book of Kells, in the sense of *house*, and it is so translated by O'Donovan. It is a word common to several languages, and its primary signification seems to be an enclosed piece of ground; "Old Arm. *lann*; Ital., Fr., Provençal *landa*, *lande*, Gothic (and English) *land*" (Ebel).

It is not found extensively in local nomenclature, and I cannot find it at all in the south; but it has given origin to the names of a few remarkable places; and it is usually anglicised *lyn*, *lynn*, or *lin*, from the oblique form *lainn* [lin: see p. 34, *supra*], as in the word *linney* quoted above. The celebrated St. Colman-Elo, patron of Lynally near Tullamore, was, according to O'Clery's Calendar, the son of St. Columba's sister. At an assembly of saints held in this

22

neighbourhood about the year 590, Columba, who
had come from the convention at *Druim-cett*, to visit
his monastery at Durrow, proposed that a spot of
ground should be given to Colman, where he might
establish a monastery; and Aedh Slaine, prince of
Meath, afterwards king of Ireland, answered that
there was a large forest in his principality, called
Fidh-Elo [Fee-Elo], i. e. the wood of Ela, where he
might settle if he wished.   Colman accepted it, and
said:—"My resurrection shall be there, and hence-
forth I shall be named [Colman-Elo] from that
place." He soon after erected a monastery there,
which became very famous, and which was called
Lann-Elo or *Land-Ealla* (O'Clery's Cal.), i. e. the
church of Ela, now anglicised Lynally (see Lanigan,
Eccl. Hist. II. 304).

Another place equally celebrated, was *Lann-léire*
or *Land-léri* [Book of Leinster], i. e. the church of
austerity, which until recently was supposed to be
the old church of Lynn, on the east side of Lough
Ennel in Westmeath. But Dr. Reeves has clearly
identified it with Dunleer in Louth, the word *dun*
being substituted for *lann*, while the latter part of the
name has been preserved with little change (see
Dr. Todd in "Wars of GG., introd., p. xl.). The
old church of Lynn, which gives name to a parish in
Westmeath, though it is not the *Lann-léire* of history, derives its name from this word *lann*.

The word appears in other, and more correct forms
in Landmore, i. e. great church, in Londonderry;
Landahussy or Lannyhussy, O'Hussy's house or
church, in Tyrone; Lanaglug in the same county,
Lann-na-gclog, the church of the bells. In Landbrock
in Fermanagh, *Lann* appears to mean simply habitation, the name being applied to a badger warren—

Lann-broc, house of badgers. Belan in Kildare, is called by the annalists *Biothlann,* which name it may have derived from a house of hospitality; *bioth,* life or existence; *Biothlann,* refection house; similar in formation to *ithlann* corn house (see p. 321).

Glenavy in Antrim is another example of the use of this word. The *g* is a modern addition; and Dr. Reeves has remarked, that the earliest authority he finds for its insertion is a Visitation Book of 1661. In the taxation of 1306, it is called *Lennewy,* and in other early English documents, Lenavy, Lynavy, &c. (Reeves Eccl. Ant., p. 47), which very well represent the pronunciation of the original Irish name, *Lann-abhaich* [Lanavy], as given in the Calendar, signifying the church of the dwarf. Colgan states that when St. Patrick had built the church there, he left it in charge of his disciple Daniel, who from his low stature, was called *abhac* [avak or ouk], i. e., dwarf, and that from this circumstance the church got its name. It is worthy of remark here, that other places have got names from a like circumstance; for example, Cappanouk in the parish of Abington, Limerick, represents the Irish *Ceapach-an-abhaich* the garden plot of the dwarf.

Baisleac. This is a loan word, little changed, from the Latin *basilica,* and bears the same meaning, viz., a church; it is of long standing in Irish, being found in very ancient MSS., and was no doubt brought in, like the preceding terms, by the first Christian teachers. I am aware of only two places in Ireland deriving their names from this word. One is Baslick, an old church giving name to a parish in Roscommon, which is often mentioned by the Four Masters, and which, in the Tripartite Life of St. Patrick, is called *Baisleac-mór,* great church. The

other place has for its name the diminutive Bas-
lickane, and is a townland in the parish of Kilcrohane, Kerry.

Disert. The word *disert* is borrowed from the Latin
desertum, and retains its original meaning in Irish,
viz., a desert, wilderness, or sequestered place. It is
used very often in Irish writings ; as for example, in
the Battle of Moyrath, p. 10 :—" *Ocus disert mbec
aigi ann sin,*" and he (the saint) had a little *desert*
(hermitage) there. It is generally used in an ecclesiastical sense to denote a hermitage, such secluded
spots as the early Irish saints loved to select for their
little dwellings ; and it was afterwards applied to
churches erected in those places.

Its most usual modern forms are Desert, Disert,
Dysart, and Dysert, which are the names of a considerable number of parishes and townlands throughout Ireland, except only in the Connaught counties
(where, however, the word is found in other forms).
Desertmartin is the name of a village in Londonderry,
and Desertserges that of a parish in Cork, the former
signifying Martin's, and the latter, Saerghus's hermitage ; Killadysert in Clare means the church of the
desert or hermitage.

The word *disert* takes various corrupt forms in the
mouths of the peasantry, both in Irish and English ;
such as *ister, exter, tirs, tristle,* &c. A good example
of one of these corruptions is found in Estersnow, the
name of a townland and parish in Roscommon. The
Four Masters call it *Disert-Nuadhan* [Nooan], St.
Nuadha's hermitage ; but the people now call it
in Irish, *Tirs-Nuadhan ;* while in an Inquisition of
Elizabeth, it is called in one place *Issetnoine,* and
in another place, *Issertnoine,* which stand as intermediate forms between the ancient and present names.

Though written Estersnow on the Ordnance maps, it
is really called by the people, when speaking English,
Easternow, which form was evidently evolved under
the corrupting influence noticed at page 38, *supra*,
(IX). The patron saint is probably the Nuadha
[Nooa] commemorated in O'Clery's Calendar at the
3rd of October; but he is now forgotten there, though
his holy well, Tobernooan, is still to be seen, and
retains his name (see O'Donovan's Four Masters,
Vol. III., p. 546, note *p*).

This root word assumes another form in Isertkelly,
an ancient church giving name to a parish in Galway, mentioned by the Four Masters, who call it
Disert-Cheallaigh, Ceallach's or Kelly's hermitage;
and in Isertkieran, a parish in Tipperary, which no
doubt received its name from St. Ciaran of Ossory
(see p. 148, *supra*). It is still further altered in
Ishartmon, a parish in Wexford, St. Munna's desert,
i. e. St. Munna of Taghmon (p. 302).

In some of the Leinster counties there are several
places whose names have been changed by the substitution of the modern word *castle* for the ancient
disert; this may be accounted for naturally enough
in individual cases, by the fact that a castle was
erected on or near the site of the old hermitage.
Castledermot in Kildare, whose ancient importance
is still attested by its round tower and crosses, is well
known by the name of *Disert Diarmada*; where
Diarmad, son of Aedh Roin, king of Ulidia, founded
a monastery about A. D. 800. The present form of
the name was, no doubt, derived from the castle built
there by Walter de Riddlesford in the time of Strong-
bow.

The Irish name of Castledillon in Kildare, is
Disert-Iolladhan [Disertillan], i. e. Iolladhan's her-

mitage.   Castlekeeran near Oldcastle in Meath, is
another example. The ancient name of this place, as
appears by the Four Masters, A.D. 868, was *Bealach-
duin* [Ballaghdoon], the road of the *dun* or fort; but
after the time of St. Ciaran the Pious, who founded
a monastery there in the eighth century, and died
in the year 770, it was generally called in the annals,
Disert-Chiarain [Disert-Kieran], St. Kieran's hermitage.   The castle that originated the present form
of the name belonged, as some think, to the Staffords,
but according to others, to the Plunkets.

Cros. *Cros* signifies a cross, and is borrowed from
the Latin *crux;* it occurs in our earliest writings;
and is found in some very old inscriptions on crosses.
It is scarcely necessary to state that, from the time
of the introduction of Christianity into this country,
crosses were erected in connection with churches and
other religious foundations; they were at first simple
and unadorned, but became gradually more elegant
in design, and more elaborate in ornamentation; and
we have yet remaining, in many parts of the country, crosses of the most beautiful workmanship, last-
ing memorials of the piety and artistic skill of our
forefathers.

These monuments were not confined to religious
buildings.   In Adamnan's Life of St. Columba, it is
related that on a certain occasion, a man whom the
saint was coming to meet, suddenly fell down and
expired. "Hence, on that spot, before the entrance
to the kiln, a cross was erected, and another where
the saint stopped, which is seen to this day" (Lib. I.,
Cap. 45); on which Dr. Reeves remarks:—"It was
usual among the Irish to mark with a cross the spot
where any providential visitation took place." This

very general custom is attested not only by history,
but also by the great number of places that have
taken their names from crosses.

The word Cross itself is the name of about thirty
townlands, and it forms the first syllable of about
150 others; there are besides numerous names in
which it assumes other forms, or in which it occurs
in the termination. Some of these places probably
took their names from cross-roads, and in others the
word is used adjectively, to signify a transverse position; but these are exceptions, and the greater number commemorate the erection of crosses.

A cross must have formerly stood near the old
parish church of Crosserlough in Cavan, the Irish
name being *Cros-air-loch*, the cross on or by the lake.
Crossmolina in Mayo, is called by the Four Masters,
Cros-ui-Mhaeilfhina [Crossyweeleena], O'Mulleeny's
cross; the family of O'Maelfhina, whose descendants
of the present day generally call themselves Mullany,
had their seat here, and were chiefs of the surrounding district. There are some townlands and a village in Down, called Crossgar, short cross; Cross-
farnoge, the name of a prominent cape near Carnsore
point, signifies the cross of the alder tree; and Gort-
nagross, the name of several places in the northern
and southern counties, is the field of the crosses—
Gort-na-gcros. The parish of Aghacross (the ford of
the cross), near Kildorrery in Cork, took its name,
no doubt, from a cross in connection with St.
Molaga's establishment (see p. 151), erected to mark
a ford on the Funcheon. There are several places
called Crossan, Crossane, and Crossoge, all which
signify little cross.

The oblique form *crois* (see p. 34, *supra*) is pronounced *crush*, and has given the name Crosh to two

townlands in Tyrone ; to Crushybracken in Antrim,
O'Bracken's cross; and to several other places. We
find the genitive in Ardnacrusha, the name of a village near Limerick city, and of a townland in Cork,
Ard-ua-croise, the height of the cross ; the diminutive, Crusheen, little cross, is the name of a small
town in Clare ; and there are townlands in Galway
called Crosheen and Crusheeny,—the last meaning
little crosses. *Crossaire* [crussera], which is a derivative from *cros*, is applied in the south of Ireland to
cross-roads, and hence we have Crossery and Crussera,
two townlands in Waterford, the latter near Dungarvan. For the form *croch*, see page 219.

CHAPTER III.

MONUMENTS, GRAVES, AND CEMETERIES.

BEFORE the introduction of Christianity, different
modes of sepulture were practised in Ireland. In
very early ages it was usual to burn the body, and
place the ashes in an urn, which was deposited in
the grave. It seems very extraordinary that all
memory of this custom should be lost to both history
and tradition ; for I am not aware that there is any
mention of the burning of bodies in any—even the
oldest—of our native writings. But that the custom
was very general we have the best possible proof ;
for in every part of Ireland, cinerary urns, containing
ashes and burned bones, have been found, in the
various kinds of pagan sepulchres.

Occasionally the bodies of kings and chieftains

were buried in a standing posture, arrayed in full
battle costume, with the face turned towards the
territories of their enemies. Of this custom we have
several very curious historical records. In the Leabhar na hUidhre it is related that King Leaghaire
[Leary] (see pp. 138, 139, *supra*) was killed "by the
sun and wind" in a war against the Lagenians; "and
his body was afterwards brought from the south, and
interred, with his arms of valour, in the south east of
the external rampart of the royal *Rath Laeghaire*
at *Temur* ('Tara), with the face turned southwards
upon the Lagenians [as it were] fighting with them,
for he was the enemy of the Lagenians in his life-
time" (Petrie's "Antiquities of Tara Hill," p. 155).
The same circumstance is related in a still older
authority, with some additional interesting details—
the "Annotations of Tirechan," in the Book of
Armagh. King Leaghaire says :—"For Neel, my
father (i. e. Niall of the Nine Hostages), did not
permit me to believe [in the preaching of St. Patrick],
but that I should be interred in the top of *Temur*,
like men standing up in war. For the pagans are
accustomed to be buried armed, with their weapons
ready, face to face [in which manner they remain]
to the day of *Erdathe*, among the Magi, i. e. the day
of judgment of the Lord " (Ibid., p. 146).

The pagan Irish believed that, while the body of
their king remained in this position, it exercised a
malign influence on their enemies, who were thereby
always defeated in battle. Thus, in the Life of St.
Kellach, it is stated, that his father, Owen Bel, great
grandson of Dathi, and king of Connaught (see pp.
103 and 138, *supra*) was killed in the battle of Sligo,
fought against the Ulstermen. And before his death
he told his people "to bury him with his red javelin

in his hand in the grave. ' Place my face towards the north, on the side of the hill by which the northerns pass when flying before the army of Connaught ; let my grave face them, and place myself in it after this manner.' And this order was strictly complied with ; and in every place where the Clanna Neill and the Connacians met in conflict, the Clanna Neill and the Northerns were routed, being panic-stricken by the countenances of their foes ; so that the Clanna Neill and the people of the north of Ireland, therefore resolved to come with a numerous host to *Rath-O'bhFiachrach* [Rathoveeragh] and raise [the body of] Owen from the grave, and carry his remains northwards across to Sligo. This was done, and the body was buried at the other side [of the river], at *Aenach Locha Gile*, with the mouth down, that it might not be the means of causing them to fly before the Connacians" (Translated by O'Donovan in " Hy Fiachrach," p. 472).

It is very curious that, in some parts of the country, the people still retain a dim traditional memory of this mode of sepulture, and of the superstition connected with it. There is a place in the parish of Errigal in Londonderry, called Slaghtaverty, but it ought to have been called *Laghtaverty*, the *laght* or sepulchral monument of the *abhartach* [avartagh] or dwarf (see p. 66, *supra*). This dwarf was a magician, and a dreadful tyrant, and after having perpetrated great cruelties on the people he was at last vanquished and slain by a neighbouring chieftain ; some say by Finn Mac Cumhail. He was buried in a standing posture, but the very next day he appeared in his old haunts, more cruel and vigorous than ever. And the chief slew him a second time and buried him as before, but again he escaped

from the grave, and spread terror through the whole
country. The chief then consulted a druid, and according to his directions, he slew the dwarf a third
time, and buried him in the same place, *with his head
downwards;* which subdued his magical power, so
that he never again appeared on the earth. The *laght*
raised over the dwarf is still there, and you may hear
the legend with much detail from the natives of the
place, one of whom told it to me.

The modes of forming receptacles for the remains,
and the monuments erected over them, were exceedingly various. It was usual in this country, as in
many others, to pile a great heap of stones, usually
called a *carn*, over the grave of any person of note;
and where stones were not abundant, clay was used
for the same purpose. This custom is mentioned
in many of our ancient writings, and I might quote
several passages in illustration, but I shall content
myself with one from Adamnan (7th cent.):—"The
old man [Artbrananus] believed, and was baptized,
and when the sacrament was administered he died
in the same spot [on the shore of the isle of Skye],
according to the prediction of the saint [i. e. of St.
Columba]; and his companions buried him there;
raising a heap of stones over his grave" (Vit.
Col. I., 33).

The same custom exists to some extent at the present day, for in many parts of Ireland, they pile up a
laght or *carn* over the spot where any person has come
to an untimely death; and every passer-by is expected
to add a stone to the heap. The tourist who ascends
Mangerton mountain near Killarney, may see a carn
of this kind near the Devil's Punch Bowl, where a
shepherd was found dead some years ago.

Our pagan ancestors had a particular fancy for

elevated situations as their final resting-place ; and
accordingly we find that great numbers of mountains
through the country have one or more of these carns
on their summit, under each of which sleeps some
person important in his day.   They are sometimes
very large, and form conspicuous objects when viewed
from the neighbouring plains.

Many mountains through every part of the country
take their names from these carns, the name of the
monument gradually extending itself to the hill.
Carnlea, a high hill north of Cushendall in Antrim,
is an example, its Irish name being *Carn-liath*, grey
carn ; the great pile on the top of Carn Clanhugh in
Longford (the carn of Clanhugh or Hugh's sons, a
sept of the O'Farrells) is visible for many miles over
the level country round the mountain; and Carron hill
near Charleville, county Cork, takes its name from a
vast pile of stones on its summit.

The word *carn* forms the whole or the beginning
of the names of about 300 townlands, in every one
of which a remarkable carn must have existed,
besides many others, of whose names its forms the
middle or end ; and there are innumerable monuments of this kind all through the country, which
have not given names to townlands.   The place
called Carn, in the parish of Coury, near the hill of
Ushnagh in Westmeath, is the ancient *Carn Fiachach*
(Four M.), Fiacha's monument, which was erected
to commemorate *Fiacha*, son of Niall of the Nine
Hostages (see p. 138, *supra*), the ancestor of the
Mageoghegans.   It is very probable that the persons
who are commemorated in such names as the following, are those over whom the carns were originally
erected.

Carutcel, now a village and parish in Tyrone, is

called by the Four Masters *Carn-tSiadhail, Siadhal's*
or Shiel's monument. There is a remarkable mountain, with a carn on its summit, called Carn Tierna,
near Rathcormack in the county Cork. According
to O'Curry (Lectures, p. 267), Tighernach [Tierna]
Tetbannach king of Munster in the time of Conor
mac Nessa, in the first century, was buried in this,
whence it was called *Carn Tighernaigh*, Tighernach's
carn ; and the sound of the old name is preserved in
the modern Carn Tierna. Carmavy (Grange) in
the parish of Killead, Antrim, Maev's carn ; Carn-
kenny near Ardstraw in Tyrone, the carn of Cainnech or Kenny ; Carnew in Wicklow probably
contains the same personal name as Rathnew—
Carn-Naoi, Naoi's carn ; Carnacally, the name of
several places, the monument of the *calliach* or hag.

It is certain that the following places have lost
their original names :—Carndonagh in Innishowen,
which got the latter part of its name merely because
the old monument was situated in the parish of
Donagh; there are some places in Antrim and Tyrone
called Carnagat, the carn of the cats, from having
been resorts of wild cats ; and a similar remark applies to Carnalughoge near Louth, the carn of the
mice. Carney in Sligo is not formed from carn ; it
is really a family name, the full designation being
Farran-O'Carney, O'Carney's land.

Other modifications of this word are seen in Carron,
the name of several townlands in Waterford, Tipperary, and Limerick ; and in Carronadavderg near
Ardmore in Waterford, the monument of the red ox,
a singular name, no doubt connected with some legend: Carnane and Carnaun, little carn, are very
often met with ; and the form Kernan is the name

of a townland near Armagh, and of another in the
county Down.

The mounds or tumuli of earth or stones, raised
over a grave, were sometimes designated by the word
tuaim [toom]. Like the cognate Latin word tumulus,
it was primarily applied to a hillock or dyke, and in
a secondary sense to a monumental mound or tomb.
These mounds, which were either of earth or stones,
are still found in all kinds of situations, and sometimes they are exceedingly large. It is often not
easy to distinguish them from the *duns* or residences;
but it is probable that these mounds that have no appearance of circumvallations are generally sepulchral.
They have given names to a great many places in
every part of Ireland, in numbers of which the old
tumuli still remain. There are about a dozen places,
chiefly in the north, called Toome, the most remarkable of which is that on the Bann, between Lough
Neagh and Lough Beg, which gives name to the two
adjacent baronies. There must have been formerly
at this place both a sandbank ford across the river,
and a sepulchral mound near it, for in the Tripartite
Life it is called *Fearsat Tuama*, the *farset* or ford of
the tumulus; but in the annals it is generally called
Tuaim.

Tomgraney in Clare is often mentioned by the
annalists, who call it *Tuaim-Greine*, the tomb of
Grian, a woman's name. The traditions of the place
still preserve the memory of the lady Grian, but the
people now call her Gillagraney—*Gill-Gréine*, the
brightness of the sun. They say that she was
drowned in Lough Graney; that her body was found
in the river Graney at a place called Derrygraney;
and that she was buried at Tomgraney. All these

places retain her name, and her monument is still in existence near the village. *Grian*, which is the Irish word for the sun, and is of the feminine gender, was formerly very usual in Ireland as a woman's name. There is a place called Carngranny near the town of Antrim, where another lady named Grian must have been buried. Her monument also remains:—" It consists of ten large slabs raised on side supporters, like a series of cromlechs, forming steps commencing with the lowest at the north east and ascending gradually for the length of forty feet towards the south west " (Reeves's Ecol. Ant., p. 66). The pile is called Granny's Grave, which is a translation of *Carn·Greiné* (see also Knockgrean in 2nd Series).

The parish of Tomfinlough in Clare took its name from an old church by a lake near Sixmile-bridge, which is several times mentioned by the Four Masters under the name of *Tuaim-Fionnlocha*, the tumulus of the bright lake. Toomona in the parish of Ogulla, same county, where are still to be seen the ruins of a remarkable old monastery, is called in the annals *Tuaim-mona*, the tomb of the bog. Toomyvara in Tipperary, exactly represents the sound of the Irish *Tuaim-ui-Mheadhra*, O'Mara's tomb; and Tomdeely, a townland giving name to a parish in Limerick, is probably the tumulus of or by the (river) Deel.

On the summit of Tomies mountain, which rises over the lower lake of Killarney, there are two sepulchral heaps of stones, not far from one another; hence the Irish name *Tuamaidhe* [Toomy], i.e. monumental mounds; and the present name, which has extended to three townlands, has been formed by the addition of the English after the Irish plural (see page 32). The Irish name of the parish of Tumna in Roscommon is *Tuaim-mna* (Four Mast.), the tumulus of the woman (*bean*, a woman, gen. *mna*). Tooman and Toomog, little tombs, are the names of several townlands in different counties.

Dumha [dooa] is another word for a sepulchral mound or tumulus; it is very often used in Irish writings, and we frequently find it recorded, that the bodies of the slain were buried in a *dumha.* These mounds have given names to numerous places, but being commonly made of earth, they have themselves in many cases disappeared. Moydow, a parish in Longford which gives name to a barony, is called by the Four Masters, *Magh-dumha* [Moy-dooa], the plain of the burial mound; and there is a townland of the same name in Roscommon.

In modern names it is not easy to separate this word from *dubh*, black, and *dumhach*, a sand bank; but the following names may be referred to it. Dooey, which is the name of several townlands in Ulster, is no doubt generally one of its modern forms, though, when that name occurs on the coast, it is more likely to be from *dumhach.* Knockadoo, the hill of the mound, is the name of some townlands in Roscommon, Sligo, and Londonderry ; and there are several places called Corradoo, Corradooa, and Corradooey, the round hill of the tumulus.

A *leacht* [laght] is a sepulchre or monument, cognate with Lat. *lectus* and Greek *lechos;* for in many languages a grave is called a bed (see *leaba*, further on); Goth. *liga :* Eng. *lie, lay;* Manx, *lhiaght.* It is often applied, like carn, to a monumental heap of stones : in Cormac's Glossary it is explained *lighedh mairbh*, the grave of a dead (person).

There are several places in different parts of the country, called Laght, which is its most correct anglicised form; Laghta, monuments, is the name of some townlands in Mayo and Leitrim, and we find Laghtagalla, white sepulchres, near Thurles. Laghtane, little *laght*, is a place in the parish of Killeenagarriff, Limerick.

In the north of Ireland, the guttural is universally suppressed, and the word is pronounced *lat* or *let ;* as we find in Latt, the name of a townland in Armagh, and of another in Cavan ; Derlett in Armagh, the oak wood of the grave (*Doireleachta*) ; Letfern in Tyrone, the *laght* of the *fearns* or alder trees ; and Corlat, the name of several places in the Ulster counties, the round hill of the sepulchres.

The word *uladh* [ulla] originally meant a tomb or carn, as the following passages will show :—"*oc denam uluidh cumdachta imat flaith,*" making a protecting tomb over thy chief (O'Donovan, App. to O'Reilly's Dict. *voce* uladh). In the Leabhar na hUidhre, it is related that Caeilte [Keeltha], Finn mac Cumhal's foster son, slew Fothadh Airgtheach, monarch of Ireland, in the battle of *Ollarba* (Larne Water), in A. D. 285. Caeilte speaks :—"The *uluidh* of Fothadh Airgtheach will be found a short distance to the east of it. There is a chest of stone about him in the earth; there are his two rings of silver, and his two *bunne doat* [bracelets ?] and his *torque* of silver on his chest; and there is a pillar stone at his carn; and an *ogum* is [inscribed] on the end of the pillar stone which is in the earth; and what is on it is, ' Eochaidh Airgtheach here '" (Petrie, R. Towers, p. 108).

The word is now, however, and has been for a long time used to denote a penitential station, or a stone altar erected as a place of devotion; a very natural extension of meaning, as the tombs of saints were so very generally used as places of devotion by the faithful. It was used in this sense at an early period, for in the "Battle of Moyrath," it is said that "Domhnall never went away from a cross without bowing, nor from an *ulaidh* without turning round, nor from an altar without praying" (p. 298). On which O'Donovan remarks :—" *Ulaidh,* a word which often occurs in ancient MSS., is still understood in the west of Ireland to denote a penitential station at which pilgrims pray, and perform rounds on their knees." These little altar tombs have given names to places all over Ireland, in many of which, especially in the west and south, they may still be seen.

Among several places in Cork, we have Glennahulla near Kildorrery, and Kilnahulla in the parish of Kilmeen, he glen and the church of the altar tomb; the latter name being the same as Killulla in Clare. In Ulusker near Castletown Bearhaven, the word seems to be used in its primary sense, as the name is understood to mean Oscar's carn *(Uladh-Oscair)*; and in this sense we must no doubt understand it in Tullyullagh near Enniskillen, the hill of the tombs. Knockanully in Antrim signifies the hill of the tomb; and Tomnahulla in Galway, would be written in Irish, *Tuaim-na-hulaidh,* the mound of the altar tomb. We have the diminutive Ullauns near Killarney, and Ullanes near Macroom in Cork, both signifying little stone altars.

" A cromlech, when perfect, consists of three or more stones unhewn, and generally so placed as to form a small enclosure. Over these a large [flat] stone is laid, the whole forming a kind of rude chamber. The position of the table or covering stone, is generally sloping ; but its degree of inclination does not appear to have been regulated by any design" (Wakeman's Handbook of Irish Antiquities,

p. 7). They are very numerous in all parts of Ireland, and various theories have been advanced to account for their origin; of which the most common is that they were "Druids' altars," and used for offering sacrifices. It is now, however, well known that they are tombs, which is proved by the fact that under many of them have been found cinerary urns, calcined bones, and sometimes entire skeletons. The popular name of "Giants' graves," which is applied to them in many parts of the country, preserves, with sufficient correctness, the memory of their original purpose. They have other forms besides that described; sometimes they are very large, consisting of a chamber thirty or forty feet long, covered by a series of flags laid horizontally, like Carngranny (p. 335); and not unfrequently the chamber is in the form of a cross.

The word cromlech—*crom-leac*, sloping stone (*crom*, bending, sloping)—is believed not to be originally Irish; but to have been in late years introduced from Wales, where it is used merely as an antiquarian term. That it is not an old Irish word is proved by the fact, that it is not used in the formation of any of our local names. It has none of the marks of a native term, for it is not found in our old writings, and—like the expression "Druids' altars"—it is quite unknown to the Irish-speaking peasantry.

These sepulchres are sometimes called *leaba* or *leabaidh*, old Irish *lebaid* [labba, labby], Manx *lhiabbee*; the word literally signifies a bed, but it is applied in a secondary sense to a grave, both in the present spoken language and in old writings. For example, in the ancient authority cited by Petrie (R. Towers, p. 350), it is stated that the great poet Rumann, who died in the year 747 at Rahan in King's County,

23*

" was buried in the same *leabaidh* with Ua Suanaigh,
for his great honour with God and man." There is
a fine sepulchral monument of this kind, hitherto
unnoticed, in a mountain glen over Mount Russell
near Charleville, on the borders of the counties of
Limerick and Cork, which the peasantry call *Labba-
Iscur*, Oscur's grave. O'Brien (Dict. *roce* Leaba) says,
"Leaba is the name of several places in Ireland,
which are by the common people called *Leabthacha-
na-bhfeinne* [Labbaha-na-veana], the monuments of
the Fenii or old Irish champions;" and it may be
remarked that Oscur was one of the most renowned
of these, being the son of Oisin, the son of Finn mac
Cumhal (see p. 90, *supra*).

Labby, which is one of the modern forms of this
term, is the name of a townland in Londonderry.
Sometimes the word is followed by a personal name,
which is probably that of the individual buried in
the monument; as in Labbyeslin near Mohill in
Leitrim, the tomb of Eslin; Labasheeda in Clare,
Sioda or Sheedy's grave. *Sioda* is the common Irish
word for silk; and accordingly many families, whose
real ancestral name is Sheedy, now call themselves
Silk. In case of Labasheeda, the inhabitants believe
that it was so called from the beautiful smooth strand
in the little bay—*Leaba-sioda*, silken bed, like the
" Velvet strand " near Malahide. Perhaps they are
right.

Cromlechs are called in many parts of the country
Leaba-Dhiarmada-agus-Grainne, the bed of Diarmaid
and Grainnĕ; and this name is connected with the
well-known legend, that Diarmaid O'Duibhne [Der-
mod O'Deena], eloped with Grainnĕ, the daughter
of king Cormac mac Art, and Finn mac Cumhail's
betrothed spouse. The pair eluded Finn's pursuit

for a year and a day, sleeping in a different place
each night, under a *leaba* erected by Diarmaid after
his day's journey ; and according to the legend there
were just 366 of them in Ireland. But this legend
is a late invention, and evidently took its rise from
the word *leabaidh,* which was understood in its literal
sense of a bed. The fable has, however, given origin
to the name of Labbadermody, Diarmaid's bed, a
townland in the parish of Clondrohid in Cork ; and
to the term Labbacallee—*Leaba-caillighe,* hag's bed—
sometimes applied to these monuments.

In some parts of Ulster a cromlech is called *cloch-
togbhala* [clogh-tōgla], i. e. raised or lifted stone, in
reference to the covering flag ; from which Cloch-
togle near Enniskillen, and Cloghogle (*t* aspirated
and omitted—p. 21), two townlands in Tyrone, have
their name. There is a hill near Downpatrick called
Slieve-na-griddle, the mountain of the *griddle ;* the
griddle is a cromlech on the top of the hill ; but the
name is half English, and very modern. It may
be remarked that cromlechs are sometimes called
"griddles" in other places ; thus Gabriel Beranger,
who made a tour through Ireland in the last century,
mentions one situated in a bog near Easky in Sligo,
which was usually called "Finn Mac Cool's Griddle."

"In many parts of Ireland, and particularly in districts where the stone circles occur, may be seen huge
blocks of stone, which evidently owe their upright
position, not to accident, but to the design and labour of an ancient people. They are called by the
native Irish *gallauns* or *leaganns,* and in character
they are precisely similar to the hoar-stones of England, the hare-stane of Scotland, and maen-gwyr
of Wales. Many theories have been promulgated
relative to their origin. They are supposed to have

been idol-stones—to have been stones of memorial—
to have been erected as landmarks, boundaries, &c.—
and, lastly, to be monumental stones" (Wakeman's
"Handbook of Irish Antiquities," p. 17). We know
that the erection of pillar stones as sepulchral monuments is often recorded in ancient Irish authorities,
one example of which will be found in the passage
quoted from Leabhar na hUidhre at page 337 ; but
it is probable that some were erected for other purposes.

There are several words in Irish to signify a pillar
stone ; one of which is *coirthe* or *cairthe* [corha,
carha]. It is used in every part of Ireland, and has
given names under various forms to many different
places, in several of which the old pillar stones are
yet standing. The beautiful valley and lake of Glencar, on the borders of Leitrim and Sligo, is called in
Irish, *Gleann-a'-chairthe* [Glenacarha], the glen of
the pillar stone ; but its ancient name, as used by
the Four Masters, was *Cairthe-Muilcheann* [Carha-
Mulkan]. Carha and Carra, the names of several
townlands in Ulster and Connaught, exhibit the word
in its simple anglicised forms. There is a place in
the parish of Clonfert, Cork, called Knockahorrea,
which represents the Irish *Cnoc-a'-chairthe*, the hill of
the pillar stone ; and in Louth we find Drumnacarra,
which has nearly the same meaning.

These stones are also, as Mr. Wakeman remarks,
called *gallauns* and *leaganns*. The Irish form of the
first is *gallán*, which is sometimes corrupted in the
modern language to *dallán*; it has given name to
Gallan near Ardstraw in Tyrone ; and to Gallane
and Gallanes in Cork. There are several low hills
in Ulster, which, from a pillar stone standing on the
top, were called Drumgallan, and some of them have

given names to townlands. Aghagallon, the field of the *gallan*, is the name of a townland in Tyrone, and of a parish in Antrim; Knockagallane (hill) is the name of two townlands in Cork, and there is a parish near Mitchelstown in the same county, called Kilgullane, the church of the pillar stone.

The word *gall*, of which *gallán* is a diminutive, was applied to standing stones, according to Cormac mac Cullenan (see p. 93, *supra*), because they were first erected in Ireland by the *Gauls*. This word is also used in the formation of names; as in Cangullia, a place near Castleisland in Kerry, the Irish name of which is *Ceann-gaille*, the head or hill of the standing stone. The adjective *gallach*, meaning a place abounding in standing stones, or large stones or rocks, has given name to several places now called Gallagh, scattered through all the provinces except Munster; and Gallow, the name of a parish in Meath, is another form of the same word.

The other term *liagán* [leegaun] is a diminutive of *liag*, which will be noticed farther on; and in its application to a standing stone, it is still more common than *gallán*. Legan, Legane, Legaun, and Leegane, all different anglicised forms, are the names of several places in different parts of the country; and the English plural, Liggins (pillar stones) is found in Tyrone. Ballylegan, the town of the standing stone, is the name of a place near Caher in Tipperary, and of another near Glanworth in Cork; there is a place called Tooralengan (*Toor*, a bleach green) near Ballylanders in Limerick; and Knockalegan, the hill of the pillar stone, is the name of half a dozen townlands in Ulster and Munster.

Fert, plural *ferta*, signifies a grave or trench. The old name of Slane on the Boyne, was *Ferta-fer-Feic,*

and the account given by Colgan (Trias Thaum.,
p. 20) of the origin of this name, brings out very
olearly the meaning of *ferta* :—" There is a place on
the north margin of the river Boyne, now called
Slaine; [but auciently] it was called *Ferta-fer-Feic,*
i. e. the trenches or sepulchres of the men of Fiac,
because the servants of a certain chieftain named
Fiac, dug deep trenches there, to inter the bodies of
the slain."

In the Book of Armagh there is an interesting
account by Tirechan, of the burial in the *ferta*, of
Laeghairo's three daughters (see p. 179, *supra*), who
had been converted by St. Patrick :—" And the days
of mourning for the king's daughters were accom-
plished, and they buried them near the well Clebach;
and they made a circular ditch like to a *ferta;* because so the Scotic people and gentiles were used to
do, but with us it is called *Reliquiæ* (Irish *Releg*), i. e.
the remains of the virgins" (Todd's Life of St.
Patrick, p. 455). *Ferta* was originally a pagan term,
as the above passage very olearly shows, but like
cluain and other words, it was often adopted by the
early Irish saints (see Reeves's "Ancient Churches of
Armagh," p. 47).

The names Farta, Ferta, and Fartha (i. e. graves),
each of which is applied to a townland, exhibit the
plural in its simple form ; with the addition of *ach*
to the singular, we have Fertagh and Fartagh, i. e. a
place of graves, which are names of frequent occurrence. Fertagh near Johnstown in Kilkenny is
called by the Four Masters *Ferta-na-gcaerach*, the
graves of the sheep ; and O'Donovan states that according to tradition, it was so called because the car-
cases of a great number of sheep which died of a
distemper, were buried there. (Four Masters, Vol. I.,

p. 498). In the parish of Maghcross, Monaghan, there is a townland called Nafarty, i. e. the graves, the Irish article *na*, forming part of the name. The parish of Moyarta in Clare which gives name to a barony, is called in Irish *Magh-fherta* (*fh* silent, see p. 20), the plain of the grave.

Reilig, old Irish *relec*, means a cemetery or grave-yard; it is the Latin *reliquiæ*, and was borrowed very early, for it occurs in the Zeuss MSS. The most celebrated place in Ireland with this name was *Reilig-na-riogh*, or "the burial place of the kings," at the royal palace of Crunchan in Connaught, one of the ancient regal cemeteries. There are only a few places in Ireland taking their names from this term. Relick is the name of two townlands in Westmeath, and there is a graveyard in the parish of Carragh near Naas, county Kildare, called The Relick, i. e. the cemetery. The parish of Relickmurry [and Athassel] in Tipperary, took its name from an old burial ground, whose church must have been dedicated to the Blessed Virgin, for the name signifies Mary's cemetery. One mile S. E. of Portstewart in Londonderry, there are two townlands called Roselick More and Roselick Beg. Roselick is a modern contraction for *Rosrelick* as we find it written in the Taxation of 1306; and the name signifies the *ros* or point of the cemetery. There is a spot in Roselick Beg where large quantities of human remains have been found, and the people have a tradition that a church once existed there; showing that the name preserves a fragment of true history (Reeves : Eccl. Ant., p. 75).

CHAPTER IV.

TOWNS AND VILLAGES.

" THE most interesting word connected with topical
nomenclature is *bally*. As an existing element it is
the most prevalent of all local terms in Ireland, there
being 6,400 townlands, or above a tenth of the sum
total, into [the beginning of] whose names this word
enters as an element. And this is a much smaller
proportion than existed at the beginning of the seventeenth century, when there was a tendency, at least
in some of the northern counties, to prefix *bally* to
almost every name whose meaning would admit of
it " (" The Townland Distribution of Ireland," by
the Rev. Wm. Reeves, D. D.: Proc. R. I. A., Vol.
VII., p. 473, where this word *baile* is fully discussed).

The Irish word *baile* is now understood to mean a
town or townland, but in its original acceptation
it denoted simply *locus*—place or situation; it is so
explained in various ancient glosses, such as those
in the Book of Armagh, Cormac's Glossary, the
Book of Lecan, &c.; and it is used in this sense in
the Leabhar na hUidhre, and in many other old
authorities.

In writings of more modern date, it is often used
to signify a residence or military station—a natural
extension of meaning from the original. For instance,
the Four Masters, at 1560, state that Owen O'Rourke,
having been kept in prison by his brother, slew his
keeper, " and ascending to the top of the *baile*,
cried out that the castle was in his power;" in which

baile evidently means the fortress in which he was confined. In the Yellow Book of Lecan, an ancient gloss explains a *rath* (i. e. a fort or residence) by *baile ;* and in the story of "The fate of the children of Lir " we read :—" She [Aeifē] went on to [the fairy residence called] *Sidh Buidhbh Deirg* [Shee-Boov-derg] ; and the nobles of the *baile* bade her welcome" (Atlantis, VII., p. 124).

This application of the term is obviously preserved in the name of the tongue of land on which the Howth lighthouse is built, which is called the Green *Bailey.* Our Annals relate that Criffan, monarch of Ireland in the first century, had his residence, *Dun-Criffan,* at *Ben Edar* or Howth, where he died in A. D. 9, "after returning from the famous expedition upon which he had gone. It was from this expedition he brought with him the wonderful jewels, among which were a golden chariot, and a golden chess-board [inlaid] with a hundred transparent gems, and a beautiful cloak embroidered with gold. He brought a conquering sword, with many serpents of refined massy gold inlaid in it; a shield with bosses of bright silver; a spear from the wound of which no one recovered ; a sling from which no erring shot was discharged ; and two greyhounds, with a silver chain between them, which chain was worth three hundred *cumhals ;* with many other precious articles " (Four Masters, A. D. 9).

Petrie and O'Donovan both believe that the lighthouse occupies the site of this ancient fortress ; and portions of the fosses by which it was defended are still clearly traceable across the neck of the little peninsula. The Rev. J. F. Shearman is of opinion that it was situated higher up, where the old Bailey lighthouse stood; but this does not invalidate the derivation of the name. And so the memory of Criffan's old *bally*, which has long been lost in popular tradition, still lives in the name of the Bailey lighthouse. In the colloquial language of the present day the word *baile* is used to signify *home*, which is obviously a relic of its more ancient application to a residence.

In modern times this word is usually translated "town;" but in this sense it is applied to the smallest village, even to a collection of only a couple of houses. It is also used to designate mere town*lands*, without any reference at all to habitations. This application is as old as the twelfth century; for we are informed by Dr. Reeves that the word was often so used in the charters of that period, such as those of Kells, Newry, Ferns, &c., in which numbers of denominations are mentioned, whose names contain it in the forms, *bali, baley, balli, balÿ*, &c. It is probable that in many old names which have descended to our own time the word *bally* is used in the sense of "residence," but it is difficult or impossible to distinguish them; and I have, for the sake of uniformity, throughout this book translated the word by "town" or "townland."

The most common anglicised form of *baile* is *bally*, which is found in a vast number of names; such as Ballyorgan near Kilfinane in Limerick, which the people call in Irish *Baile-Aragáin*, the town of *Aragan*, an ancient Irish personal name, the same as the modern Horgan or Organ. In Ballybofey (Donegal) the *bally* is a modern addition; and the place, if it had retained an anglicised form of the old name, *Srath-bo-Fiaich* (Four Masters), should have been called *Srathbofey*. Some old chief or occupier named Fiach must have in past times kept his cows on the beautiful holm along the river Finn near the town; for the name signifies the *srath* or river holm of Fiach's cows. Ballyheige in Kerry has its name from the family of O'Teige, its full Irish name being *Baile-ui-Thady;* and Ballylanders is in like manner called from the English family of Landers. Indeed, a considerable proportion of these *Ballys* take their names from families, of which many are so plain as to tell their own story.

When *bally* is joined to the article followed by a noun in the genitive singular, if the noun be masculine, the Irish *Baile-an-* is generally contracted to *Ballin-*; as we find in Ballinrobe in Mayo, which the Four Masters write *Baile-an-Rodhba* [Roba], the town of the (river) Robe; and in Ballincurry, Ballincurra, and Ballincurrig, all of which are in Irish *Baile-an-churraigh,* the town of the moor or marsh. But it is occasionally made *Ballyn-,* as in Ballyneety, the name of a dozen places, chiefly in Waterford, Tipperary, and Limerick, which represents the sound of the Irish *Baile-an-Fhaeite,* the town of White, a family name of English origin. If the following noun be feminine, or in the genitive plural, the Irish *Baile-na-* is made either *Ballina-* or *Ballyna-;* as in the common townland names, Ballynahinch and Ballinahinch, the town of the island; Ballynaglogh, the town of the stones (*cloch,* a stone).

In the counties on the eastern coast, *bally* is very often shortened to *bal,* of which there are numerous examples, such as Baldoyle near Dublin, which is written in the Registry of All Hallows, Balydowyl, and in other old Anglo-Irish authorities, Ballydub-gaill, Balydugil, Ballydowill, &c.—Irish, *Baile-Dubh-ghoill,* the town of *Dubhghall* or Doyle, a personal name meaning black *Gall* or foreigner. Balbriggan,

the town of Brecan, a very usual personal name;
Balrath is generally the town of the fort; but Balrath in the parish of Castletown-Kindalen in Westmeath, is *Bile-ratha* (Four M.), the *bile* or ancient
tree of the rath. Baltrasna, cross-town, i. e. placed
in a transverse direction, the same name as Bally-
trasna, Ballytarsna, and Ballytarsney.

The plural of *baile* is *bailte*, which appears in names
as it is pronounced, *bally*. There is a townland in
Wicklow, near Hollywood, called Baltyboys, i. e.
Boioe's townlands; and a further step in the process
of anglicisation appears in its *alias* name of Boystown,
which form has given name to the parish. Baltylum
in Armagh, bare townlands, i. e. bare of trees;
Baltydaniel in Cork, Donall's or Domhnall's townlands. The diminutives Balleen and Balteen (little
town) are the names of several places in Kilkenny
and the Munster counties; Balteenbrack in Cork,
speckled little town.

Baile is not much liable to changes of form further
than I have noticed; yet in a few names we find it
much disguised. For instance, Coolbullow in the
parish of Kerloge, Wexford, represents *Cul-bhaile*,
back town, the same as we find in Coolbally and
Coolballyogan (Hogan's) in Queen's County, and
Coolballyshane (John's) in Limerick. The proper
original of Baurille in Innishowen, Donegal, is *Bo-
bhaile*, cowtown; Loughbollard near Clane, Kildare,
the lake of the high-town; Derrywillow in Leitrim
represents *Doire-bhaile*, which, with the root words
reversed, is the same name as Ballinderry, the town
of the *derry* or oak wood.

Sráid [sraud] signifies a street, and appears to be
borrowed from the Latin *strata*. The Four Masters
use it once when they mention *Sraid-an-fhiona*

[Sraud-an-eena], the street of the wine, now Wine-tavern-street in Dublin. There are several town-lands in Antrim, Donegal, and Londonderry, called Straid, which is one of its English forms, and which enters into several other names in the same counties; we find Strade in Mayo, and Stradeen, little street, in Monaghan. It is also sometimes made *strad*, as in Stradreagh in Londonderry, grey-street; Strad-avoher near Thurles, the street of the road: Strad-brook near Monkstown, Dublin, is very probably a translation of *Sruthan-na-sraide* [Sruhanasrauda], the brook of the street.

A village consisting of one street, undefended by either walls or castle—a small unfortified hamlet—was often called *Sradbhaile*, i. e. street-town; which, in its English form, Stradbally, is the name of several villages, parishes, and townlands, in the southern half of Ireland. Stradbally in Queen's County, is men-tioned by the Four Masters, who call it "*Sradbhaile* of Leix.*"

Buirghes [burris] signifies a *burgage* or borough. This word was introduced by the Anglo-Normans, who applied it to the small borough towns which they established, several of which have retained the original designations. After the twelfth century, it is often found in Irish writings, but always as a part of local names.

It is usually spelled in the present anglicised names Borris, Burris, and Burges, which are met with forming the whole or part of names in several of the Munster, Connaught, and Leinster counties; it does not occur in Ulster. Burriscarra, Borris-in-Ossory, Borrisoleagh, and Burrishoole, were so called to dis-tinguish them from each other, and from other Borrises; being situated in the ancient territories of

Carra, Ossory, Ileagh or *Ui-Luighdheach*, and *Umhall*, or "The Owles." Borrisnafarney, the name of a parish in Tipperary, signifies the borough of the alder-plain (see Farney) ; Borrisokane, O'Keane's borough town.

Graig, a village. It is supposed by many to have been introduced by the Anglo-Normans, but its origin is very doubtful. It is used extensively in the formation of names, there being upwards of sixty places called Graigue, and a great many others of whose names it forms a part. It does not occur at all in Ulster.

The name of Graiguenamanagh in Kilkenny, bears testimony to its former ecclesiastical eminence, for it signifies the village of the monks ; Graiguealug and Graiguenaspiddogue, both in Carlow, the village of the hollow, and of the robin-redbreasts ; Graiguefrahane in Tipperary, the *graig* of the *freaghans* or whortleberries. Gragane and Graigeen in Limerick, Gragan in Clare, and Grageen in Wexford, all signify little village, being different forms of the diminutive ; Ardgraigue in Galway, and Ardgregane in Tipperary, the height of the village.

CHAPTER V.

FORDS, WEIRS, and BRIDGES.

THE early inhabitants of a country often, for obvious reasons, selected the banks of rivers for their settlements ; and the position most generally chosen was opposite a part of the stream sufficiently shallow to be fordable by foot passengers. Many of our important towns, as their names clearly indicate, derive their origin from these primitive and solitary settlements; but most of the original fords have been long since spanned by bridges.

But whether there was question of settlements or not, the fordable points of rivers must have been known to the very earliest colonists, and distinguished by names; for upon this knowledge depended, in a great measure, the facility and safety of intercommunication, before the erection of bridges. Fords were, generally speaking, natural features, but in almost all cases they were improved by artificial means, as we find mentioned by Boate:—"Concerning the fords: it is to be observed that not everywhere, where the high-ways meet with great brooks or small rivers, bridges are found for to pass them, but in very many places one is constrained to ride through the water itself, the which could not be done if the rivers kept themselves everywhere enclosed between their banks; wherefore they are not only suffered in such places to spread themselves abroad, but men help thereto as much as they can, to make the water so much the shallower, and consequently the easier to be passed" (Nat. Hist., C. VII., Sect. VII.). Very often also, when circumstances made it necessary, a river was rendered passable at some particular point, even where there was no good natural ford, by laying down stones, trees, or wicker work. For these reasons I have included "Fords" in this third part among artificial structures.

There are several Irish words for the different kinds of fords, of which the most common is *ath*, cognate with Latin *cadum*. In the various forms *ath, ah, augh, agh, a,* &c., it forms a part of hundreds of names

24

all over Ireland (see p. 44, *supra*). The Shannon must have been anciently fordable at Athlone; and there was a time when the site of the present busy town was a wild waste, relieved by a few solitary huts, and when the traveller—directed perhaps by a professional guide—struggled across the dangerous passage where the bridge now spans the stream. It appears from the "Battle of Moylena" (p. 60), that this place was first called *Athmore*, great ford, which was afterwards changed to *Ath-Luain*, the ford of Luan, a man's name, formerly very common. I know nothing further of this Luan, except that we learn his father's name from a passage in the tale called "The fate of the children of Tuireann," in which the place is called *Ath-Luain-mic-Luighdheach*, the ford of Luan the son of Lewy.

Athleague on the Suck in the county Roscommon, is called by the Four Masters *Ath-liag*, the ford of the stones, or more fully, *Ath-liag-Maenagain*, from St. Maenagan, who was formerly venerated there, though no longer remembered. The people say that there is one particular stone which the river never covers in its frequent inundations, and that if it were covered, the town would be drowned. There was another *Ath-liag* on the Shannon, which is also very often mentioned in the Annals; it crossed the river at the present village of Lanesborough, and it is now called in Irish *Baile-atha-liag*, or in English Bally-league (the town of the ford of the stones), which is the name of that part of Lanesborough lying on the west bank of the Shannon. Another name nearly the same as this, is that of Athlacca in Limerick, which was so called from a ford on the Morning Star river, called in Irish *Ath-leacach*, stony or *flaggy* ford. And it will appear as I go on, that a great many other

places derive their names from these stony fords.
There was another ford higher up on the same river,
which the Four Masters call *Bel-atha-na-nDeise* [Bel-
lananeasy], the ford-mouth of the Desii, from the
old territory of *Deis-beag*, which lay round the hill of
Knockany ; and in the shortened form of *Ath-nDeise*
it gives name to the surrounding parish, now called
Athneasy.

Ath is represented by *aa* in Drumaa, the name of
two townlands in Fermanagh, in Irish, *Druim-atha*,
the ridge of the ford.   A ford on the river Inny, formerly surrounded with trees, gave name to the little
village of Finnea in Westmeath, which the Four
Masters call *Fidh-an-atha* [Fee-an-aha], the wood of
the ford.   Affane, a well-known place on the Blackwater, took its name from a ford across the river
about two miles below Cappoquin ; it is mentioned
by the Four Masters, when recording the battle fought
there in the year 1565, between the rival houses of
Desmond and Ormond, and they call it *Ath-mheadh-
on* [Ah-vane], middle ford.   At the year 524, we read
in the Four Masters, " the battle of *Ath-Sidhe* [Ah-
shee] (was gained) by Muircheartach (king of Ireland)
against the Leinstermen, where Sidhe, the son of Dian,
was slain, from whom *Ath-Sidhe* [on the Boyne:
the ford of Sidhe] is called ;" and the place has preserved this name, now changed to Assey, which, from
the original ford, has been extended to a parish.   The
same authority states (A. D. 526), that Sin [Sheen],
the daughter of Sidhe, afterwards killed Muircheartach, by burning the house of Cletty over his head,
in revenge of her father's death.

Ath is very often combined with *baile*, forming the
compound *Baile-atha* [Bally-aha], the town of the
ford ; of which Ballyboy in the King's County, a

village giving name to a parish and barony, is an
example, being called in various authorities, *Baile-
atha-buidhe* [Ballyaboy], the town of the yellow ford.
There are many townlands in different counties, of
the same name, but it probably means yellow town
[*Baile-buidhe*] in some of these cases. Ballylahan in
the parish of Templemore, Mayo, is called in the
annals *Baile-atha-leathain*, the town of the broad
ford. The parish of Ballee in Down is written in
the taxation of 1306, *Baliath*, which shows clearly
that the original name is *Baile-atha* (Reeves: Eccl.
Ant., p. 41).

The diminutive *athán* [ahaun] is of frequent occurrence; in the forms of Ahane and Ahaun (little ford),
it gives names to several townlands in the southern
counties; and there is a parish in Derry called Agh-
anloo, or in Irish *Athan-Lugha*, Lewy's little ford.

The word *bél* or *béal* [bale] primarily signifies a
mouth, but in a secondary sense it was used, like the
Latin *os*, to signify an entrance to any place. In
this sense, it appears in Bellaugh, the name of a village lying west of Athlone. Between this village
and the town there was formerly a slough or miry
place, called in Irish a *lathach* [lahagh], which the
Four Masters mention by the name of *Lathach-Caich-
tuthbil;* and the spot where the village stands was
called *Bel-lathaigh*, the entrance to the *lathach*, which
is now correctly enough anglicised Bellaugh. Bel-
laghy, another and more correct form, is the name of
a village in Londonderry, of another in Sligo, and of
a townland in Antrim.

This word *bél* is very often united with *ath*, forming the compound *bél-atha* [bellaha or bella], which
signifies ford-entrance—an entrance by a ford—literally *mouth of a ford;* it is applied to a ford, and

has in fact much the same signification as *ath* itself.
It is so often used in this manner that the word *bél*
alone sometimes denotes a ford. Belclare, now the
name of a parish in Galway, was more anciently applied to a castle erected to defend a ford on the road
leading to Tuam, which was called *Bel-an-chlair*, the
ford or entrance of the plank. There is also a townland in Mayo, called Belclare, and another in Sligo,
which the Four Masters call *Bel-an-chlair*. Phale
near Enniskeen in Cork, is called in the Annals of
Innisfallen, *Inis-an-bheil* [Innishaneale], the island or
river holm of the mouth, the last syllable of which is
preserved in the present name.

The proper anglicised form of *bel-atha*, is *bella*,
which is the beginning of a great many names. Bel-
lanagare in Roscommon, formerly the residence of
Charles O'Conor the historian, is called in Irish *Bel-
atha-na-gearr*, the ford-mouth of the cars (see for cars
2nd Ser., chap XI.); Lisbellaw in Fermanagh, *Lios-
bel-atha*, the *lis* of the ford-mouth. Sometimes the
article intervenes, making *bel-an-atha* in the original,
the correct modern representative of which is *bellana*,
as we find in Bellanacargy in Cavan, the ford-mouth
of the rock

Bél-atha is often changed in modern names to *balli*
or *bally*, as if the original root were *baile* a town;
and *bel-an-atha* is made *ballina*. Both of these
modern forms are very general, but they are so
incorrect as to deserve the name of corruptions.
Ballina is the name of about twenty-five townlands
and villages in different parts of Ireland, several of
which are written *Bel-an-atha* in the annals. Ballina
in Tipperary, opposite Killaloe, was so called from
the ford—now spanned by a bridge—called *Atha-na-
borumha*, the ford of the cow tribute; and here no

doubt the great monarch Brian was accustomed to cross the Shannon when returning to his palace of Kincora, with the herds of cattle exacted from the Leinstermen (see Boro, below). Ballina in Mayo, on the Moy, is somewhat different, and represents a longer name, for it is called in an ancient poem in the Book of Lecan, *Bel-atha-an-fheadha* [Bellahanā], the ford-mouth of the wood. We find this compound also in Ballinafad in Sligo, which the Four Masters call *Bel-an-atha-fada* [Bellanafada], the mouth of the long ford; and there is a village in Leitrim and several townlands in other counties, called Ballina-more, the mouth of the great ford.

Bel-atha is reduced to *bally* and *balli* in the following names. The ford on the river Erne round which the town of Ballyshannon rose, is called by the annalists, *Ath-Seanaigh* and *Bel-atha-Seannaigh* [Bellashanny]; from the latter, the modern name is derived, and it means the mouth of Seanach's or Shannagh's ford, a man's name in common use. The *on* in Ballyshannon is a modern corruption; the people call the town *Ballyshanny*, which is nearer the original; and in an Inquisition of James I., it is given with perfect correctness, *Bealashanny*. Bally-shannon in Kildare, west of Kilcullen Bridge, is also called in Irish *Ath-Seanaigh* (Four Masters), Sean-ach's ford; and the present name was formed, as in case of the northern town, by prefixing *Bel*. It appears from a record in the Annals of Ulster, that this place in Kildare was also called *Uchba*.

There is a ford on the river Boro in Wexford, called *Bel-atha-Borumha*, which preserves the memory of the well-known *Borumha* or cow tribute, long exacted from the kings of Leinster by the monarchs of Ireland (see p. 157). From the latter part

of the name, *Borumha* [Boru], this river—so lovingly
commemorated in Mr. Kennedy's interesting book,
" The banks of the Boro "—derives its name. The
ford is called *Bealaborowe*, in an inquisition of
Charles I., and in the modern form Ballyboro, it
gives name to a townland. Ballylicky, on the road
from Glengarriff to Bantry in Cork, where the river
Ouvane enters Bantry Bay, is called in Irish *Bel-
atha-lice*, the ford-mouth of the flag stone, and whoever has seen it will acknowledge the appropriateness
of the name. All the places called Bellanalack,
derive their names from similar fords.

When a river spread widely over a craggy or rugged spot, the rough shallow ford thus formed was
often called *scairbh* [scarriv], or as O'Reilly spells it,
scirbh. A ford of this kind on a small river in Clare,
gave name to the little town of Scarriff; and there
are several townlands of the same name in Cork,
Kerry, and Galway. Near Newtownhamilton in
Armagh, there are two adjoining townlands called
Skerriff; and the same term is found shortened in
Scarnageeragh in Monaghan, *Scairbh-na-gcaerach*, the
shallow ford of the sheep.

The syllable *ach* is sometimes added to this word
in the colloquial language, making *scairbheach* [scar-
vagh], which has the same meaning as the original;
this derivative is represented by Scarva, the name of
a village in Down; Scarvy in Monaghan ; and Scar-
ragh in Tipperary and Cork.

In the end of names, when the word occurs in the
genitive, it is usually, though not always, anglicised
scarry, as in Ballynascarry in Westmeath and Kilkenny, the town of the ford; and Lackanascarry in
Limerick, the flagstones of the shallow ford. A ford
of this kind, where the old road crosses the Cookstown

river, gave name to Enniskerry in Wicklow. This spot is truly described by the term *scairbh*, being rugged and stony even now ; the natives call it *Annaskerry*, and its Irish name is obviously *Ath-na-scairbhe* [Anascarry], the ford of the *scarriff* or rough river-crossing. Other forms are seen in Bellanascarrow and Bellanascarva in Sligo, the ford-mouth of the *scarriff* (see p. 357).

The word *fearsad* [farsad] is applied to a sandbank formed near the mouth of a river, by the opposing currents of tide and stream, which at low water often formed a firm, and comparatively safe passage across. The term is pretty common, especially in the west, where these *farsets* are of considerable importance, as in many places they serve the inhabitants instead of bridges. Colgan translates the word, " *vadum* vel *trajectus*."

A sandbank of this kind across the mouth of the Lagan gave name to Belfast, which is called in Irish authorities *Bel-feirsdě*, the ford of the *farset ;* and the same name, in the uncontracted form Belfarsad, occurs in Mayo. There is now a bridge over the old sandbank that gave name to the village of Farsid near Aghada on Cork harbour : the origin of this name is quite forgotten, and the people call it *Farside*, and understand it to be an English word ; but the name of the adjacent townland of Ballynafarsid proves, if proof were necessary, that it took its name from a *farset*. Callanafersy in Kerry, between the mouths of the rivers Maine and Laune, is somewhat softened down from the Irish name *Cala-na-feirtse*, the ferry of the *farset*. On the river Swilly where it narrows near Letterkenny, there was a *farset* which in old times was evidently an important pass, for the Four Masters record several battles fought near it :

it is now called Farsetmore, and it can still be crossed at low water.

A *kish* or *kesh*, in Irish *ceis* [kesh], is a kind of causeway made of wickerwork, and sometimes of boughs of trees and brambles, across a small river, a marsh, or a deep bog. The word means primarily wicker or basket work ; and to this day, in some parts of Ireland, they measure and sell turf by the *kish*, which, originally meant a large wicker basket. These wickerwork bridges or *kishes*, were formerly very common in every part of Ireland, and are so still in some districts. The Four Masters record at 1483, that O'Donnell on a certain occasion constructed a *censaigh-droichet* [cassy-drohet] or wicker bridge across the Blackwater in Tyrone, for his army ; and when they had crossed, he let the bridge float down the stream. The memory of this primitive kind of bridge is preserved in many places by the names.

This word appears in its simple form in Kesh, a small town in Fermanagh ; and in Kish, a townland near Arklow ; and I suppose the Kish light, outside Dublin Bay, must have been originally floated on a wicker framework. A causeway of brambles and clay made across a marsh, not far from a high limestone rock, gave name to the village of Keshcarrigan in Leitrim, the *kesh* of the *carrigan* or little rock. There is a place not far from Mallow, called Anna-kisha (*Ath-na-cise*) the ford of the wickerwork causeway—a name that points clearly to the manner in which the ford on the river was formerly rendered passable.

Sometimes *ceiseach*, or in English *kishagh*, is the form used, and this in fact is rather more common than *kish* : we find it as Kisha near Wexford ; and the same form is preserved in Kishaboy (*boy*, yellow) in Armagh. Other modifications are seen in Casey Glebe in Donegal; Cassagh in Kilkenny; and in Cornakessagh in Fermanagh, the round hill of the wicker causeway. Kishoge, little *kish*, is the name of a place near Lucan in Dublin.

Those wickerwork causeways were also often de-signated by the word *cliath* [clee], which primarily means a hurdle; the diminutive *clethnat* glosses *tigillum* in the Sg. MS. of Zeuss (Gram. Celt., p. 282); and it is cognate with Lat. *clitellæ* and Fr. *claie*. An artificial ford of this kind was constructed across the Liffey (see p. 45), in very early ages; and the city that subsequently sprung up around it was from this circumstance called *Ath-cliath* [Ah-clee], the ford of hurdles, which was the ancient name of Dublin. This is the name still used by speakers of Irish in every part of Ireland; but they join it to *Bally—Baile-atha-claith* (which they pronounce *Blaa-clee*), the town of the hurdle ford.

The present name, Dublin, is written in the annals *Duibh-linn*, which in the ancient Latin Life of St. Kevin, is translated *nigra therma*. i. e. black pool; it was originally the name of that part of the Liffey on which the city is built, and is sufficiently descriptive at the present day. *Duibh-linn* is sounded *Durlin* or *Divlin*, and it was undoubtedly so pronounced down to a comparatively recent period, by speakers of both English and Irish; for in old English writings, as well as on Danish coins, we find the name written *Divlin, Dyflin*, &c., and even yet the Welsh call it *Dulin*. The present name has been formed by the restoration of the aspired *b* (see p. 45, *supra*).

There are several other places through Ireland

called *Duibhlinn*, but the aspiration of the *b* is observed in all, and consequently not one of them has taken the anglicised form *Dublin.* Devlin is the name of eight townlands in Donegal, Mayo, and Monaghan ; Dowling occurs near Fiddown in Kilkenny, Doolin in Clare, and Ballindoolin, the town of the black pool, in Kildare.

In several of these cases, the proper name was *Ath-cliath*, hurdle ford, which was formerly common as a local name ; and they received their present names merely in imitation of Dublin ; for, as the people when speaking Irish, always called the metropolis, *Baile-atha-cliath*, and in English, Dublin, they imagined that the latter was a translation of the former, and translated the names of their own places accordingly.

A row of stepping stones across a ford on a river, is called in every part of Ireland by the name of *clochan*, pronounced *clackan* in the north of Ireland and in Scotland. This mode of rendering a river fordable was as common in ancient as it is in modern times ; for in the tract of Brehon Laws in the Book of Ballymote, regulating the stipend of various kinds of artificers, it is stated that the builder of a *clochan* is to be paid two cows for his labour.

These stepping stones have given names to places in all parts of Ireland, now called Cloghan, Cloghane, and Cloghaun, the first being more common in the north, and the two last in the south. Cloghanaskaw in Westmeath, was probably so called from a ford shaded with trees, for the name signifies the stepping stones of the shade or shadow ; Cloghanleagh, grey stepping stones, was the old name of Dunglow in Donegal ; Cloghanenagleragh in Kerry, the stepping stones of the clergy ; Ballycloghan and Ballincloghan,

the town of the *cloghan*, are the names of several
townlands.

Clochan is sometimes applied to a stone castle, and
in some of the names containing this root, it is to be
understood in this sense. And in Cork and Kerry it
is also used to denote an ancient stone house of a
beehive shape.

When there were no means of making a river fordable, there remained the never-failing resource of
swimming. When rivers had to be crossed in this
manner, certain points seem to have been selected,
which were considered more suitable than others for
swimming across, either because the stream was nar-
rower there than elsewhere, or that it was less dangerous on account of the stillness of the water, or that
the shape of the banks afforded peculiar facilities.
Such spots were often designated by the word *snamh*
[snauv], which literally means swimming ; a word
often met with in our old historical writings in the
sense of a swimming ford, and which forms part of
several of our present names.

Lixnaw on the river Brick in Kerry, is called in
the Four Masters *Lic-snamha* [Licksnawa], the flag-
stone of the swimming ; the name probably indicating that there was a large stone on the bank, from
which the swimmers were accustomed to fling themselves off ; and Portnasnow near Enniskillen (*port*, a
bank), is a name of similar origin. About midway
between Glengarriff and Bantry, the traveller crosses
Snave bridge, where before the erection of the bridge,
the deep transparent creek at the mouth of the Coomhola river must have been generally crossed by swimming. So with the Shannon at Drumsna in Leitrim ;
the Erne at Drumsna, one mile south-east of Enniskillen ; and the narrow part of the western arm of Lough

Corrib at Drumsnauv; all of which names are from the Irish *Druim-snamha* [Drum-snauva], the hill of the swimming-ford.

When the article is used with this word *snamh* the *s* is eclipsed by *t*, as we see in Carrigatna in Kilkenny, which is in Irish *Carraig-a'-tsnamha*, the rock of the swimming; and Glanatnaw in the parish of Caheragh, Cork, where the people used to swim across the stream that runs through the *glan* or glen. In the north of Ireland the *n* of this construction is replaced by *r* (see p. 51, *supra*), as in Ardatrave on the shore of Lough Erne in Fermanagh, *Ard-a'-tsnamha* [Ardat-nauva], the height of the swimming. Immediately after the Shannon issues from Lough Allen, it flows under a bridge now called Ballintra; but Weld, in his "Survey of Roscommon," calls it *Ballintrace*, which points to the Irish *Bél-an-tsnamha* [Bellant-nauva], the ford of the swimming, and very clearly indicates the usual mode of crossing the river there in former ages.

The lower animals, like the human inhabitants, had often their favourite spots on rivers or lakes, where they swam across in their wanderings from place to place. On the shore of the little lake of Muckno in Monaghan, where it narrows in the middle, there was once a well-known religious establishment called in the annals *Mucshnamh* [Mucknauv], the swimming place of the pigs (*muc*, a pig), which has been softened to the present name Muckno. Some of our ecclesiastical writers derive this name from a legend; but the natural explanation seems to be, that wild pigs were formerly in the habit of crossing the lake at this narrow part. Exactly the same remark applies to the Kenmare river, where it is now spanned by the suspension bridge at the town. It was nar-

rowed at this point by a spit of land projecting from
the northern shore ; and here in past ages, wild pigs
used to swim across so frequently and in such numbers, that the place was called *Mucsnamh* or Mucksna,
which is now well known as the name of a little hamlet near the bridge, and of the hill that rises over it,
at the south side of the river.

A weir across a river, either for fishing or to divert
a mill stream, is called in Irish *cora* or *coradh* [curra].
Brian Borumha's palace of Kincora was built on a
hill in the present town of Killaloe, and it is repeatedly mentioned in the annals, by the name of *Ceann-
coradh*, the head or hill of the weir ; from which we
may infer that there was a fishing weir across the
Shannon at this point, from very early times. There
is another Kincora in King's County, in which was a
castle mentioned by the Four Masters, and called by
the same Irish name. And we find Ti*kincor* in Waterford, the house at the head of the weir.

Ballinacor in Glenmalure in Wicklow, which gives
name to two baronies, is called in the Leabhar
Branach, *Baile-na-corra*, the town of the weir. There
are several other places of the same name in Wicklow
and Westmeath ; and it is modified to Ballinacur
in Wexford, and to Ballinacurra or Ballynacorra in
several counties, the best known place of the name
being Ballynacorra on Cork harbour. Corrofin in
Clare is called by the Four Masters *Coradh-Finne*, the
weir of Finna, a woman's name (see p. 173, *supra*) ;
in the same authority we find Drumcar in Louth,
written *Druim-caradh* [Drumcara], the ridge of the
weir ; and here the people still retain the tradition
of the ancient weir on the river Dee, and point out
its site ; Smith (Hist. of Cork, II., 254) states that
there was formerly an eel-weir of considerable profit

at the castle of Carrignacurra on the river Lee near Inchigeelagh; and the name bears out his assertion, for it signifies the rock of the weir.

"The origin of stone bridges in Ireland is not very accurately ascertained; but this much at least appears certain, that none of any importance were erected previous to the twelfth century" (Petrie, "Dub. Pen. Journal," I., 150). *Droichet*, as it is given in Cormac's Glossary, or in modern Irish, *droichead* [drohed], is the word universally employed to denote a bridge, and under this name, bridges are mentioned in our oldest authorities. The fourteenth abbot of Iona, from A. D. 726 to 752, was Cilline, who was surnamed *Droichteach*, i. e. the bridge maker; and Fiachna, the son of Aedh Roin, king of Ulidia in the eighth century, was called Fiachna Dubh Droichtech, black Fiachna of the bridges, because "it was he that made *Droichet-na-Feirsi* (the bridge of the *farset*, see p. 360), and *Droichet-Mona-daimh* (the bridge of the bog of the ox), and others." It is almost certain, however, that these structures were of wood, and that bridges with stone arches were not built till after the arrival of the Anglo-Normans.

Many places in Ireland have taken their names from bridges, and the word *droichead* is often greatly modified by modern corruption. It is to be observed that the place chosen for the erection of a bridge was very usually where the river had already been crossed by a ford; for besides the convenience of retaining the previously existing roads, the point most easily fordable was in general most suitable for a bridge. There are many places whose names preserve the memory of this, of which Drogheda is a good example. This place is repeatedly mentioned in old authorities, and always called *Droichead-atha* [Drohed-aha], the bridge of the ford; from which the present name was easily formed; pointing clearly to the fact, that the first bridge was built over the ford where the northern road along the coast crossed the Boyne.

There is a townland in Kildare called Drehid, and another in Londonderry called Droghed; Drehid-tarsna (cross-bridge) is a parish in Limerick; Bally-drehid and Balliudrehid, the town of the bridge, are the names of some townlands, the same as Ballindrait in Donegal. The memory of the two modes of crossing is preserved in the name of Belladrihid near - Bullysadare in Sligo, which the Four Masters write *Bel-an-droichit*, the ford of the bridge. Five miles east of Macroom, *near a bridge* over the Lee, there is a rock in the river on which stands a castle, called Carrigadrohid, the rock of the bridge: according to a legend told in the neighbourhood, the castle was built by one of the Mac Carthys with the money extorted from a leprechaun (see p. 190, *supra*).

The word is obscured in Knockadreel, the hill of the bridge, in Wicklow, which same name is correctly anglicised Knockadrehid in Roscommon. A like difference is observable between Drumadrehid and Drumadried, the ridge of the bridge, the former in Clare, and the latter in Antrim; and between Ros-drehid in the south of King's County, and Rossdroit south west of Enniscorthy, both meaning the wood of the bridge. The parish of Kildrought in Kildare took its name from a bridge over the Liffey, the Irish form being *Cill-droichid*, the church of the bridge. Though the parish retains the old name, that of the original spot is changed by an incorrect translation; the first part was altered to *Cel*, and the last part translated, forming Celbridge, the name of a well-known town. What renders this more certain is, that the place is called *Kyldroghet*, in an Inquisition of William and Mary.

CHAPTER VI.

ROADS AND CAUSEWAYS.

"According to the Irish annals, and other fragments of our native history, the ancient Irish had many roads which were cleaned and kept in repair according to law. The different terms used to denote road, among the ancient Irish, are thus defined in Cormac's Glossary, from which a pretty accurate idea may be formed of their nature" (O'Donovan, Book of Rights, Introd., p. lvi.). O'Donovan then quotes Cormac's enumeration of the different terms, several of which are still used. According to the Dinnsenchus, there were anciently five great roads leading to Tara, from five different directions; and it would appear from several authorities, that they were constructed in the reign of Felimy the lawgiver, in the second century (see p. 128, *supra*). Besides these great highways, numerous other roads are mentioned in our annals and tales, many of which are enumerated in O'Donovan's valuable introduction to the Book of Rights.

Among the different Irish words to denote a road, the most common and best known is *bóthar* [bōher]; and its diminutive *bohereen* is almost on the eve of acknowledgment as an English word. It originally meant a road for cattle, being derived from *bo*, a cow; and Cormac defines its breadth to be such that "two cows fit upon it, one lengthwise, the other athwart, and their calves and yearlings fit on it along with them."

The word is scarcely used at all in Ulster; but in the other provinces, the anglicised forms Boher, and Bohereen or Borheen, constitute part of a great number of names, and they are themselves the names of several places. There is a townland in Galway called Bohercuill, the road of the hazel (*coll*); and this same name becomes Boherkyle in Kilkenny, Boherkill in Kildare, and Boherquill in Westmeath; while with the diminutive, it is found as Bohereenkyle in Limerick.

Sometimes the word is contracted to one syllable; as we find, for instance, in Borleagh and Bornacourtia in Wexford, grey road, and the road of the court or mansion; and Borderreen in King's County, the road of the little wood. When the word occurs as a termination, the *b* is often aspirated (p. 19), as in the common townland name, Ballinvoher, the town of the road; and in this case, we also sometimes find it contracted, as in Cartronbore near Granard, the quarter-land of the road. For the change of *bothar* to *batter*, see p. 44, *supra*.

Slighe or *Slighcadh* [slee] was anciently applied by the Irish to the largest roads; the five great roads leading to Tara, for instance, were called by this name. The word is still in common use in the vernacular, but it has not entered very extensively into names.

Sleo near Enniskillen, preserves the exact pronunciation of the original word; Clonaslee, a village in Queen's County, is the meadow of the road; Bruslee in Antrim, indicates that a *brugh* or mansion stood near the old road; and Sleemanagh near Castletownroche in Cork, is middle road. Sleehaun, little road, is the name of some places in Longford and Donegal ; and in Roscommon we find Cornaslechan, the round hill of the little road.

Bealach [ballagh], signifies a road, or pass. It forms part of the well-known battle cry of the 88th Connaught Rangers, *Fág-a'-bealach*, clear the road. Ballagh, the usual modern form, constitutes or begins the names of a number of places ; near several of these the ancient roadways may be traced ; and in some cases they are still used. Ballaghboy, yellow road, was formerly the name of several old highways, and is still retained by a number of townlands. Ballaghmoon, two miles north of Carlow, where the battle in which Cormac Mac Cullenan was killed, was fought in the year 903, is called in the Book of Leinster, *Bealach-Mughna*, Mughan's or Mooan's pass ; but we know not who this Mughan was.

The great road from Tara to the south-west, called *Slighe Dala*, is still remembered in the name of a townland in Queen's County, which enables us to identify at least one point in its course. This road was also called *Ballaghmore Moydala* (the great road of the plain of the conference), and the first part of this old name is retained by the townland of Ballaghmore near Stradbally. There are several other places in Leinster and Munster called Ballaghmore, but none with such interesting associations as this.

Several other well-known places retain the memory of those old *bealachs*. Ballaghadereen in Mayo, is called in Irish *Bealach-a'-doirtn*, the road of the little oak wood ; the village of Ballaghkeen in Wexford, was originally called *Bealach-cucin*, beautiful road ; and Ballaghkeeran near Athlone, must have been formerly shaded with *keerans* or quicken trees.

When this word occurs as a termination, it is very often changed to *rally* by the aspiration of the *b*, and the disappearance of the final guttural. There are townlands scattered through the four provinces called Ballinvally and Ballyvally, the town of the road; which in Limerick is made Ballinvallig, by the restoration of the final *g* (p. 31). So also Moyvally, the name of a place in Carlow, and of another in Kildare —the latter a station on the Midland railway—the plain or field of the road. The word has another form still in Revallagh near Colerane, clear or open (*reidh*) road—so called, no doubt, to distinguish it from some other road difficult of passage. For the word *ród*, a road, see Second Series, chap. XIII.

Casán signifies a path. It is a term that does not often occur, but we find a few places to which it gives names; such as Cassan in Fermanagh; Cussan in Kilkenny; and Cossaun near Athenry in Galway— all of which mean simply "path :" the same name is corrupted to Carsan in Monaghan ; and the plural Cussana (paths) is the name of two townlands in Kilkenny. Ardnagassan near Donegal, and Ardna-gassane in Tipperary, are both called in the original *Ard-na-gcasan*, the height of the paths.

It is curious that the river Cashen in Kerry derives its name from this word. It is called Cashen as far as it is navigable for *curraghs*, i. e. up to the junction of the Feale and the Brick ; and its usual name in the annals is *Casan-Kerry*, i. e. the path to Kerry—being as it were the high road to that ancient territory. But the term was also applied to other streams. The mouth of the Ardee river in Louth, was anciently called *Casan-Linne* ("Circuit of Ireland "); and the village of Annagassan partly preserves this old name—*Ath-na-gcasan*, the ford of the *paths*—probably in reference to the two rivers, Glyde and Dee, which join near the village (see Dr. Todd in " Wars of GG.," Introd., p. lxi., note *t*).

In early ages, before the extension of cultivation and drainage, the roads through the country must have often been interrupted by bogs and morasses, which, when practicable, were made passable by causeways. They were variously constructed; but the materials were generally branches of trees, bushes, earth, and stones, placed in alternate layers, and trampled down till they were sufficiently firm; and they were called by the Irish name of *tóchar*.

These *tóchars* were very common all over the country; our annals record the construction of many in early ages, and some of these are still traceable. They have given names to a number of townlands and villages, several of them called Togher, and many others containing the word in combination. Ballintogher, the town of the causeway, is a very usual name (but Ballintogher in Sligo appears to be a different name — see this in 2nd Series); and Templetogher (the church of the *togher*) in Galway was so called from a celebrated causeway across a bog, whose situation is still well known to the inhabitants.

CHAPTER VII.

MILLS AND KILNS.

MANY authorities concur in showing that water mills were known in this country in very remote ages, and

that they were even more common in ancient than in
modern times. We know from the Lives of the Irish
saints, that several of them erected mills where they
settled, shortly after the introduction of Christianity,
as St. Senanus, St. Ciaran, St. Mochua, St. Fechin,
&c. ; and in some cases mills still exist on the very
sites selected by the original founders—as, for instance, at Fore in Westmeath, where " St. Fechin's
mill " works as busily to-day as it did twelve hundred
years ago. We may infer, moreover, from several
grants and charters of the eleventh and twelfth centuries, that, where circumstances permitted, a mill
was a usual appendage to a ballybetagh, or ancient
townland.

It appears certain that water mills were used in
Ireland before the introduction of Christianity. For
we have reliable historical testimony that Cormac
mac Art, monarch of Ireland in the third century,
sent across the sea for a millwright, who constructed
a mill on the stream of Nith, which flowed from the
well of *Neamhnach* [Navnagh] at Tara. "The ancient
Irish authorities all agree in stating that this was the
first mill ever erected in Ireland ; and it is remarkable
that this circumstance is still most vividly preserved
by tradition, not only in the neighbourhood, where a
mill still occupies its site, but also in most parts of
Ireland. Tradition adds that it was from the king
of Scotland the Irish monarch obtained the millwright,
and it can be shown that the probability of its truth
is strongly corroborated by that circumstance "* (see
Mullenoran in 2nd Series).

---

* From the Ordnance memoir of the parish of Templemore.
See also O'Donovan's article on the antiquity of corn in Ireland
in the Dublin Penny Journal, and Petrie's Essay on Tara.

The Irish word for a mill is *muilenn* [mullen], and this term exists in several of the Indo-European languages :—Sansc. *malana*, the action of grinding ; Lat. *molo* to grind ; Goth. *malan ;* Eng. *mill.* A very considerable number of places in Ireland have taken their names from mills, and the most usual anglicised form of *muilenn* is Mullen or Mullin.

Mullennakill in Kilkenny, is in Irish, *Muilenn-na-cille*, the mill of the church ; and Mullinavat, in the same county is *Muilenn-a'-bhata*, the mill of the stick. When this word occurs as a termination the *m* is often changed to *w* by aspiration (p. 19), as in Ma-william in Londonderry, *Magh-mhuilinn*, the plain of the mill. Ballywillin is the name of a parish on the borders of Antrim and Londonderry, and of several townlands in these and other counties ; while the form Ballinwillin is very frequent in some of the southern counties ; this name signifies the town of the mill, and it is often so translated, from which has originated the very common name Milltown. Cloona-willen is the name of five townlands, the same as Clonmullin and Cloonmullin, all signifying the *cloon* or meadow of the mill ; there is a parish in Monaghan called Aghnamullen, and two townlands in Leitrim called Aghawillin, the former the field of the mills, and the latter, of the mill ; Killawillin on the Black-water, near Castletownroche in Cork, is called in Irish by the people *Cill-a'-mhuilinn*, the church of the mill ; Killywillin, the name of a townland in Fer-managh, and of another in Cavan, is different, the latter place being called by the Four Masters, *Coill-an-mhuilinn*, the wood of the mill.

A quern or hand mill is designated by the word *bro*, which is also applied to the mill stone used with water mills; genitive *brón* or *broin* [brone], plural *bróinte* [broanty]. We find this word in the names of several places, where it is likely there were formerly water mills or hand mills, the owners of which made their living by grinding their neighbours' corn. Coolnabroue, the hill-back of the quern or mill-stone, is the name of two townlands in Kilkenny; and in the same county near Fiddown, is Tobernabrone, the well of the quern; Clonbrone and Cloonbrone, the meadow of the mill-stone, are the names of some townlands in King's County, Galway, and Mayo.

Before the potato came into general use it was customary for families—those especially who were not within easy reach of a mill—to grind their own corn for home consumption; and the quern was consequently an instrument of very general use. We may presume that there were professional quern makers, and we know for a certainty, that some places received names from producing stones well suited for querns. Such a place is Carrigeenamronety, a hill near Ballyorgan in Limerick, on whose side there is a ridge of rocks, formerly much resorted to by the the peasantry for quern stones; its Irish name is *Carraigín-na-mbrointe*, the little rock of the mill-stones; and there are other rocks of the same name in Limerick. So also Bronagh in Leitrim, i. e. a place abounding in mill-stones.

Aith [ah] denotes a kiln of any kind, whether a lime-kiln or a kiln for drying corn. It is generally found in the end of names, joined with *na*, the gen. fem. of the article, followed by *h*, by which it is distinguished from *ath*, a ford, which takes *an* in the genitive. There are several places in Monaghan and

Armagh, called Annahaia and Annahagh, all of
which are from the Irish, *Ath-na-haithe*, the ford
of the kiln; we find Ballynahaha in Limerick, and
Ballynahaia in Cavan (*Bally*, a town); in Antrim,
Lisnahay (*Lis*, a fort); Gortnahey in Londonderry, Gortnahaha in Clare and Tipperary, and
Aughnahoy in Antrim, all of which signify the field
of the kiln.

PART IV.

NAMES DESCRIPTIVE OF PHYSICAL FEATURES.

CHAPTER I.

MOUNTAINS, HILLS, AND ROCKS.

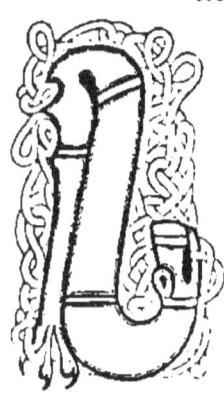

IKE most other countries, Ireland has a large proportion of its territorial names derived from those of hills. For hills, being the most conspicuous physical features, are naturally often fixed upon, in preference to others, to designate the districts in which they stand. There are at least twenty-five words in the Irish language for a hill, besides many others to denote rocks, points, slopes, and cliffs; and all without exception have impressed themselves on the nomenclature of the country. Many of these are well distinguished one from another, each being applied to a hill of some particular shape or formation; but several, though they may have been formerly different in meaning, are now used synonymously, so that it is impossible to make any distinction between them. I will here enumerate them, and illustrate the manner in which names are formed from each.

Sliabh [sleeve] signifies a mountain; and according to O'Brien, it was sometimes applied to any heath-land, whether mountain or plain. It occurs in the Zeuss MSS. in the old Irish form *sliab*, which glosses *mons.* The word in the anglicised form of *sliere* is applied to great numbers of the principal mountains in Ireland; and it is almost always followed by a limiting term, such as an adjective or a noun in the genitive case. For example, Slievesnaght, the name of a mountain in Innishowen, and of several others in different parts of the country, represents the Irish *Sliabh-sneacht,* the mountain of the snow; Slieve Anierin in Leitrim, *Sliabh-an-iarainn,* the mountain of the iron, in allusion to its well-known richness in iron ore; Slieve Bernagh in the east of Clare, gapped mountain.

This word is occasionally so very much disguised in modern names, that it is difficult to recognise it; and of such names I will give a few examples. There is a mountain west of Lough Arrow in Sligo called Bricklieve, the proper Irish name of which is *Breic-shliabh* (Four Mast.), speckled mountain, and the *s* has disappeared by aspiration. The same thing occurs in Finliff in Down, white mountain; in Gortin-lieve in Donegal, the little field of the mountain; and in Beglieve in Cavan, small mountain. The parish of Killevy in Armagh took its name from an old church situated at the foot of Slieve Gullion, which the annalists usually call *Cill-shleibhe,* i. e. the church of the mountain; the pronunciation of which is well preserved in the modern spelling.

Sometimes the *r* sound is omitted altogether, and this often happens when the word comes in as a termination. Sleamaine in Wicklow is anglicised from *Sliabh-meadhoin*, middle mountain; Illaunslea in Kerry, the island of the mountain. Slemish in Antrim is well known as the mountain where St. Patrick passed his early days as a slave, herding swine; the full Irish name is *Sliabh-Mis*, the mountain of Mis, a woman's name; and there is another almost equally celebrated mountain in Kerry, of the same name, now called Slieve Mish, "the Mountain of Mis, the daughter of Mureda, son of Cared" (Four Masters).

In other cases both the *s* and *r* are lost, as for example in Crotlie or Cratlie, the name of several hills, *Croit-shliabh*, hump-backed mountain—which in other places is made Cratlieve. In a great many cases the sound of *s* is changed to that of *t* by eclipse (p. 23, as in Ballintlea, the name of about fifteen townlands in the Munster and Leinster counties, *Baile-an-tsleibhe*, the town of the mountain; the same name as Ballintleva in Galway and Mayo, Ballintlevy in Westmeath, and Ballintlieve in Meath and Down; Baunatlea in the parish of Ballingaddy, Limerick, the *bawn* or green field of the mountain.

The plural *sleibhte* [slcaty] appears in Sleaty, a celebrated church giving name to a village and parish in Queen's County. There can be no doubt as to the original form and meaning of this name, as it is written *Sleibhte* by all Irish authorities; and Colgan translates it *Montes*, i. e. mountains. The name must have been originally given to the church from its contiguity to the hills of Slieve Margy, as Killevy was called so from its proximity to Slieve Gullion.

Sleibhin [slayveen], a diminutive of *sliabh*, is applied to a little hill; in modern nomenclature it is usually made Sleveen, which is the name of a hill

rising over Macroom in Cork, of a village in Waterford, and of nine townlands chiefly in the southern
counties. Slevin in Roscommon, is the same word;
and Slievinagee in the same county, signifies the
little mountain of the wind (*gaeth*).

Cnoc signifies a hill; its most common anglicised
form is Knock, in which the *k* is usually silent, but in
the original the first *c*, which the *k* represents, was
sounded [*cnoc*, pron. *kännäck*, the first *u* very short].
There is a conspicuous isolated hill near Ballingarry
in Limerick, called Knockfierna, a noted fairy haunt.
It serves as a *weather glass* to the people of the circum-
jacent plains, who can predict with certainty, whether
the day will be wet or dry, by the appearance of the
summit in the morning; and hence the mountain is
called *Cnoc-firinne*, the hill of truth, i. e. of truthful
prediction. Knockea is the name of a hill near Glen-
nosheen, three miles south from Kilfinane in Limerick, and of several townlands, all of which are called
in Irish *Cnoc-Aedha*, Aedh's or Hugh's hill, probably from some former proprietors. The well-known
hill of Knocklayd in Antrim was so called from its
shape, *Cnoc-leithid* [Knocklehid], literally the hill of
breadth, i. e. broad hill.

The diminutives Knockane, Knockaun, Knockeen,
and Knickeen, with their plurals, form the names of
more than seventy townlands, all so called from a
"little hill." Ballyknockan and Ballyknockane, the
town of the little hill, are the names of about twenty-
five townlands; and the places called Knockauneevin
in Galway and Cork are truly described by the name,
Cnocán-aoibhinn beautiful little hill.

Cnuic, the genitive of *cnoc*, is often made *knick* and
nick in the present names, as the diminutive *cnuicín*
is sometimes represented by Knickeen; and these

modern forms give correctly the pronunciation of the
originals—except of course the silent *k*. Thus Bally-
knick in the parish of Grange, Armagh, which is the
same as the very common name, Ballyknock, the
town of the hill; Tinnick in Wexford, and Ticknick
or Ticknook on the side of the Three Rock mountain
in Dublin, *Tigh-cnuic*, the house of the hill, which
under the forms Ticknock and Tiknock, is the name
of several townlands in the eastern counties.

The word is still further modified by the change of
n to *r*, already noticed (p. 51), which prevails chiefly
in the northern half of Ireland, and which converts
knock into *crock* or *cruck*. Crockacapple in the parish
of Kilbarron, Donegal, means the hill of the horse
(*capall*), and Crocknagapple near Killybegs, same
county, the hill of the horses (*Cnoc-na-geapall*); and
these two names are the same respectively as Knock-
acappul and Knocknagappul, which are found in
other counties. Crockshane near Rathcoole in Dublin, John's hill; Crockanure near Kildare, the hill of
the yew tree. The diminutives suffer this corruption also, and we find many places called Crock-
aun, Crickaun, Crockeen, Cruckeen and Crickeen, all
meaning little hill. The syllable *Knock* begins the
names of about 1800 townlands, and *Crock* of more
than fifty.

Beann [ban], genitive and plural *beanna* [banna],
signifies a horn, a gable, a peak, or pointed hill; but
it is often applied to any steep hill: cognate with
Latin *pinna*. In anglicised names, it is generally
spelled *ben* or *bin*, each of which begins about thirty
townland names; but it undergoes various other
modifications; in Cork and Kerry, it is often anglicised Beoun, to represent the southern pronunciation.

Beann is not applied to *great* mountains so much

in Ireland as in Scotland, where they have Ben Lo-
mond, Ben Nevis, Benledi, &c.; but as applied to
middle and smaller eminences, it is used very extensively.   There is a steep hill in Westmeath, called
the Ben (i. e. the peak) of Fore, from the village
near its base ; the Irish name of Bengore Head in
Antrim is *Beann-gabhar*, the peak of the goats.
Benburb, now the name of a village in Tyrone, the
scene of the battle in 1646, was originally applied to
the remarkable cliff overhanging the Blackwater, on
which the castle ruins now stand ; the Irish name as
given in the annals is *Beann-borb*, which O'Sullivan
Bear correctly translates *Pinna superba*, the proud
peak.

   The Twelve Pins, a remarkable group of mountains
in Connemara, derive their name from the same
word ; *Pins* being a modification of *Bens*.   They are
commonly called " The Twelve Pins of Bunnabeola,"
in which the word *beann* occurs twice: for Bunnabeola is *Beanna-Beola*, the peaks of Beola.   This
Beola, who was probably an old Firbolg chieftain, is
still vividly remembered in tradition ; and a remarkable person he must have been, for the place of his
interment is also commemorated, namely Toombeola,
Beola's tumulus, which is a townland south of the
Twelve Pins, at the head of Roundstone bay, containing the ruins of an abbey.

   The adjective form *beannach* is applied to a hilly
place—a place full of *bens* or peaks ; and it has given
name to Bannagh in Cork, and to Benagh in Down
and Louth.   This word appears in Bannaghbane and
Bannaghroe (white, red) in Monaghan ; and Agha-
vannagh, Irish *Achadh-bheannach*, hilly field, is the
name of three townlands in Wicklow.   The plural,
beanna, is found in Bannamore and Benamore in

Tipperary, great peaks: and in the form Bauna, it
occurs several times in Kerry. Benbo, a conspicuous
mountain near Manorhamilton, is written by the
Four Masters, *Beauna-bo,* the peaks or horns of the
cow; it is still so called in Irish, and it appears to
have got the name from its curious double peak,
bearing a rude resemblance to a cow's horns.

The word assumes various other forms, and enters
into many combinations, of which the following
names will be a sufficient illustration. The old name
of Dunmanway in Cork, was *Dun-na-mbeann* [Dun-
naman: Four Mast.], the fortress of the gables or
pinnacles; and the name was probably derived from
the ridge of rocks north of the town, or perhaps from
the shape of the old *dun.* In a grant made in the
time of Elizabeth, the place is called *Downemanroy,*
from which, as well indeed as from the tradition of
the inhabitants, it appears that the last syllable,
ray—which must be a modern addition, as it does
not appear in the older documents—is a corruption
of the Irish *buidhe,* yellow (*b* changed to *w* by aspiration; p. 19):—Dunmanway, the fortress of the
yellow pinnacles. Dunnaman, which is a correct
anglicised form of *Dun-na-mbeann,* is still the name
of a townland in Down, and of another near Croom
in Limerick. Ballycangour in Carlow, is in Irish,
Baile-bheanna-gabhar, the town of the pinnacle of the
goats, the latter part (-vangour), being the same as
Bengore in Antrim (see last page); Knockbine in
Wexford, the hill of the peak; Dunnavenny in Londonderry, the fortress of the peak.

The word has several diminutive forms, the most
common of which is *beinnín* [benneen], which gives
name to several mountains now call Binnion or
Bignion, i. e. small peak. Another diminutive, *bean-*

nachán, appears in Meenavanaghan in Donegal, the *meen* or mountain flat of the small peak.

Beannchar or *beannchor* [banagher] is a modification of *beann*, and signifies horns, or pointed hills or rocks, and sometimes simply peaked hill; it is a word of frequent topographical use in different parts of Ireland, and it is generally anglicised *banagher* or *bangor*. Banagher in King's County (*Beannchor*, Four Mast.) is said to have taken its name from the sharp rocks in the Shannon; and there are seven townlands in different counties bearing the same name.

Bangor in Down is written *Beannchar* by various authorities, and Keating and others account for the name by a legend; but the circumstance that there are so many *Beannchars* in Ireland renders this of no authority; and there is a hill near the town, from which it is more likely that the place received its name. Coolbanagher or Whitechurch, a church giving name to a parish in Queen's County, where Aengus the Culdee began his celebrated *Felire* (see p. 157), is written in Irish authorities, *Cuil-beannchair*, the angle or corner of the pinnacle. "There is a Lough Banagher (the lake of the pinnacles) in Donegal; Drumbanagher in Armagh; Movanagher on the Bann, parish of Kilrea, Derry (*Magh-bheannchair*, the plain of the pinnacles); and the ancient church of *Ross-bennchuir* (*ross*, a wood), placed by Archdall in the county of Clare" (Reeves, Ecclesiastical Antiquities, p. 199, where the word *beannchar* is exhaustively discussed).

Ard is sometimes a noun meaning a height or hill, and sometimes an adjective, signifying high: cognate with Lat. *arduus*. In both senses it enters extensively into Irish nomenclature; it forms the beginning of about 650 townland names; and there are at least as many more that contain it otherwise combined.

There is a little town in Waterford, and about twenty-six townlands in different counties, called Ardmore, great height; but only two bear the correlative name, Ardbeg, little height. Ardglass in Down, is called *Ard-glass* by the Four Masters, i. e. green height; which is also a usual townland name; and there are many places scattered over the country, called Ardkeen, that is, *Ard-caein*, beautiful height. Ardorin in the Queen's County is the highest of the Slieve Bloom range; and the inhabitants of the great central plain who gave it the name, signifying the height of Ireland, unaccustomed as they were to the view of high mountains, evidently believed it to be one of the principal elevations in the country.

When *ard* is followed by *tighe* [tee], a house, the final *d* is usually omitted; as in Artiferrall in Antrim, *Ard-tighe-Fearghaill*, the height of Farrell's house; Artimacormick near Ballintoy, same county, the height of MacCormack's house, &o.

This word has two diminutives, *airdín* and *ardán* [ardeen, ardaun]; the former is not much in use, but it gives name to some places in Cork and Kerry, called Ardeen, and it forms a part of a few other names. The latter, under the different forms Ardan, Ardane, and Ardaun, all meaning little height or hillock, is by itself the name of several places in the midland counties; and it helps to form many others, such as Ardanreagh in Limerick, grey hillock; and Killinardan near Tallaght in Dublin, the church or wood of the little height.

Leath-ard [lahard], which means literally half height, is used topographically to denote a gently sloping eminence; and the anglicised form Lahard, and the diminutives Lahardan, Lahardane, and Lahardaun, are the names of many places, chiefly in Connaught and Munster. Derrylahard, the oak wood of the gentle hill, occurs near Skull, in Cork; and the same name, in the shortened form, Derrylard, is found in the parish of Tartaraghan, Armagh.

The word *alt* primarily denotes a height, cognate with Lat. *altus;* it occurs in Cormac's Glossary, where it is derived "*ab altitudine:*" in its present topographical application, it is generally understood to mean a cliff, or the side of a glen. It is pretty generally spread throughout the country, forming the first syllable of about 100 townland names, which are distributed over the four provinces. Alt stands alone as the name of some places in Mayo and Donegal; and Alts (heights or glen sides) occurs in Monaghan. Altnahullion in Cavan is the cliff of the holly; in Limerick and Queen's County we have Altavilla, *Alt-a'-bhile,* the glen-side of the old tree; Altinure in Derry and Cavan, the cliff of the yew.

There is a place in the parish of Tulloghobegly, Donegal, called Altan, little cliff; and the plural Altans occurs in Sligo. Altanagh in Tyrone signifies a place abounding in cliffs and glens. In the end of names, this word is sometimes made *alta*, and sometimes *ilt*, representing two forms of the genitive, *alta* and *ailt*, as we see in Lissanalta in Limerick, the fort of the height; and Tonanilt in Cavan, the backside of the cliff.

The primary meaning of *cruach* is a rick or stack, such as a stack of corn or hay; but in an extended sense, it is applied to hills, especially to those presenting a round, stacked, or piled up appearance;

26 *

Welsh *crug*, a heap ; Cornish *cruc.* It is used pretty
extensively as a local term, generally in the forms
Croagh or Crogh ; and the diminutive *Cruachán* is
still more common, giving names to numerous mountains, townlands, and parishes called Croaghan,
Croaghaun, Croghan, and Crohane, all originally
applied to a round-shaped hill. *Cruachán* was the
original name of the village of Crookhaven on the
south coast of Cork ; the present name signifying the
haven of the *cruach* or round hill.

Croghan hill in King's County, was anciently
called *Bri-Eile*, the hill of Eilě, daughter of Eochy
Feilench, and sister of Meave, queen of Connaught in
the first century (see p. 126, *supra*) ; it afterwards
received the name of *Cruachan*, and in the annals it
is sometimes called *Cruachan-Bri-Eile*, which looks
tautological, as *Cruachan* and *Bri* both signify a hill.
Croaghan near Killashandra in Cavan, the inauguration place of the O'Rourkes, is often mentioned in
the Irish authorities by two names—*Cruachan O'Cup-
roin*, O'Cupron's round hill, and *Cruachan-Mic-
Tighearnain*, from the Mac Tighearnans or Mac-
Kiernans, the ancient possessors of the barony of
Tullyhunco, the chief of whom had his residence
there. The word is somewhat disguised in Bally-
crogue, the name of a parish in Carlow, the same as
Ballycroghan near Bangor in Down, only that in the
latter the diminutive is used. Kilcruaig, a townland
near Ballyorgan in the south-east of Limerick, obviously got its name, which means the church of the
round hill, from the detached mountain now called
Carrigeenamronety, on whose side the place in question lies.

Tulach, a little hill—a hillock ; often written *tealach*
in old documents. It occurs in Cormac's Glossary,

where it is given as the equivalent of *bri*. It is anglicised Tulla, Tullow, and Tullagh, but most commonly Tully (see p. 34). Tullanavert near Clogher in Tyrone represents *Tulach-na-bhfeart*, the hill of the graves; Tullaghacullion near Killybegs, Tullaghcullion near Donegal, and Tullycullion in Tyrone, the hill of the holly. The parish of Tully near Kingstown in Dublin was anciently called *Tulach-na-nespuc*, which signifies the hill of the bishops; and according to the Life of St. Brigid, it received this name from seven bishops who lived there, and on one occasion visited the saint at Kildare (O'Curry, Lect., p. 382). Tullymongan, the name of two townlands near Cavan, was originally applied to the hill over the town, now called Gallows Hill; the Four Masters call it *Tulach-Mongain*, the hill of Mongan, a man's name.

The parish of Kiltullagh in Roscommon was so called from an old church, the name of which perfectly describes its situation—*Cill-tulaigh*, the church of the hill; and the parish of Kiltullagh in Galway, near Athenry, is called *cill-tulach* (church of the little hills) in "Hy Many." In the Munster counties, the *g* in *tulaigh*, is pronounced hard, giving rise to a new form Tullig, which is found in the names of many places, the greater number being in Cork and Kerry.

There are two diminutive forms in use, *tulán* and *tulachán*. From the former comes Tullen in Roscommon, Tullin near Athlone, and Tullans near Coleraine; but the other is more common, and gives origin to Tullaghan, Tullaghaun, and Tullaghans (little hills), found in several counties as the names of townlands and villages. The word is sometimes spelled in Irish *tealach* [tallagh], which orthography

is often adopted by the Four Masters; this form
appears in the name of Tallow, a town in Waterford,
which is called in Irish *Tealach-an-iarainn* [Tallow-
anierin], the hill of the iron, from the iron mines
worked there by the great Earl of Cork.

Bri [bree], signifies a hill or rising ground, the
same as the Scotch word *brae;* in Cormac's Glossary
it is explained by *tulach;* Cornish and Breton *bre;*
Gaulish *brega, briga.* The word occurs frequently
as a topographical term in our ancient writings, of
which *Bri-Eile* (p. 388), is an example. Brigown,
a village near Mitchelstown in Cork, once a celebrated ecclesiastical establishment, where are still to
be seen the remains of a very ancient church and
round tower, is called in Irish, *Bri-gobhunn* (Book
of Lismore: *gobha*, a smith), the hill of the smith.
In our present names this word does not occur very
often; it is found simply in the form of Bree, in
Donegal, Monaghan, and Wexford; while in Tyrone
it takes the form of Brigh.

Bray which is the name of several places in Ireland, is another form of the same word. Bray in
Wicklow is called *Bree* in old church records and
other documents; and it evidently received its name
from Bray head, which rises abruptly 793 feet over
the sea. In the Dinnsenchus there is a legendary
account of the origin of the name of this place, viz.,
that it was so called from Brea, son of Seanboth, one
of Parthalon's followers, who first introduced single
combat into Ireland (see p. 160). The steep promontory on the south-western extremity of Valentia
island, is also called Bray head. At the head of
Glencree in Wicklow, is a small mountain lake, well
known to Dublin excursionists, called Lough Bray,

whose name was, no doubt, derived from the rocky
point—a spur of Kippure mountain—which rises
perpendicularly over its gloomy waters.

Lagh [law] a hill, cognate with Ang.-Sax. *law*,
same meaning. It is not given in the dictionaries,
but it undoubtedly exists in the Irish language, and
has given names to a considerable number of places
through the country, of which the following may be
taken as examples :—

Portlaw on the Suir in Waterford took its name
from the steep hill at the head of the village—*Port-
lagha*, the bank or landing place of the hill ; there are
some townlands in Kilkenny and the Munster counties called Ballinla and Ballinlaw, the town of the
hill ; Luggelaw in Wicklow, the *lug* or hollow of the
hill, the name of the valley in which is situated the
beautiful Lough Tay ; Clonderalaw in Cork and
Clare, the meadow between the two hills.

O'Brien explains *ceide* [keady] " a hillock, a com-
pact kind of hill, smooth and plain at the top;" and
this is the sense in which it is understood at the
present day, wherever it is understood at all. The
Four Masters write it *crideach*, when mentioning
Keadydrinagh in Sligo, which they call *Ceideach-
droighneach*, the flat-topped hill of the black-thorns.
The word is not in very general use, and is almost
confined to the northern and north-western counties ; but in these it gives name to a considerable
number of places now called Keadew and Keady.
It takes the forms of Keadagh, Cady, and Caddagh,
in several counties ; the diminutive Keadeen is the
name of a high hill east of Baltinglass in Wicklow, and another modification, Cadian, occurs in
Tyrone.

Mullach, in its primary meaning, signifies the top

or summit of anything—such as the top of a house.
Topographically it is generally used to denote smaller
eminences, though we find it occasionally applied to
hills of considerable elevation ; and as a root word, it
enters very extensively into the formation of names,
generally in the forms Mulla, Mullagh, Mully, and
Mul, which constitute of themselves, or form the beginning of, upwards of 400 names.

Mulla is well known as the name given by the
poet Spenser to the little river Awbeg, which flows
by Kilcolman castle, where he resided, near Buttevant
in Cork:—

> "Strong Allo tombling from Slewlogher steep,
> And Mulla mine whose waves I whilom taught to weep."
>   "Faerie Queene," Book IV., Canto xi.

In another place he says that Kilnamulla (now
Buttevant), took its name from the Mulla:—

> "It giveth name unto that ancient cittie,
> Which Kilnemulla clepped is of old."

But this is all the creation of the poet's fertile
imagination ; for the Awbeg was never called Mulla
except by Spenser himself, and Kilnamullagh, the
native name of Buttevant, has a very different
origin (see Bregogo in 2nd Series).

The peasantry of the locality understand Kilnamullagh to mean the church of the curse (*mallacht*),
in connection with which they relate a strange legend;
but the explanation is erroneous, and the legend an
invention of later times. At the year 1251, the
Four Masters, in recording the foundation of the
monastery, call it *Cill-na-mullach*, which O'Sullivan,
in his History of the Irish Catholics, translates *ecclesia
tumulorum*, the church of the hillocks or summits,

and the name admits of no other interpretation. The present name Bultevant is said to have been derived from *Boutez-en-avant*, a French phrase meaning "Push forward!" the motto of the Barrymore family.

The village of Mullagh in Cavan got its name from the hill near it, which the Four Masters call *Mullach-Laeighill*, the hill of *Laeighell* or Lyle, a man's name formerly common in Ireland.   The Hill of Lloyd near Kells, is called in the Annals *Mullach-Aidi*, Aidē's hill; and it still retains this same name with those who speak Irish; Mullaghattin near Carlingford, the hill of the furze; Mullaghsillogagh near Enniskillen, the hill of the sallows; Mullaghmeen, smooth summit.   Mul, the shortened form, appears in Mulboy in Tyrone, yellow summit; and in Mulkeeragh in Derry, the summit of the sheep.

Mullan, little summit, is a diminutive of *mullach*, and it is generally applied to the top of a low, gently sloping hill.   In the forms Mullan, Mullaun, and in the plural Mullans and Mullauns, it is the name of nearly forty townlands, and of course helps to form many others.   Glassavullaun near Tallaght in Dublin, represents *Glaise-a'-mhullain*, the streamlet of the little summit; and Mullanagore in Monaghan, and Mullanagower in Wexford, signify the little eminence of the goats.   In Carlow, Wicklow, and Wexford, this word is understood to mean simply a green field; but it has evidently undergone a change of meaning, the transition being sufficiently easy from a gentle green hill to a green field.   Mulkaun in Leitrim, exhibits another diminutive, namely *mulcán* or *mullachán* which also appears in Meenawullaghan in the parish of Inver, Donegal, the *meen* or

mountain flat of the little summit; and in Meena-
mullaghan, parish of Lower Fahan, same county,
Min-na-mullachan, the mountain flat of the little
summits.

Iomaire [ummera] signifies a ridge or hill-back'; as
a local term it is found in each of the four provinces,
being, however, more common in Ulster and Connaught than in the other provinces; but in any part
of Ireland it does not enter extensively into names.
Its most common modern forms are Ummera, Um-
mery, and Umry, which form or begin the names of
more than twenty townlands.

Ummeracam in Armagh, and Umrycam in Done-
gal and Derry, are called in Irish *Iomaire-cam,* crooked
ridge; Ummeraboy in Cork, yellow ridge: Ummera-
free in Monaghan, the ridge of the heath; Kil-
lanummery, a townland giving name to a parish in
Leitrim, is called by the Four Masters, *Cill-an-iomaire,*
the church of the ridge, and the word is somewhat
altered in Clonamery in Kilkenny, the meadow of
the ridge.

The primary meaning of *meall* [mŭl] is a lump,
mass, or heap of anything; and it is applied locally
to a small round hillock. It does not occur very
often except in Munster, where it is met with pretty
extensively; its most usual anglicised form is *maul,*
which begins the names of near sixty townlands, all
in Cork and Kerry. Take for example, Maulanim-
irish and Maulashangarry, both near Dunmanway,
the first meaning the hillock of the contention (*im-
reas*), and the second, of the old garden (*sean,* old;
garrdha, a garden). Maulagh near Killarney signifies a place abounding in hillocks.

Millin [milleen] is a diminutive of this word,

usually represented in the present names by Milleen,
which forms the whole or the beginning of fifteen
townland names, all except one in Cork; Milleenna-
horna has the same meaning as Maulnahorna, the
hillock of the barley (*corna*). Near Rathcormack,
there is a place called Maulane, the only example I
find of the diminutive in *an*. In anglicised names it
is often difficult to distinguish this word from *mael*
and its modifications, as both often assume the same
form.

Mael [mwail or moyle] as an adjective signifies
bald, bare, or hornless; and it is often employed as
a noun to denote anything having these shapes or
qualities. It is, for instance, applied to a cow without horns, which in almost every part of Ireland is
called a *mael* or *maeelleen*. It is also used synonymously with *giolla*, to denote in a religious sense, a
person having the head shorn or tonsured; it was
often prefixed to the name of a saint, and the whole
compound used to denote a person devoted to such a
saint; and as a mark of reverence this kind of name
was often given to men at their baptism, which originated such surnames as Mulholland, Mulrony,
Moloney, Mulronin, Malone, &c.

It is applied to a church or building of any kind
that is either unfinished or dilapidated—most commonly the latter; thus Templemoyle, the bald or
dilapidated church, is the name of some places in
Derry, Galway, and Donegal; there are five townlands in Antrim and one in Longford called Kilmoyle
which have the same meaning; Kilmoyle near
Ballymoney is in Latin records translated *Ecclesia
calra*, which gives the exact sense. And Castlemoyle,
bald castle, occurs in Galway, Wexford, and Tipperary. The word is used to designate a moat or

mound flat on top, or dilapidated by having the materials carted away ; and hence we have such names
as Rathmoyle, Lismoyle, and Dunmoyle.

Mael is applied to hills and promontories, and in
this sense it is very often employed to form local
names. Moyle, one of its usual forms, and the plural
Moyles, gives names to several places in the middle
and northern counties ; Knockmoyle, a usual townland name, bald hill. In the south and west it often
assumes the form *mweel*, which preserves the pronunciation more nearly than *moyle :* thus Mweela-
horna near Ardmore in Waterford, the bald hill of
the barley ; and in Fermanagh also, this form is
found in Mweelbane, white hill. It sometimes takes
the form of *meel*, as in Meelshane in Cork, John's
bald hill ; Meelgarrow in Wexford, rough hill (*garbh,*
rough) ; Meeldrum near Kilbeggan in Westmeath,
bare ridge.

There are two diminutives in pretty common use,
maclán and *macilin* [mweelaun, mweeleen] ; the former is often applied to round-backed islands in the
sea, or to round bare rocks ; and we find accordingly
several little islands off the south and west coast,
called Moylaun, Moylan, and Mweelaun. The same
word is seen in Meelon near Bandon, and Milane,
near Dunmanway, both in Cork ; and in Mellon near
where the Maigue joins the Shannon in Limerick.
The second diminutive is more frequent, and it is
spelled in various ways ; it is found as Moyleen and
Mweeleen in Galway, Kerry, and Mayo ; Mweeling
near Ardmore in Waterford ; and Meeleen in the
parish of Kilquane, Cork.

Meelaghans near Geashill in King's County (little
bare hills), exhibits another diminutive, *Maclachán ;*
and we have still another in Milligan in Monaghan,

and Milligans in Fermanagh, little hills. Mealough
is the name of a townland in the parish of Drumbo,
Down, meaning either a round hill or a place abounding in hillocks.   In Scotland, the word *mael* is often
used, as, for instance, in the Mull of Galloway and
the Mull of Cantire; in both instances the word
Mull signifying a bare headland.   From the Mull of
Cantire, the sea between Ireland and Scotland was
anciently called the " Sea-stream of Moyle ;" and
Moore has adopted the last name in his charming
song, " Silent, O Moyle, be the roar of thy water."

Mael combines with the Irish preposition *for*, forming the compound *formael*, which is used to signify
a round hill; and which, in the forms Formoyle, Fer-
moyle, and Formil, constitutes the names of twenty-
nine townlands, scattered through the four provinces ;
in Meath it is made Formal, and in Galway it retains
the more Irish form, Formweel.   This name occurs
twice in the Four Masters ; first at A. D. 965, where
a battle is recorded to have been fought at *Formacil*
of Rathbeg, which O'Donovan identifies with Formil in the parish of Lower Bodoney, Tyrone ; and
secondly, at 1051, where mention is made of Slieve-
Formoyle, which was the ancient name of Slieve-
O'Flynn, west of Castlerea in Roscommon.

The word *cor*, as a topographical term, has several
meanings, the most common being a round hill; but
it is also applied to a round pit or cup-like hollow, to
a turn or bend, such as the bend of a road, &c.; and
as an adjective, it means odd, and also round.   In
consequence of this diversity, it is often difficult to
determine its exact sense ; and to add to the com-
plexity, the word *corr*, a crane, is liable to be confounded with it.

This word is used very extensively in local nomen-

clature; and in its various senses, it forms the first
syllable of more than 1000 townland names, in the
greater number of which it means a round hill. Cor-
beagh in Longford and Cavan, is in Irish, *Cor-beith-
each*, the round hill of the birch; Corkeeran in
Monaghan, of the *keerans* or rowan-trees; Cornagee
and Cornageeha, the hill of the wind; Cornaveagh,
of the ravens (*fiach*). The diminutives Corrog and
Corroge, give names to some places in Down and
Tipperary; and we find Correen in several of the
north western counties; Correenfeeradda near Knock-
ainy in Limerick, is called in Irish, *Coirin-feir-fhada*,
the round hill of the long grass.

Cruit means a hump on the back; from this it is
applied to round *humpy-looking* hills; and it is commonly represented by Crott, Crut, or Crit, which are
the names of places in Fermanagh, Longford, Mayo,
and Kilkenny. There is an island called Cruit off
the coast of Donegal, i.e. humpy-backed island; and
two townlands in King's County and Roscommon
are called by the same name. The plural Crotta, or
Crutta, humps, and the English plural Crottees, give
names to some places in Kerry, Tipperary, and Cork;
and Crottan, little hump, occurs in Fermanagh.

The word is variously combined to form other
names; such as Kilcruit in Carlow, the wood of the
hump-backed hill; Loughcrot near Dromdaleague
in Cork, the lake of the hillocks; Drumacruttan in
Monaghan, and Drumacrittin in Fermanagh, the
ridge of the little hump; Barnagrotty in King's
County, *Barr-na-gcrotta*, the hill-top of the hum-
mocks.

Cnap [knap, *c* pronounced as in *cnoc*, p. 381] is a
button, a knob, a lump of anything, a knot in timber,
&c.; and it is cognate with Ang.-Sax. *cnaep*, Ger.

knopf, Eng. *knob.* In a secondary sense it is applied
to small round hillocks, and gives names to a considerable number of places. In anglicised names it takes
various forms, such as *knap, nap,* &c.; and in the
northern counties, it becomes *crap* and *crup,* just as
knock becomes *crock* (see p. 51). The diminutives in
óg and *án* occur oftener than the original; Knoppoge,
little knob or hill, is the name of thirteen townlands
in Cork, Kerry, and Clare; and in the slightly different form Knappoge, it occurs twice in Longford,
and once in Clare.

There are many places in the northern and north
western counties, called Knappagh, which represents
the Irish *cnapach,* hilly land—a place full of knobs or
hillocks; Nappagh near Ardagh in Longford, is the
same name, but it has lost the *k;* and the same thing
has happened in Nappan in Antrim, which is the
diminutive *Cnapan,* a little hillock; in this last place
is an old burial ground called Killycrappin (*cill-a'-
cnapain:* see Reeves, Eccl. Ant., p. 87), which preserves the name in another form. In the following
names, the *n* is changed to *r:*—Crappagh in Monaghan
and Galway, which is the same name as Knappagh;
Crippaun in Kildare, the same as Nappan in Antrim;
Carrickcroppan in Armagh, *Carraig-cnapain,* the rock
of the little hillock; and Lisnacroppan in Down, the
fort of the hillock.

Tor signifies a tower, and corresponds to Latin
turris. Although the word properly means an artificial tower, yet in many parts of Ireland, as for
instance in Donegal, it is applied to a tall rock resembling a tower, without any reference to an artificial structure. It is pretty common as forming part
of names, and its derivatives occur oftener than the
original. Toralt in Fermanagh, signifies the tower

of the *alt* or cliff; Tormore, great tower, is the name
of several islands, of one for instance off the coast of
Donegal; Tornaroy in Antrim is the kings' tower;
and in the parish of Culfeightrin, same county, there
are five townlands whose names begin with *Tor.* In
some few cases, especially in the central counties,
the syllable *tor* may have been corrupted from *tuar*,
a bleach green; but the physical aspect of the place
will generally determine which is the correct root.

Tory Island off the coast of Donegal, is known in
ancient writings by two distinct names, *Toirinis* and
Torach, quite different in meaning, but both derived
from *tor.* This island is mentioned in our bardic
histories as the stronghold of the Fomorian pirates
(see p. 161), and called in these documents, *Toir-inis*,
the island of the tower; and according to all our
traditional accounts, it received this name from *Tor-
Conaing* or Conang's tower, a fortress famous in
Irish legend, and called after Conang, a Fomorian
chief.

In many other ancient authorities, such as the Life
of St. Columbkille, "The Wars of GG.," &c., it is
called *Torach;* and the present name Tory, is derived
from an oblique case of this form (*Toraigh*, pron.
Torry: see p. 34, *supra*). The island abounds in
lofty isolated rocks which are called *tors* or towers;
and the name *Torach* means simply towery—abounding in *tors* or tower-like rocks. The intelligent
Irish-speaking natives of the Donegal coast give it
this interpretation; and no one can look at the island
from the mainland, without admitting that the name
is admirably descriptive of its appearance.

Tortán, a diminutive of *tor*, forms a part of several
modern names, and it is applied to a small knoll or
tummock, or a high turf bank. It gives name to

Turtane in Carlow, to Toortane in Queen's County, Waterford, and Kilkenny, and to Tartan in Roscommon.

Fornocht is a bare, naked, or exposed hill. It gives name to a parish in Kildare, now called Forenaghts, in which the plural form has prevailed, very probably in consequence of the subdivision of the original townland into two parts. There are also several townlands called Fornaght in Cork and Waterford; and Farnaght, another modern form, is the name of some places in Fermanagh and the Connaught counties.

Cabhán [cavan] means a hollow or cavity, a hollow place, a hollow field; and this is undoubtedly its primary meaning, for it is evidently cognate with Lat. *carea*, Fr. *caban*, Welsh *cabane*, and Eng. *cabin*. Yet in some parts of Ulster it is understood to mean the very reverse, viz., a round dry hill; and this is the meaning given to it by O'Donnell in his Life of St. Columba, who translates it *collis* (Reeves, Colt. Vis. 133). This curious discrepancy is probably owing to a gradual change of meaning, similar to the change in the words *lug, mullan,* &c. Which of the two meanings it bears in each particular case, depends of course on the physical confirmation of the place. In its topographical application this word is confined to the northern half of Ireland, and is more frequent in the Ulster counties than elsewhere; its universal anglicised form is *cavan.*

The town of Cavan is well described by its name, for it stands in a remarkable hollow; Racavan, the name of a parish in Antrim, is *Rath-cabhain*, the fort of the hollow. There are more than twenty townlands called Cavan, and the word begins the name of about seventy others. In the counties of

Tyrone, Donegal, and Armagh, there are several places called Cavanacaw, which represents the Irish *Cabhan-a'-chátha*, the round hill of the chaff, from the custom of winnowing corn on the top; Cavanaleck near Enniskillen, the hill of the flagstone or stony surface. The word *cabhanach* is an adjective formation from *cabhan*, and means a place abounding in round hills; in the modern form Cavanagh it is found in Cavan and Fermanagh; and in Monaghan, the same word occurs under the form Cavany.

Eiscir [esker] means a ridge of high land, but it is generally applied to a sandy ridge, or a line of low sand hills. It enters pretty extensively into local names, but it is more frequently met with across the middle of Ireland than in either the north or south. It usually takes the form of Esker, which by itself is the name of more than thirty townlands, and combines to form the names of many others; the word is somewhat altered in Garrisker, the name of a place in Kildare, signifying short sand ridge.

The most celebrated *esker* in Ireland is *Esker-Riada*, a line of gravel hills extending with little interruption across Ireland, from Dublin to Clarin-Bridge in Galway, which was fixed upon as the boundary between the north and south halves of Ireland, when the country was divided, in the second century, between Owen More and Conn of the Hundred Battles (see p. 133).

As a termination, this word assumes other forms, all derived from the genitive *eiscreach* [eskera]. Clashaniskera in Tipperary is called in Irish *Clais-an-eiscreach*, the trench or pit of the sand hill. Ahas-cragh in Galway signifies the ford of the *esker*; but its full name as given by the Four Masters is *Ath-eascrach Cuain* [Ahascra Cuan], the ford of St. Cuan's

sand-hill; and they still retain the memory of St.
Cuan, the patron, who is commemorated in O'Clery's
Calendar at the 15th of October; Tiranascragh, the
name of a townland and parish in Galway, the land
of the esker. Eskeragh and Eskragh are the names
of several townlands in the Ulster and Connaught
counties, the Irish *Eiscreach* signifying a place full
of eskers or sand hills.

Tiompan is generally understood, when used topographically, to mean a small abrupt hill, and sometimes a standing stone; it occurs as a portion of a
few townland names, and it does not appear to be
confined to any particular part of the country. It
is pronounced Timpan in the north, and Timpaun
in the south and west, and modernised accordingly;
the former being the name of a place in the parish of
Layd, Antrim, and the latter of another in Roscommon. In the townland of Reanadimpaun, parish
of Seskinan, Waterford, there is an ancient monument consisting of a number of pillar stones, which
has given name to the townland—*Reidh-na-dtiompan*,
the *rea* or mountain-flat of the standing stones. The
word is slightly varied in Tempannroe (*roe*, red) in
Tyrone; and Timpany in the same county is from
Tiompannach, a place full of *timpans* or hillocks. Craig-
atempin near Ballymoney, Antrim, is the rock of the
hillock; and Curraghnadimpaun in Kilkenny, the
curragh or marsh of the little hills.

The word *learg* [larg] signifies the side or slope of
a hill; it is used in local names, but not so often as
leargaidh [largy], a derivative from it, with the same
meaning. Largy, the most usual modernised form,
is found only in the northern half of Ireland, and is
almost confined to Ulster; it gives names to many
townlands, both by itself and in combination. Lar-

gysillagh and Largynagreana are the names of two places near Killybegs in Donegal, the former signifying the hill-side of the sallows, and the latter, sunny hill-slope, from its southern aspect. The diminutive Largan, meaning still the same thing. is also of very common occurrence as a townland name, both singly and compounded with other words; Larganreagh in Donegal, grey hill-side,

Leitir [letter]. According to Peter O'Connell, this word means the side of a hill, a steep ascent or descent, a cliff; and O'Donovan translates it " hillside," " wet or spewy hill-side," "hill side with the tricklings of water," &c. It is still understood in this sense in the west of Connaught; and that this is its real meaning is further shown by the Welsh *llethr*, which signifies a slope. In Cormac's Glossary it is thus explained:—" *Leitir,* i. e. *leth tirim agus leth fliuch ;*" " *leitir,* i. e. half dry and half wet ;" from which it appears that Cormac considered it derived from *leth-tirim, half-dry.* This corresponds so far as it goes, with present use.

This word is often found in ancient authorities, as forming the names of places. At 1584, the Four Masters mention an island called *Leitir-Mcallain,* Meallan's *letter* or hill side, which lies off the Connemara coast, and is still called Lettermullen. Latteragh in Tipperary is very often mentioned in the annals and Calendars, and always called *Letrecha-Odhrain* (Latraha-Oran : O'Cler. Cal.), Odhran's wet hill-slopes. St. Odhran [Oran], the patron, who is commemorated in the Calendar at the 26th of November, died, according to the Four Masters, in the year 548. Other modifications of the plural (*leatracha,* pron. *latraha*) are seen in Lettera and Letteragh, the names of places in various counties ; Lattery in Armagh; and Lettery in Galway and Tyrone; all meaning "wet hill-slopes." Lettreen, little *letter*, occurs in Roscommon; and another diminutive Letteran, in Londonderry.

A considerable number of places derive their names from this word, especially in the western half of Ireland, where it prevails much more than elsewhere; I have not found it at all towards the eastern coast. Its most usual form is Letter, which is by itself the name of about twenty-six townlands, and forms the beginning of about 120 others. Letterbrick in Donegal and Mayo, is *Leitir-bruic*, the hill-side of the badger; Letterbrock, of the badgers; Lettersheudony in Derry, the old man's hill-side; Letterkeen in Fermanagh and Mayo, beautiful *letter;* Letterlicky in Cork, the hill side of the flag-stone or flag-surfaced land; Lettergeeragh in Longford, of the sheep; and Lettermacaward in Donegal, the hill-slope of Mac Ward or the son of the bard.

Rinn means the point of anything, such as the point of a spear, &c.; in its local application, it denotes a point of land, a promontory, or small peninsula. O'Brien says in his dictionary:—" It would take up more than a whole sheet to mention all the necklands of Ireland, whose names begin with this word *Rinn.*" It is found pretty extensively in names in the forms Rin, Rinn, Reen, Rine, and Ring; and these constitute or begin about 170 townland names.

Names containing this word are often found in Irish authorities. In the county Roscommon, on the western shore of Lough Ree, is a small peninsula about a mile in length, now called St. John's or Randown, containing the ruins of a celebrated castle;

there must have been originally a *dun* on the point,
for the ancient name as given in the annals is *Rinn-
duin*, the peninsula of the *dun* or fortress.   The ancient name of Island Magee, a peninsula near Larne,
was *Rinn-Scimhne* [Rin-Sevnĕ], from the territory in
which it was situated, which was called *Seimhne;* in
the Taxation of 1306 it is called by its old name, in
the anglicised form *Ransvryn*. It received its present name from its ancient proprietors, the Mac
Aedhas or Magees, not one of whose descendants is
now living there. (See Reeves, Eccl. Ant., pp. 58,
270).

In the parish of Kilconry, Clare, is a point of land
jutting into the Shannon, called Rineanna, which
the Four Masters call *Rinn-eanaigh*, the point of the
marsh; there is an island in Lough Ree called
Rinanny, and a townland in Mayo, called Rinanagh,
both of which are different forms of the same name.
Ringcurran is a peninsula forming a modern parish
near Kinsale; it is a place very often mentioned in
the annals, and its Irish name is *Rinn-chorrain*,
which Philip O'Sullivan Beare correctly translates,
cuspis falcis, the point of the reaping-hook, so called
from its shape. It is curious that the same sickle
shape has given the name of Curran to a little peninsula near Larne. On a point of land near Kinsale,
are the ruins of Ringrone castle, the old seat of the
De Courcys; the name, which properly belongs to
the little peninsula on which the castle stands, is
written in the Annals of Innisfallen, *Rinn-roin*, the
point of the seal. The little promontory between
the mouths of the rivers Ouvane and Coomhola near
Bantry, is called Reenadisert, the point of the wilderness or hermitage, a name which is now applied

to a ruined castle, a stronghold of the O'Sullivans.
The next peninsula, lying a mile southward, is called
Reenydonagan, O'Donogan's point.

Ring stands alone as the name of many places in
different counties, in all cases meaning a point of
land; Ringaskiddy near Spike Island in Cork, is
Skiddy's point. I think it very probable that the
point of land between the mouth of the river Dodder
and the sea, gave name to Ringsend near Dublin,
the second syllable being English :—Ringsend, i. e.
the end of the *Rinn* or point. There is a parish
forming a peninsula near Dungarvan in Waterford,
called Ringagonagh in Irish, *Rinn-O-gCuana*, the
point of the O'Cooneys.

Ringville in Waterford, though it looks English,
is an Irish name, *Rinn-bhile*, the point of the *bile* or
ancient tree ; this is also the name of two townlands
in Cork and Kilkenny; and Ringvilla in Fermanagh,
is still the same. There is a little peninsula in Galway, opposite Inishbofin island, called Rinville, and
another of the same name, with a village on it, projecting into Galway bay, east of Galway; both are
written in our authorities, *Rinn-Mhil*, the point of
Mil; and according to Mac Firbis, they were so
called from Mil, an old Firbolg chief. " Ringhaddy
is a part of Killinchy parish in Down, lying in
Strangford Lough. It was originally an island; but
having been from time immemorial united to the
mainland by a causeway, it presents on the map the
appearance of an elongated neck of land, running
northwards into the Lough. Hence, probably, the
name *Rinn-fhada*, the long point." (Reeves, Eccl.
Ant. p. 9). In the same county there is a townland
called Ringfad, which is another modification of the
same name.

Reen is another form of this word, which is confined to Cork, Kerry, and Limerick, but in these
counties it occurs very often, especially on the coasts.
Rinn and Rin are more common in the western and
north-western counties than elsewhere; as in Rin-
rainy island near Dunglow in Donegal, the point of
the ferns. In Clare the word is pronounced Rine,
and anglicised accordingly; Rinecaha in the parish of
Kilkeedy, signifies the point of the chaff or winnowing. The diminutive Rinneen, little point, is the name
of several townlands in Galway, Clare, and Kerry.

Stuaic [stook] is applied to a pointed pinnacle, or
a projecting point of rock. Although the word is
often used to designate projecting rocky points, especially on parts of the coast of Donegal, it has not
given names to many townlands. Its usual English
form is *stook*, which, in Ireland at least, has taken
its place as an English word, for the expression, " a
stook of corn " is used all over the country, meaning
the same as the English word *shock*. Stook is the
name of a place in Tipperary; but the two diminutives, Stookan and Stookeen, occur more frequently
than the original.

Visitors to the Giant's Causeway will remember
the two remarkable lofty rocks called the Stookans—
little stooks or rock pinnacles—standing in the path
leading to the causeway, which afford a very characteristic example of the application of this term. We
find Stookeens, the same word, in Limerick, and the
singular, Stookeen, occurs in Cork. Near Loughrea
in Galway, is a townland called Cloghastookeen, the
stone fortress of the little pinnacle, which received its
name from a castle of the Burkes, the ruins of which
still remain; Baurstookeen in Tipperary, the summit
of the pinnacle.

The words *aill* and *faill* [oil, foil], mean a rock, a cliff, or a precipice; both words are radically the same, the latter being derived from the former by prefixing *f* (see p. 27). I have already observed that this practice of prefixing *f* is chiefly found in the south, and accordingly it is only in this part of Ireland that names occur derived from *faill*.

Faill is generally made *foil* and *foyle* in the present names, and there are great numbers of cliffs round the Munster coasts, especially on those of Cork and Kerry, whose names begin with these syllables; they also begin the names of about twenty-five townlands, inland as well as on the coast. Foilyoleara in Limerick and Tipperary, signifies O'Clery's cliff; Foilnaman in the latter county *Faill-na-mban*, the cliff of the women. The diminutive is seen in Falleenadatha in the parish of Doon, Limerick, *Faillín-a'-deata*, the little cliff of the smoke. When *foyle* comes in as a termination, it is commonly derived, however, not from *faill*, but from *poll*, a hole; for instance, Ballyfoyle and Ballyfoile, the names of several townlands, represent the Irish *Baile-phoill*, the town of the hole.

While *faill* is confined to the south, the other form *aill*, is found all over Ireland, under a variety of modern forms. Ayle and Aille are the names of a number of places in Munster and Connaught; Allagower near Tallaght, Dublin, is the cliff of the goat. Lisnahall in Tyrone, signifies the fort of the cliff; and Aghnahily in Queen's County, the field of the cliff. The diminutive Alleen is found in Tipperary and Galway; in the former county there are four townlands, two of them called Alleen Hogan, and two, Alleen Ryan, Hogan's and Ryan's little cliff.

Carraig or *carraic* [carrig, carrick], signifies a rock; it is usually applied to a large natural rock, not lying flat on the surface of the ground like *leac*, but more or less elevated. There are two other forms of this word, *craig* and *creag*, which, though not so common as *carraig*, are yet found in considerable numbers of names, and are used in Irish documents of authority. *Carraig* corresponds with Sansc. *karkara*, a stone; Armoric, *karrek*, and Welsh, *careg* or *craig*, a rock.

Carrick and Carrig are the names of nearly seventy townlands, villages, and towns, and form the beginning of about 550 others; *craig* and *creag* are represented by the various forms, Crag, Craig, Creg, &c., and these constitute or begin about 250 names; they mean primarily a rock, but they are sometimes applied to rocky land.

Carrigafoyle, an island in the Shannon, near Ballylongford, Kerry, with the remains of Carrigafoyle castle near the shore, the chief seat of the O'Conors Kerry, is called in the annals, *Carraig-an-phoill*, the rock of the hole; and it took its name from a deep hole in the river immediately under the castle. Ballynagarrick in Down, represents the Irish *Baile-na-gcarraig*, the town of the rocks; Carrigallen in Leitrim was so called from the rock on which the original church was built, the Irish name of which was *Carraig-álainn*, beautiful rock. In Inishargy in Down, the initial *c* has dropped out by aspiration; in the Taxation of 1306 it is called *Inyscargi*, which well represents *Inis-carraige*, the island of the rock; and the rising ground on which the old church stands was formerly, as the name indicates, an island surrounded by marshes, which have been converted into cultivated fields (see Reeves, Eccl. Ant., p. 19).

The form *craig* occurs more than once in the Four
Masters; for instance, they mention a place called
Craig-Corcrain, Corcran's rock; and this name in the
corrupted form of Cahercorcaun, is still applied to a
townland in the parish of Rath, Clare; they also
mention *Craig-ui-Chiardubhain,* O'Kirwan's rock, now
Craggykerrivan in the parish of Clondagad, same
county. Craigavad on Belfast Lough was so called,
probably from a rock on the shore, to which a boat
used to be moored; for its Irish name is *Craig-a'-
bhaid,* the rock of the boat.

The form Carrick is pretty equally distributed over
Ireland; Carrig is much more common in the south
than elsewhere; Cregg and Creg are found oftener in
the north and west than in the south and east; and
with three or four exceptions, Craig is confined to
Ulster. The diminutives Carrigeen, Carrigane, and
Carrigaun, prevail in the southern half of Ireland;
and in the northern, Carrigan, Cargan, and Cargin,
all signifying little rock, or land with a rocky surface;
and with their plurals, they give names to numerous
townlands and villages. There are also a great many
places in the north and north west, called Creggan,
and in the south and west, Creggane and Creggaun,
which are diminutives of *creag,* and are generally
applied to rocky land; Cargagh and Carrigagh,
meaning a place full of rocks, are the names of
several townlands.

Cloch signifies a stone—any stone either large or
small, as, for instance, *cloch-shneachta,* a hail-stone,
literally snow-stone; *cloch-teine,* fire-stone, i.e. a flint.
So far as it is perpetuated in local names, it was
applied in each particular case to a stone sufficiently
large and conspicuously placed to attract general
notice, or rendered remarkable by some custom or

historical occurrence. This word is also, in an extended sense, often applied to a stone building, such
as a castle; for example, the castle of Glin on the
Shannon in Limerick, the seat of the Knight of Glin,
is called in Irish documents, *Cloch-gleanna*, the stone
castle of the glen or valley. It is often difficult to
determine with certainty which of these two meanings it bears in local names.

Cloch is one of our commonest topographical roots;
in the English forms Clogh and Clough, it constitutes
or begins more than 400 townland names; and it helps
to form innumerable others in various combinations.
Cloghbally and Cloghvally, which are common townland names, represent the Irish *Cloch-bhaile*, stony-
town; scattered over Munster, Connaught, and Ulster,
are many places called Cloghboley and Cloghboola,
stony *booley* or dairy place; and Cloghvoley, Clogh-
voola, and Cloghvoula, are varied forms of the same
name; Shannaclogh and Shanclogh in Munster and
Connaught, old stone or stone castle.

Sometimes the final guttural drops out and the
word is reduced to *clo;* as in Clomantagh in Kilkenny,
in which no guttural appears, though there is one in
the original *Cloch-Mantaigh*, the stone or stone-castle
of Mantach, a man's name signifying toothless (see
p. 108), said to have taken its name from a stone
circle on the hill; Clonmoney and Clorusk in Carlow, the former signifying the stone of the shrubbery,
and the latter, of the *rusk* or marsh. And very often
the first *c* becomes *g* by eclipse (see p. 22), as in
Carrownaglogh, which conveys the sound of *Ceath-
ramhadh-na-gclogh* (Book of Lecan), the quarter-land
of the stones.

Names formed from this word, variously combined,
are found in every part of Ireland: when it comes in

as a termination, it is usually in the genitive (*cloiche,*
pron. *clohy*), and in this case it takes several modern
forms, which will be illustrated in the following
names : — Ballyclogh, Ballyclohy, Ballinaclogh,
Ballynaclogh, and Ballynacloghy, all names of frequent occurrence, mean stone town, or the town of
the stones. Kilnacloghy, in the parish of Cloontuskert, in Roscommon, is called *Coill-na-cloiche* in the
Four Masters, the wood of the stone. Aughnacloy is
a little town in Tyrone ; and there are several townlands in other counties of the same name, all called
in Irish *Achadh-na-cloiche* [Ahanaclohy], the field of
the stone.

There are three diminutives of this word in common use—*cloichin, clochóg,* and *cloghán*—of which the
third has been already dealt with (p. 363). The first
is generally anglicised Cloheen or Clogheen, which is
the name of a town in Tipperary, and of several
townlands in Cork, Waterford, and Kildare. Clogh-
oge or Clohoge, though literally meaning a small
stone like Clogheen, is generally applied to stony
land, or to a place full of round stones ; it is the
name of about twenty townlands, chiefly in Ulster—
a few, however, being found in Sligo and in the
Leinster counties.

There are several derivative forms from this word
cloch. The most common is *clochar,* which is generally applied to stony land—a place abounding in
stones, or having a stony surface ; but it occasionally
means a rock. Its most usual anglicised form is
Clogher, which is the name of a well-known town in
Tyrone, of a village, and a remarkable headland in
Louth, and of nearly sixty townlands scattered over
Ireland ; and, compounded with various words, it
helps to form the names of numerous other places.

For Clogher in Tyrone, however, a different origin
has been assigned.   It is stated that there existed
anciently at this place a stone covered with gold,
which was worshipped as Kermann Kelstach, the
principal idol of the northern Irish; and this stone, it
is said, was preserved in the church of Clogher down
to a late period : hence the place was called *Cloch-oir*,
golden stone.   O'Flaherty makes this statement in
his Ogygia, on the authority of Cathal Maguire, arch-
deacon of Clogher, the compiler of the Annals of
Ulster, who died in 1495 ; and Harris, in his edition
of Ware's Bishops, notices the idol in the following
words :—" Clogher, situated on the river Lanny,
takes its name from a Golden Stone, from which, in
the Times of Paganism, the Devil used to pronounce
juggling answers, like the Oracles of *Apollo Pythius*,
as is said in the Register of Clogher."

With this story of the idol I have nothing to do;
only I shall observe that it ought to be received with
caution, as it is not found in any ancient authority ;
it is likely that Maguire's statement is a mere record
of the oral tradition, preserved in his time.   But that
the name of Clogher is derived from it—i. e. from
Cloch-oir—I do not believe, and for these reasons.
The prevalence of the name Clogher in different parts
of Ireland, with the same general meaning, "is rather
damaging to such an etymon," as Dr. Reeves remarks, and affords strong presumption that this
Clogher is the same as all the rest.   The most ancient
form of the name, as found in Adamnan, is *Clochur
Filiorum Daimeni* (this being Adamnan's translation of the proper Irish name, *Clochur-mac-Daimhin,
Clochur* of the sons of Daimhin); in which the final
syllable *ur* shows no trace of the genitive of *ór*, gold
(*ór*, gen. *óir*); and, besides, the manner in which

Clochur is connected with *mac-Daimhin* goes far to
show that it is a generic term, the construction being
exactly analogous to *Inis-mac-Nessan* (p. 108).

But farther, there is a direct statement of the
origin of the name in a passage of the Tain-bo-
Chuailnge in Leabhar na Uidhre, quoted by Mr. J.
O'Beirne Crowe in an article in the Kilkenny Archæo-
ological Journal (April, 1869, p. 311). In this passage we are told that a certain place on which was
a great quantity of stones, was called for that reason
Mag Clochair, the plain of the stones; and Mr. Crowe
remarks:—" Clochar, as any Irish scholar might
know, does not mean a *stone of gold;* the form *clochar*
from *cloch*, a stone, is like that of *sruthar* from *sruth*,
a stream, and other nouns of this class with a cumu-
lative signification."

This place retains its ancient name in the latest
Irish authorities. Daimhin, whose sons are commemorated in the name, was eighth in descent from
Colla-da-Chrich (p. 136), and lived in the sixth
century. His descendants were in latter times called
Clann-Daimhin [Clan Davin]; and they were represented so late as the fourteenth century, by the family
of Dwyer.

Cloghereen, little stony place, a diminutive of
clogher, is well known to tourists as the name of
a village near Killarney. *Cloichrcán*, or *cloithrcán*
[cloherawn], another diminutive, signifies also a
stony place, and is found in every part of Ireland in
different modern forms. It is Cloghrane in Kerry
and Waterford; and in the county of Dublin it gives
name to two parishes called Cloghran. In many
cases the guttural has dropped out, reducing it to
Cloran in Westmeath, Tipperary and Galway; Clo-
rane and Clorhane in Limerick, King's and Queen's

County. It undergoes various other alterations—
as for instance, Clerran in Monaghan : Cleighran in
Leitrim ; Cleraun in Longford ; and Clerhaun in
Mayo and Galway.

Clochar has other developments, one of which,
clocharach or *cloithreach*, meaning much the same as
clochar itself—a stony place—is found pretty widely
spread in various modern forms ; such as Cloghera
in Clare and Kerry ; and Clerragh in Roscommon.
Another offshoot is *cloichearnach*, with still the same
meaning ; this is anglicised Cloghernagh in Donegal
and Monaghan ; Clahernagh in Fermanagh ; Cloher-
nagh in Wicklow and Tipperary ; while in Tyrone
it gives the name of Clogherny to a parish and four
townlands.   .

The word *leac, lic,* or *liag* [lack, lick, leeg]—for it is
written all three ways—means primarily a great stone,
but it is commonly applied to a flag or large flat
stone ; thus the Irish for ice is *leac-oidhre* [lack-ira],
literally snow-flag. The most ancient form is *liac* or
liacc, which is used to translate *lapis* in the Wb. and
Sg. MSS of Zeuss ; and it is cognate with the Welsh
llech ; Lat. *lapis ;* and Greek *lithos.*

This word occurs very often in Irish names, and
in its local application it is very generally used to
denote a flat-surfaced rock, or a place having a level
rocky surface. Its most common forms are Lack,
Leck, and Lick, which are the names of many townlands and villages through Ireland as well as the diminutives Lackeen and Lickeen, little rock. The form
liag is represented by Leeg and Leek in Monaghan,
and by Leeke in Antrim and Londonderry.

Lickmolassy, a parish in Galway—St. Molaise's
flag-stone—was so called, because the hill on which
the church was built that gave name to the parish,

is covered on the surface with level flag-like rocks.
Legvoy, a place in Roscommon, west of Carrick-on-
Shannon, is called by the Four Masters *Leagmhagh*
[Legvah], the flag-surfaced plain. The celebrated
mountain Slieve League in Donegal, is correctly
described by its name :—"A quarry lately opened
here, shows this part of the mountain to be formed
of piles of thin small flags of a beautiful white
colour. . . . . And here observe how much there is
in a name; for Slieve League means the mountain of
flags." *

I have already observed (p. 355) that stony fords
are very often designated by names indicating their
character; and I will give a few additional illustrations here. Belleek in Fermanagh, on the Erne, east of
Ballyshannon, is called in Irish authorities, *Bél-leice*
[Bellecka] "translated *os rupis* by Philip O'Sullivan
Beare in his history of the Irish Catholics. The name
signifies ford-mouth of the flag-stone, and the place
was so called from the flat-surfaced rock in the ford,
which, when the water decreases in summer, appears
as level as a marble floor" (O'Donovan, Four Mast. V.,
p. 134). Belleek is also the name of a place near Ballina in Mayo, which was so called from a rocky ford
on the Moy; there is a village of the same name near
Newtown Hamilton, Armagh, and also two townlands in Galway and Meath. Ballinalack is the name
of a village in Westmeath, a name originally applied
to a ford on the river Inny, over which there is now a
bridge; the correct name is *Bel-atha-na-leac* [Bella-
nalack], the mouth of the ford of the flag-stones, a
name that most truly describes the place, which is
covered with limestone flags. In some other cases,

* From " The Donegal Highlands," Murray and Co., Dublin.

however, Ballinalack is derived from *Baile-na-leac*
the town of the flag-stones.

Several derivative forms from *leac* are perpetuated
in local names; one of these, *leacach*, signifying stony,
is applied topographically to a place full of stones or
flags, and has given the name of Lackagh to many
townlands in different parts of Ireland. Several places
of this name are mentioned in the annals; for instance, Lackagh in the parish of Innishkeel, Donegal,
and the river Lackagh, falling into Sheephaven, same
county, both of which are noticed in the Four
Masters.

Leacan is one of the most widely extended of all
derivatives from *leac*, and in every part of the country
it is applied to a hill-side. In the modern forms
of Lackan, Lacken, Lackaun, Leckan, Leckaun, and
Lickane, it gives name to more than forty townlands,
and its compounds are still more numerous. Lackan-
darra, Lackandarragh, and Lackendarragh, all signify the hill-side of the oak; Ballynalackan and
Ballynalacken, the town of the hill-side. Lackan in
the parish of Kilglass in Sligo was formerly the
residence of the Mac Firbises, where their castle, now
called Castle Forbes (i. e. Firbis), still remains; and
here they compiled many Irish works, among others,
the well-known Book of Lecan. The form Lacka is
also very common in local names, with the same
meaning as *leacán*, viz., the side of a hill; Lackabane
and Lackabaun, white hill-side.

The two words, *leaca* and *leacán*, also signify the
cheek; it may be that this is the sense in which they
are applied to a hill-side, and that in this application
no reference to *leac*, a stone was intended.

" *Boireann* (burren), a large rock; a stony, rocky

district. It is the name of several rocky districts in
the north and south of Ireland" (O'Donovan, App. to
O'Reilly's Dict. *in voce*). In a passage from an ancient
MS. quoted by O'Donovan, it is fancifully derived
from *borr*, great, and *onn*, a stone.

A considerable number of local names are derived
from this word ; one of the best known is Burren in
Clare, an ancient territory, very often mentioned in
the annals, which is as remarkable for its stony
character as it is celebrated for its oyster bank.
Burren is the name of eleven townlands, some of
which are found in each of the provinces ; there is a
river joining the Barrow at the town of Carlow,
called Burren, i. e. rocky river ; and in Dublin, the
word appears in the name of the Burren rocks near
the western shore of Lambay island.

There are many places whose names are partly
formed from this word :—Burrenrea in Cavan, and
Burrenreagh in Down, both meaning grey burren.
Cloonburren on the west bank of the Shannon, nearly
opposite Clonmacnoise, is frequently mentioned in the
annals, its Irish name being *Cluain-boireann*, rocky
meadow. Rathborney, a parish in Clare, received
its name—*Rath-Boirne*, the fort of Burren—from
the district in which it is situated. The plural, *boirne*
(bourny), is modernized into Burnew, i. e. rocky
lands in the parish of Killinkere, Cavan ; in the form
Bourney, it is the name of a parish in Tipperary ;
and near Aghada in Cork, is a place called Knock-
anemorney, in Irish *Cnocan-na-mboirne*, the little hill
of the rocks.

The word *carr*, though not found in the dictionaries, is understood in several parts of Ireland to
mean a rock, and sometimes rocky land. It is pro-

28*

bable that *curraig*, a rock, *carn*, a monumental heap
of stones, and *cairthe*, a pillar-stone, are all etymologically connected with this word.

Carr is the name of three townlands in Down,
Fermanagh, and Tyrone ; and it forms part of several
names ; such as Carcullion in the parish of Clonduff,
Down, the rock or rocky land of the holly ; Gortahar
in Antrim, *Gort-a'-chairr*, the field of the rock.   In
the parish of Clonallan, Down, is a place called
Carrogs, little rocks.   There is another diminutive
common in the west of Ireland, namely, *cairthin*,
which is anglicised as it is pronounced, Carheen ; it
generally means rocky land, but in some places it is
understood to mean a *cahereen*, that is, a little *caher*
or stone fort, and occasionally a little *cairthe*, or
pillar-stone (see pp. 283, 342); the English plural
Carheens, and the Irish Carheeny, both meaning
little rocks or little stone forts, are the names of
several places in Galway, Mayo, and Limerick.

The third diminutive, *carran*, is more generally used
than either of the two former, and it has several anglicised forms, such as Caran, Caraun, Carran, and
Carraun.   It is often difficult to fix the meaning of
these words ; they generally signify rocky land, but
they are occasionally understood to mean a reaping
hook, applied in this sense, from some peculiarity of
shape ; and Caran and Carran are sometimes varied
forms of *carn*.   Craan, Craane, and Crane, which are
the names of a number of places, are modifications
which are less doubtful in meaning; they are almost
confined to Carlow and Wexford, and are always
applied to rocky land—land showing a rocky surface.

Sceir [sker] means, according to the dictionaries, a
sharp sea rock ; *sceire* [skerry], sea rocks ; Scandina-

vian *sker*, a reef, *skere*, reefs.   It is applied to rocks
inland, however, as well as to those in the sea, as is
proved by the fact, that there are several places far
removed from the coast whose names contain the
word.   It enters pretty extensively into local nomenclature, and its most usual forms are either Soar,
Skerry, or the plural Skerries, which are the names
of several well-known places.

Sceilig [skellig], according to O'Reilly, means a
rock; the form *scillic* occurs in Cormac's Glossary in
the sense of a splinter of stone; and O'Donovan, in
the Four Masters, translates *Sceillic*, sea rock.   There
are, however, as in the case of *sceir*, some places inland whose names are derived from it.

The most remarkable places bearing the name of
Sceilig are the great and little Skelligs, two lofty
rocks off the coast of Kerry.   Great Skellig was selected, in the early ages of Christianity, as a religious
retreat, and the ruins of some of the primitive cells
and oratories remain there to this day; the place
was dedicated to the Archangel Michael, and hence
it is called in Irish authorities, *Sceilig Mhichil*, Michael's *skellig* or sea rock.   From these rocks the
Bay of Ballinskelligs, on the coast of Iveragh, took
its name.

One of the little ruined churches in Glendalough,
which is situated under the crags of Lugduff mountain, is called Templenaskellig, the church of the
rock, and this *skellig* or rock is often mentioned in
the old Lives of St. Kevin.   Bunskellig, the foot of
the rock, is a place near Eyeries on Kenmare Bay;
and in Tyrone there are two townlands called Skel-
gagh, an adjective formation from *sceilig*, signifying
rocky land.

Spcilic is used in Louth in the sense of a splintery

rock, but it is very probably a corruption of *sceilig;*
it has given name to Spellickanee in the parish of
Ballymascanlan, which is in Irish, *Speilic-an-fhiaich,*
the rock of the raven. Among the Mourne mountains it is pronounced *spellig* ; and the adjective form
speilgeach [spelligagh], is understood there to denote
a place full of pointed rocks.

Spinc [spink] is used in several parts of Ireland to
denote a point of rock, or a sharp overhanging cliff;
but it is employed more generally on the coast of
Donegal than elsewhere. It has not given names to
many places, however, even in Donegal, where it is
most used. There is a townland in King's County,
called Spink ; and near Tallaght in Dublin, rises a
small hill called Spinkan, little *spink* or pinnacle.

There are other terms for hills, such as *druim*, *eudan*,
ceann, &c., but these will be treated of in another
chapter.

CHAPTER II.

PLAINS, VALLEYS, HOLLOWS, AND CAVES.

Magh [maw or moy] is the most common Irish word
for a plain or level tract; Welsh *ma.* It is generally
translated *campus* by Latin writers, and it is rendered *planities* in the Annals of Tighernach. It is a
word of great antiquity, and in the Latinized form
magus,—which corresponds with the old Irish orthography *mag*—it is frequently used in ancient Gaulish
names of places, such as Cæsaromagus, Drusomagus,
Noviomagus, Rigomagus, &c. (Gram. Celt., p. 9). It
occurs also in the Zeuss MSS., where it is given as

the equivalent of *campus.* The word appears under various forms in anglicised names, such as *magh, moy, ma, mo,* &c.

Several of the great plains celebrated in former ages, and constantly mentioned in Irish authorities, have lost their names, though the positions of most of them are known. *Magh-breagh* [Moy-bra], the great plain extending from the Liffey northwards towards the borders of the present county of Louth, may be mentioned as an example. The word *breagh* signifies fine or beautiful, and it is still preserved both in sound and sense in the Scotch word *brave ; Magh-breagh* is accordingly translated, in the Annals of Tighernach, *Planities amœna,* the delightful plain ; and our "rude forefathers" never left us a name more truly characteristic.* In its application to the plain, however, it has been forgotten for generations, though it is still preserved in the name of Slieve Bregh, a hill between Slane and Collon, signifying the hill of *Magh-breagh.*

Many of the celebrated old plains still either partly or wholly retain their original names, and of these I

* Notwithstanding the authority of Tighernach, I fear this translation is incorrect. Any one who examines the way in which the name *Breg* (in all its inflections) is used in old Irish writings, will see at once that it is not an adjective, but a plural noun ; that it is never used in the singular ; and further, that it was the name of a people : *Brega* (the nom. plural form) being a term exactly corresponding with *Angli, Germani, Celti,* &c. According to this, *Mag-Breg,* or in later Irish, *Magh-Breagh,* signifies, not delightful plain, but the plain of the *Brega,* who were I suppose the original inhabitants. As a further confirmation of this, and as a kind of set-off against the authority of Tighernach, we find *Sliabh-Breagh* translated in the Lives of SS. Fanchea and Columbkille, *Mons-Bregarum,* the mountain of the Bregians. See J. O'Beirne Crowe's note in Kilk. Arch. Jour., 1872, p. 181.

will mention a few. Macosquin, now a parish in
Londonderry, is called in the annals, *Magh-Cosgrain*,
the plain of Cosgran, a man's name, very common
both in ancient and modern times. There is a village
called Movilla near Newtownards in Down, where a
great monastery was founded by St. Finnian in the
sixth century; its Irish name is *Magh-bile* (O'Cler.
Cal.), the plain of the ancient tree; and there is
another place with the same Irish name in the east
of Inishowen in Donegal, now called Moville, which
was also a religious establishment, though not equally
ancient or important.

Mallow in Cork is called in Irish *Magh-Ealla*,
[Moyalla: Four Mast.], the plain of the river *Ealla*
or Allow. The stream now called the Allow is a small
river flowing into the Blackwater through Kanturk,
ten or eleven miles from Mallow; but the Blackwater
itself, for at least a part of its course, was anciently
called Allow;[*] from this the district between Mallow
and Kanturk was called *Magh-Ealla*, which ultimately settled down as the name of the town of
Mallow. The river also gave name to the territory
lying on its north bank, west of Kanturk, which is
called in Irish authorities, *Duthaigh Ealla* [Doohy-
alla], i. e. the district of the Allow, now shortened to
Duhallow.

Magunihy, now a barony in Kerry, is called by
the Four Masters, in some places, *Magh-gCoincinne*,
[Magunkinny], and in others, *Magh-O-gCoinchinn*,
i. e. the plain of the O'Coincinns; from the former
of which the present name is derived. The territory,
however, belonged 250 years ago to the O'Donohoes,

* See a Paper by the author, on " Spenser's Irish Rivers,"
Proc. R. I. A., Vol. X., p. 1.

and, according to O'Heeren, at an earlier period to the O'Connells: of the family of O'Conkin, who gave name to the territory, I have found no further record.

The form Moy is the most common of any. It is itself, as well as the plural Moys (i. e. plains), the name of several places, and forms part of a large number. Moynalty in Meath represents the Irish *Magh-nealta*, the plain of the flocks; this was also the ancient name of the level country lying between Dublin and Howth (see p. 160); and the bardic Annals state that it was the only plain in Ireland not covered with wood, on the arrival of the first colonies. The district between the rivers Erne and Drowes is now always called the Moy, which partly preserves a name of great antiquity. It is the celebrated plain of *Magh-gCedne* [genně], so frequently mentioned in the accounts of the earliest colonists; and it was here the Fomorian pirates of Tory (p. 162), exacted their oppressive yearly tribute from the Nemedians.

This word assumes other forms in several counties, such as Maw, Maws, Moigh, and Muff. In accordance with the Munster custom of restoring the final *g* (p. 31), it is modified to Moig in the name of some places near Askeaton, and elsewhere in Limerick; and this form, a little shortened, appears in Mogeely, a well-known place in Cork, which the Four Masters call *Magh-Ilě*, the plain of Ilě or Eilě, a man's name. There is a parish in Cork, east of Macroom, called Cannaway, or in Irish *Ceann-a'-mhaighe* [Cannawee], the head of the plain; the same name is anglicised Cannawee in the parish of Kilmoe, near Mizen Head in the same county; while we find Kilcannavee in the parish of Mothell, Waterford, and Kilcannway near Mallow in Cork, both signifying the church at the head of the plain.

There is one diminutive, *maighin* [moyne], which
is very common, both in ancient and modern names;
it occurs in the Zeuss MSS. in the form *magen*, where it
is used in the sense of *locus;* and we find it in the Four
Masters, when they record the erection, in 1460, by
Mac William Burke, of the celebrated abbey of *Maighin* or Moyne in Mayo.   The ruins of this abbey still
remain near the river Moy, in the parish of Killala,
county Mayo.   This, as well as the village of Moyne
in Tipperary, and about a dozen places of the same
name in the three southern provinces, were all so
called from *maighin* or little plain. Maine and Mayne,
which are the names of several places from Derry to
Cork, are referable to the same root, though a few
of them may be from *meadhon* [maan], middle.

Machaire [maghera], a derivative from *magh*, and
meaning the same thing, is very extensively used
in our local nomenclature.   It generally appears
in the anglicised forms of Maghera and Maghery,
which are the names of several villages and townlands; Maghera is the more usual form, and it begins
the names of nearly 200 places, which are found in
each of the four provinces, but are more common in
Ulster than elsewhere.   The parish of Magheradrool
in Down, is called in the Reg. Prene, *Machary-edar-
gawal,* which represents the Irish, *Machaire-eadar-
ghabhal* [Maghera-addrool], the plain between the
(river) forks. (Reeves, Eccl. Ant., p. 316. See Addergoole).

Reidh [ray] signifies a plain, a level field; it is more
commonly employed in the south of Ireland than elsewhere, and it is usually applied to a mountain flat, or
a coarse, moory, level piece of land among hills.
Its most general anglicised forms are *rea, re,* and
rey.

In the parish of Ringagonagh, Waterford, there is a townland called Readoty, which is modernized from *Reidh-doighte*, burnt mountain-plain: Reanagishagh in Clare, the mountain flat of the *kishes* or wicker causeways; Remeen in Kilkenny, smooth plain; Ballynarea, near Newtown Hamilton, Armagh, the town of the mountain-flat. The plural Rehy, i. e. mountain-flats, is the name of a place in Clare. *Reidhleach* [Relagh], a derivative from *reidh*, and meaning the same thing, gives names to some places in Tyrone, Fermanagh, and Cavan, in the modernized form, Relagh.

Reidh is also used as an adjective, signifying ready or prepared; and from this, by an easy transition, it has come to signify clear, plain, or smooth; it is probable indeed that the word was primarily an adjective, and that its use as a noun to designate a plain is merely a secondary application. There is a well-known mountain over the Killeries in Connemara, called Muilrea; and this name characterizes its outline, compared with that of the surrounding hills, when seen from a moderate distance :—*Mael-reidh*, smooth flat mountain (see *Mael*, p. 395). Rehill is the name of some places in Kerry and Tipperary, which are called in Irish, *Reidh-choill*, smooth or clear wood, probably indicating that the woods to which the name was originally applied were less dense or tangled, or more easy to pass through, than others in the same neighbourhood.

Clar is literally a board, and occurs in this sense in the Zeuss MSS. in the old form *claar*, which glosses *tabula*. It is applied locally to a flat piece of land; and in this sense it gives name to a considerable number of places. Ballyclare is the name of a town in Antrim, and of half a dozen townlands in Roscommon

and the Leinster counties, signifying the town of
the plain. Ballinclare is often met with in Leinster
and Munster, and generally means the same thing;
but it may signify in some places the ford of the
plank, as it does in case of Ballinclare in the parish
of Kilmactoige in Sligo, which is written *Bel-an-
chlair* by the Four Masters (see for plank bridges,
2nd. Ser., chap. xiii.) There is a place in Galway
which was formerly called by this name, where a great
abbey was founded in the thirteenth century, and a
castle in the sixteenth, both of which are still to be
seen in ruins; the place is mentioned by the Four
Masters, who call it *Baile-an-chlair*, but it retains only
a part of this old name, being now called Clare-Gal-
way to distinguish it from other Clares.

Clare is by itself the name of many places, some of
which are found in each of the four provinces. The
county of Clare was so called from the village of the
same name; and the tradition of the people is, that it
was called Clare from a board formerly placed across
the river Fergus to serve as a bridge. Very often
the Irish form *clar* is preserved unchanged: as in
Clarcarricknagun near Donegal, the point of the rock
of the hounds; Clarbane in Armagh, white plain;
Clarderry in Monaghan, level oak wood. Clarkill in
Armagh, Down, and Tipperary, and Clarehill in
Derry, are not much changed from the original,
Clarchoill, level wood. In the three last names *clar*
is used as an adjective.

The form Claragh, signifying the same as *clar* itself
—a level place— is much used as a townland name;
Claraghatlea in the parish of Drishane in Cork, *Clar-
ach-a'-tsleibhe*, the plain of (i. e. near) the mountain.
Sometimes this is smoothed down to Clara, which is
the name of a village in King's County, and of

several other places ; Clarashinnagh near Mohill in Leitrim, the plain of the foxes. And lastly, there are several places called Clareen, little plain.

The word *gleann* [pron. *gloun* in the south, *glan*, elsewhere], has exactly the same signification as the English word *glen*. Though they are nearly identical in form, one has not been derived from the other, for the English word exists in the Ang.-Saxon, and on the other hand, *gleann* is used in Irish MSS. much older than the Anglo-Norman invasion, as for instance in *Lebor-na-h Uidhre.*

The two words Glen and Glan form or begin the names of more than 600 places, all of them, with an occasional exception, purely Irish ; and they are sprinkled through every county in Ireland. The most important of these are explained in other parts of this book, and a very few illustrations will be sufficient here. Glennamaddy, the name of a village in Galway, is called in Irish, *Gleann-na-madaighe,* the valley of the dogs ; Glennagross near Limerick, of the crosses ; Glenmullion near the town of Antrim, the glen of the mill ; Glendine and Glandine, the names of several places in the Munster and Leinster counties, *Gleann-doimhin,* deep glen ; and the same name, in the form of Glendowan, is now applied to a fine range of mountains in Donegal, which must have been so called from one of the " deep valleys " they enclose.

Sometimes it is made Glin, of which one of the best known examples is Glin on the Shannon, in Limerick, from which a branch of the Fitzgeralds derives the title of the Knight of Glin. The full name of the place, as given by the Four Masters, is *Gleann-Corbraighe* [Corbry], Corbrach's or Corbry's Valley. And occasionally we find it Glyn or Glynn, of which

we have a characteristic example in the village and
parish of Glynn in Antrim, anciently *Gleann-fhin-
neachta.* The genitive of *gleann* is *gleanna* [glanna],
and sometimes *glinn*, the former of which is represented by *glanna* in the end of names; as in Ballin-
glanna in Cork, Kerry, and Tipperary, the town of
the glen; the same as Ballinglen and Ballyglan in
other counties.

There are two diminutives in common use; the
one, *gleannán*, is found in the northern counties in
the form of Glennan, while in Galway it is made
Glennaun. The other, *gleanntán*, is very much used
in the south and west, and gives names to several
places now called Glantane, Glantaun, Glentane, and
Glentaun—all from a "little glen."

The plural of *gleann* is *gleannta* or *gleanntaidhe*
[glanta, glenty], the latter of which, with the English plural superadded to the Irish (p. 32), gives
name to the village of Glenties in Donegal: it is
so called from two fine glens at the head of which it
stands, viz., the glen of Stracashel (the river holm of
the *cashel* or stone fort), and *Glenfada-na-scalga*, or
the long valley of the hunting.

When this word occurs in the end of names, the *g*
is sometimes aspirated, in which case it disappears
altogether both in writing and pronunciation. Old-
Leighlin in Carlow, a place once very much celebrated as an ecclesiastical establishment, is called in
the annals, *Leith-ghlionn* [Lehlin], half glen, a name
derived from some peculiarity of configuration in the
little river bed. Crumlin is the name of a village
near Dublin, and of another in Antrim; there are
also eighteen townlands of this name in different
counties through the four provinces, besides Crimlin
in Fermanagh, and Cromlin in Leitrim. In every

one of these places there is a winding glen, and in the
Antrim Crumlin, the glen is traversed by a river,
whose name corresponds with that of the glen, viz.,
Camline, which literally signifies crooked line. Crumlin near Dublin takes its name from a pretty glen
traversed by a little stream passing by Inchicore and
under the canal into the Liffey. The Four Masters,
in mentioning this Crumlin, give the true Irish form
of the names of all those places, *Cruimghlinn,* curved
glen, the sound of which is exactly conveyed by
Crumlin. Sometimes in pronouncing this compound,
a short vowel sound is inserted between the two root
words, which preserves the *g* from aspiration ; and in
this manner was formed Cromaglan, the name of the
semicircularly curved glen traversed by the Crinnagh
river, which falls into the upper lake of Killarney.
From this, the fine hill rising immediately over the
stream, and overlooking the upper lake, borrowed
the name of Cromaglan ; and it is now hardly necessary to add that this name does not mean "drooping
mountain," as the guide books absurdly translate it.
There is a townland of the same name in the parish
of Tullylease in Cork, now called Cromagloun.

Lug or *lag* signifies a hollow ; when used topographically, it is almost always applied to a hollow in a
hill ; and *lag, lig, leg,* and *lug* are its most common
forms, the first three being more usual in Ulster, and
the last in Leinster and Connaught. The word is not
so much used in Munster as in the other provinces.

There is a place near Balla in Mayo called Lag-
namuck, the hollow of the pigs ; Lagnaviddoge in
the same county signifies the hollow of the plovers.
Leg begins the names of about 100 townlands, almost
all of them in the northern half of Ireland. The
places called Legacurry, Legachory, and Lagacurry,

of which there are about a dozen, are all so called
from a caldron-like pit or hollow, the name being in
Irish, *Lag-a'-choire*, the hollow of the *coire* or caldron. When the word terminates names it takes
several forms, none differing much from *lug*; such as
Ballinlig, Ballinlug, Ballinluig, Ballylig, and Bally-
lug, all common townland names, signifying the town
of the *lug* or hollow.

As this word was applied to a hollow in a mountain,
it occasionally happened that the name of the hollow
was extended to the mountain itself, as in case of
Lugduff over Glendalough in Wicklow, black hollow;
and Lugnaquillia, the highest of the Wicklow mountains, which the few old people who still retain
the Irish pronunciation in that district, call *Lug-na-
gcoilleach*, the hollow of the cocks, i. e. grouse.

The diminutives Lagan and Legan occur very often
as townland names, but it is sometimes difficult to
separate the latter from *liagan*, a pillar stone. The
river Lagan, or Logan, as it is called in the map of
eschcated estates, 1609, may have taken its name
from a "little hollow" on some part of its course;
there is a lake in Roscommon called Lough Lagan,
the lake of the little hollow; and the townland of
Leggandorragh near Raphoe in Donegal, is called
in Irish *Lagan-dorcha*, dark hollow.

Cúm [coom] a hollow; a nook, glen, or dell in a
mountain; a valley enclosed, except on one side, by
mountains; corresponding accurately with the Welsh
cwm, and English *comb*. The Coombe in Dublin is
a good illustration, being, as the name implies, a
hollow place.

This word is used very often in the neighbourhood
of Killarney to designate the deep glens of the surrounding mountains; as in case of Coomnagoppul

under Mangerton, whose name originated in the practice of sending horses to graze in it at certain seasons—*Cum-na-gcapall*, the glen of the horses; and there is another place of the same name in Waterford.

The most usual forms are *coom* and *coum*, which form part of many names in the Munster counties, especially in Cork and Kerry; thus Coomacheo in Cork, the valley of the fog; Coomnahorna in Kerry, the valley of the barley; Coomnagun near Killaloe, of the hounds. Lackenacoombe in Tipperary—the hill-side of the hollow—exhibits the word as a termination. Commaun, Commeen, and Cummeen, little hollow, are often met with; but as the two latter are sometimes used to express a "common," the investigator must be careful not to pronounce too decidedly on their meaning, without obtaining some knowledge of the particular case. Sometimes the initial *c* is eclipsed, as in case of Baurtrigoum, the name of the highest summit of the Slieve Mish mountains near Tralee, which signifies the *barr* or summit of the three *coms* or hollows: and the mountain was so called because there are on its northern face three glens from summit to base, each traversed by a stream.

Bearn or *bearna* [barn, barna], a gap; it is usually applied to a gap in a mountain or through high land; and in this sense it is very generally applied in local nomenclature, commonly in the form of Barna, which is the name of about a dozen townlands, and enters into the formation of a very large number. Barnageehy and Barnanageehy, the gap of the wind, is a name very often given to high and bleak passes between hills; and the mountain rising over Bally-organ in Limerick, is called Barnageeha, from a pass

29

of this kind on its western side. Very often it is
translated Windygap and Windgate: there is, for
instance, a remarkable gap with the former name in
the parish of Addergoole, Mayo, which the Four
Masters call by its proper Irish name, *Bearna-na-
gaeithe.* Ballinabarny, Ballybarney, Ballynabarna,
Ballynabarny, Ballynabearna, and Ballynaberny, all
signify the town of the gap.

There are several places in different counties, called
by the Irish name, *Bearna-dhearg* [Barna-yarrig],
red gap, and anglicised Barnadarrig and Barnaderg.
The most remarkable of these for its historic associations is *Bearna-dhearg* between the two hills of
Knockea and Carrigeenamronety, on the road from
Kilmallock in Limerick to Kildorrery in Cork. It
is now called in English Redchair or Richchair,
which is an incorrect form of the old Anglo-Irish
name Redsherd, as we find it in Dymmok's "Treatise
of Ireland," written about the year 1600 (Tracts relating to Ireland, Vol. II., p. 18 : Irish Arch. Soc.),
i. e. red gap, a translation of the Irish ; *sheard*, being
a West-English term for a gap.   There is a gap in
the mountain of Forth in Wexford, which, according
to the Glossary quoted at page 44, *supra*, is also called
Reed-sheard or Red-gap, by the inhabitants of Forth
and Bargy.

This word takes other forms, especially in the
northern counties, where it is pretty common ; it is
made *barnet* in several cases, as in Drumbarnet, the
ridge of the gap, the name of some places in Donegal
and Monaghan ; Lisbarnet in Down, the fort of the
gap. There is another Irish form used in the north,
namely, *bearnas;* it has the authority of the annals,
in which this term is always used to designate the
great gap of Barnismore near Donegal ; and in the

forms Barnes and Barnish, it gives name to several
places in Antrim, Donegal, and Tyrone. All the preceding modifications are liable to have the *b* changed
to *v* by aspiration (p. 19), as in Ardvarness in Derry,
Ardvarney and Ardvarna in several other counties,
high gap; Ballyvarnet near Bangor in Down (Bally-
vernock: Inq., 1623), the town of the gap.

The diminutive *Bearnán* is the real name of the
remarkable gap in the mountain now called the
Devil's Bit in Tipperary, whose contour is so familiar
to travellers on the Great Southern and Western
Railway; and it gives name to the parish of Bar-
nane-Ely, i. e. the little gap of *Eile*, the ancient territory in which it was situated.

A *scealp* [scalp] is a cleft or chasm; the word is
much in use among the English-speaking peasantry
of the south, who call a piece of anything cut off by
a knife or hatchet, a *skelp*. The well-known mountain chasm called the Scalp south of Dublin near
Enniskerry, affords the best known and the most
characteristic application of the term; and there are
other places of the same name in the counties of
Clare, Galway, Dublin, and Wicklow. Scalpnagoun
in Clare is the cleft of the calves; Moneyscalp in
Down, the shrubbery of the chasm.

Poll, a hole of any kind; Welsh *pwll*; Manx *powll*;
Breton *poull*; Cornish *pol*; Old High German *pful*;
English *pool*. Topographically it is applied to holes,
pits, or caverns in the earth, deep small pools of water,
very deep spots in rivers or lakes, &c.; in the beginning of anglicised names it is always made *poll*,
poul or *pull*; and as a termination it is commonly
changed to *foyle*, *phuill*, or *phull*, by the aspiration
of the *p* (p. 20), and by the genitive inflexion; all
which forms are exhibited in Ballinfoyle, Ballin-

phuill and Ballinphull, the town of the hole, which
are the names of many places all over the country.
Often the *p* is eclipsed by *b* (p. 22) as in Ballyna-
boll and Ballynaboul, *Baile-na-bpoll,* the town of the
holes.

The origin of the name Poolbeg, now applied to
the lighthouse at the extremity of the South Wall in
Dublin bay, may be gathered from a passage in
Boate's Natural History of Ireland, written, it must
be remembered, long before the two great walls, now
called the Bull Wall and the South Wall, were built.
He states:—"This haven almost all over falleth dry
with the ebbe, as well below Rings-end as above it,
so as you may go dry foot round about the ships
which lye at an anchor there, except in two places,
one at the north side, and the other at the south side,
not far from it.   In these two little creeks (whereof
the one is called the pool of Clontarf, and the other
Poolbeg) it never falleth dry, but the ships which
ride at an anchor remain ever afloat" (Chap. III.,
Sect. II.). The "Pool of Clontarf" is still called "The
Pool;" and the other (near which the lighthouse was
built), as being the smaller of the two, was called *Poll-
beag,* little pool.

There is a place near Arklow called Pollahoney,
or in Irish, *Poll-a'-chonaidh* the hole of the firewood ;
Pollnaranny in Donegal, Pollrane in Wexford, and
Pollranny in Roscommon and Mayo, all signify the
hole of the ferns; Polldorragha near Tuam, dark
hoe; Pollaginnive in Fermanagh, sandpit ; Polfore
near Dromore, Tyrone, cold hole.   So also Pouldine
in Tipperary, deep hole ; Poulaculleare near Whitechurch, same county, and Pollacullaire in Galway,
the quarry hole.

The diminutive in various forms is also pretty ge-

neral. The Pullens (little caverns) near Donegal,
" is a deep ravine through which a mountain torrent
leaps joyously, then suddenly plunges through a cleft
in the rock of from thirty to forty feet in depth," and
after about half a mile " it loses itself again in a dark
chasm some sixty feet deep, from which it emerges
under a natural bridge " (The Donegal Highlands,
p. 68). There are some very fine sea caves a little
west of Castletown Bearhaven in Cork, which, as well
as the little harbour, are well known by the name
of Pulleen, little hole or cavern ; and this is the
name of some other places in Cork and Kerry. We
have Pullans near Coleraine in Derry, and in the
parish of Clontibret, Monaghan ; Pollans in Donegal ;
and Polleens and Polleeny in Galway, all signifying
little holes or caverns. The adjective form *pollach* is
applied to land full of pits or holes, and it has given
name to about thirty-five townlands in the three
southern provinces, in the forms Pollagh and Pullagh.

We have several words in Irish for a cave. Sometimes, as we have seen, the term *poll* was used, and
the combination *poll-talmhan* [Poultalloon : hole of
the earth] was occasionally employed as a distinctive
term for a cavern, giving name, in this sense, to Poll-
talloon in Galway, and to Poultalloon near Fedamore
in Limerick.

Dearc or *derc* [derk] signifies a cave or grotto, and
also the eye. The latter is the primary meaning,
corresponding with Gr. *derkō*, I see, and its application to a cave is figurative and secondary. The word
is often found in the old MSS. ; as, for instance, in
case of *Derc-ferna* (cave of alders), which was the
ancient name of the Cave of Dunmore near Kilkenny,
and which is still applied to it by those speaking Irish.
In the parish of Rathkenny in Meath, is a place

called Dunderk, the fortress of the cave; so named,
probably, from an artificial cave in connection with
the *dun;* there are several places called Derk and
Dirk, both meaning simply a cave; and Aghadark in
Leitrim, is the field of the cavern.

Cuas is another term for a cave, which has also
given names to a considerable number of places: Coos
and Coose are the names of some townlands in Down,
Monaghan, and Galway; there is a remarkable cavern
near Cong called Cooslughoga, the cave of mice;
and it is very likely that Cozies in the parish of Billy,
Antrim, is merely the English plural of Cuas, meaning "caves." Clooncoose, Clooncose, Cloncose, and
Cloncouse, are the names of fourteen townlands spread
over the four provinces; the Irish form is *Cluain-cuas*
(Four Masters), the meadow of the caves. Sometimes
the *c* is changed to *h* by aspiration, as in Corrahoash
in Cavan, the round hill of the cave; and often we
find it eclipsed by *g* (p. 22), as in Drumgoose and
Drumgose, the names of some places in Armagh,
Tyrone, and Monaghan, which represent the Irish
Druim-gcuas, cave ridge. There are several places
called Coosan, Coosane, Coosaun, and Coosheen, all
signifying little cave. Round the coasts of Cork and
Kerry, and perhaps in other counties, *cuas* or *coos* is
applied to a small sea inlet or cove, and in these
places the word must be interpreted accordingly.

There is yet another word for a cave in very general use, which I find spelled in good authorities in
three different ways, *uagh, uaimh,* and *uath* [ooa];
for all these are very probably nothing more than
modifications of the same original. There is a class
of romantic tales in Irish "respecting various occurrences in caves: sometimes the taking of a cave,
when the place has been used as a place of refuge or

habitation; sometimes the narrative of some adven-
ture in a cave; sometimes of a plunder of a cave;
and so on " (O'Curry, Lect., p. 283).   A tale of this
kind was called *uath*, i. e. cave.

The second form *uaimh* is the one in most general
use, and its genitive is either *uamha* or *uamhain* [oon,
ooan], both of which we find in the annals.   Cloyne
in Cork, has retained only part of its ancient name,
Cluain-uamha, as it is written in the Book of Leinster
and many other authorities, i. e. the meadow of the
cave; this was the old pagan name, which St. Colman
Mac Lenin adopted when he founded his monastery
there in the beginning of the seventh century; and
the cave from which the place was named so many
hundred years ago, is still to be seen there.   At A. M.
3501, the Four Masters record the erection by Emh-
ear, of *Rath-uamhain*, i. e. the fort of the cave
(O'Donovan's Four Masters, I., 27), which exhibits
the second form of the genitive.

Both of these genitives are represented in our present names.   The first very often forms the termina-
tion *oe* or *oo*, or with the article, *nahoe*, or *nahoo;* as
Drumnahoe in Antrim and Tyrone, and Drumahoe
in Derry, i. e. *Druim-na-huamha*, the ridge of the cave;
Farnahoe near Inishannon in Cork (*Farran*, land);
Glennoo near Clogher in Tyrone, and Glennahoo in
Kerry, the glen of the cave.   And occasionally the r
sound of the aspirated *m* comes clearly out, as in
Cornahoova in Meath, and Cornahove in Armagh,
the round hill of the cave; the same as Cornahoe in
Monaghan and Longford.

The other genitive, *uamhain* [ooan], is also very
often used, and generally appears in the end of names
in the form of *one* or *oon*, or with the article, *nahone*
or *nahoon;* in this manner we have Mullennahone in

Kilkenny, and Mullinahone in Tipperary, *Muilenn-na-huamhain*, the mill of the cave, the latter so called from a cave near the village through which the little river runs: Knockeennahone in Kerry (little hill); and Lisnahoon in Roscommon, so called, no doubt, from the artificial cave in the *lis* or fort. Both forms are represented in Gortnahoo in Tipperary, and Gornahoon in Galway, the field of the cave; and in Knocknahoe in Kerry and Sligo, and Knocknahooan in Clare, cave hill.

Occasionally we find this last genitive form used as a nominative (p. 34), for, according to O'Donovan (App. to O'Reilly's Dict.), "*Uamhuinn* is used in Thomond to express a natural or artificial cave." Nooaff and Noonn are the names of some places in Clare; they are formed by the attraction of the article (p. 23), the former representing *n'uaimh*, and the latter *n'uamhainn*, and both signifying "the cave." The Irish name of Owenbristy near Ardrahan in Galway is *Uamhainn-brisde*, broken cave.

Uamhainn with the *mh* sounded, would be pronounced *ooran*; and this by a slight change, effected under the corrupting influence noticed at page 38, has given name to "The Ovens," a small village on the river Bride, two miles west of Ballincollig in Cork. For in this place "is a most remarkable cave, large and long, with many branches crossing each other" (Smith's Cork, I., 212), which the people say runs as far as Gill Abbey near Cork; and by an ingenious alteration, they have converted their fine caves or *oorans* into ovens! The ford at the village was anciently called *Ath-'n-uamhain* [Athnoonn], the ford of the cave, and this with the *c* sound suppressed has given the name of Athnowen to the parish.

CHAPTER III.

ISLANDS, PENINSULAS, AND STRANDS.

THE most common word for an island is *inis*, cognate with Welsh *ynys*, Arm. *enes*, and Lat. *insula*. It is also applied in all parts of Ireland to the holm, or low flat meadow along a river; and a meadow of this kind is generally called an *inch* among the English-speaking people, especially in the south. This, however, is obviously a secondary application, and the word must have been originally applied to islands formed by the branching of rivers; but while many of these, by gradual changes in the river course, lost the character of islands, they retained the name. It is not difficult to understand how, in the course of ages, the word *inis* would in this manner gradually come to be applied to river meadows in general, without any reference to actual insulation.

The principal modern forms of this word are Inis, Inish, Ennis, and Inch, which give names to a vast number of places in every part of Ireland; but whether, in any individual case, the word means an island or a river holm, must be determined by the physical configuration of the place. In many instances places that were insulated when the names were imposed are now no longer so, in consequence of the drainage of the surrounding marshes or lakes; as in case of Inishargy (p. 410).

Inis and Inish are the forms most generally used, and they are the common appellations of the islands round the coast, and in the lakes and rivers; they are also applied, like *inch*, to river meadows   There is an island in Lough Erne, containing the ruins of

an ancient church, which the annalists often mention
by the name of *Inis-muighe-samh* [moy-sauv], the
island of the plain of the sorrel; this island is
now, by a very gross mispronunciation, called Inishmacsaint, and has given name to the parish on the
mainland.

Near the town of Ennis in Clare, is a townland
called Clonroad, which preserves pretty well the
sound of the name as we find it in the annals,
Cluain-ramhfhoda, usually translated the meadow
of the long rowing: the spot where Ennis now
stands must have been originally connected in some
way with this townland, for the annals usually
mention it by the name of *Inis-Cluana-ramfhoda*,
i. e. the river meadow of Clonroad. Inishnagor in
Donegal and Sligo, is a very descriptive name,
signifying the river meadow of the *corrs* or cranes;
there are several places in both north and south,
called Enniskeen and Inishkeen, in Irish *Inis-cacin*
(Four Mast.), beautiful island or river holm. Inistioge in Kilkenny is written *Inis-Teoc* in the Book
of Leinster, Teoc's island; and Ennistimon in Clare
is called by the Four Masters *Inis-Diomain*, Diman's
river meadow.

This word very often occurs in the end of names,
usually forming with the article the termination *na-
hinch*, as in Coolnahinch, the corner or angle of the
island or river meadow. Sometimes it is contracted,
as we see in Cleenish, an island near Enniskillen,
giving name to a parish, which ought to have been
called *Cleeninish;* for the Irish name, according to
the Four Masters, is *Claen-inis*, i. e. sloping island.

Oilean or *oilen* is another word for an island which
is still used in the spoken language, and enters pretty
extensively into names. It is commonly anglicised

Illan and Illaun, and these words give names to
places all over the country, but far more numerously
in Connaught than elsewhere. Thus Illananummera
in Tipperary, the island of the ridge, so called no
doubt from its shape; Illanfad in Donegal, long
island, the same as Illaunfadda in Galway; Illaun-
inagh near Inchigeelagh in Cork, ivy island; and
there are several little islets off the coast of Galway
and Mayo, called Roeillaun, red island.

A peninsula is designated by the compound *leith-
insi* [lehinshi] literally half-island; and this word
gives name to all places now called Lehinch or La-
hinch, of which, besides a village in Clare (which is
mentioned by the Four Masters), there are several in
other parts of Ireland. The word is shortened in
Loughlynch in the parish of Billy, Antrim, which
ought to have been called *Loughlehinch*, as it is written in the Four Masters *Loch-leithinnsi*, the lake of
the peninsula; for a lake existed there down to a recent period.

The word *ros* signifies, first, a promontory or peninsula; secondly, a wood; and it has other signifi-
cations which need not be noticed here. Colgan
translates it *nemus* in Act. SS., p. 791 *b*, n. 15; and
in Tr. Th., p. 383 *a*, n. 17, it is rendered *peninsula*.
By some accident of custom, the two meanings are
now restricted in point of locality; for in the southern half of Ireland, *ros* is generally understood only
in the sense of wood, while in the north, this application is lost, and it means only a peninsula.

Yet there are many instances of the application of
this term to a peninsula in the south, showing that
it was formerly so understood there. A well-known
example is Ross castle on the lower lake of Killarney,
so called from the little *ros* or point on which it was

built. Between the middle and lower lakes is the
peninsula of Muckross, so celebrated for the beauty
of its scenery, and for its abbey; its Irish name is
Muc-ros, the peninsula of the pigs; which is also the
name of a precipitous head-land near Killybegs in
Donegal, and of several other places. And west of
Killarney, near the head of Dingle bay, is a remarkable peninsula called Rossbehy or Rossbegh, the
latter part of which indicates that it was formerly
covered with birch trees :—birchy point.

There is a parish in Leitrim called Rossinver, which
takes its name from a point of land running into the
south part of Lough Melvin—*Rosinbhir*, the Peninsula of the *inver* or river mouth ; and Rossorry near
Enniskillen is called in the Four Masters, *Ros-airthir*
[Rossarher], eastern peninsula, of which the modern
name is a corruption. Portrush in Antrim affords an
excellent illustration of the use of this word ; it takes
its name from the well-known point of basaltic rock
which juts into the sea :—*Post-ruis*, the landing place
of the peninsula. The district between the bays of
Gweebarra and Gweedore in Donegal is called by
the truly descriptive name, The Rosses, i. e. the
peninsulas.

While it is often difficult to know which of the
two meanings we should assign to *ros*, the nature of
the place not unfrequently determines the matter.
Rush north of Dublin, is called in Irish authorities
Ros-eó [Rush-ō], from which the present name has
been shortened ; and as the village is situated on a
projection of land three-fourths surrounded by the
sea, we can have no hesitation about the meaning of
the first syllable : the whole name therefore signifies
the peninsula of the yew-trees.

Traigh or *tracht* [trū, traght] signifies a strand ;

it is found in the Zeuss MSS., and corresponds with
Lat. *tractus*, Welsh *traeth*, and Cornish *trait*. The first
form is that always adopted in modern names, and it
is generally represented by *tra*, *traw*, or *tray*. One
of the best known examples of its use is Tralee in
Kerry; the Four Masters call it *Traigh-Li*, and the
name is translated in the Life of St. Brendan, *Littus
Ly*, which is generally taken to mean the shore or
strand of the Lee, a little river which runs into the
sea there, but which is now covered over. In the
Annals of Connaught, however, the place is called
"Traigh Li mic Dedad," the strand of Li the son
of Dedad; from which it would appear that it took
its name from a man named Li (which is consistent
with the translation in the Life of St. Brendan); and
this is probably the true origin of the name. Tralee
in the parish of Ardtrea, Derry, has a different
origin, the Irish name being *Traigh-liath*, grey
strand. Tramore near Waterford, great strand;
Trawnamaddree in Cork, the strand of the dogs.
Baltray, strand-town, is the name of a village near
the mouth of the Boyne; there is a place called
Ballynatray, a name having the same meaning, on
the Blackwater, a little above Youghal; and near the
same town, on the opposite shore of the river,
is Monatray, the bog of the strand. There is a
beautiful white strand at Ventry in Kerry, from
which the place got the name of *Fionn-traigh* [Fin-
tra: *Fionn*, white]; Hanmer calls it *rentra*, which
is an intermediate step between the ancient and
modern forms. This same name is more correctly
modernised Fintra in Clare, and Fintragh near
Killybegs in Donegal.

CHAPTER IV.

WATER, LAKES, AND SPRINGS.

THE common Irish word for water is *uisce* [iska] ; it occurs in the Zeuss MSS., where it glosses *aqua*, and it is cognate with Lat. *unda*, and Gr. *hudōr*. It is pretty extensively used in local names, and it has some derivatives, which give it a wider circulation. It occurs occasionally in the beginning of names, but generally in the end, and its usual forms are *iska*, *isky*, and *isk*. Whiskey is called in Irish *uisce-beatha* [iska-baha], or as it is often anglicised, *usquebaugh*, which has exactly the same meaning as the Latin *aqua ritæ*, and the French *eau-de-vie*, water of life ; and the first part of the compound, slightly altered, now passes current as an English word—whiskey.

At A.D. 465, the Four Masters record that Owen, son of Niall of the Nine Hostages (see p. 138, *supra*), died of grief for his brother Conall Gulban, and that he was buried at *Uisce-chacin*, whose name signifies beautiful water. This place is now called Eskaheen, preserving very nearly the old sound ; it is situated near Muff in Inishowen, and it received its name from a fine spring, where, according to Colgan, there anciently existed a monastery. No tradition of Owen is preserved there now (see O'Don. Four Mast. I., 146).

Knockaniska, the name of some places in Waterford, is the hill of the water ; there is a parish in Wicklow, called Killiskey, the church of the water, and the little stream that gave it the name still runs by the old church ruin ; the same name exists in Wexford, shortened to Killisk, and in King's County

it is made Killiskea. Balliniska and Ballynisky are
the names of two townlands in Limerick, both
signifying the town of the water ; and the village of
Ballisk near Donabate in Dublin, has the same name,
only without the article. Ballyhisky in Tipperary
is a different name, viz., *Bealach-uisce*, the road of
the water, the *h* in the present name representing
the *ch* of *bealach*.

According to Cormac's Glossory, *esc* is another ancient Irish word for water—"*esc*, i. e. *uisce:*" its
original application is lost, but in some parts of Ireland, especially in the south, it is applied to the track
of a stream or a channel cut by water, either inland
or on the strand. It has given name to some townlands called Esk in Kerry ; and to Eskenacartan in
Cork, the stream-track of the forge. The glen under
the south slope of Cromaglan mountain at Killarney
is called Esknamucky, the stream-track of the pig ;
and this is also the name of a townland in Cork.
The name of Lough Eask near Donegal may be
formed from this word (the lake of the channel) ; but
more probably it is from *iasc*, fish—*Loch-eisc*, the lake
of the fish.

Loch signifies a lake, cognate with Lat. *lacus*, English, *lake*, &c. The word is applied both in Ireland
and Scotland, not only to lakes, but to arms of the
sea, of which there are hundreds of examples round
the coasts of both countries. The almost universal
anglicised form in this country is *lough*, but in Scotland they have preserved the original *loch* unchanged.
As the word is well known and seldom disguised in
obscure forms, a few examples of its use will be sufficient here.

The lake names of Ireland are generally made up
of this word, followed by some limiting term, such as

a man's name, an adjective, &c. Thus the lakes of
Killarney were anciently, and are often still, called
collectively, Lough Leane; and according to the
Dinnsenchus, they received that name from Lean of
the white teeth, a celebrated artificer who had his
forge on the shore. Lough Conn in Mayo is called
in the Book of Ballymote and other authorities, *Loch-
Con*, literally the lake of the hound; but it is probable that Con, or as it would stand in the nominative, Cu, is here also a man's name. Loughrea in
Galway is called in the annals, *Loch-riabhach*, grey
lake.

Great numbers of townlands, villages, and parishes,
take their names from small lakes, as in the widely-
extended names Ballinlough and Ballylough, the
town of the lake. In numerous cases the lakes have
been dried up, either by natural or artificial drainage, leaving no trace of their existence except the
names.

The town of Carlow is called in Irish authorities,
Cetherloch, quadruple lake; and the tradition is that
the Barrow anciently formed four lakes there, of
which, however, there is now no trace. The Irish
name is pronounced Caherlough, which was easily
softened down to the present name. By early English writers, it is generally called Catherlogh or
Katherlagh, which is almost identical with the Irish;
Boate calls it "Catherlogh or Carlow," showing that
in his time the present form was beginning to be developed.

The diminutive *lochan* is of very general occurrence in the anglicised forms Loughan, Loughane,
and Loughaun, all names of places, which were so
called from "small lakes." There is a place in Westmeath, near Athlone, called Loughanaskin, whose

Irish name is *Lochán-easgann*, the little lake of the eels; in the county Clare is a townland called Lough-aunaweelaun, *Lochún-na-bhfaeileán*, the little lake of the seagulls; Loughanreagh near Coleraine in Londonderry, grey lakelet; and Loughanstown, the name of several places in Limerick, Meath, and Westmeath, is a translation from *Baile-an-locháin*, the town of the little lake; which is retained in the untranslated forms Ballinloughan, Ballyloughan, and Ballylough-aun, in other counties. But Ballinloughane in the parish of Dunmoylan, near Shanagolden in Limerick, is a different name; for it is corrupted from *Baile-Uí-Gheileachain* [Ballygeelahan], as the Four Masters write it, which signifies O'Geelahan's town (see 2nd Series, Chap. VIII).

Turlough is a term very much used in the west of Ireland; and it is applied to a lake which dries up in summer, exhibiting generally, at that season, a coarse, scrubby, marshy surface, which is often used for pasture. It gives names to several places in the counties west of the Shannon (including Clare), a few of which are mentioned by the Four Masters, who write the word *turlach*. There are two townlands in Roscommon called Ballinturly, the town of the *turlach*. The root of this word is *tur*, which, according to Cormac's Glossary, signifies · dry; but the *lach* in the end is a mere suffix (see this suffix in 2nd Ser., Chap. I), and not *loch*, a lake, as might naturally be thought:—*turlach*, a dried up spot (which had formerly been wet). This appears evident from the fact that the Four Masters write its genitive, *turlaigh*, in which *laigh* is the proper genitive of the postfix *lach*, and not of *loch*, a lake, which makes *locha* in the genitive.

Wells have been at all times held in veneration in

Ireland.   It appears from the most ancient Lives of
St. Patrick, and from other authorities, that before
the introduction of Christianity, they were not only
venerated, but actually worshipped, both in Ireland
and Scotland.   Thus in Adamnan's Life of St. Columba we read :—"Another time, remaining for some
days in the country of the Picts, the holy man (Columba) heard of a fountain famous amongst this hea-
then people, which foolish men, blinded by the devil,
worshipped as a divinity. . . . . . The pagans, se-
duced by these things, paid divine honour to the
fountain" (Lib. II. Cap. xi).   And Tirechan relates
in the Book of Armagh, that St. Patrick, in his progress through Ireland, came to a fountain called
Slan [Slaun], which the druids worshipped as a God,
and to which they used to offer sacrifices.   Some of
the well customs that have descended even to our
own day, seem to be undoubted vestiges of this pagan
adoration (see 2nd Series, Chap. v.).

After the general spread of the Faith, the people's
affection for wells was not only retained but intensi-
fied ; for most of the early preachers of the Gospel
established their humble foundations—many of them
destined to grow in after years into great religious
and educational institutions—beside those fountains,
whose waters at the same time supplied the daily
wants of the little communities, and served for the
baptism of converts.   In this manner most of our
early saints became associated with wells, hundreds
of which still retain the names of these holy men,
who converted and baptized the pagan multitudes on
their margins.

The most common Irish name for a well is *tobar ;*
it enters into names all over Ireland, and it is subject to very little alteration from its original form.

Tober is the name of about a dozen townlands, and begins those of more than 130 others, all of them called from wells, and many from wells associated with the memory of patron saints. The following are a few characteristic examples. At Ballintober in Mayo, there was a holy well called Tober Stingle, which was blessed by St. Patrick; and the place was therefore called Ballintober Patrick, the town of St. Patrick's well, which is its general name in the annals. It was also called *Baile-na-craibhi* [Ballynacreeva: Book of Lecan], the town of the branchy tree, which is still partly retained in the name of the adjacent townland of Creevagh. This well has quite lost its venerable associations; for it is called merely Tobermore (great well), and is not esteemed holy. The place is now chiefly remarkable for the fine ruins of the abbey erected by Cathal of the red hand, king of Connaught, in the year 1216 (see O'Don. in "Hy Fiachrach," p. 191). Ballintober and Ballytober (the town of the well), are the names of about twenty-four townlands distributed through the four provinces (see p. 263, *supra*).

Tobercurry in Sligo is called in Irish, and written by Mac Firbis, *Tobar-an-choire*, the well of the caldron, from its shape. Carrowntober, the name of many townlands, signifies the quarter-land of the well. Toberbunny near Cloughran in Dublin signifies the well of the milk (*Tobar-bainne*), and Toberlownagh in Wicklow has nearly the same meaning (*Tobar-leamhnachta* : *leamhnacht* [lownaght], new milk); both being so called probably from the softness of their waters. Some wells take their names from the picturesque old trees that overshadow them, and which are preserved by the people with great veneration; such as Toberbilly in Antrim, *Tobar-*

bile, the well of the ancient tree; the same name as
Toberavilla north-east of Moate in Westmeath.

In case of some holy wells, it was the custom to
visit them and perform devotions on particular days
of the week; and this has been commemorated by
such names as Toberaheena, which is that of a well
and village in Tipperary, signifying the well of Friday. A great many wells in different parts of the
country are called *Tobar-righ-an-domhnaigh* [Tober-
reendowney: see p. 318], literally the well of the
King of Sunday (i. e. of God); one of which gave
name to the village of Toberreendoney in Galway.
It is probable that these were visited on Sundays,
and they are generally called in English, Sunday's
Well, as in case of the place of that name near Cork.

Sometimes *tobar* takes the form of Tipper, which is
the name of a parish in Kildare, and of two townlands
in Longford; Tipperstown in Dublin and Kildare is
only a half translation from *Baile-an-tobair*, the town
of the well; Tipperkevin, St. Kevin's well. Of similar formation is Tibberaghny, the name of a townland
and parish in Kilkenny, which the annalists write
Tiobraid-Fachtna [Tibbradaghna], St. Faghna's well.
Occasionally the *t* is changed to *h* by aspiration,
as in Mohober in the parish of Lismalin in Tipperary,
which Clyn, in his annals, writes Moytobyr, the field
or plain of the well.

In Cormac's Glossary and other ancient documents,
we find another form of this word, namely, *tipra*,
whose genitive is *tiprat*, and dative *tiprait*. In accordance with the principle noticed at p. 34, *supra*,
the dative *tiprait*, or as it is written in the later
Irish writings, *tiobraid* [tubbrid], gives name to
sixteen townlands scattered through the four provinces, now called Tubbrid. Geoffrey Keating the

historian was parish priest of Tubbrid near Cahir
in Tipperary, where he died about the year 1650,
and was buried in the churchyard.   The word takes
other modern forms, as we find in Clontibret in
Monaghan, which the annalists write *Cluain-tiobrat*,
the meadow of the spring.   The well that gave
name to the town of Tipperary, and thence to the
county, was situated near the Main-street, but it is
now closed up; it is called in all the Irish authorities,
Tiobraid-Arann [Tubrid-Auran] the well of Ara
(*Ara*, gen. *Arann*), the ancient territory in which it
was situated.   Other forms are exhibited in Aghatub-
rid in Donegal, Cork and Kerry, the field of the
well; in Ballintubbert and Ballintubbrid, the same
as Ballintober; and in Kiltubbrid, the same name as
Kiltober, the church of the well.

Uaran or *fuaran* is explained by Colgan, " a living
fountain of fresh or cold water springing from the
earth."   It is not easy to say whether the initial *f* is
radical or not; if it be, the word is obviously derived
from *fuar*, cold; if not, it comes from *ur*, fresh; and
Colgan's explanation leaves the question undecided.

This word gives name to Oranmore in Galway,
which the Four Masters call *Uaran-mór*, great spring.
Oran in Roscommon was once a place of great consequence, and is frequently mentioned in the annals;
it contains the ruins of a church and round tower;
and the original *uaran* or spring is a holy well, which
to this day is much frequented by pilgrims.

Oran occurs pretty often in names, such as Knock-
anoran (*knock*, a hill), in Queen's County and Cork
Ballinoran and Ballynoran (*Bally*, a town), the names
of many townlands through the four provinces; Tin-
oran in Wicklow, *Tigh-an-uarain*, the house of the

spring ; Carrickanoran in Kilkenny and Monaghan
(Carrick, a rock) ; and Lickoran, the name of a parish
in Waterford, the flag-stone of the cold spring.

CHAPTER V.

RIVERS, STREAMLETS, AND WATERFALLS.

The Irish language has two principal words for a
river—*abh* or *abha* [aw or ow] and *abhainn*, which
are identified in meaning in Cormac's Glossary, in
the following short passage :—"*Abh*, i. e. *abhainn*."
There are many streamlets in Ireland designated by
abh ; and it also enters into the names of numerous
townlands and villages, which have a stream flowing
through or by them. So far as I have yet observed,
I find that *abh* is used only in the southern half of
Ireland.

The word is used simply as the name of a small
river in Wicklow, the Ow, i. e. the river, rising on the
south-eastern slope of Lugnaquillia ; Awbeg, Owbeg,
or Owveg, little river, is the name of many streams,
so called to distinguish them from larger rivers near
them, or to which they are tributary. The Ounageeragh, the river of the sheep ('*Abh-na-geacrach*), is a
tributary of the Funcheon in Cork ; Finnow is the
name of several small streams, signifying white or
transparent river ; there is a place a few miles east of
Tipperary called Cahervillahowe, the stone fort of
the old tree (*bile*) of the river ; and Ballynahow, the
town of the river, is a townland name of frequent
occurrence in Munster, but not found elsewhere.

Abhainn [owen], which corresponds with the Sanscrit *aruni*, is in much more general use than *abh* ; and
it is the common appellative in the spoken language
for a river.   It is generally anglicised *aron* or *owen*,
and there are great numbers of river names through
the country formed from these words.   *Abhainn-mór*,
great river, is the name of many rivers in Ireland,
now generally called Avonmore or Owenmore ; this
was and is still, the Irish name of the Blackwater in
Cork (often called Broadwater by early Anglo-Irish
writers), and also of the Blackwater in Ulster, flowing
into Lough Neagh by Charlemont.

The word *abhainn* has three different forms in the
genitive, viz. *abhann*, *abhanna*, and *aibhne* [oun, ouna,
ivnĕ], which are illustrated in the very common
names Ballynahown, Ballynahone, Ballynahowna,
and Ballynahivnia, all signifying the town of the
river.

Abhnach [ounagh] is an adjective formation from
abhainn, signifying literally " abounding in rivers,"
but applied to a marshy or watery place ; and it gives
name to Ounagh in Sligo ; and to Onagh in Wicklow.
The name of Glanworth in Cork is written in the Book
of Rights, *Gleann-amhnach* [Glanounagh], i. e. the
watery or marshy glen ; but its present Irish name is
Gleann-iubhair [Glanoor], the glen of the yew tree ;
and I believe that it is from this, and not from *Gleann-*
amhnach, the anglicised form has been derived.   The
parish of Boyounagh in Galway takes its name from
the original church, which is situated in a bog, and
which the Four Masters call *Buidheamhnach* [Bwee-
ounagh], i. e. yellow marsh, probably from the
yellowish colour of the grass or flowers.   Boyanagh
and Boyannagh, the names of places in Roscommon,
Leitrim, and Westmeath, are slightly different in

form though identical in meaning, the latter part
being *canach,* another name for a marsh (see p.
461 *infra*); and Boynagh in Meath may be either
the one or the other.

Glaise or *glais* or *glas* [glasha, glash, glas], signifies a small stream, a rivulet; it is very often used to
give names to streams, and thence to townlands, all
over Ireland, and its usual anglicised forms are *glasha,
glash,* and *glush.* Glashawee and Glashaboy, yellow
streamlet, are the names of several little rivers and
townlands in Cork; and there is a place near Ard-
straw in Tyrone, called Glenglush, the glen of the
streamlet. The little stream flowing into the sea
at Glasthule near Kingstown in Dublin, has given
the village the name:—*Glas-Tuathail,* Thoohal's or
Toole's streamlet. Douglas is very common both as
a river and townland designation all over the country, and it is also well known in Scotland; its Irish
form is *Dubhghlaise,* black stream; and in several parts
of the country it assumes the forms of Douglasha and
Dooglasha, which are the names of many streams.

There is a little streamlet at Glasnevin near Dublin, which winds in a pretty glen through the classic
grounds of Delville, and joins the Tolka at the bridge.
In far remote ages, beyond the view of history, long
before St. Mobhi established his monastery there in
the sixth century, some old pagan chief named
Naeidhe [Nee] must have resided on its banks; from
him it was called *Glas-Naeidhen* [Glasneean : Four
Mast.], i. e. Naeidhe's streamlet; and the name gradually extended to the village, while its original application is quite forgotten. This ancient name is
modernized to Glasnevin by the change of *dh* to *r*
(see p. 54, *supra*).

The diminutive Glasheen is also in frequent use as

a territorial designation; Glasheenaulin near Castlehaven in Cork, signifies literally beautiful little streamlet; Glasheena or Glashina is "a place abounding in little streams;" and Ardglushin in Cavan, signifies the height of the little rivulet.

Sruth [sruh] means a stream, and is in very common use both in the spoken and written language. It is an ancient and primitive word in Irish, being found in the Wb. MS. of Zeuss, where it glosses *flumen, rivus;* it is almost identical with Sansc. *sróta*, a river; and its cognates exist in several other languages, such as Welsh *frut*, Cornish *frot*, Slavonic *struja*, Old High German *stroum*, Eng. *stream* (Ebel).

Sruth occurs pretty often in names, and its various derivatives, especially the diminutives, have also impressed themselves extensively on the nomenclature of the country. In its simple form it gives names to Srue in Galway; to Sruh in Waterford; and to Shrough in Tipperary: Ballystrew near Downpatrick is the town of the stream.

Sruthair [sruhar], a derivative from *sruth*, is in still more general use, and signifies also a stream; it undergoes various modern modifications, of which the commonest is the change of the final *r* to *l* (see p. 48). Abbeyshrule in Longford was anciently called *Sruthair*, i. e. the stream, and it took its present name from a monastery founded there by one of the O'Farrells. Abbeystrowry in Cork is the same name, and it was so called from the stream that also gives name to Bealnashrura (ford-mouth of the stream), a village situated at an ancient ford. Struell near Downpatrick is written *Strohill* in the Taxation of 1306, showing that the change from *r* to *l* took place before that early period; but the *r* is retained in a grant of about the year of 1178, in which the place is called

Tirestruther, the land of the streamlet   The celebrated wells of St. Patrick are situated here, which
in former times were frequented by persons from all
quarters; and the stream flowing from them must
have given the place its name (see Reeves's Eccl.
Ant., pp. 42, 43). The change of *r* to *l* appears also
in Sroolane and Srooleen, which are often applied to
little streams in the south, and which are the names
of some townlands.

Sruthan [sruhaun], the diminutive of *sruth*, enters
very often into local names in every part of Ireland;
and it is peculiarly liable to alteration, both by corruption and by grammatical inflexion, so that it is
often completely disguised in modern names.   In its
simple form it gives name to Sroughan in Wicklow;
and with a *t* inserted (p. 60), and the aspirate omitted,
to Stroan in Antrim, Kilkenny, and Cavan.   The
sound of *th* in this word is often changed to that of *f*
(p. 52), converting it to *sruffan* or *sruffaun*, a term in
common use in some parts of Ireland, especially in
Galway, for a small stream.   And lastly, the substitution of *t* for *s* by eclipse (p. 22), leads to still
further alteration, which is exemplified in Killeena-
truan in Longford, *Cillin-a'-tsruthain*, the little church
of the stream; Carntrone in Fermanagh, the *carn* or
monumental heap of the streamlet.

Feadan [faddaun] is a common word for a brook,
and it enters largely into local names; it is a diminutive of *fead* [fad], and the literal meaning of both
is a pipe, tube, or whistle; whence in a secondary
sense, they came to be applied to those little brooks
whose channels are narrow and deep, like a tube.

From this word we get such names as Faddan,
Feddan, Fiddan, Fiddane, &c.; Fiddaunnageeroge
near Crossmolina in Mayo, is the little brook of the

keeroges or chafers. With the *f* sound suppressed under the influence of the article (p. 27), we have Ballyneddan in Down and Ballineddan in Wicklow, *Baile-an-fheadain*, the town of the streamlet. Fedany in Down, is from the Irish *Feadanach*, which signifies a streamy place.

Inbhear [inver], old Irish *inbir* (Cor. Gl.), means the mouth of a river; "a bay into which a river runs, or a long narrow neck of the sea, resembling a river" (Dr. Todd). The word is pretty common in Ireland, and equally so in Scotland, generally in the form of *inver*, but it is occasionally obscured by modern contraction. At A.D. 639, the Four Masters record the death of St. Dagan of *Inbhear-Dacile* [Invereela], i.e. the mouth of the river Deel; this place, which lies in Wicklow, four miles north from Arklow, retains the old name, modernized to Ennereilly, though the river is no longer called the Deel, but the Pennycomequick. The townland of Dromineer in Tipperary, which gives name to a parish, is situated where the Nenagh river enters Lough Derg; and hence it is called in Irish *Druim-inbhir*, the ridge of the river mouth.

It would appear that waterfalls were objects of special notice among the early inhabitants of this country, for almost every fall of any consequence in our rivers has a legend of its own, and has impressed its name on the place in which it is situated. The most common Irish word for a waterfall is *eas* [ass] or *ess*, gen. *easa* [assa]; and the usual modern forms are, for the nominative, *ass* and *ess*, and often for the genitive, *assa* and *assy*, but sometimes *ass* or *ess*.

Doonass near Castleconnell was so called from the great rapid on the Shannon, the Irish name being

Dun-easa, the fortress of the cataract; but its ancient name was *Eas-Danainne* [Ass-Danniny; Four Most.], the cataract of the Lady Danann (for whom see p. 163, *supra*). The old name of the fall at Cuherass near Croom in Limerick, was *Ess-Maighe* [Ass-Ma: Book of Leinster], i. e. the waterfall of the river Maigue; and the name Caherass was derived, like Doonass, from a fort built on its margin. There is a fall on the river that flows through Mountmellick in Queen's County, which has given to the stream the name of Owenass; in Glendalough is a well-known dell where a rivulet falls from a rock into a deep clear pool, hence called Pollanass, the pool of the waterfall; and the same name in another form, Poulanassy, occurs in the parish of Kilmacow, Kilkenny.

The Avonbeg forms the Ess fall, at the head of Glenmalure in Wicklow; and the Vartry as it enters the Devil's Glen, is precipitated over a series of rocky ledges, from which the place is called Bonanass, a local corruption of Bellananass, the ford of the cataracts (as Ballinalee in the same county, properly Bellanalee, is locally called Bonalee: (see p. 470, *infra*). Ballyness, the town (or perhaps in some cases the ford) of the waterfall, is the name of seven townlands in the northern counties; and the diminutive Assan, Assaun, Essan, and Essaun, are also very common.

The beautiful rapid on the Owenmore river at Ballysadare in Sligo, has given name to the village. It was originally called *Easdara* [Assdara], the cataract of the oak; or according to an ancient legend, the cataract of Red Dara, a Fomorian druid who was slain there by Lewy of the long hand (see pp. 161, 201). It afterwards took the name of *Baile-*

easa-Dara [Ballyassadarra: Four Mast.], the town of
Dara's cataract, which has been shortened to the
present name.

CHAPTER VI.

MARSHES AND BOGS.

THERE are several words in Irish to denote a marsh,
all used in the formation of names; but in thousands
of cases the marshes have been drained, and the land
placed under cultivation, tho names alone remaining
to attest the existence of swamps in days long past.
One of these words, *eanach* [annagh], signifies literally a watery place, and is derived from *ean*, water.
In some parts of the country it is applied to a out-
out bog, an application easily reconcilable with the
original signification. It appears generally in the
forms Annagh, Anna, and Anny, and these either
simply or in combination, give names to great numbers of places in every part of the country.

Annaduff in Leitrim is called by the Four Masters,
Eanagh-dubh, black marsh; Annabella near Mallow
has an English look; but it is the Irish *Eanach-bile*,
the marsh of the *bile* or old tree: Annaghaskin in
Dublin, near Bray, the morass of the eels (*easgan*, an
eel). As a termination this word generally becomes
-anny or *-enny*, in accordance with the sound of the
genitive *eanaigh*; as in Gortananny in Galway, the
field of the marsh; Inchenny in Tyrone, which the
Four Masters call *Inis-eanaigh*, the island or river
holm of the marsh. There are several places in
Munster called Rathanny, the fort of the marsh;
and Legananny the *lug* or hollow of the marsh, is
the name of two townlands in Down. In some of

the northern counties, this form is adopted in the beginning of names (p. 34), as in Annyalty in Monaghan, the marsh of the flocks (*ealta*).

Carcach, a marsh—low swampy ground : it is used in every part of Ireland, and assumes various forms, which will be best understood from the following examples.

After St. Finbar. in the sixth century, had spent some years in the wild solitude of *Loch Irc*, now Gougane Barra, St. Barra's or Finbar's rock-cleft, at the source of the Lee, he changed his residence, and founded a monastery on the edge of a marsh near the mouth of the same river, round which a great city subsequently grew up. This swampy place was known for many hundred years afterwards by the name of *Corcach-mor* or *Corcach-mor-Mumhan* [Moonn], the great marsh of Munster; of which only the first part has been retained, and even that shortened to one syllable in the present name of Cork. The city is still, however, universally called *Corcach* by those who speak Irish ; and the memory of the old swamp is perpetuated in the name of The Marsh, which is still applied to a part of the city.

Corkagh is the name of several places in other counties ; while in the form of Corkey it is found in Antrim and Donegal. And we often meet with the diminutives, Curkeen, Curkin, and Corcaghan, little marsh. *Corcas*, another form of the word, is also very common, and early English topographical writers on Ireland often speak of the corcasses or marshes as very numerous. It has given names to many places in the northern counties, now called Corkish, Curkish, Corcashy, Corkashy, &c.

Cuirreach, or as it is written in modern Irish, *currach*, has two meanings, a race course, and a morass.

In its first sense it gives name to the Curragh of Kildare, which has been used as a racecourse from the most remote ages.* In the second sense, which is the more general, it enters into names in the forms Curra, Curragh, and Curry, which are very common through the four provinces. Curraghmore, great morass, is the name of nearly thirty townlands scattered over the country; Currabaha and Currabeha, the marsh of the birch trees. There are more than thirty places, all in Munster, called Curraheen, little marsh ; and this name is sometimes met with in the forms Currin and Curreen.

Sescenn, a quagmire, a marshy, boggy, or sedgy place; it occurs in Cormac's Glossary, where it is given as the equivalent of *cuirreach.* It is used in giving names to places throughout the four provinces; and its usual modern forms are Sheskin and Seskin. Seskinrea in Carlow, grey marsh ; Sheskinatawy in the parish of Inver, Donegal, *Sescenn-a'-tsamhaidh*, the marsh of the sorrel. When it comes in as a termination, the initial *s* is often eclipsed by *t* (p. 23); as we see in Ballinteskin, the name of several places in Leinster, in Irish *Baile-an-tsescinn*, the town of the quagmire.

Riasg or *riasc* [reesk] signifies a moor, marsh, or fen. There are twenty-two townlands scattered through the four provinces, called Riesk, Reisk, Risk, and Reask ; and near Finglas in Dublin, is a place called Kilreisk, the church of the morass. *Rusg* is another form of the same word, which is much used in local nomenclature, though it is not given in the dictionaries; occurring commonly as Roosk and Rusk. The old church that gave name to the parish of Tul-

* See Mr. Hennessy's interesting paper "On the Curragh of Kildare," Proc. R. I. A.

lyrusk in Antrim, stood in the present graveyard,
which occupies the summit of a gentle hill, rising from
marshy ground: hence the name, which Colgan writes
Tulach-ruisc, the hill of the morass (Reeves, Eccl.
Ant., p. 6). The adjective forms *rusgach* and *rus-
gaidh* [roosky], are in still more general use; they
give names to all those places called Roosky, Roosk-
agh, Roosca, Rousky, and Rusky, of which there are
about fifty in the four provinces, all of which were
originally fenny or marshy places; Ballyroosky in
Donegal, the town of the marsh.

Cala or *caladh* [colla] has two distinct meanings,
reconcilable, however, with each other: 1. In some
parts of Ireland it means a ferry, or a landing place for
boats; 2. In Longford, Westmeath, Roscommon, Galway, &c., and especially along the course of the Shannon, it is used to signify a low marshy meadow along
a river or lake which is often flooded in winter, but
always grassy in summer. Callow, the modernized
form, is quite current as an English word in those
parts of the country, a "callow meadow" being a
very usual expression; and it forms part of the names
of a great many places.

There is a parish in Tipperary called Templea-
chally, the church of the *callow.* Ballinchalla is now
the name of a parish verging on Lough Mask in
Mayo. The Four Masters call it the *Port* of Lough
Mask, and it is also called in Irish the *Cala* of Lough
Mask, both meaning the landing place of Lough
Mask: the present name is anglicised from the Irish
Baile-an-chala, the town of the *callow* or landing
place.

Maethail [mway-hill] signifies soft or spongy land,
from the root *maeth* [mway] soft. The best known
example of its use is Mohill in the county Leitrim,

which is called in Irish authorities, *Maethail-Manchain*, from St. Manchan or Monaghan, who founded a monastery there in the seventh century, and who is still remembered. The parish of Mothel in Waterford is called *Moethail-Bhrogain* in O'Clery's Calendar, from St. Brogan, the patron, who founded a monastery there ; and there is another parish in Kilkenny called Mothell ; in both of which the aspirated *t* is restored (see p. 43). The term is very correctly represented by Moyhill in Clare and Meath ; and we find it also in other names, such as Cahermohill or Cahermoyle in Limerick, the stone fort of the soft land ; Knockmehill in Tipperary, the soft surfaced hill ; and Corraweehill in Leitrim, the round hill of the wet land (see Dr. Reeves's learned essay "On the Culdees," Trans. R. I. A., XXIV., 175).

Imleach [imlagh] denotes land bordering on a lake, and hence a marshy or swampy place ; the root appears to be *imeal*, a border or edge. It is a term in pretty common use in names, principally in the forms Emlagh and Emly. The most remarkable place whose name is derived from this word, is the village of Emly in Tipperary, well known as the ancient see of St. Ailbhe, one of the primitive Irish saints. In the Book of Lismore, and indeed in all the Irish authorities, it is called *Imleach-iubhair*, the lake-marsh of the yew tree. The lake, on the margin of which St. Ailbhe selected the site for his establishment, does not now exist, but it is only a few years since the last vestige of it was drained.

Miliuc [meelick], is applied to low marshy ground, or to land bordering on a lake or river, and seems synonymous with *imleach*. It occurs in Leinster, Munster, and Ulster, but it is much more general in Connaught than in the other provinces ; and in the

31

form Meelick, it is the name of about 30 townlands.
The old anglicised name of Mountmellick in Queen's
County, which is even still occasionally heard among
the people, is *Montiaghmeelick*, i. e. the bogs or boggy
land of the *meelick* or marsh; and the latter part of
the name is still retained by the neighbouring townland of Meelick.

Murbhach [Murvagh], a flat piece of land extending along the sea; a salt marsh. The word occurs
as a general term in Cormac's Glossary (*voce* "tond"),
where the sea waves are said to "*share* the grass
from off the *murbhach*." In the Book of Rights it is
spelled *murmhagh*, which points to the etymology:—
muir, the sea, and *magh*, a plain—*murmhagh*, sea
plain.

The name occurs once in the Four Masters, when
they mention *Murbhach* in Donegal, which is situated
near Ballyshannon, and is now called Murvagh. In
that county the word is still well understood, and
pretty often used to give names to places. In other
counties it is changed to Murvey, Murragh, Murroogh,
and Murreagh; and it is still further softened in the
"Murrow of Wicklow," which is now a beautiful
grassy sward, and affords a good illustration of the
use of the word. There is a small plain called *Murbhach*, in the north-west end of the great island of
Aran, from which the island itself is called in "Hy
Fiachrach," *Ara* of the plain of *Murbhach;* and the
name still lives as part of the compound *Cill-Mur-
bhaigh*, the church of the sea-plain, now anglicised
Kilmurvy.

Muirisc [murrisk] is a sea-shore marsh, and is
nearly synonymous with *murbhach*. Two places in
Connaught of this name are mentioned in the annals:—one is a district in the north of Sligo, lying

to the east of the river Easky ; and the other a narrow plain between Croagh Patrick and the sea, where
an abbey was erected on the margin of the bay,
which was called the abbey of Murrisk, and which in
its turn gave name to the barony.

Móin [mone] a bog, corresponds with Lat. *mons*,
a mountain, and the Irish word is sometimes understood in this sense. As may be expected from the
former and present abundance of bogs in Ireland, we
have a vast number of places named from them in
every part of the country ; but in numerous cases the
bogs are cut away, and the land cultivated. The
syllable *mon*, which begins a great number of names,
is generally to be referred to this word ; but there are
many exceptions, which, however, are in general
easy to be distinguished.

Monabraher, near Limerick, is called by the Four
Masters, *Moin-na-mbrathar*, the bog of the friars ; and
there are two townlands in Cork, one in Galway, and
another in Waterford, of the same name, but spelled
a little differently ; the two latter, Monambraher and
Monamraher, respectively. Monalour near Lismore,
signifies the bog of the lepers ; Monamintra, a parish
in Waterford, is anglicised from *Moin-na-mbaintreabh-
aigh* [Monamointree], the bog of the widows ; Mon-
anearla near Thurles, the earl's bog ; Moanmore,
Monmore, and Monvore, great bog.

As a termination, this word often takes the form
of *mona*, as is seen in Ballynamona and Ballinamona,
the town of the bog, the names of a great many
places in Leinster, Connaught, and Munster ; Knock-
namona, the hill of the bog. Sometimes the *m* of
this termination is aspirated (p. 19), as in Ardvone
near Ardagh in Limerick, which is in Irish *Ard
mhoin*, high bog.

The diminutive Moneen is also very much used, being the name of more than twenty townlands in all the four provinces. Moneenagunnel in King's County, is the little bog of the candles; Moneena-brone in Cavan, the little bog of the quern; Bally-mooneen, the town of the little bog. There are two other diminutives, *Mointín*, and *Mointeán*. The first is the most common, and takes the anglicised forms Moanteen, Moncteen, and Monteen: Monteena-sudder in Cork, the little bog of the tanner (see for tanners, 2nd Series, chap. VI.). The adjective *mointeach* signifies a boggy place, and it gives name to several places now called Montiagh and Mon-tiaghs.

CHAPTER VII.

ANIMALS.

ALL our native animals, without a single exception, have been commemorated in names of places. In the course of long ages, human agency effects vast changes in the distribution of animals, as well as in the other physical conditions of the country; some are encou-raged and increased; some are banished to remote and hilly districts; and others become altogether ex-tinct. But by a study of local names we can tell what animals formerly abounded, and we are able to identify the very spots resorted to by each particular kind.

Some writers have attempted to show that certain animals were formerly worshipped in Ireland, so that the literary public have lately become quite familiar-

ised with such terms as "bovine cultus," "porcine
cultus," &c.; and the main argument advanced is,
that the names of those animals are interwoven with
our local nomenclature. But if this argument be
allowed, it will prove that our forefathers had the most
extensive pantheon of any people on the face of the
earth :—they must have adored all kinds of animals
indiscriminately—not only cows and pigs, but also
geese, sea-gulls, and robin-redbreasts, and even pismires, midges, and fleas.* I instance this, not so
much to illustrate the subject I have in hands, as to
show to what use the study of local names may be
turned, when not ballasted by sufficient knowledge,
and directed by sound philosophy.

The cow. From the most remote ages, cows formed
one of the principal articles of wealth of the inhabitants of this country; they were in fact the standard
of value, as money is at the present day; and prices,
wages, and marriage portions, were estimated in cows
by our ancestors. Of all the animals known in Ireland, the cow is, accordingly, the most extensively
commemorated in local names.

The most general Irish word for a cow is *bo*, not
only at the present day, but in the oldest MSS.: in
the Sg. MS. of Zeuss it glosses *bos*, with which it is
also cognate. It is most commonly found in our
present names in the simple form *bo*, which, when it
is a termination, is usually translated " of the cow,"
though it might be also " of the cows."

* We have many names from all these :—Coumshingaun, a
well-known valley and lake in the Cummeragh mountains, south
east of Clonmel, the glen of the pismires; Cloonnameeltoge in
the parish of Kilmaimmore, Mayo, the meadow of the midges:
and in the parish of Rath, county Clare, is a hill called Knock-
aunnadrankaly, the little hill of the fleas. See 2nd Ser. chap.
XVIII.

Aghaboe in Queen's County, where St. Canice of
Kilkenny had his principal church, is mentioned by
many Irish authorities, the most ancient of whom is
Adamnan, who has the following passage in Vit. Col.,
II. 13, which settles the meaning:—"St. Canice being
in the monastery which is called in Latin *Campulus
boris* (i. e. the field of the cow), but in Irish *Achad-
bou*." This was the name of the place before the
time of St. Canice, who adopted it unchanged. The
parish of Drumbo in Down is called *Druimbo* by the
Four Masters, that is, the cow's ridge : Dunboe in
Londonderry, and Arboe in Tyrone, the fortress and
the height of the cow.

When the word occurs in the end of names in the
genitive plural, the *b* is often eclipsed by *m* (p. 22),
forming the termination *-namoe*, of the cows ; as in
Annamoe in Wicklow, which would be written in
Irish *Ath-na-mbo*, the ford of the cows, indicating
that the old ford, now spanned by a bridge at the
village, was the usual crossing-place for the cows of
the neighbourhood. At Carrigeennamoe near Mid-
dleton in Cork, the people were probably in the habit
of collecting their cows to be milked, for the name
signifies the little rock of the cows.

Laegh [lea] means a calf; it enters into names
generally in the form of *lee ;* and this, and the articled
terminations, *-nalee* and *-nalea*, are of frequent occurrence, signifying "of the calves." Ballinalee in
Longford and Wicklow, is properly written in Irish,
Bel-atha-na-laegh, the ford-mouth of the calves, a name
derived like Annamoe ; Clonleigh near Lifford is
called by the four Masters, *Cluain-laegh*, the calves'
meadow ; in Wexford there is a parish of the same
name, and in Clare another, which is called Clonlea.

Another Irish word for a calf is *gamhan* [gowan],

or in old Irish *gamuin* (Cor. Gl.), which is also much
used in the formation of names, as in Clonygowan in
King's County, which the annalists write *Cluain-na-
ngamhan*, the meadow of the calves. This word must
not be confounded with its derivative, *gamhnach*
[gownah], which, according to Cormac's Glossary,
means "a milking cow with a calf a year old;" but
which in modern Irish is used to signify simply a
stripper, i. e. a milk-giving cow in the second year
after calving. Moygownagh is the name of a parish
in Mayo; we find it written in an old poem in the
Book of Lecan, *Magh-gamhnach*, which Colgan translates " *Campus foetarum sire lactescentium vaccarum*,"
the plain of the milch cows. Cloongownagh in the
parish of Tumna in Roscommon, is written *Cluain-
gamhnach* by the Four Masters, the meadow of the
strippers; and there is a place of the same name
near Adare in Limerick. In anglicised names it is
hard to distinguish between *gamhan* and *gamhnach*,
when no authoritative orthography of the name is
accessible.

A bull is called in Irish *tarbh*, a word which exists
in cognate forms in many languages; in the three
Celtic families—Old Irish, Welsh, and Cornish—it is
found in the respective forms of *tarb, taru*, and *tarow*,
while the old Gaulish is *tarros;* and all these are
little different from the Gr. *tauros* and Lat. *taurus*.
A great number of places in every part of Ireland
have taken their names from bulls, and the word
tarbh is in general easily recognised in all its modern
forms.

There are several mountains in different counties
called Knockaterriff, Knockatarriv, and Knockatarry,
all signifying the hill of the bull. Mountarriv near
Lismore in Waterford, the bull's bog. Sometimes

the *t* is aspirated to *h* (p. 21), as in Drumherriff and
Drumharriff, a townland name common in the Ulster
counties and in Leitrim, the ridge of the bull.   Clontarf near Dublin, the scene of the great battle fought
by Brian Borumha against the Danes in 1014, is
called in all the Irish authorities *Cluain-tarbh*, the
meadow of the bulls; and there are several similar
names through the country, such as Cloontariff in
Mayo, and Cloontarriv in Kerry.   Loughaterriff and
Loughatarriff are the names of many small lakes
through the country, the original form of which is
Loch-an-tairbh (Four M.), the lake of the bull.

   Damh [dauv], an ox; evidently cognate with Lat.
dama, a deer.   How it came to pass that the same
word signifies in Irish an ox, and in Latin a deer, it
is not easy to explain.*   Devenish island near Enniskillen, celebrated in ancient times for St. Molaise's
great establishment, and at present for its round
tower and other ecclesiastical ruins, is called in all
the Irish authorities *Daimh-inis* [Davinish], which, in
the Life of St. Aidus, is translated the island of the
oxen; and there are three other islands of the same
name in Mayo, Roscommon, and Galway.   There is
a peninsula west of Ardara in Donegal, called Dawros
Head, the Irish name of which is *Damh-ros*, the headland of the oxen; and there are several other places
of the same name in Galway, Sligo, and Kerry.   We
find the word also in such names as Dooghcloon,

---

* The transfer of a name from one species of animals or
plants to another, is a curious phenomenon, and not unfrequently
met with.   The Greek *phēgos* signifies an oak, while the corresponding Latin, Gothic, and English terms—*fagus*, *bóka*, and
brech—are applied to the beech tree; and I might cite several
other instances.   See this question curiously discussed in Max
Müller's Lectures, 2nd Series, p. 222.

Doughcloyne, and Doughloon, which are modern forms of *Damh-chluain* (Hy Fiachrach), ox-meadow.

In the end of names this word undergoes a variety of transformations. It is often changed to -*duff*, or some such form, as in Clonduff in Down, which is called in O'Clery's Calendar *Cluain-Daimh*, the meadow of the ox (see Reeves, Eccles. Ant., p. 115); Legaduff in Fermanagh, and Derrindiff in Longford, the hollow, and the oak-wood of the ox. In other cases the *d* disappears under the influence of aspiration (p. 20) as in Cloonaff, Clonuff, Cloniff, and Clooniff, all the same names as Clonduff. And often the *d* is eclipsed by *n* (p. 22), as in Coolnanav near Dungarvan in Waterford, *Cuil-na-ndamh*, the corner of the oxen; Derrynanaff in Mayo, and Derrynananmph in Monaghan, the oak grove of the oxen.

The sheep. A sheep is called in Irish *caera* [kaira], gen. *caerach*, which are the forms given in the Zeuss MSS. The word seems to have been originally applied to cattle in general, for we find that Irish *caerachd* denotes cattle, and in Sanscrit, *caratha* signifies *pecus.* It is found most commonly in the end of names, forming the termination -*nageeragh*, or without the article, -*keeragh*, " of the sheep," as in Ballynageeragh, the town of the sheep; Meenkeeragh, the *meen* or mountain pasture of the sheep. The village of Glenagearey near Kingstown in Dublin, took its name from a little dell, which was called in Irish, *Gleann-na-ycaerach*, the glen of the sheep; and Glennageeragh near Clogher in Tyrone, is the same name in a more correct form. There are several islands round the coast called Inishkeeragh, the island of sheep, or mutton island, as it is sometimes translated, which must have been so called from the custom of

sending over sheep to graze on them in spring and
summer.

The horse. We have several Irish words for a
horse, the most common of which are *each* and *capall.*
Each [agh] is found in several families of languages;
the old Irish form is *ech;* and it is the same name as
the Sansc. *açra,* Gr. *hippos* (Eol. *ikkos*), Lat. *equus,*
and old Saxon *ehu.* *Each* is very often found in the
beginning of names, contrary to the usual Irish order,
and in this case it generally takes the modern form
of *augh.* At A. D. 598, the Four Masters mention
Aughris head in the north of Sligo, west of Sligo bay,
as the scene of a battle, and they call it *Each-ros,* the
ros or peninsula of the horses ; there is another place
of the same name, west of Ballymote, same county ;
and a little promontory north-west from Clifden in
Galway, is called Aughrus, which is the same name.
Aughinish and Aughnish are the names of several
places in different parts of the country, and are anglicised from *Each-inis* (Four Mast.), horse island.
They must have been so called because they were
favourite horse pastures, like "The Squince," and
Horse Island, near Glandore, "which produce a
wonderful sort of herbage that recovers and fattens
diseased horses to admiration" Smith, Hist. of
Cork, I., 271).

In the end of names it commonly forms the postfix
·agh; as in Russagh in Westmeath, which the Four
Masters write *Ros-each,* the wood of horses ; Dellan-
anagh in Cavan, *Bél-atha-na-neach,* the ford-mouth
of the horses ; Cloonagh and Clonagh, horse meadow.
Sometimes it is in the genitive singular, as in Kin-
neigh near Iniskeen in Cork, *ceann-ech* (Four Mast.),
the head or hill of the horse ; the same name as

Kineigh in Kerry, Kineagh near Kilcullen in Kildare, and Kinnea in Cavan and Donegal.

Capall, the other word for a horse, is the same as Gr. *kaballēs*, Lat. *caballus*, and Rus. *kobyla*. It is pretty common in the end of names in the form of *capple*, or with the article, -*nagappul* or -*nagapple*, as in Gortnagappul in Cork and Kerry, the field of the horses; Pollacappul and Poulacappul, the hole of the horse.

Lárach [lawragh] signifies a mare, and it is found pretty often forming a part of names. Cloonlara, the mare's meadow, is the name of a village in Clare, and of half a dozen townlands in Connaught and Munster; Gortnalaragh, the field of the mares.

The goat. The word *gabhar* [gower], a goat, is common to the Celtic, Latin, and Teutonic languages; the old Irish form is *gabar*, which corresponds with Welsh *gafar*, Corn. *gavar*, Lat. *caper*, Ang.-Sax. *haefer*. This word very often takes the form of *gover*, *gour*, or *gore* in anglicised names, as in Glenagower in Limerick, *Gleann-na-ngabhar*, the glen of the goats; Ballynagore, goats' town.

The word *gabar*, according to the best authorities, was anciently applied to a horse as well as to a goat. In Cormac's Glossary it is stated that *gabur* is a goat, and *gobur*, a horse; but the distinction was not kept up, for we find *gabur* applied to a horse in several very ancient authorities, such as the Leabhar na hUidhre, the Book of Rights, &c. Colgan remarks that *gabhur* is an ancient Irish and British word for a horse; and accordingly the name *Loch-gabhra*, which occurs in the Life of St. Aidus, published by him, is translated *Stagnum-equi*, the lake of the horse. This place is situated near Dunshaughlin in Meath, and it is now called Lagore; the lake has been long dried up, and many curious antiquities have been found in its bed.

The deer. Ireland formerly abounded in deer; they were chased with greyhounds, and struck down by spears and arrows; and in our ancient writings—in poems, tales, and romances—deer, stags, does, and fawns, figure conspicuously. They are, as might be expected, commemorated in great numbers of local names, and in every part of the country. The word *fiadh* [fee] originally meant any wild animal, and hence we have the adjective *fiadhan* [feean], wild; but its meaning has been gradually narrowed, and in Irish writings it is almost universally applied to a deer. It is generally much disguised in local names, so that it is often not easy to distinguish its modern forms from those of *fiach*, a raven, and *each*, a horse. The *f* often disappears under the influence of the article (p. 27), and sometimes without the article, as will be seen in the following examples:—

The well-known pass of Keimaneigh, on the road from Inchigeelagh to Glengarriff in Cork, is called in Irish, *Ceim-an-fhiaidh*, the *keim* or pass of the deer, which shows that it was in former days the route chosen by wild deer when passing from pasture to pasture between the two valleys of the Lee and the Ouvane; Drumanee in Derry, and Knockanee in Limerick and Westmeath, both signify the deer's hill. There is a parish in Waterford, and also a townland, called Clonea, which very well represents the correct Irish name, *Cluain-fhiadh*, the meadow of the deer. In some parts of the south the final *g* is sounded, as in Knockaneag in Cork, the same as Knockanee. When the *f* is eclipsed in the genitive plural (see p. 22), it usually forms some such termination as *na-veigh*: Gortnaveigh in Tipperary, and Gortnavea in

Galway, both represent the sound of the Irish, *Gort-na-bhfiadh*, the field of the deer ; Annaveagh in Mo-naghan, *Ath-na-bhfiadh*, deer ford.

Os signifies a fawn. The celebrated Irish bard and warrior, who lived in the third century of the Christian era, and whose name has been changed to Ossian by Macpherson, is called in Irish MSS., *Oisin* [Osheen], which signifies a little fawn ; and the name is ex-plained by a Fenian legend.

In the end of names, when the word occurs in the genitive plural, it is usually made -*nanuss*, while in the singular, it is anglicised *ish*, or with the article, -*anish*. Glenish in the parish of Currin, Monaghan, is written in Irish *Glenois*, the fawn's glen ; and there is a conspicuous mountain north of Macroom in Cork, called Mullaghanish, the summit of the fawn. Not far from Buttevant in the county of Cork, is a hill called Knocknanuss — *Cnoc-na-nos*, the hill of the fawns—where a bloody battle was fought in No-vember, 1647 : in this battle was slain the celebrated Mac-Colkitto, Alasdrum More, or Alexander Mac-donnell, the ancestor of the Macdonnells of the Glens of Antrim, whose chief was the late Right Ho-nourable Sir Alexander Macdonnell, of the board of Education.

Eilit, gen. *eilte* [ellit, eltĕ] is a doe ; Gr. *ellos*, a fawn ; O. H. Ger. *elah* ; Ang. Sax. *elch*. The word occurs in Irish names generally in the forms *elty*, *illy*, *elt*, or *ilt* ; Clonelty in Limerick and Fermanagh, and Cloonelt in Roscommon, the meadow of the doe : Rahelty in Kilkenny and Tipperary (*rath*, a fort) ; Annahilt in Down, *Eanach-eilte*, the doe's marsh.

The pig. If Ireland has obtained some celebrity in modern times for its abundance of pigs, the great numbers of local names in which the animal is com-

memorated show that they abounded no less in the
days of our ancestors. The Irish language has several words for a pig, but the most usual is *muc*,
which corresponds with the Welch *moch*, and Cornish
moh. The general anglicised form of the word is
muck; and *-namuck* is a termination of frequent occurrence, signifying " of the pigs." There is a well-
known hill near the Galties in Tipperary, called
Slievenamuck, the mountain of the pigs. Ballyna-
muck, a usual townland name, signifies pig-town ;
Tinamuck in King's County, a house (*tigh*) for pigs.
In Lough Derg on the Shannon, is a small island,
much celebrated for an ecclesiastical establishment ;
it is called in the annals, *Muic-inis*, hog island, or
Muic-inis-Riagail, from St. Riagal or Regulus, a contemporary of St. Columkille. This name would be
anglicised Muckinish, and there are several other
islands of the name in different parts of Ireland.

In early times when woods of oak and beech
abounded in this country, it was customary for kings
and chieftains to keep great herds of swine, which
fed in the woods on masts, and were tended by swine-
herds. St. Patrick, it is well known, was a swine-herd
in his youth to Milcho, king of Dalaradia ; and numerous examples might be quoted from our ancient
histories, romances, and poems, to show the prevalence
of this custom.

There are several words in Irish to denote a place
where swine were fed, or where they resorted or slept ;
the most common of which is *muclach*, which is much
used in the formation of names. Mucklagh, its most
usual form, is the name of many places in Leinster,
Ulster, and Connaught ; and scattered over the same
provinces, there are about twenty-eight townlands
called Cornamucklagh, the round hill of the piggeries.

Muiccannach [muckanagh] also signifies a swine haunt, and it gives names to about nineteen townlands in the four provinces, now called Muckanagh, Muckenagh, and Mucknagh. Muckelty, Mucker, Muckern, and Muckery, all townland names, signify still the same thing—a place frequented by swine for feeding or sleeping.

Torc [turk] signifies a boar; it is found in the Sg. MS. of Zeuss, as a gloss an *aper*. Wild boars formerly abounded in Ireland; they are often mentioned in old poems and tales; and hunting the boar was one of the favourite amusements of the people. *Turk*, the usual modern form of *torc*, is found in great numbers of names. Kanturk in Cork is written by the Four Masters, *Ceann-tuirc*, the head or hill of the boar; the name shows that the little hill near the town must have been formerly a resort of one or more of these animals; and we may draw the same conclusion regarding the well-known Toro mountain at Killarney, and Inishturk, an island outside Clew bay in Mayo, which is called in "Hy Fiachrach" *Inis-tuirc*, the boar's island, a name which also belongs to several other islands.

By the aspiration of the *t*, the genitive form, *tuirc* becomes *hirk*; as in Drumhirk, a name of frequent occurrence in Ulster, which represents the Irish, *Druimthuirc*, the boar's ridge. And when the *t* is changed to *d* by eclipse (p. 23), the termination *durk* or *nadurk* is formed; as in Edendurk in Tyrone the hill-brow of the boars.

The dog. There are two words in common use for a dog, *cu* and *madadh* or *madradh* [madda, maddra], which enter extensively into local names. Of the two forms of the latter, *madradh* is more usual in the south, and *madadh* in the rest of Ireland; they often form the terminations *-namaddy*, *-namaddoo*, and *-na-maddra*, of the dogs; as in Ballynamaddoo in Cavan, Ballynamaddree in Cork, and Ballynamaddy in Antrim, the town of the dogs: or if in the genitive singular, *-araddy*, *-araddoo*, and *-araddra*, of the dog; as in Knockaraddra, Knockaraddy, Knockawaddra, and Knockawaddy, the dog's hill.

The other word, *cu*, is in the modern language always applied to a greyhound, but according to O'Brien, it anciently signified any fierce dog. It is found in many other languages as well as Irish, as for example, in Greek, *kuōn*; Latin, *canis*; Welsh, *ci*; Gothic, *hunds*; English, *hound*; all different forms of the same primitive word. This term is often found in the beginning of names. The parish of Connor in Antrim appears in Irish records in the various forms, *Condcire*, *Condaire*, *Condere*, &c.; and the usual substitution of modern *nn* for the ancient *nd* (see p. 64), changed the name to *Conncire* and Connor. In a marginal gloss in the Martyrology of Aengus, at the 3rd Sept., the name is explained as "*Doire-na-con*, the oak-wood in which were wild dogs formerly, and she wolves used to dwell therein" (See Reeves's Eccl. Ant., p. 85).

Conlig in Down signifies the stone of the hounds; Convoy in Donegal, and Convra in Cork, both from *Con-mhagh*, hound-plain. And as a termination it usually assumes the same form, as in Clooncon and Cloncon, the hound's meadow; except when the *c* is eclipsed (p. 22), as we find in Coolnagun in Tipperary and Westmeath, the corner of the hounds.

The rabbit. It is curious that the Irish appear to have grouped the rabbit and the hare with two very different kinds of animals—the former with the dog, and the latter with the deer. *Coinín* [cunneen], the

Irish word for a rabbit, is a diminutive of *cu*, and means literally a little hound; the corresponding Latin word, *cuniculus*, is also a diminutive; and the Scandinavian *kanina,* Danish *kanin,* and English *coney,* all belong to the same family.

The word *coiuln* is in general easily recognised in names; for it commonly forms one of the terminations, *-coneen, -nagoneen,* or *-nagoneeny,* as in Kylenagoneeny in Limerick, *Coill-na-gcoininidhe,* the wood of the rabbits; Carrickoonoen in Tipperary, rabbit rock. The termination is varied in Lisnagunnion in Monaghan, the fort of the rabbits.

A rabbit warren is denoted by *coinicér* [cunnickere], which occurs in all the provinces under several forms —generally, however, easily recognised. In Carlow it is made Coneykeare; in Galway, Conicar; in Limerick, Conigar; and in King's County, Conicker. It is Connigar and Connigare in Kerry; Cunnaker in Mayo; Cunnicar in Louth; Cunnigar in Waterford; and Kinnegar in Donegal. In the pronunciation of the original the *c* and *n* coalesce very closely (like *c* and *n* in *cnoc,* p. 381), and the former is often only faintly heard. In consequence of this, the *c* sometimes disappears altogether from anglicised names, of which Nicker in Limerick, and Nickeres (rabbit warrens) in Tipperary, afford characteristic examples.

The wolf. This island, like Great Britain, was formerly much infested with wolves; they were chased like the wild boar, partly for sport, and partly with the object of exterminating them: and large dogs of a particular race, called wolfdogs, which have only very recently become extinct, were kept and trained for the purpose. After the great war in the seventeenth century, wolves increased to such an extent,

and their ravages became so great, as to call for state
interference, and wolf-hunters were appointed in various parts of Ireland.   The last wolf was killed only
about 160 years ago.

In Irish there are two distinct original words for a
wolf, *fael* and *bréach*. *Fael*, though often found in
old writings, is not used by itself in the modern language, the general word for a wolf now being *faelchu*,
formed by adding *cu*, a hound, to the original.   There
is a little rocky hill near Swords in Dublin, called
Feltrim, the name of which indicates that it must
have been formerly a retreat of wolves; in a gloss in
the Felire of Aengus, it is written *Faeldruim* [Fail-
drum], i. e. wolf-hill.

The other term *bréach* is more frequently found in
local names, especially in one particular compound,
written by the Four Masters *Breach-mhagh* [breagh-
vah], wolf-field, which in various modern forms gives
names to about twenty townlands.   In Clare, it occurs eight times, and it is anglicised Breaghra, except in one instance where it is made Breaffy; in
Donegal, Longford, and Armagh, it is Breaghy; in
Sligo and Mayo, Breaghwy; while in Fermanagh
(near Enniskillen) it becomes Breagho; and in Kerry,
Breahig.   In Cork it is still further corrupted to
Britway, the name of a parish, which in Pope Ni-
cholas's Taxation, is written *Breghmagh*.   The worst
corruption of all however is Brackley, now the name
of a lake in the north of the parish of Templeport in
Cavan.   It contains a little island on which the celebrated St. Maidoc of Ferns was born, called in old
authorities *Inis-breachmhaighe* [Inish-breaghwy], the
island of the wolf-field ; and the latter part of this
was made Brackley, which is now the name of both
island and lake.   Caherbreagh in the parish of Bally-

macelligot, east of Tralee, took its name from a stone
fort which must have been at one time a haunt of
these animals :— *Cathair-breach*, the *caher* of wolves.

There is still another term—though not an original
one—for a wolf—namely, *mac-tire* [macteera], which
is given as the equivalent of *brech* in a gloss on an
ancient poem in the Book of Leinster ; it literally
signifies "son of the country," in allusion to the
lonely haunts of the animal. By this name he is
commemorated in Knockaunvicteera, the little hill of
the wolf, a townland in the parish of Kilmoon, Clare,
where, no doubt, some old wolf long baffled the huntsman's spear and the wolfdog's fang. There is a lake
in the parish of Dromod in Kerry, about four miles
nearly east of Lough Curraun or Waterville Lake,
called Iskanamacteera, the water (*uisce*) of the wolves.

The fox. Sionnach [shinnagh] is the Irish word
for a fox—genitive *sionnaigh* [shinny] ; it often occurs
in the end of names, in the forms -*shinny* and -*shin-
nagh ;* as in Monashinnagh in Limerick, the bog of
the foxes ; Coolnashinnagh in Tipperary, and Cool-
nashinny in Cavan, the foxes' corner.

The badger. These animals like many others, must
have been much more common formerly than now, as
there are numbers of places all over Ireland deriving
their names from them. The Irish word for a badger
is *broc* [bruck] ; it is usually anglicised *brock*, and it
is very often found as a termination in the forms
-*brock*, -*nabrock*, and -*namrock*, all signifying "of the
badgers." Clonbrock in Galway, the seat of Lord
Clonbrock, is called in Irish, *Cluain-broc*, the meadow
of the badgers ; and the same name occurs in King's
and Queen's Counties ; while it takes the form of
Cloonbrock in Longford ; Meenabrock in Donegal,
the *meen* or mountain meadow of the badgers.

Brocach signifies a haunt of badgers—a badger
warren, and gives names to a great many townlands
in the four provinces, now called Brockagh, Brocka,
and Brockey. In Cormac's Glossary the form used
is *broiccannach*, which is represented by Bruckana in
Kilkenny, and by Brockna in Wicklow. There are
several Irish modifications of this word in different
parts of the country, which have given rise to corresponding varieties in anglicised names; such as
Brockernagh in King's County, Brocklagh in Longford; Brockley in Cavan; Brockra and Brockry in
Queen's County; all meaning a badger warren.

Birds. Among the animals whose names are found
impressed on our local nomenclature, birds hold a
prominent place, almost all our native species being
commemorated. *En* [ain] is the Irish for a bird at
the present day as well as from the most remote antiquity, the word being found in the Sg. MS. of Zeuss,
as a gloss on *aris.* It appears under various modifications in considerable numbers of names, often forming the termination -*nancane*, of the birds; as in
Rathnaneane and Ardnaneane in Limerick, the fort,
and the height, of the birds.

The eagle. In several wild mountainous districts,
formerly the haunts of eagles, these birds are remembered in local names. *Iolar* [iller] is the common
Irish word for an eagle, and in anglicised names it
usually forms the terminations, -*iller*, -*ilra*, and -*ulra*;
as in Slieveanilra, the eagle's mountain, in Clare;
and Coumaniller, the eagle's hollow, on the side of
Keeper Hill in Tipperary, under a rocky precipice.
The word assumes other forms—as for example, in
Drumillard, the name of four townlands in Monaghan, which is the same as Drumiller in Cavan, the
ridge of the eagle. There is a hill on the borders of

Tyrone and Derry called Craiganuller, the eagle's rock.

Seabhac [shouk or shoke], old Irish *seboc*, means a hawk, and is cognate with the Welsh *hebawg*, Ang.- Sax. *hafok*, and Eng. *hawk*. It forms part of the name of Carrickshock, a well-known place near Knocktopher in Kilkenny, which is called in Irish, *Carraig-seabhaic*, the hawk's rock, nearly the same name as Carricknashoke in Cavan. The initial *s* is often eclipsed by *t*, as in Craigatuke in Tyrone, and Carrigatuke near Keady in Armagh, *Craig-a'-tseabhaic* and *Carraig-a'-tseabhaic*, both the same name as Carrickshock.

Crows. The different species of the crow kind are very well distinguished in Irish, and the corresponding terms are often found in local names. *Préachán* [prēhaun] is a generic term, standing for any ravenous kind of bird, the various species being designated by qualifying terms: standing by itself, however, it usually signifies a crow, and as such occurs in Ardnapreaghaun in Limerick, *Ard-na-bpreach-an*, the hill of the crows; Knockaphreaghaun in Cork, Clare, and Galway, the crow's hill.

Feannog [fannoge], signifies a royston or scald crow: we find it in Tirfinnog near Monaghan, the district of the scald crows; in Carnfunnock in Antrim, where there must have been an old monumental heap, frequented by these birds; and Toberfinnick in Wexford is the scald crows' well. Buffanoky in Limerick represents the Irish *Both-fionnoice*, the hut or tent of the royston crow. Very often the *f* is eclipsed (p. 22), as in Mullanavannog in Monaghan, *Mullach-na-bhfeannog*, the scald crows' hill.

A raven is designated by the word *fiach* [feeagh], which, in anglicised names, it is often difficult to dis-

linguish from *fiadh*, a deer. There is a remarkable
rock over the Barrow, near Graiguenamanagh, called
Benaneha, or in Irish *Beann-an-fheiche*, the cliff of
the raven ; Lissaneigh in Sligo is the raven's fort ;
Carrickoneagh in Tipperary, and Carrickanee in Donegal, the raven's rock. The genitive plural with
an eclipse (p. 22) is seen in Mulnaveagh near Lifford,
and Mullynaveagh in Tyrone, the hill of the ravens.

Bran is another word for a raven : it is given in
Zeuss (Gram. Celt., p. 46) as the equivalent of *cor-
rus*, and it is explained *fiach* in Cormac's Glossary.
Brankill, the name of some places in Cavan, signifies
raven wood ; Brannish in Fermanagh, a contraction
for *Bran-inis*, raven island; and Rathbranagh near
Croom in Limerick, the fort of the ravens.

The seagull. This bird is denoted by the two
diminutives, *faileán* and *faeileóg* [feelaun, feeloge] ;
and both are reproduced in modernized names, often
forming the terminations -*naweelaun* -*naweeloge*, and
-*eelan*. Carrownaweelaun in Clare represents the
sound of the Irish *Ceathramhadh-na-bhfaeilcán*, the
quarter-land of the sea-gulls; Loughnaweeloge and
Loughaunnaweelaun, the names of some lakes and
townlands in different counties, signify the sea-gulls'
lake ; and the same name is reduced to Lough
Wheelion in King's County; Ardeclan in Donegal,
the height of the sea-gulls.

The plorer. *Feadog* [faddoge], a plover ; derived I
suppose from *fead*, a whistle, from the peculiar note
uttered by the bird. *Feadóg* generally occurs in the
end of names in the forms -*riddoge*, -*raddoge*, -*faddock*,
&c.; as in Ballynavaddog in Meath, and Balfeddock
in Louth, the townland of the plovers ; Barranafad-
dock near Lismore, the plovers' hill-top ; Moanavid-
doge near Oola in Limerick, the bog of the plovers.

The crane. *Corr* means any bird of the crane kind, the different species being distinguished by qualifying terms. Standing alone, however, it is always understood to mean a heron—generally called a crane in Ireland; and it is used very extensively in forming names, especially in marshy or lake districts, commonly in the forms *cor*, *gor*, and *gore*. Loughanagore near Kilbeggan in Westmeath, in Irish *Lochan-na-gcorr*, signifies the little lake of the cranes; the same as Corlough, the name of several lakes and townlands in different counties. Edenagor in Donegal, Annagor in Meath, and Monagor in Monaghan, signify respectively the hill-brow, the ford, and the bog, of the cranes; and the little *ros* or peninsula that juts into Lough Erne at its western extremity, must have been a favorite haunt of these birds, since it got the name of Rosscor.

The corncrake. *Tradhnach* or *treanach* means a corncrake; it is pronounced *tryna* in the south and west, but *traina* elsewhere, and anglicised accordingly. Cloonatreane in Fermanagh signifies the meadow of the corncrakes; Lugatryna in Wicklow, the corncrake's hollow. In the west and north west the word is often made *tradhlach*, as we see in Carrowntreila in Mayo, and Carrowntryla in Galway and Roscommon, the quarter-land of the corncrake.

The goose. The Irish word *gédh* [gay] a goose, has its cognates in many languages:—Sansor. *hansa*; Gr. *chen*; Lat. *anser*; O. H. Ger. *kans*; Ang-Sax. *gos* and *gandra*; Eng. *goose* and *gander*. It occurs in names almost always in the form *gay*; as in Monagay, a parish in Limerick, which is called in Irish *Moin-a'-ghedh*, the bog of the goose, probably from being frequented by flocks of wild geese: it is not easy to conjecture what gave origin to the singular name,

Ballingayrour, i. e. *Baile-an-ghédh-reamhair*, the town
of the fat goose, which we meet with in the same
county, but it might have been from the fact, that the
place was considered a good pasture for fattening
geese.   Gay Island in Fermanagh is not an English
name, as it looks; it is a half translation from *Inis-
na-ngédh*, i. e. goose island.

The duck.   The word *lacha*, gen. *lachan*, a duck, is
occasionally, though not often, found in names; the
townland of Loughloughan in the parish of Skerry,
Antrim, took its name from a little lake called *Loch-
lachan*, the lake of the ducks; and this and Loughna-
loughan are the names of several other lakelets and
pools in different parts of the country.

In the west of Ireland, the word *cadhan* [coin] is
in common use to denote a barnacle duck; and it is
a word long in use, for it occurs in old documents,
such as Cormac's Glossary, &c.   We find it in Gort-
nagoyne, i. e. *Gort-na-gcadhan*, the name of a townland in Galway, and of another in Roscommon;
and there is a lake in the parish of Burriscarra, Mayo,
called Loughnagoyne—these two names meaning,
respectively, the field and the lake of the barnacle
ducks.

The cuckoo—Irish *cuach* [coogh].   From the great
number of places all over the country containing this
word, it is evident that the bird must have been a
general favourite.   The following names include all
the principal changes in the word: Derrycoogh in
Tipperary is in Irish *Doire-cuach*, the oak-grove of
the cuckoos; Cloncough in Queen's County, the
cuckoos' meadow.   The word occurs in the gen. singular in Cloncoohy in Fermanagh, the meadow of
the cuckoo; and in Drumnacooha in Longford, the
cuckoo's ridge.   It appears in the gen. plural with an

eclipse (p. 22) in Knocknagoogh in Tipperary, and Boleynagoagh in Galway, the hill, and the dairy place, of the cuckoos. And it is still further softened down in Clontycoe in Queen's County, and Clontycoo in Cavan, the cuckoo's meadows; and in Ballynacoy in Antrim, the town of the cuckoo.

The woodcock. Creabhar [crour] means a woodcock, and is in general easy to be distinguished in names, as it is usually made either -*crour* or -*grour*, the *g* taking the place of *c* in the latter, by eclipse (p. 22). Lacka-nagrour near Bruree in Limerick, is written in Irish *Leaca-na-gcreabhar*, the hill-side of the woodcocks; Gortnagrour in Limerick (*Gort*, a field); Coolna-grower in King's County and Tipperary, the wood-cock's corner.

The blackbird. The Irish word for a blackbird is *lon* or *londubh*, and the former is found, though not often, in names. The Four Masters mention a place in Tyrone, called *Coill-na-lon*, the wood of the black-birds; and this same name occurs in Meath in the modernized form, Kilnalun.

The thrush. Smól or *smólach* [smole, smólagh] is a thrush. The best known name containing the word is *Gleann-na-smól*, the valley of the thrushes, the scene of a celebrated Irish poem, which is believed to be the same place as Glennasmole, a fine valley near Tallaght, Dublin, where the river Dodder rises. Near Lifford in Donegal, is a townland called Glensmoil, which represents the Irish *Gleann-a-smoil*, the thrush's glen.

The skylark. Fuiseóg [fwishoge] is a lark. It occurs in Rathnafushogue in Carlow, the fort of the larks; in Knocknawhishoge in Sligo, lark-hill; and in Kilnabushoge near Clogher in Tyrone, the wood of the larks.

Birds' nests. The word *nead* [nad] signifies a

nest ; in Cormac's Glossary it is given in the old Irish
form *net ;* Welsh, *nyth ;* Cornish, *neid ;* Breton, *neiz ;*
Manx, *edd.* It is of very frequent occurrence in
names, generally in the forms *nad, ned,* and *nid.*
There are three townlands in Cavan, Fermanagh,
and Derry, called Ned ; Nedeen, little nest, is the
name of the spot on which Kenmare stands, and the
town itself is often called by that name. There are
many high cliffs in mountainous districts, the resorts
of eagles in times gone by, which still retain the name
of Nadanuller, the eagle's nest ; and they have in
some cases given names to townlands. Nadnaveagh
in Roscommon, and Nadneagh in King's County,
signify—the first, the nest of the ravens ; the second,
of the raven ; Nadaphreaghane, a hill six miles north
of Derry, the crow's nest. Athnid, the ford of the
nest, is a parish in Tipperary ; Drumnid is a townland near Mohill in Leitrim ; and there is another in
the parish of Magherally, Down, called Drumneth,
both meaning the ridge of the nests ; Derrynaned
in Mayo, the oakwood of the birds' nests.

CHAPTER VIII.

PLANTS.

As with the animal world, so it is with the vegetable—
all the principal native species of plants are commemorated in local names, from forest trees down to
the smallest shrubs and grasses ; and where cultivation has not interfered with the course of nature,
there are still to be found many places, that to this
day produce in great abundance the very species
that gave them names many hundreds of years ago.

Woods. All our histories, both native and English, concur in stating that Ireland formerly abounded
in woods, which covered the country down to a comparatively recent period; and this statement is fully
borne out by the vast numbers of names that are
formed from words signifying woods and trees of
various kinds. According to our historians, one of
the bardic names of Ireland was *Inis-na-bhfiodh-
bhaidh* [Inish-na-veevy], woody island. If a wood
were now to spring up in every place bearing a name
of this kind, the country would become once more
clothed with an almost uninterrupted succession of
forests.

There are several words in Irish for a wood, the
principal of which are *coill* and *fidh.* *Coill* is represented by various modern forms, the most common
being *kil* and *kyle;* and as these also are the usual
anglicised representatives of *cill,* a church, it is often
difficult, and not unfrequently impossible, to distinguish them. Whether the syllables *kil* and *kyle* mean
church or wood, we can ascertain only by hearing the
names pronounced in Irish—for the sounds of *cill* and
coill are quite distinct—or by finding them written
in some Irish document of authority.

I have already conjectured (p. 313) that about a
fifth of the *kils* and *kills* that begin names are woods :
the following are a few examples:—Kilnamanagh, a
barony in Tipperary, the ancient patrimony of the
O'Dwyers, is called by the Four Masters, *Coill-
na-manach,* the wood of the monks. The barony of
Kilmore near Charleville in Cork, whose great forest
was celebrated in the wars of Elizabeth, is called
Coill-mhor, great wood, in the annals; but the vast
majority of the Kilmores, of which there are about
eighty—are from *Cill-mór,* great church. O'Meyey,

who killed Hugh de Lacy at Durrow, fled, according
to the Four Masters, "to the wood of *Coill-an-chlair*"
(the wood of the plain); this wood is gone, but it
was situated near Tullamore, and the place is still
known by the name of Kilclare. The word Kyle,
which very often stands for *cill*, in many cases also
means a wood; as in Kylemore (lake), great wood,
near the Twelve Pins in Connemara.

Coill assumes other forms, however, in which it is
quite distinguishable from *cill*; as in Barnacullia, a
hamlet on the eastern face of the Three Rock mountain near Dublin, *Barr-na-coille*, the top of the wood;
and this wood is still in existence; Barnakillew in
Mayo, and Barnakilly in Derry, same meaning; Lis-
nacullia in Limerick, wood fort; Ballynakillew, the
town of the wood. The diminutive *coillin* gives names
to several places, now often called either in whole or
part, Culleen; Ardakillen in the parish of Killukin,
Roscommon, is called by the Four Masters, *Ard-an-
choillin*, the height of the little wood; and *coilltean*
[kyle-tawn], which is sometimes applied to a growth
of underwood, sometimes to a "little wood," is represented by Kyletaun near Rathkeale in Limerick.

The plural of *coill* is *coillte* [coiltha], which is often
found in some of the Connaught counties in the forms
of *cuilty*, *cuiltia* and *cultia*; as in Cuiltybo in Mayo
and Roscommon, the woods of the cows. In Clare
there are some places called Quilty, which is the same
word; and we also find Keelty and Keelties, as the
names of several townlands. But its most common
form is *kilty*, except in Munster, where it is not much
used; this begins the names of about forty townlands,
chiefly in the western and north western counties,
several, however, occurring in Longford; Kiltyclogher
and Kiltyclogh in Leitrim, Longford, and Tyrone,

signify stony woods; Killybegs in Longford and
Monaghan, little woods; Kiltynashinnagh in Leitrim,
the woods of the *shinnaghs* or foxes. *Coillidh* [quilly]
is a derivative of *coill* in common use to signify woodland; it is found frequently in the form of Cully—as,
for example, Cullycapple in Londonderry, the woodland of the horses; and it is very often made Quilly,
which is the name of some places in Derry, Waterford, and Down.

Fidh or *fiodh* [fih], the other term for wood, is
found in both the Celtic and Teutonic languages.
The old Irish form is *fid*, which glosses *arbor* in Sg.
(Zeuss, p. 65); and it corresponds with the Gaulish
eidu, Welsh *guid*, O. H. German *witu*, Ang.-Saxon
vudu, English *wood*. Its most usual modern forms
are *fee, fi*, and *feigh*; thus Feebane, white wood, near
Monaghan; Feebeg and Feemore (little and great)
near Borrisokane; and it is occasionally made *foy*,
but this may be also a modern form of *faithche*, a
play-green (see p. 295). At the mouth of the river
Fergus in Clare, there is an island called Feenish, a
name shortened from *Fidh-inis*, woody island; we find
the same name in the form of Finish in Galway, while
it is made Finnis in Cork and Down. The parish
of Feighcullen in Kildare is mentioned by the Four
Masters, who call it *Fiodh-Chuilinn*, Cullen's Wood;
and Fiddown in Kilkenny, they write *Fidh-duin*, the
wood of the fortress.

Sometimes the aspirated *d* in the end is restored
(p. 42), as we find in Fethard, a small town in Tipperary, which the annalists write *Fiodh-ard*, high
wood; there is also a village in Wexford of the same
name; and Feeard in the parish of Kilballyowen in
Clare, exhibits the same compound, with the *d* aspirated. So also in Kilfithmone in Tipperary; the

latter part (fithmone) represents the ancient Irish
name, *Fiodh-Mughaine*, the wood of *Mughain* (a woman):—Kilfithmone, the church of Mugania's wood.

There are two baronies in Armagh called Fews,
which are mentioned in the Four Masters at A. D.
1452, by the name of *Feadha* [Fä], i. e. woods ; which
is modernized by the adoption of the English plural
form (p. 32) ; and Fews, the name of a parish in
Waterford, has the same origin. There was a district in Roscommon, west of Athlone, which in the
annals is also called *Feadha* ; but it is now commonly
called the Faes (i. e. the woods) of Athlone.

This word has some derivatives which also con-
tribute to the formation of names. *Fiodhach* [feeagh]
signifies a woody place, and all those townlands now
called Feagh and Feeagh, which are found distributed over the four provinces, derive their names
from it. *Fiodhnach* [Feenagh], which has exactly
the same meaning, was the old name of Fenagh in
Leitrim (Four Masters) ; and though now bare of
trees, it was wooded so late as the seventeenth century. There are several other places called Fenagh
and Feenagh, which have the same original name.
Feevagh in Roscommon, is called in Irish, *Fiodhbhach*,
which also signifies a place covered with wood.

Ros, as I have already stated, has several meanings, one of which is a wood ; and in this sense we
often find it in names, especially in the south. There
is a place called Rosserk near Killala at the mouth
of the Moy in Mayo. It is called in Irish *Ros-Serce*
(Searc's wood), and we learn from Mac Firbis (Hy
Fiachrach, p. 51) that "it is so called from Searc the
daughter of Carbery, son of Awley (see p. 138, *supra*),
who blessed the village and the wood which is at the
mouth of the river Moy." The original church

founded by the virgin saint Searc in the sixth century, has long since disappeared ; but the place contains the ruins of a beautiful little abbey. Roscrea in Tipperary is written in the Book of Leinster, *Ros-Cre*, Cre's wood. Roskeen, the name of several places, represents the Irish *Ros-cacin*, beautiful wood ; Rossnamanniff near Templemore in Tipperary, the wood of the *bonnires* or young pigs (*b* eclipsed, see p. 22).

New Ross in Wexford, notwithstanding its name, is an old place ; for Dermot Mac Murrough built a city there in the twelfth century, the ruins of which yet remain.   It is called in the annals, *Ros-mic-Treoin* [Rosmicrone], the wood of the son of Treun, a man's name ; the people still use this name corrupted to *Rosemacrone* ; and they think the town was so called from a woman named Rose Macrone, about whom they tell a nonsensical story. St. Coman, from whom was named Roscommon (Coman's wood), founded a monastery there, and died, according to the Four Masters, in 746 or 747, but other authorities place him much earlier. Ross Carbery in Cork, was formerly a place of great ecclesiastical eminence ; and it was "so famous for the crowds of students and monks flocking to it, that it was distinguished by the name of *Ros-ailithir*" [allihir : Four Masters], the wood of the pilgrims. Rusheen, a diminutive, and the plural Rusheens, are the names of a great many townlands in Munster and Connaught ; the word is often applied to a growth of small bushy trees or underwood, as well as to a wood small in extent. The word *ros* is often written with *a* instead of *o*, both in old records and in anglicised names ; as in Rasheen Wood, near the Dundrum station of the Great Southern and Western railway.

Fásach [faussagh], a very expressive word, derived from *fas*, growth, signifies a wilderness or an uncultivated place. It gives names to some townlands now called Fasagh and Fassagh ; the territory along the river Dinin in Kilkenny, which now forms a barony, is called Fassadinin, the wilderness of the Dinin : Fassaroe in Wicklow, red wilderness.

Scairt [scart] denotes a cluster of bushes, a thicket, a scrubby place. In the form Scart, with the diminutive Scarteen, it gives names to numerous places, but only in the Munster counties and Kilkenny. Scartlea, grey thicket, is the name of a village in Cork, and of some townlands in Waterford and Kerry ; Scartaglin near Castleisland, the thicket of the glen ; Ballinascarty in the parish of Kilmaloda, Cork, the town of the thicket.

Muine [munny], a brake or shrubbery. It occurs frequently in names, generally in the form of *money*, which constitutes or begins about 170 townland names through the four provinces. The word is also sometimes applied to a hill, so that its signification is occasionally doubtful. It is probably to be understood in the former sense in the name of Monaghan, which is called in Irish *Muineachán* (Four Mast.), a diminutive of *muine*, signifying little shrubbery. There are three townlands in Down called Moneydorragh, i. e. *Muine-dorcha*, dark shrubbery ; Ballymoney, the town of the shrubbery, is the name of many places through the country ; Magheraculmoney in Fermanagh, the plain of the back of the shrubbery ; Monivea in Galway is called in Irish authorities, *Muine-an-mheadha* [Money-an-va : Four Mast.], the shrubbery of the mead, very probably because the drink was brewed there.

The compound *Liathmhuine* [Leewinny], grey

shrubbery, is often used to form names, and is variously modified; such as we see in Leaffony in Sligo, Leafin in Meath, Liafin and Lefinn in Donegal, and Leighmoney in Cork; Cloghleafin, near Mitchelstown in Cork, the castle of the grey thicket.

Gaertha [gairha], is used in the south to denote a woodland along a river, overgrown with small trees, bushes, or underwood; it is almost confined to Cork and Kerry, and generally appears in the forms of Gearha and Gearagh; and occasionally Geeragh and Gairha. There is a well-known place of this kind near Macroom, where a dense growth of underwood extends for three or four miles along the Lee, and it is universally known by the name of Gearha. Tourists who have seen Coomiduff near Killarney, will remember the Gearhameen river which flows through it into the upper lake of Killarney; the postfix *meen*, Irish *min*, signifies literally smooth, fine, or small, indicating that this *gearha* was composed of a growth of small delicate bushes. There is also a Gearhameen west of Bantry in Cork.

Garrán is a shrubbery. There are a great many places in Munster and Connaught called Garran, Garrane, and Garraun, all derived from this word. It is also found in Leinster, but not often, except in Kilkenny; and it occurs half a dozen times in Monaghan, but I have not found it elsewhere in Ulster. Garranamanagh, the name of a parish in Kilkenny, signifies the shrubbery of the monks; and there is another parish in Cork called Garranekinnefeake, the shrubbery of Kinnefeake, a family name. Ballingarrane, Ballygarran, Ballygarrane, and Ballygarraun, all townland names, signify the town of the shrubbery.

A tree. The common word for a tree is *crann*, and

it has retained this form unchanged from the earliest
ages, for *crann* occurs in the Zeuss MSS. as a gloss
on *arbor*: Welsh *pren*; Armoric *prenn*. This word
forms part of the names of many places, in every one
of which there must have once stood a remarkable tree,
and for a time sufficiently long to impress the name.

In the nominative, it generally takes the forms
Crann and Cran, which are the names of townlands
in Armagh, Cavan, and Fermanagh; and constitute
the beginning of many names; such as Crandaniel in
Waterford, Daniel's tree; Crancam in Roscommon
and Longford, crooked tree; Cranlome in Tyrone,
bare tree; Cranacrower in Wexford, the woodcocks'
tree.

The genitive case, *crainn*, is usually pronounced
crin or *creen*, and the form is modified accordingly
when it occurs as a termination: Crossmacrin in
Galway is written in Irish, *Cross-maighe-crainn*, the
cross of the plain of the tree. Drominacreen in Limerick, the little hill of the tree; Corcrain in Armagh
(*Cor*, a round hill); and Carrowcrin, the name of
several places, the quarter-land of the tree. With
the *c* eclipsed, the termination is usually -*nagran*, as
in Ballynagran, a common townland name, *Baile-na-
gcrann*, the town of the trees. The adjective *cran-
nach* signifies arboreous—a place full of trees; and
from this a great many townlands and rivers, now
called Crannagh, have received their names.

Bile [billa] signifies a large tree; it seems connected with Sanso. *bala*, a leaf, the more so as *bilcóg*,
the diminutive of the Irish word, also denotes a leaf.
Bile was generally applied to a large tree, which, for
any reason, was held in veneration by the people;
for instance, one under which their chiefs used to be
inaugurated, or periodical games celebrated.

Trees of this kind were regarded with intense reverence and affection; one of the greatest triumphs that a tribe could achieve over their enemies, was to cut down their inauguration tree, and no outrage was more keenly resented, or when possible, visited with sharper retribution. Our annals often record their destruction as events of importance; at 981 for example, we read in the Four Masters, that the *bile* of *Magh-adhar* [Mah-ire] in Clare, the great tree under which the O'Briens were inaugurated—was rooted out of the earth, and cut up, by Malachy, king of Ireland; and at 1111, that the Ulidians led an army to Tullahogue, the inauguration place of the O'Neills, and cut down the old trees; for which Niall O'Lough-lin afterwards exacted a retribution of 3000 cows.

These trees were pretty common in past times; some of them remain to this day, and are often called *Bell* trees, or *Bellow* trees, an echo of the old word *bile*. In most cases, however, they have long since disappeared, but their names remain on many places to attest their former existence. The word *bile* would be correctly anglicised *billa*, as we find it in Lisnabilla in Antrim, the fort of the ancient tree.

As a termination it assumes several forms; and it is in some places used in the masouline, and in others in the feminine (see p. 518). It is very often made -*rilla*, in which case it is likely to be mistaken for the English word *rilla*. The well-known song "Lovely Kate of Garnavilla," will be in the recollection of many people. The home of the celebrated beauty lies near the town of Caher in Tipperary, and its Irish name is *Garran-a'-bhile*, the shrubbery of the ancient tree. Gortavella and Gortavilly are the names of two townlands in Cork and Tyrone (*Gort*, a field); Knockavilla in several counties (*knock*, a hill); and

33*

there are many places called Aghavilla, Aghaville,
and Aghavilly, the field (*achadh*) of the old tree. At
Rathvilly in Carlow, one of these trees must have, at
some former time, flourished on or near an ancient
fort, for it is written by the annalists *Rath-bile;* and
in the King's County, there is a place of the same
name, but spelled Rathvilla.

In some parts of Ireland, especially in the south,
the word is pronounced *bella*, as if spelled *beile*, and
this form is perpetuated in the names of many places,
for instance Bellia, a village in Clare, and Bellew in
Meath; Ballinvella in Waterford, the town of the
old tree, the same as Ballinvilla, the name of places
in various counties. Near the entrance to Cork harbour there is a small peninsula called Ringabella, the
rinn or point of the ancient tree, which has given
name to the little bay near it.

Craebh [crave] signifies either a branch or a large
wide-spreading tree. The name, like *bile*, was given
to large trees, under whose shadows games or religious
rites were celebrated, or chiefs inaugurated; and we
may conclude that one of these trees formerly grew
wherever we find the word perpetuated in a name.
Creeve, the most usual modern form, is the name of
a great many places. In several cases, the *bh* is represented by *w*, changing the word to Crew, which
is the name of ten or twelve places in the northern
counties. Crewhill in Kildare, is merely the phonetic
representation of *Craebh-choill*, branchy wood, or a
wood of branchy trees; Loughcrew, a small lake in
Meath, giving name to a parish, is called in Irish,
Loch-craeibhe, the lake of the branchy tree; and the
village of Mullacrew in Louth is *Mullach-craeibhe*,
the hill' of the tree. There are more than thirty
townlands called Creevagh, i. e. branchy or bushy

land. The name of the parish of Cruagh at the base of the mountains south of Dublin city, has the same original form, for we find it written "Creuaghe" and "Crevaghe" in several old documents; and Creevy, which is a modification of the same word, is the name of about twenty others: in Monaghan and Tyrone we find some places called Derrycreevy, which signifies branchy *derry* or oak wood. Near the town of Antrim, is a townland called Creevery, and another in Donegal called Crevary; both of which are from the Irish *Craebhaire*, a branchy place.

The oak. We know as a historical fact, that this country formerly abounded in forests of oak, and that for many ages the timber continued to be exported to England; it appears to have been the most plentiful of all Irish trees; and we find it commemorated in local names to a greater extent than any other vegetable production.

Dair [dŭr], the common Irish word for oak, is found in many of the Indo-European languages; the Sansc. *dru* is a tree in general, which is probably the primary meaning, whence it came to signify "oak," which is the meaning of the Greek *drus;* Welsh *dar;* and Armoric *deró*.

The old Irish form of the word, as found in the Zeuss MSS., is *daur*, and this is preserved nearly in its purity in the name of the Daar, a little river flowing by Newcastle in Limerick, which the people call *Ahhainn-na-dárach*, the river of the oak. There is a place near Foynes in the Shannon, called Durnish; Dernish is the name of three islands in Clare, Fermanagh, and Sligo, ; and we have also Derinch and Derinish; all of which are from *Dair-inis*, as we find it written in "Wars of GG.," signifying oak island.

The genitive of *dair* is *darach* or *dara*, which is

very common in the end of names, in the forms of
-*daragh*, -*dara*, and -*dare*.   Adare in Limerick is
always called in Irish documents, *Ath-dara*, the ford
of the oak tree, a name which shows that a great oak
must have for many generations shaded the ford
which in ancient times crossed the Maigue.   There
is a place of the same Irish name near Dromore in
Tyrone, but now called Aghadarragh ; and we have
Clondarragh in Wexford, the meadow of the oak ;
Lisnadarragh, the fort of the oak.   *Darach*, an adjective formation, signifies a place full of oaks; the
ancient form is *daurauch*, which in the Zuess MSS.,
glosses *quercetum*, i. e. an oak grove.   It gives name
to Darragh, a parish in the south east of Limerick,
where oaks still grow ; and there are places of the
same name in Down and Clare.

Doire or *daire* [derry] is an oak wood, and is
almost always represented in anglicised names by
derry or *derri*.   Derrylahan, a very usual name, signifies broad oak-wood ; the wood still remains on the
side of a hill at Glendalough in Wicklow, that gave
it the name of Derrybawn (*bán*, whitish), and this is
also the name of other places ; Derrykeighan, a
parish in Antrim, is called in Irish, *Doire-Chaechain*
(Four Mast.), Caechan's, or Keeghan's grove.   When
doire is joined with the gen. masc. of the article, it
becomes in English *derrin*, which begins many names.
Thus Derrinlaur, a townland in which are the ruins
of a castle, in Waterford, not far from Clonmel, is
mentioned by the Four Masters, who write the name
Doire-an-lair, middle *derry*.   And sometimes it is
contracted to *der*, as in Dernagree in Cork, the same
as Derrynagree in other places, the wood of the cattle ; Derradd in Westmeath, and Derrada in the
Connaught counties, which are the same as Derryadd

in the middle and north of Ireland, Derryadda in
Mayo, and Derryfadda in the south and west—all
from *Doire-fhada*, long oak-wood, the *f* being aspirated
and omitted in some (see p. 20).

The most ancient name of Londonderry, according
to all our authorities, was *Daire-Calgaich* [Derry-
Calgagh]; Adamnan, in one place uses this name,
and elsewhere he translates it *Roboretum-Calgachi*,
the oak wood of Calgach. Calgach was a man's name
common among the ancient Irish, signifying " fierce
warrior;" and in the Latinized form of Galgacus,
readers of Tacitus will recognise it, as the name of
the hero who led the Caledonians at the battle of the
Grampians.

Daire-Calgaich was the old pagan name, used for
ages before St. Columba erected his monastery there
in 546: it was retained till the tenth or eleventh century, when the name Derry-Columkille began to prevail, in memory of its great patron, and continued
down till the time of James I., whose charter, granted
to a company of London merchants, imposed the
name " *Londonderry.*"

We have several interesting notices of the *derry*, or
oak wood, that gave name to this place; we find it
in existence more than 600 years after the time of
St. Columba; for the Four Masters, at 1178, record :—
"A violent wind-storm occurred this year; it caused
a great destruction of trees. It prostrated oaks. It
prostrated one hundred and twenty trees in Derry-
Columkille.

The word *doire* is one of the most prolific roots in
Irish names; and if we recollect that wherever it occurs an oak wood once flourished, we shall have a
good idea of the great abundance of this tree in past
ages. Over 1300 names begin with the word in its

various forms, and there are innumerable places
whose names contain it as a termination. Derreen,
little oak wood, is also of very frequent occurrence,
chiefly in Munster and Connaught, and occasionally
in Leinster and Ulster; Derreenataggart in Cork, the
little oak grove of the *sagart* or priest. We have at
least one example of the diminutive in *án*, in Derrane
in Roscommon, which is mentioned by the Four
Masters under the name of *Doireán*.

There is yet another derivative of *dair* in pretty
common use, namely *dairbhre*, which is now universally pronounced *darrery*, the aspirated *b* being wholly
sunk. According to O'Reilly, it sometimes means an
oak; but it is generally used to signify an oak forest,
or a place abounding in oaks. Valentia island is well
known in our ancient literature by the name of *Dairbhre*, as the principality of the great druid Mogh-
Ruith, who played so important a part at the siege
of Knocklong (see p. 101). The island is now always
called *Darrery* in Irish, by the people of Munster—
a conclusive proof that the word *darrery* in the modern language, is identical with the ancient *dairbhre*.

There are two townlands in Galway, one in Cork,
and one in Limerick, called Darrery; we find Darra-
ragh in Mayo, and Darrary in Cork and Galway;
Dorrery occurs near Carrick-on-Shannon; and this
same form is preserved in Kildorrery, the church of
the oaks, a village in the north of the county Cork,
where the ruins of an old church are still to be seen;
written Kill-darire in the Registry of Clonmacnoise.
Carrigdarrery in the parish of Kilmurry in Cork,
the rock of the oaks. We have one notable example
of the preservation of the full ancient pronunciation
in Lough Derravara in Westmeath, whose Irish

name, as used in the annals is *Loch Dairbhreac*
the lake of the oaks.

Ráil or *rál* [rawl] is another term for an oak, which
we find used in the best authorities; and it often occurs in names, but nearly always in the genitive form,
rálach [rawlagh]. Drumralla near Newtown Butler
in Fermanagh is written by the Four Masters, *Druim-
rálach*, the ridge of the oak. There is a place in
Queen's County called Ballinrally, the town of the
oak; another near Athlone, called Cloonrollagh
(meadow); and a third in Cork, called Ardraly
(height). Ralaghan, the name of some townlands in
Cavan and Monaghan; and Rallagh near Banagher
in Derry, both signify a place of oaks.

There is yet another word for an oak, namely, *omna;*
it occurs in Cormac's Glossary and in the Book of
Armagh, but it is less used in names than the others;
and as it is not liable to corruption, it is plainly dis-
cernible when it occurs. It forms part of the name
of Portumna, a little town on the Galway side of the
Shannon, which the Four Masters write *Port-omna*,
the *port* or landing place of the oak; it is also seen
in Gortnahomna near Castlemartyr in Cork, the field
of the oak; and in Drumumna in Clare, oak ridge.

The ash. In the south and west of Ireland there
are three names for the common ash—all modifications of the same original, viz.:—*fuinnse, fuinnseann,*
and *fuinnseóg* [funsha, funshan, funshoge]; the last,
which is the most modern, is almost universally used,
and the others are nearly forgotten. In the north
the *f* is omitted (see p. 27), and the word always employed is *uinnseann* [unshan].

The name of the river Funcheon in Cork—the ash-
producing river—preserves one of the old forms; and
we find it also in Funshin and Funshinagh, the names

of several places in Connaught; while the northern form appears in Unshinagh and Inshinagh, which are common townland names :—all these mean land abounding in ash trees. Funchoge, which has the same signification, occurs in Wexford, and we find this form as far north as Louth ; while without the *f*, it becomes Unshog in the parish of Tynan, Armagh, and Hinchoge near Raheny in Dublin.

The birch. Beith [beh]. the birch tree ; cognate with the first syllable of the Latin *betula*, which is a diminutive. Great numbers of places have received their names from this tree : and some of the most common derivatives are Beagh, Behagh, Bahagh, Behy, and Beaghy ; which are all modifications of *Beitheach* and *Beithigh*, birch land, and are found in every part of Ireland. We find several other places called Bahana, Behanagh, Beheenagh, and Behernagh—all meaning a place abounding in birch. The village of Kilbeheny in Tipperary, near Mitchelstown, is called in the Four Masters, *Coill-beithne*, birch-wood ; and this interpretation is corroborated by the fact, that the place is situated at the point where the little river Behanagh (birch-producing river) joins the Funcheon.

In the end of names, the word takes various forms, the most common of which is *behy ;* as we find in Ballaghbehy in Limerick, and Ballaghnabehy in Leitrim, the birchy road. Other forms are seen in the following :—the Irish name of Ballybay in Monaghan, is *Bel-atha-beithe* [Bellabehy], the ford-mouth of the birch ; and they still show the ford, on which a few birches grow, or grew until recently, that gave name to the town. Aghavea in Fermanagh is always called in the annals, *Achadh-beithe* (Four Masters), birch-field, the same name as Aghaveagh in Donegal and Tyrone. Coolavehy near Ballyorgan in Limerick,

the corner of the birch; Kilbaha in Kerry and Clare,
birch wood.

The elm. This tree is denoted by *leamh* [lav],
which has relatives in several other languages, such
as Latin *ulmus*, Ang-Sax. *ellm*, Eng. *elm*, &c. The
simple Irish form is hardly ever heard in the present
spoken language, the diminutive *leamhan* [lavaun]
being used in the south, and *sleamhan* [slavan] in the
north. These words enter largely into names, and
are subject to some curious transformations; but the
most general recognisable forms are *leran, leevan*, and
leraun, which are generally terminations, and signify
abounding in elms.

In the parish of Inishmacsaint in Fermanagh, there
is a place called Glenlevan, elm glen; Ballylevin, the
town of elms, in King's County and Donegal; Lis-
levane, elm fort, in the parish of Abbeymahon, Cork;
Drumleevan in Leitrim, and Dromalivaun near
Tarbert in Kerry, elm ridge. The form with an
initial *s* is often found in the northern counties; as
in Carrickslavan in Leitrim, the rock of the elms;
Mullantlavan in the parish of Magheracloone, Monaghan, elm hill, the *s* being eclipsed—*Mul'-an-tsleamh-
ain* (see p. 23).

The river Laune, flowing from the lower lake of
Killarney, is called *Leamhain* in the Irish annals, i. e.
the elm river; and this is its Irish name at the present day, for the nasal sound of the aspirated *m* is
distinctly heard in the pronunciation. *Leamhain*
[Lavin] is also the original name of the river Leven
in Scotland, for so we find it written in Irish documents, such as the Irish version of Nennius, &c.; and
the river has given name to the territory of Lennox,
which is merely a modern corruption of its old name
Leamhna (Reeves' Adamnan, p. 379).

As a termination, the simple form *leamh* is seen in Drumlamph, elm ridge, near Maghera in Derry. There is a derivative term, *leamhraidhe* [lavree], signifying a place of elms, which is anglicised Lowery in Fermanagh and Donegal, and which also gives name to Mullanalamphry, a townland near Donegal town, the little hill of the elms. Lavagh, the English form of *Leamhach*, a place of elms, is the name of some townlands in the midland and western counties. The oblique form *Leamhaidh* [Lavy : see p. 34], is very correctly anglicised Lavey, the name of a parish in Cavan; and with the aspirated *m* restored (see p. 44), we see the same word in Lammy, the name of some townlands in Tyrone and Fermanagh.

An elm wood was called *Leamhchoill* [lavwhill], and this compound, subject to various alterations, exists at the present day, showing where these woods formerly flourished. The usual anglicised forms are Laughil, Laghil, Laghile, Loghill, and Loughill—the names of many places in the middle, south, and west of Ireland; Cloonlaughil in Leitrim and Sligo, the meadow of the elm wood. But the most curious transformation is Longfield (for which see p. 40); in Tyrone, near Lough Neagh, occurs a kind of metamorphic form in Magheralamfield the plain of the elm wood.

The yew. Of all European trees the yew is believed to attain the greatest age; there are several individual yews in England which are undoubtedly as old as the Christian era, and some are believed to be much older. We have some very old yews in Ireland also; one, for instance, at Clontarf, has probably reached the age of six or seven hundred years; and at the ruined castle of Aughnanure (field of the yews) near Oughterard in Galway, there is yet to be

seen one venerable solitary yew, the sole survivor of
those that gave name to the place, which cannot be
less than 1000 years old.

We have two words for the yew tree, evidently of
the same origin, and both very common in names,
viz. *eó* [o or yo] and *iubhar* [oor or yure]. *Eó* is
common to the Celtic, Teutonic, and Classical languages :—Low Lat. *irus*, Fr. *if*, Welsh *yw*, Arm. *irin ;*
Ang.-Sax. *ir*, Eng. *yew*. "As the yew is distinguished by its remarkable longevity, one may conjecture a connection of the O. H. German *iwa* with
éwa eternity, Gr. *aíōn*, Lat. *œvum*, Goth. *airs* "[Eng.
age and *ever*] (Pictet, "Origines "). Cormac mac
Cullenan made the same observation a thousand years
ago in his Glossary, when he derived *iubhar* from *eó*,
ever, and *barr*, top, "because it never loses its top ;
i. e. it is ever-green."

In the seventh century, St. Colman, an Irish monk,
having retired from the see of Lindisfarne, returned
to his native country, and erected a monastery at a
place called *Magh-eó* or *Mageo* (Bede), the plain of
the yews, in which he settled a number of English
monks whom he had brought over with him. For
many ages afterwards, this monastery was constantly
resorted to by monks from Britain, and hence it
is generally called in the annals *Magheo-na-Saxan*
i. e. Mayo of the Saxons. The ruins of the old abbey
still remain at the village ; and from this place the
county Mayo derives its name. Mayo is also the
name of several other places, and in all cases it has
the same signification. There is a parish in Clare,
taking its name from an old church, called in the
annals *Magh-neó*, now Moynoe, which is the same
name as Mayo, only with the addition of the *n* of the
old genitive plural. The word *eó* is very often re-

presented by *o* or *oe* as a termination, as in Killoe in
Longford, *Cill-eó* (O'Cl. Cal.), the church of the
yews : Gleno and Glenoe, yew glen.

The compound *eóchaill* [ohill], signifying yew wood,
in various modern forms gives names to a great many
places.   The best known is Youghal at the mouth of
the Blackwater (*Eochaill;* Four Mast.), which was so
called from an ancient yew wood that grew on the
hill slope where the town now stands ; and even yet
some of the old yews remain there.   The term is
more common, however, in the form Oghill, which is
the name of about twenty townlands in various counties.   It occurs in Tipperary as Aughall, and in Derry
as Aughil; the plural forms, Oghilly, Oghly, and
Aghilly (yew woods), are found in Galway and Donegal ; and the English plural, Aughils and Aghills,
in Kerry and Cork.   Donohill in Tipperary, the fortress of the yew wood ; the parish of Cloonoghill in
Sligo is called in "Hy Fiachrach" *Cluain-eochaille*
the meadow of the yew wood; and there is another
place of the same name in Roscommon ; while the
form Clonoghill is found in King's and Queen's
Counties.

The other term, *iubhar*, is the word now used in
the spoken language, and it is still more common in
local nomenclature than *eó*.   As a termination it occurs in the form of *-ure*, or with the article *-nure*,
in great numbers of names all over the country.
Terenure is a place near Dublin whose name signifies the land of the yew (*Tir-an-iubhair*), and the
demesne contains, or contained until lately, some
very large yew trees.   The village—now a suburb
of Dublin—that was built on this townland, was
called from its shape, Roundtown ; but the good
taste of the present proprietor has restored the old

name Terenure, and "Roundtown" is now fast falling
into disuse. Ballynure and Ballinure, the name of
a great many places, yew-town; Ahanure, the ford
of the yew. In the parish of Killelagh, Londonderry, there is a townland called Gortinure, which
the Four Masters call *Gort-an-iubhair*, the field of
the yew; and this is also the name of several other
townlands. There are many old churches giving
names to townlands and parishes, called Killure and
Killanure, the church of the yew, no doubt from the
common practice of planting yew trees near churches.
The townland and parish of Uregare in Limerick,
must have received the name from some remarkable
yew tree, for the name is *Iubhar-ghearr* [Yure-yar],
short yew.

Newry in Down, was anciently called *Iubhar-cinn-
tragha* [Yure-kintraw], the yew tree at the head of
the strand, of which the oldest form is found in the
Leabhar na hUidhre, viz., *Ibur-cind-trachta*. It appears by a curious entry in the Four Masters to have
derived its name from a tree planted by St. Patrick,
and which continued to flourish for 700 years after
him :—"A.D. 1162. The monastery of the monks at
Iubhar-cinn-tragha was burned, with all its furniture
and books, and also the yew which St. Patrick himself had planted." The tree must have been situated
near the highest point to which the tide rises, for this
is what the word *crann-tragha*, strand-head, denotes.
In after ages, the full name was shortened to *Iubhar*,
which by prefixing the article (p. 23), and making
some other alterations, was reduced to the present
name.

We have also other places called Newry; and the
shortened form, Nure, is the name of several townlands. Uragh, a place abounding in yews, is some-

times met with, and the same name, by the attraction
of the article (p. 23), becomes Newragh, which in
many cases, especially in the Loinster counties, is
corrupted to Newrath.

The quicken tree. *Caerthainn* [keeran or caurhan],
is the Irish word for the quicken tree, mountain ash,
or rowan tree. It enters into names very often, in
the form of Keeran, which is the name of several townlands; but it undergoes many other modifications,
such as Keerhan in Louth; Carhan in Kerry, as in
case of the river Carhan (quicken-tree river), at
Cahersiveen; Kerane and Keraun in Tipperary and
King's County:—all these places must have produced
this tree in abundance, for the names mean simply
mountain ash. Drumkeeran, the ridge of the quicken
tree, is the name of a village in Leitrim, of a parish
in Fermanagh, and of several townlands in the northern counties.

The holly. This tree is denoted by *Cuillion* [oul-
lion], which, as a root word, is very widely diffused
over the country, and is in general very easily recognised. There are fifteen townlands, all in the Ulster
counties, called Cullion, signifying holly or holly-
land; another form, Cullen, is the name of a parish
in Cork, and of some townlands in other counties.
Cullen in Tipperary is called by the Four Masters,
Cuilleann-O-g Cuanach [O-goonagh], from the old territory of Coonagh, to which it must have formerly
belonged. This word enters into numerous compounds, but generally in the form *cullen;* as in Drumcullen in King's County, *Druim-cuillinn* (Four Mast.),
holly ridge; Moycullen in Galway, the plain of holly;
Knockacullen, holly hill. Many have believed that
Slieve Gullion in Armagh took its name from the
great artificer Culann, who had his forge on it (see

2nd Ser., c. VIII). But if this were the case, the ancient name should be written *Sliabh-Culainn*; whereas we know that in the oldest and best authorities, it is *Sliabh-Cuillinn*, which admits of only one interpretation, the mountain of holly. There are two derivatives of this word, Cullenagh and Cullentragh or Cullentra, which gives names to about sixty townlands and villages; the former is more usual in the south, and the latter in the north; and both were originally applied to a place abounding in holly.

The hazel. This tree was formerly held in great estimation in Ireland: we are told that Mac Cuill (literally "son of the hazel"), one of the three last kings of the Tuatha De Dananns, was so called because he worshipped the hazel. When the old writers record, as they frequently do, that the country prospered under the benign rule of a good king, they usually state, as one of the indications of plenty, that the hazels bended with abundance of nuts; and the salmon that ate the nuts which fell from the nine hazel trees growing round certain great river fountains, became a "salmon of knowledge;" for whoever took and ate one of these fish, became immediately inspired with the spirit of poetry.

Coll is the Irish word for a hazel, corresponding with Lat. *corylus*. It is often difficult to distinguish the modern forms of this word from those of several others; in the beginning of names it is usually represented by *coll, col, cole, cull,* and *cul,* but some of these syllables are often of doubtful signification. Cullane and Cullaun are the names of some townlands in Kilkenny and the Munster counties; Cullan occurs in Mayo; and Collon is a village and parish in Louth: all these signify a place where hazels grow. The name of the celebrated Slieve Callan in

Clare has the same signification; for it is written *Collán* in the old authorities. *Collchoill* [culhill], hazel wood, like *leamh-choill* (p. 508) is subject to considerable variations of form : as Cullahill, we find it in Tipperary and Queen's County; Colehill in Donegal, King's County, Longford, and Meath; and Callowhill in Fermanagh, Leitrim, Monaghan, and Wicklow.

As a termination, the word *coll* takes the different forms, -*kyle*, -*quill*, and -*coyle*, all representing the genitive, *cuill;* Barnakyle near Mungret in Limerick, and Barnacoyle in Wicklow, hazel gap ; Monaquill in Tipperary, Carnquill in Monaghan, and Lisaquill in Longford and Monaghan, the bog, the *carn*, and the fort, of the hazel.

The alder. This tree is called *fearn* [farn] in Irish ; but in the present spoken language the diminutive *fearnóg* (farnoge) is always used. The syllables *farn* and *fern*, which are found in names in every part of Ireland, indicate the prevalence of this tree : thus we have several places called Farnagh, Fernagh, and Ferney, denoting a place producing alders ; and Farnane and Farnoge are used in the same sense. Ferns in Wexford is well known in ecclesiastical and other records by the name of *Fearna* —i. e. alders, or a place abounding in alders. Glenfarne, a beautiful valley near Manorhamilton, is called by the Four Masters *Gleann-fearna*, the alder glen. When the *f* is eclipsed (p. 22), the terminations, -*nacarn*, -*navern*, -*nararna*, &c., are formed : Gortnavern in Donegal and Gortnavarnoge in Tipperary, alder field ; Leoknavarna in Galway, the flagstone of the alders.

The celebrated territory of Farney in Monaghan is called *Fearnmhagh* [Farnvah] in the Book of Rights

and other Irish documents, which was softened down
to the present form by the aspiration of the *m* and *g*.
This name signifies alder plain ; and even so late as
the seventeenth century, the alder woods remained
in considerable abundance (see Mr. E. P. Shirley's
account of the barony of Farney, page 1).

The apple tree.   *Abhall* or *ubhall* signifies both an
apple and an apple tree :—pronounced *owl* or *ool*, and
sometimes *avel*. The ancient Irish form, as found in
the Zeuss MSS., is *aball*, which corresponds with the
Ang.-Sax. *appel*, Eng. *apple*.

This word enters largely into local names, and
very often assumes the forms *owl*, *ool*, *owle*, &c.
Aghowle in Wicklow is called in Irish documents
Achadh-abhla, the field of the apple trees ; the same
name is found in Fermanagh, in the slightly different
form Aghyowle ; and in Leitrim Aghyowla. Bally-
hooly on the Blackwater, below Mallow, is called in
the Book of Lismore, *Ath-ubhla* [Ahoola], the ford
of the apples ; and the present name was formed by
prefixing *Bally:—Baila-atha-ubhla* (now pronounced
Blaa-hoola), the town of the apple ford.

In many places, and especially in some parts of
the north, the word *abhall* is used in the sense of
"orchard ;" as, for instance, in Avalreagh in Monaghan, gray orchard ; Annahavil in Londonderry
and Tyrone, the marsh of the orchard. Very much
the same meaning has Oola on the Limerick and
Waterford railway, which preserves exactly the sound
of the Irish name, *Ubhla*, i. e. apple trees, or a place
of apples.

The proper and usual word for an orchard, however, is *abhalghort* [oulart], literally apple-garden,
which is of pretty frequent occurrence, subject to
some variations of spelling. The most common form

is Oulart, the name of several places in Wexford;
Ballinoulart in Wexford and King's County, and
Ballywhollart in Down, both signify the town of the
orchard.   Another form appears in Knockullard in
Carlow, orchard hill; but Ullard in Kilkenny has a
different origin.

The elder tree. The elder or boortree is called *tromm*
or *trom*, gen. *truim* [trim].   The best known place
named from this tree is Trim in Meath, which was
so called from the elder trees that grew near the
old ford across the Boyne : it is called in the Book of
Armagh *Vadum-Truimm*, a half translation of its
Irish name, *Ath-Truim*, the ford of the boortrees, of
which only the latter part has been retained.   We
have numerous names terminating in -*trim* and -*trime*
which always represent the genitive of *trom;* Gal-
trim in Meath, once a place of some importance, is
called in the annals, *Cula-truim*, the *callow* or holm
of the elder; Gortvunatrime near Emly in Tipperary,
the *gort* or field of the bottom land (*bun*) of the
elder.   The old name of the mountain now called
Bessy Bell, near Newtownstewart, was *Sliabh-truim*
(Four M.), the mountain of the elder.

A place where elders grow is often called *tromaire*
[trummera], from which Trummery in Antrim derives its name; it is shortened to Trummer, as the
name of a little island in the Clare part of the Shannon ; and in Wexford it takes the form of Trimmer.
Tromán, a diminutive of *tromm*, meaning either the
elder tree or a place producing elder, has given name
to Tromaun in Roscommon, to Tromman in Meath,
and to Trumman in Donegal.

The blackthorn. *Draeighean* [dreean] is the black-
thorn or sloe-bush; the old Irish form as given in
Cormac's Glossary is *droigen;* Welsh *draen;* Cornish

drain. The simple word gives names to several places in Antrim, Derry, and Tyrone, now called Dreen, Drain, and Drains, i. e. black-thorn. Drinan near Kinsaley in Dublin is called *Draighnen* by the Four Masters, i. e. a place producing black-thorns. This diminutive form is much more common than the primitive, and in most parts of Ireland the sloe-bush is called *drinan*, or *drinan-donn* (brown). It gives names to various places now called Dreenan, Drinane, and Drinaun. The adjective form, *draeighneach*, and its diminutive, *draeighneachán*, are also very common as townland names, in the modern forms, Dreenagh, Drinagh, Driny, and Drinaghan—signifying a place abounding in sloe-bushes; Aghadreenagh, Aghadreenan, Aghadrinagh, and Aghadreen, are the names of townlands in various counties, all meaning the field of the sloe bushes.

The sloe is designated by the Irish word *airne* [arny], which is found pretty often in the end of names, in the form of *-arny*. For the original name of Killarney in Kerry, we have not, as far as I am aware, any written authority; but I see no reason to question the opinion already advanced by others, that the Irish name is *Cill-airneadh*, the church of the sloes. This opinion is corroborated by the frequency of the same termination: thus we have a Killarney in Kilkenny, another in Roscommon, and a third near Bray in Wicklow. Near Clones, there is a townland called Magherarny, the plain of the sloes; Clonarney in Westmeath and Cavan, sloe-meadow; Mullarney in Kildare, the summit of the sloes, &c.

The white thorn or haw tree—Irish, *sceach* [skagh]. From these thorn bushes, so plentifully diffused over the whole country, a vast number of places have received their names. There are numerous townlands

called Skagh, Skea, and Skeagh, i. e. simply a thorn
bush; and these, along with the shorter form, Ske,
begin the names of many others, such as Skeagh-
anore in Cork, the bush of the gold, and Skenarget
in Tyrone, of the silver—both probably so called
because the bushes marked the spots where the peasantry dreamed of, and dug for money.

As a termination, the word takes these same forms,
in addition to several others, such as -*ske*, -*skeha*,
-*skehy*, &c.; as in Gortnaskeagh, Gortnaskehy, and
Gortnaskey, all which are the names of townlands,
and signify the field of the white-thorns; Tullyna-
skeagh, and Knocknaskeagh, both signifying white-
thorn hill; Baunskeha in Kilkenny, the green field
of the bush; Aghnaskeha, Aghnaskeagh, and Aghna-
skew, bushy field (*achadh*); Clonskeagh in Dublin,
and Cloonskeagh in Mayo, the *cloon* or meadow of the
white-thorn bushes. Lisnaskea in Fermanagh (the
fort of the bush), took its name from the celebrated
tree called *Sceath-ghabhra*, under which the Maguire
used to be inaugurated. There are some places in
Donegal, Fermanagh, and Tyrone, called Skeoge,
and we have several townlands with the name of
Skeheen, both these signifying a little bush, or a
little bushy brake. Skehanagh and Skahanagh, a
bushy place, are the names of townlands in every
part of Ireland, except Ulster.

The furze. Aileann [attan] is our word for the
furze; old Irish, *aitten* (Cor. Gl.), Welsh *eithin*; and
it is found chiefly as a termination in two different
forms, -*attin*, and -*attina*. The first is seen in Cool-
attin, the name of some places in Limerick, Wicklow, and Wexford, signifying the corner of the
furze; and the second in Ballynahattina in Galway,
the same as Ballynahatten in Down and Louth, and

Ballinattin in Waterford and Tipperary, the town of the furze. The Irish scholar will remark that in these names the word is used in the masculine in the south, and in the feminine in the north and west; and I may remark here, once for all, that I have also observed this difference of gender inflexion according to locality, in case of the names of some other natural productions.

The heath. The common heath—*erica vulgaris*—is denoted by the word *fraech;* as may be expected, it enters extensively into names, and oftener as a termination than otherwise. In the beginning of names, and when it stands alone, it is usually represented by Freagh and Freugh; thus Freaghillaun is the name of several little islands round various parts of the coast, signifying heathy island ; Freaghmore in Westmeath, and Freughmore in Tyrone, great heath. We find, however, Freeduff—black heath—in Armagh and Cavan, the same as Freaghduff in Tipperary.

As a termination it takes the form -*free*, which exactly represents the pronunciation of the genitive, *fraeigh.* Inishfree, a little island in Lough Gill, is called by the Four Masters, *Inisfraeich*, heathy island ; and there are islands of the same name off the coast of Donegal, and elsewhere. Coolfree, heathy corner, is a townland near Ballyorgan in Limerick. When the article is used, the *f* disappears by aspiration (p. 20), and the word becomes -*ree ;* but then this syllable is often also the modern form of *righ*, a king :—Thus Ballinree, which is the name of about a dozen townlands, might represent either *Baile-an-righ*, the town of the king, or *Baile-an-fhraeigh*, of the heather.

The diminutives *fraechán* and *fraechóg*—but prin-

cipally the former—are used to denote the bilberry,
or whortleberry, or "hurt," as it is called over a
great part of Munster, a contraction of "hurtle" or
"whortle." In other parts of Ireland, these berries
got their proper Irish name; and the citizens of Dublin are well accustomed to see "fraughans" exposed
for sale in baskets, by women who pick them on
the neighbouring hills. Freahanes and Frehans, i. e.
whortleberries, are the names of two townlands, one
near Ross Carberry, the other in Tipperary; and by
a change of *ch* to *f* (p. 52), it becomes Froffans in
Meath. On the Northern side of Seefin mountain
over Glenosheen in Limerick, there is a deep glen
called Lyronafreaghaun, which represents the Irish
Ladhar-na-bhfracchán, the river-branch of the whortleberries; and it produces them as plentifully to-day as
when it got the name. Kilnafrehan in Waterford,
and Kylefreaghane in Tipperary, bilberry wood;
Binnafreaghan in Tyrone, the peak of the whortleberries.

The ivy. The different kinds of ivy are denoted by
the term *eidhneán* [ine-aun], which is a diminutive of
the older form *eden*, as given in Cormac's Glossary;
Welsh *eiddew*. In its simple form it gives name
to Inan in Meath, and to Inane in Cork and Tipperary, both meaning an ivy-covered place. The
adjective form *eidhnach* [inagh], abounding in ivy,
is, however, much more common, and it occurs in
MSS. of authority. There is a river in Clare called
Inagh, from which a parish takes name, and also a
river in Donegal, flowing into Inver Bay, called
Eany (which gives name to Gleneany, through
which it flows), both of which the Four Masters
mention by the name of *Eidhneach*, i. e. the ivy-pro-
ducing river.

The celebrated monastery of Clonenagh in Queen's County was founded by St. Fintan in the middle of the sixth century. It is called in O'Clery's Calendar and other Irish documents, *Cluain-eidhnech*, which, in the Latin Life of the founder is translated *Latibulum hederosum*, the retreat, (i. e. the *cloon*) of the ivy. It is interesting to observe that this epithet is as applicable to-day as it was in the time of St. Fintan ; for the place produces a luxuriant growth of ivy, which clothes the gable of the old church, and all the trees in the neighbourhood.

CHAPTER IX.

SHAPE AND POSITION.

A REAL or fancied resemblance to different parts of the human body, has originated a great variety of topographical names all over the country. Most of the bodily members have been turned to account in this manner: and the natural features compared with, and named from them, are generally, but not always, hills.

The head. The word *ceann* [can], a head, is used much in the same way as the English word, to denote the head, front, or highest part of anything ; and it commonly appears in anglicised names, in the forms *can, ken, kin*. There is a place near Callan in Kilkenny called Cannafahy, whose Irish name is *Ceann-na-faithche*, the head of the exercise-green ; Kincon in Mayo and Armagh, the hound's head, so called from some peculiarity of shape ; Kinard, high head or hill ; Kinturk, the head or hill of the boar.

The highest point reached by the tide in a river, was sometimes designated by the term *ceann-mara*, i. e. the head of the sea; from a spot of this kind on the river Roughty, the town of Kenmare in Kerry received its name; and Kinvarra in Galway originated in the same way, for the Four Masters call it *Ceannmhara.* Another compound, *ceannsaile* [cansauly], also used to express the same idea, means literally the head of the brine, and from this we have the name of Kinsale in Cork, of Kinsalebeg in Waterford (*beg*, little, to distinguish it from the preceding), of Kinsaley, a parish north of Dublin; and of Kintale in the parish of Killygarvan in Donegal, in which last the *s* is eclipsed by *t*.

The forehead is denoted in Irish by the word *eudan* [edan]. which is used topographically to signify a hill brow. There is a small town in King's County, another in Antrim, and half a dozen townlands in several counties, called Edenderry; all of which are from the Irish *Eudan-doire*, the hill brow of the oak wood. This word, Eden—always with the same meaning— is much used in the northern and north-western counties in local nomenclature; it is itself the name of about a dozen places; and it forms the beginning of more than 100 other names. It is occasionally contracted; as in Ednashanlaght in Tyrone, the hill brow of the old sepulchre (*leacht*).

The nose. Srón [srone], the nose, is often applied to prominent points of hills, or abrupt promontories; and in this sense we sometimes find it in townland names; as in Sroankeeragh in Roscommon, the sheep's nose; Shronebeha in Cork, the nose or point of the birch.

The throat. The word *braghad* [braud], which literally signifies the gullet or windpipe, is locally applied to a gorge or deeply-cut glen; and of this application, the river and valley of the Braid near Ballymena in Antrim, form a very characteristic example. The diminutive Bradoge, little gorge, is the name of a small stream flowing by Grangegorman into the Liffey on the north side of Dublin, and of another flowing into the sea at Bundoran in Donegal; and the same word gives name to a townland in Monaghan now called Braddocks. *Scórnach* is another term for the windpipe; it is applied to a remarkable glen cut through the hills near Tallaght in Dublin, now called the gap of Ballinascorney, i.e. the town of the gorge; and there is a place called Scornagh on the Lee, three miles above Ballincollig.

The shoulder. Guala or *gualann* [goola, goolan] signifies the shoulder, and was often applied to a hill. The village of Shanagolden in Limerick is called in Irish authorities, *Seangualann*, old shoulder or hill, and this is also the Irish name still in use.

The back. The literal meaning of the word *druim* [drum] is a back, exactly the same as the Latin *dorsum*, with which it is also cognate. In its local application, it signifies a long low hill or ridge; and in this sense also it is often translated by *dorsum*. It is one of the most common of all root words in Irish names; its most usual anglicised forms are *drum*, *drom*, and *drim*; and these syllables begin about 2400 names of townlands, towns, and villages, besides the countless names that contain this very prolific root otherwise combined. In Munster it is very generally pronounced *droum*, and in many names it is modernized accordingly.

There are several places in the southern and western counties, called Dromada and Dromadda, the Irish name of which is *Druim-fhada*, long ridge, the

sound of *f* being wholly sunk by aspiration (p. 20);
in some of the northern counties the *f* is retained,
and the name becomes Drumfad. Drumagh in
Queen's County, Drimagh in Wexford, and Dromagh
in Cork, signify ridged land, a place full of *drums* or
ridges.

In many combinations of this word, the *d* sound
is lost by aspiration. Aughrim near Ballinasloe in
Galway, the scene of the battle of 1691, has its name
formed in this way; it is called in Irish authorities,
Each-dhruim, which Colgan translates *equi-mons*, i. e.
horse-hill; and the pronunciation of the ancient name
is well preserved in the modern. There are, besides
this, about twenty Aughrims in Ireland. Sometimes
the *d* sound is changed to that of *t*, as in Leitrim, the
name of one of the counties, and of more than forty
townlands scattered over Ireland : — *Liath-dhruim*
(Four Mast.), grey ridge (see Sheetrim, p. 184).

The diminutive *Druimin* [Drimmeen], has given
names to various places now called Drimeen, Dro-
meen, and Drummeen. *Dromainn* [drumin], which
is perhaps a diminutive, also means a ridge, much
the same as *druim* itself, and this word originated
the names of all those places called Dromin, Drum-
min, and Drummans; in the northern counties it is
often corrupted to Drummond (p. 62), which is the
name of about twenty townlands. Another develop-
ment of *druim* is *druimneach* or *druimne*, meaning
ridges or ridged land, originating a new growth of
names. For example, Drimnagh castle and parish,
three miles south west from Dublin, took the name
from the little sand-ridges now called the Green
Hills. Drimna, Dromnagh, and Drumina, the names
of places in various parts of Ireland, are all different
forms of this word.

The Irish word *tón* [thone] signifies the *backside*, exactly the same as the Latin *podex*. It was very often used to designate hills, and also low-lying or *bottom* lands ; and it usually retains the original form, *ton ;* as we see in Tonduff, Tonbaun, and Tonroe, black, white, and red, backside, respectively ; Toneel, in Fermanagh, the bottom land of the lime.

One particular compound, *Ton-le-gaeith*, which literally signifies "backside to the wind," seems to have been a favourite term ; for there are a great many hills all through the country with this name, which are now called Tonlegee. Sometimes the preposition *re* is used instead of *le*—both having the same meaning—and the name in this case becomes Tonregee. In this last, a *d* is often inserted after the *n* (p. 62), and this with one or two other trifling changes, has developed the form Tanderagee, the name of a little town in Armagh, and of ten townlands, all in the Ulster counties, except one in Meath, and one in Kildare.

The side. Irish *taebh* [teev]. This, like the corresponding English word, is applied to the side of a hill ; and its usual anglicised forms are *tieve* and *teer*. Tievenavarnog in Fermanagh represents the Irish, *Taebh-na-bhfearnog*, the hill side of the alders ; Teevnabinnia in Mayo, the side of the pinnacle.

The thigh. The word *más* [mauce] the thigh, is locally applied to a long low hill. It gives name to several places in the western counties, now called Mace ; Masreagh in Sligo, Massreagh in Donegal, and Mausrevagh in Galway, grey hill. Mausrower in Kerry, *fat* or thick hill. There is a castle near Antrim town called Massereene, giving name to two baronies ; this name, which originally belonged to a small friary of Franciscans, founded about the year

1500 by one of the O'Neills, is written in O'Mellan's
Journal of Phelim O'Neill, *Masareghna*, which is
little different from the correct Irish form, *Más-a'-
rioghna*, the queen's hill (Reeves, Eccl. Ant., p. 389).

The shin. Irish, *lurga* or *lurgan.* This word, like
the last, was often applied to a long low ridge, or to
a long stripe of land. From the first form, some
townlands, chiefly in the south, are called Lurraga.
The second form was much used in the northern and
western counties, in which there are about thirty
places called Lurgan, and more than sixty others of
whose name it forms a part.

The foot. The word *cos* [cuss], a foot, is used
locally to express the foot, or bottom, or lower end
of any thing; the form found in anglicised names is
generally *cush*, which represents, not the nominative
but the dative (*cois*, pron. *cush*), of the original word
(p. 34). Cush and Cuss, i. e. foot, are the names of
some places in the middle and southern counties.
Cushendun in Antrim is called by the Four Masters,
Bun-abhann-Duine, the end, i. e. the mouth of the
river Dun; this was afterwards changed to *Cos-
abhann-Duine* [Cush-oun-dunny], which has the same
meaning, and which has been gradually compressed
into the present name. Cushendall was in like manner contracted from *Cois-abhann-Dhalla*, the foot or
termination of the river Dall (Reeves, Eccl. Ant.,
pp. 83, 283). In the Ordnance Memoir of the
parish of Templemore (p. 213), it is conjectured that
the stream which flows by Coshquin near Londonderry, was anciently called *Caein* [keen], i. e. beautiful; whence the place got the name of *Cois-Caeine*,
the end of the river *Caein*, now shortened to Coshquin.

The barony of Coshlea in Limerick, was so called

from its position with respect to the Gulty mountains; its Irish name being *Cois-sleibhe* [Cushleva], i. e. (at) the foot of the mountain; and this signification is still preserved in the name of a place, now called Mountain-foot, situated at the base of this fine range. Sometimes the word *cois* (which is in this case a remnant of the compound preposition, *a-gcois* or *a-cois*), is used to express contiguity or nearness; in this sense it appears in the name of the barony of Coshma in Limerick, *Cois-Maighe* (the district) near or along the river Maigue; and in that of Coshbride in Waterford, the territory by the river Bride.

Besides the names enumerated in the preceding part of this chapter, many others are derived from their resemblance to various objects, natural or artificial; and many from their position, or from their direction with respect to other places. Of these the following will be a sufficient specimen.

Bun means the bottom or end of anything; Bunlahy in Longford, the end of the *lahagh* or slough. It is very often applied to the *end*, that is, the mouth of a river, and many places situated at river mouths have in this manner received their names; as Bunorana in Donegal, the mouth of the river Crana; Bunratty in Clare, the mouth of the river formerly called the Ratty, but now the Owen Ogarney, because it flows through the ancient territory of the O'Carneys. Bonamargy in the parish of Culfeightrin, Antrim, the mouth of the Margy or Carey river; Bunmahon in Waterford, the mouth of the river Mahon.

Bárr [baur] is the top of anything. Barmona in Wexford, the top of the bog; Barravore in Wicklow, great top; Barmeen in Antrim, smooth top; Barreragh in Cork, western top. In some of the northern

counties, the *barr* of a townland means the high or
hilly part; and from this we derive such names as
the Barr of Slawin in Fermanagh, i. e. the top or
highest part of the townland of Slawin.

Gabhal [goul, gowal, and gole], a fork, old Irish,
gabul, from the verb *gab*, to take. It is a word in
very extensive local use in every part of Ireland, being
generally, though not always, applied to river forks;
and it assumes a variety of forms, in accordance with
different modes of pronunciation. The simple word
is seen in such names as Gole, Gowel, and Goul; and
the plural Gola (forks) is pretty common in the
northern counties. At Lisgoole near Enniskillen,
there was formerly a monastery of some note, which
the Four Masters call *Lis-gabhail*, the fort of the
fork. There is a remarkable valley between the
mountains of Slieve-an-ierin and Quilcagh, near
the source of the Shannon, now called Glengavlin;
but the Four Masters give the true name at A. D.
1390, *Gleann-gaibhle* [gavla], the glen of the fork.

The land enclosed by two branches of a river was
often designated by the compound *Eadar-dha-ghabhal*
[Adragoul], or *Eadar-ghabhal* [Addergoul], i. e. (a
place) between two (river) prongs; and this has
given names to many places, in the various forms,
Addergoole, Adderagool, Addrigoole, Adrigole, Ad-
rigool, Edergole, and Edergoole.

The diminutives are still more widely spread than
the original; and they give names to those places
called Golan, Goleen, Goulaun, Gowlan, Gowlane,
and Gowlaun, all signifying a little fork, commonly
a fork formed by rivers. At the village of Golden ·
in Tipperary, the river Suir divides for a short distance, and encloses a small island; this small bifur-
cation was, and is still, called in Irish, *Gabhailin*

[gouleen], which has been corrupted to the present name of the village, Golden.

In some parts of the south, this word is pronounced *gyle*, and hence we have Gyleen, the name of a village near Trabolgan, just outside Cork harbour. There are two conical mountains a little west of Glengariff in Cork, between which ran the old road to Castletown Bearhaven; they stand up somewhat like the prongs of a fork, and hence they are called Goulmore and Goulbeg, great and little fork; but the former is now better known by the name of Sugarloaf. This very remarkable mountain is also often called *Sliabh-na-gaibhle*, the mountain of the fork, which is pronounced *Slieve-na-goila;* and many people now believe that this signifies *the mountain of the wild men!*

Another word for a fork is *ladhar* [pron. *lyre* in the south, *lear* in the north], which is also much used in forming names, and like *gabhal*, is applied to a fork formed by streams or glens. There are many rivers and places in the south called Lyre, and others in the north called Lear, both of which are anglicised forms of this word; and the diminutives Lyreen, Lyrane, and Lyranes (little river forks), are the names of some places in Cork, Kerry, and Waterford. Near Inchigeela in Cork, there is a townland called, from its exposed situation, Lyrenagehla, the fork of the wind; Lyranearla in Waterford, near Clonmel, the earl's river fork. On the southern side of Seefin mountain, three miles south of Kilfinane in Limerick, is a bright little valley traversed by a sparkling streamlet; which, from its warm, sunny aspect, is called Lyrenagreana, in Irish *Ladhar-na-greine*, the river-branch of the sun.

Cúil [cooil], *accessus* (Colgan)—a corner or angle;

35

it is very extensively used in forming local names, generally in the forms of *cool* and *cole*, but it is often difficult to tell whether these syllables, especially the first, represent *cúil*, a corner, or *cúl* [cool], a back. The barony of Coole in Fermanagh received its name from a point of land extending into Upper Lough Erne, which was anciently called *Cúil-na-noirear* (Four M.), the angle of the coasts or harbours. There is a place in King's County called Coleraine ; Coolrain is the name of a village and of some townlands in Queen's County ; and we find Coolrainey in Wexford, Coolrahnee near Askeaton, and Coolraine near Limerick city. All these names are originally the same as that of Coleraine in Londonderry, which is explained in an interesting passage in the Tripartite Life of St. Patrick. When the saint, in his journey through the north, arrived in this neighbourhood, he was received with great honour, and hospitably entertained by a chieftain named Nadslua, who also offered him a piece of ground on which to build a church. And when the saint inquired where the place was, it was pointed out to him on the bank of the river Bann : it was a spot overgrown with ferns, and some boys were at the moment amusing themselves by setting them on fire. From this circumstance the place received the name of *Cuil-rathain* [Coolrahen], translated by Colgan, *Secessus filicis,* the corner of the ferns, which it retains to this day with very little alteration.

INDEX OF NAMES.

N.B.—Many names that do not occur in the body of the work are explained in this Index.

35 *

INDEX OF ROOT WORDS,

WITH PRONUNCIATION, MEANING, AND REFERENCE.